The Bobby Girls

Johanna Bell cut her teeth on local newspapers in Essex, eventually branching into magazine journalism with stints as a features writer and then commissioning editor at *Full House* magazine. She now has more than sixteen years' experience in print media. Her freelance life has seen her working on juicy real-life stories for the women's weekly magazine market, as well as hard-hitting news stories for national newspapers and prepping her case studies for TV interviews. When she's not writing, Johanna can be found walking her dog with her husband or playing peek-a-boo with her daughter.

To hear more from Johanna, follow her on Twitter, @JoBellAuthor and on Facebook, /johannabellauthor.

The Bobby Girls

Book One in the Bobby Girls Series

JOHANNA BELL

HODDER

First published in Great Britain in 2019 by Hodder & Stoughton
An Hachette UK company

1

A CIP catalogue record for this title is available from the British Library

Paperback ISBN 978 1 529 33085 4
eBook ISBN 978 1 529 33084 7

Typeset in Plantin Light by Palimpsest Book Production Limited,
Falkirk, Stirlingshire

Printed and bound in Great Britain by Clays Ltd, Elcograf S.p.A.

Hodder & Stoughton policy is to use papers that are natural, renewable and
recyclable products and made from wood grown in sustainable forests.
The logging and manufacturing processes are expected to conform to the
environmental regulations of the country of origin.

Hodder & Stoughton Ltd
Carmelite House
50 Victoria Embankment
London EC4Y 0DZ

www.hodder.co.uk

★ For Adam (Gilly) ★
I will always cherish that final game of cards

Dear readers,

I hope you enjoy this first book in the Bobby Girls series. Although I've been a journalist and writer for more than fifteen years, this is the first book I have ever written – and I'm so excited to share it with you.

My fascination with the great wars started when I was young. I loved hearing my granddad's World War Two stories. He didn't talk about his experiences with the Royal Electrical and Mechanical Engineers a lot, which made our chats about them all the more special. He ignited my passion for learning about what the soldiers went through, as well as unlocking a curiosity about what life was like for everybody left behind at home.

When my cousin Adam joined the Royal Marines as a member of 42 Commando, my interest in it all deepened. He was fifteen years older than me and I had always looked up to him, but this achievement knocked my socks off – especially when I learned about how extreme the training was. I sat and played cards with Adam on his bed during his final visit home before he was killed on duty in Northern Ireland. He was just twenty-one years old when we lost him. When my granddad passed at the ripe old age of ninety-one, many years later, he was still heartbroken by Adam's death.

After losing both these incredible men I became even more passionate about learning as much as I could about how war affects not only those on the front line but their families and communities. That's why researching for *The Bobby Girls* was such a delight for me. It was refreshing to delve into the lives of some of the strongest, feistiest women I've ever heard of. The negativity and backlash the first recruits came up against was astounding but they kept on going – determined to get what they had set out for.

I was shocked to learn about how unfairly women were treated at the time. My editor also found it hard to believe that the reality was so awful – so much so that she questioned many of the details, and was staggered when I produced my sources! The establishment of the WPV was a real turning point for women's liberation and I've got great respect for everyone involved.

I thoroughly enjoyed developing the characters in this book – especially Maggie, Annie and Irene. I hope you grow to love them as much as I do. As a journalist I'm so used to writing about facts that it felt quite liberating to be able to build my own stories around the historical facts and what I discovered about the WPV in London during World War One. I can't wait to come up with more adventures for the girls and I'd love for you all to join me on the journey.

The Bobby Girls

THE VOTE, June 19, 1914. ONE PENNY.

ARREST OF OUR HON. TREASURER.

THE VOTE

THE ORGAN OF THE WOMEN'S FREEDOM LEAGUE.

VOL. X. No. 243. [Registered at the General Post Office as a Newspaper.] FRIDAY, JUNE 19, 1914.

20 PAGES. Edited by C. DESPARD. FOUR PAGES EXTRA.

OBJECTS: To secure for Women the Parliamentary vote as it is or may be granted to men; to use the power thus obtained to establish equality of rights and opportunities between the sexes, and to promote the social and industrial well-being of the community.

WHY

WOMEN POLICE

ARE

URGENTLY NEEDED

Prologue

August 1914

Sarah

As Sarah put the finishing touches to her article, the sound of excited chatter made its way across the offices of *The Vote* towards her desk. She had been working at the paper for the last year. Normally there was a sense of calm and relief as everyone met the final deadline and relaxed before the latest edition went to press. But today was different.

She pulled her work out of the typewriter and left it at the end of her desk to be picked up, before making her way to the crowd that had gathered around Nina. Peering over a few shoulders, Sarah could just manage to see the page proof that had everyone so giddy. It was there, in big, bold letters: *RECRUITING*. Squinting her eyes, she strained to make out the small print underneath. She could read enough to work out that a corps of female volunteer police was being put together.

'Finally!' she exclaimed, as Nina grinned at her through the small crowd. Nina, *The Vote*'s political secretary, had been campaigning for women to be allowed to become special constables for a long time. She had written about it in the paper and had even started recruiting a few months ago, before the Chief Commissioner of Police gave her permission to form the group. The paper had run a big front-page call-to-arms back in June, along with an article outlining all the reasons why women police were needed. Sarah had been outraged when Nina told her what the commissioner had said in response to her ideas: 'You will get yourselves knocked on the head, and you surely don't expect me to look after a lot of women.' It was just typical of men – why couldn't they see that women could look after themselves perfectly well?

'The commissioner finally gave in,' smiled Nina. 'It seems all his manpower is off to fight so he has no choice but to draft in female help. Now we can start enrolling the women who have already come forward, and begin officially recruiting.'

Sarah felt a sudden rush of adrenaline as the enormity of the news sunk in. 'This is our chance to show everyone what we can do,' she said to her friend Daisy as they made their way back to their desks.

'Will you be signing up, then?' Daisy asked, nervously.

'Of course,' Sarah said. 'Why on earth wouldn't I?' At twenty-one, Sarah was the youngest writer at the paper. Her age along with her short and slight frame led people to assume she was shy and meek. They were always surprised to discover that, though she was small, her personality was big.

'It's just . . . well . . .' stammered Daisy, avoiding eye contact and staring uncomfortably at the floor. 'I know this is what we've been fighting for for so long . . . but now it's actually happening, I think I would be a little too scared to sign up.'

'Are you pulling my leg?' Sarah scoffed. 'This is it, Daisy – *this* is what all the hard work has been about! Female bobbies! All the campaigning has worked! This is our opportunity to show the men we can do just as good a job as them!' Sarah's eyes watered as emotion took over. She paused before continuing.

'This is our chance to protect all those poor women getting dragged through the court system by male police officers, male solicitors, male court staff and male judges – whether they've done something that deserves justice or been a victim. We need to do this for them!'

Sarah could feel all eyes on her as her voice increased in volume, as it tended to do when she got going on this topic. She couldn't help it – she was just so passionate about it. She had been devastated when her beloved suffragettes had ceased hostilities at the outbreak of the war earlier that month. Yes, she agreed everyone needed to work together to help win the war – but she had been worried it would be at the sacrifice of all the progress that had been made.

Lowering her voice, she added, 'Now that Nina has permission to go ahead, I'll be drawing up my application. You should really think about doing the same thing, Daisy. We need to stick together and show everyone we can do this'

As she sat back down at her desk, Sarah's thoughts turned to what life in the police could be like, and how it would feel to walk the streets of London acting as a protector for vulnerable women. She was desperate to do her bit for the women's lib movement, and if she could help those being let down by the all-male justice system – well, she could really make a difference.

As Sarah left the offices that evening, the latest issue of *The Vote* was going to press. She smiled to herself as she thought about it landing on doormats and desks in the morning, delivering all the hope and promise she had felt herself when she had first laid eyes on that groundbreaking cover.

Maggie

Sitting down with her morning cup of tea, Maggie froze when she saw the newspaper lying at the other end of the kitchen table, the words 'The Vote' emblazoned across the front. She looked around furtively to make absolutely sure she was alone, then grabbed the corner and pulled it towards her.

Her heart thumped hard in her chest as she flicked through. Her eyes were drawn to a section about Women Police Volunteers. She had to take a moment to process the news that the women behind the campaign had been given permission to start recruiting. After taking a deep breath, she drank in the words, every single one of them making her feel braver and more empowered.

She knew that the suffragettes had been campaigning for this for years, but it just hadn't seemed like something that could ever become a reality. Now they had the backing of the police commissioner, her tummy flipped as she dared herself to dream of getting involved in something so exciting.

I'd love to join these women, but Daddy would never let me, she thought sadly. At that moment, she heard her father's footsteps coming down the stairs, and her heart pounded faster. Quick as a flash, she closed the paper, put it back facing the way it had been before she had touched it, and stared innocently into her cup of tea.

'Good morning, Margaret,' her father said stiffly as he walked into the room. Her father insisted on calling her Margaret even though she had begged to be known as Maggie for as long as she could remember. Her father was the strictest she had ever heard of. She lived with him, her mother and her brother Eddie in a big house in Kensington. She often thought that it was a good job the house was so big, as she was hardly ever allowed to go out and do anything on her own. She regularly wandered up and down the long corridors, pretending she was out in the fresh air for a stroll. The vast space also meant there were plenty of hiding places. Maggie had squeezed herself into many a secret spot over the years to avoid her father when he was in one of his moods. She had learned at a very young age that it was best to stay out of his way when he lost his temper, and she was now an expert at spotting the warning signs, and making a quick escape.

At eighteen, Maggie was desperate to get out into the world and start living her life, but her father was convinced she would do something shameful before he had a chance to present her at a Debutante Ball and find her a suitor. Maggie found it hard to keep friendships going when she'd only ever been allowed out of the house on her own to attend school. The few friends she had were always trying to convince her to sneak out, but she never dared to. No amount of fun was worth the punishment her father would dish out if he discovered her defiance. Her friends had no idea about his treatment of her, and the secret meant she found it hard to get close to anyone. Then there were all the bruises she had been forced to explain away over the years. How could she form proper friendships with these girls when they didn't know the real her?

Maggie couldn't think of anything worse than being married off young. She would rather go out and live her life how she wanted – and maybe find herself a husband along the way. She most certainly didn't want to spend the rest of her days answering to a tyrant, like her mother had to. But her father's work in politics and his affluent upbringing meant he was strongly against women's liberation. The one time Maggie had mentioned the suffragettes in front of him, you'd have thought she had said a swear word. He only got *The Vote* to keep abreast of the opposition, and she didn't normally get even a sniff of it. All her information about the women's movement came from her few friends and sometimes from their cook, Florence – when her father was safely out of the house.

Maggie breathed a sigh of relief when her father walked past the paper on the table without seeming to notice it had been disturbed.

'I trust you will be putting a jacket on before leaving the house today,' he said, without even looking at her. 'We don't want to give out the wrong impression.' He had a thing about women showing off their arms. Maggie had known she was taking a risk putting on a short-sleeved dress this morning – but it was so hot outside.

It was bad enough her parents tried to dictate her every move – but her clothes? 'Oh, Daddy!' In her frustration, the words came out before she could stop them, and she braced herself. The outburst seemed to have shocked her father so much he had stopped dead in his tracks. Maggie couldn't ever remember a time when he had been lost for words like this.

She knew she had only moments to prevent a full-scale row. 'What I meant to say was, it's really very hot to be wearing long sleeves or a jacket, and it doesn't matter anyhow as there aren't any eligible young men around to notice.' She held her breath as she waited for his response. She didn't often answer him back. The few times she had done, he had become so angry that she'd instantly regretted it. He didn't hit her regularly, but he always made it clear that he was considering it. It was normally enough to make her think twice before standing up to him, so she wasn't sure what had come over her this morning.

She flinched when he stepped closer to her and raised his hand in the air, a menacing look on his face. As he towered over her, he spoke in a snarl, his teeth and jaw clenched in anger as she cowered in her chair.

'Keep talking back to me, Margaret Smyth, and I will have no choice but to make you see the error of your ways,' he spat furiously. Instinctively, Maggie put a hand up to cover her face. She wasn't sure why – he had never struck her face before, always opting for parts of her body that were easier to hide with clothes.

The only time he had slipped up was when her mother had stepped in to protect her a few years before. He'd caught her mother's cheek and sent her flying into the corner of a table. She had nearly lost her sight as a result and now suffered regular migraines. Maggie wasn't sure if her mother actually got migraines as often as she claimed – she suspected she used them as an excuse to take to her bed and stay out of her father's way. She didn't blame her. Her poor mother was normally his first port of call for a beating when he was feeling angry.

Suddenly, footsteps rang out on the stairs and her father moved back and dropped his hand. Maggie breathed a sigh of relief and silently thanked whoever it was who had unknowingly saved her.

'We've spoken about that dress and it is not to be worn out of the house,' Mr Smyth said firmly, his voice calm now, as though he hadn't just threatened to hurt her. The way he could change moods within a heartbeat made her shiver. 'Go and get changed before I send a maid up to your room to dress you in something I have picked out myself.' Before she had a chance to say anything, he turned on his heel and left the room, leaving her alone once again with the newspaper. Maggie breathed a second sigh of relief before looking up to see her brother walking into the room.

'Hey kiddo,' he beamed, ruffling her blonde hair and kissing her on the forehead. Maggie quickly rearranged her hair. She always wore it long so that it covered her ears, and she hated it when Eddie messed it up. They both had ears that stuck out slightly, but while Maggie was self-conscious about hers, Eddie couldn't give a hoot about his. He took a step back to study Maggie's face. She realised then that she was shaking.

'What's wrong? You're white as a ghost,' he said, his voice full of concern.

'Oh, Eddie, it's just the usual,' Maggie muttered, shrugging her shoulders and sighing. He scowled and put his arm around her, giving her a comforting squeeze. They both knew there was nothing he could say to make it better. They stayed in the embrace for a minute or so before Eddie pulled away to sit down and pour himself a cup of tea from the pot on the table.

'One day he'll get what's coming to him,' he muttered, staring angrily at the brown liquid in his cup. He took a deep breath and sighed before continuing. 'He's a bully, and bullies never win – not in the end.' They sat in silence for a few minutes before Eddie rose abruptly.

'We're better than this life, Mags,' he said, sounding positive now. 'We'll find a way to leave this all behind. But let's bide our time and try not to antagonise Father in the meantime, eh?' he added encouragingly, giving Maggie's hair another ruffle before leaving her on her own once more.

Maggie angrily brought the newspaper around to face her again. She turned back to the section about Women Police Volunteers and stared at the words on the page. *I'll show Daddy who I can really be*, she thought, smiling grimly as she imagined the look on his face as she revealed a year or so down the line that she had been doing a 'man's job'. It was enough to make her want to post off an application there and then.

Suddenly, she remembered Eddie's words about not antagonising their father, and she groaned in frustration. But then, wouldn't this be a superb way of giving the man his comeuppance? Eddie would be so proud of her! She found herself imagining what it would be like to gain enough independence that she could leave this house and make something of her life all by herself.

Maggie had grown up watching her mother walk on eggshells around this man. She knew that didn't always work for her – she had heard the cries and seen the bruises. They never spoke about it, of course, even after the table incident, which Maggie had seen for herself. She knew the hell her mother was living in. What if she could escape and build enough of a life that she could rescue her mother, too? And maybe even her brother?

Hearing footsteps coming back towards the kitchen, Maggie hurriedly placed the paper back in its original position.

Annie

As Annie worked fastidiously on her balaclava, she tried to block out the chorus of knitting needles and chatter in the room around her. She didn't really enjoy these gatherings – she would rather knit for the troops in the quiet of her own home – but she went along regularly with her mum out of a sense of duty. Since war had broken out she had felt so helpless. At least this way she knew she was directly helping those poor men fighting on the front line. Annie had had to rush from her job as a typist to get to tonight's meet-up. As she worked away in her usual silence, she wondered whether the balaclava helmet she was knitting would be the one to finally reach her fiancé, Richard.

Ever since joining the group, she had been putting a little mark inside each balaclava she completed. She had let Richard know to look out for them when she'd written to him soon after finishing her first one, but she hadn't heard back yet. She knew it was silly, but it helped her feel that little bit closer to him. Perhaps it would help him, too, if he knew he was wearing something she had made with her own loving hands. After all, he was all she thought about as she knitted away. The chance to keep him warm and a little more protected made her smile through the pain of being without him and the constant worry about whether or not he would make it home safely.

Annie drifted off as she remembered the night she had met Richard at a local dance. It was a year ago now. She nearly didn't make it that night, but she had persuaded her parents it would be mostly girls there and definitely no funny business. She grinned as the rush of excitement she'd felt when Richard had introduced himself came flooding back to her. His easy charm had overcome her usual shyness, and they had clicked straight away. They were courting seriously within weeks.

Richard was a bank clerk and Annie's parents had been delighted when she had brought him home to meet them. It was a relief as they could be sniffy when it came to potential suitors for their little girl, even if she was now in her twenties. Annie knew they were just looking out for her, though. She'd had a modest upbringing and she had always been aware of the fact her father wished he could have provided more for her and her siblings. It upset her as they were all so happy – they had so much love from their parents, how could they possibly want for anything more? But her father was obsessed with her marrying into at least a little bit of money. She had heard him commenting on Richard's 'healthy earnings' and the fact he was a good match for her when she'd been seeing him out after dinner.

'No prizes for guessing what you're thinking about, my girl – or should I say, who?' Annie's mum's friend June interrupted her musings. As Annie blushed furiously, June shoved a newspaper under her nose. 'Look at this,' June said eagerly. Annie could see straight away it was a copy of *The Vote*. She had been following the women's lib movement closely over the last few years, although she had never plucked up the courage to get involved. The thought was exciting to her – but at the same time terrifying for someone so timid. She didn't think her parents would approve, and she was quite sure Richard would have something to say, too. She didn't like upsetting people and going against their expectations of her.

'They've finally got the go-ahead for female bobbies,' June added as Annie's eyes devoured the recruitment call.

'Oh gosh, I never thought it would actually happen,' Annie whispered, putting down her needles and picking the paper up for a closer look. It said that they were looking for '*healthy, self-reliant and reliable, punctual and regular, and not undersized*' women to join the corps.

'I can't see it working myself,' June sniffed, turning her nose up and continuing with her knitting. 'Can you see any man taking orders from a woman, even if she *is* in a fancy uniform? It's just not the way the world works, is it?'

Annie pondered this for a moment. She couldn't imagine any man taking orders from *her*, that was for sure. She wouldn't dream of trying to boss a man around, let alone a stranger who was disobedient enough to be breaking the law. But with more and more men heading off to fight, she'd heard the female police would be focused on protecting the naïve young women who kept flocking to the army camps to be around the soldiers. Cara at work told her they often got carried away with it all. Annie hadn't been sure what she had meant, and had been shocked when Cara explained that many of the girls ended up falling into prostitution.

'They're worried the Contagious Diseases Act will be brought back in, and they want to protect the women who are carrying on with the soldiers,' Annie said, suddenly finding her voice.

'No, no, no,' June shook her head with her eyes closed, still knitting away at a rate of knots. Annie didn't know how she could work so fast, all the while barely glancing at what she was doing. 'I'm all for women's liberation, my dear, but this is a step too far,' she said firmly.

'Yes, I suppose you're right,' Annie agreed, backing down and nodding quickly. In truth, she thought it was a brilliant idea, and she wished she was brave enough to get involved. She didn't have the confidence to say that to June, though. When June, her eyes still closed, started humming to herself, Annie's mum, who had been sitting on her other side, quietly reached over, picked up the newspaper and slipped it into Annie's bag.

'What are you doing?' Annie whispered in confusion.

'You'd be perfect,' her mum smiled, placing her hand lovingly on Annie's arm.

Annie stared at her, completely taken aback. 'But what about—'

'Don't worry about your father,' she said in a hushed voice, 'I'll deal with him. You need to do your bit and I'll make him see this is the best way. You can't be his little girl forever.'

'But I have a job,' Annie said in confusion. She only worked in the mornings and the pay was just a bit of pocket money, really – but she insisted on contributing a little towards the household costs and took pride in the fact she did so.

'If you need to give up work in order to volunteer then I'm sure we can make do without your help for a little while,' her mum reasoned.

'But who's going to listen to me?' Annie argued quietly, fear coursing through her at just the thought of having to approach a stranger in the street, let alone tell them what to do or reprimand them. With her loose, mousey curls and fresh, round face, she had always looked younger than her twenty-two years.

'You'd be in uniform, love. Just think of the status and confidence that would give you! And you would look so grown up,' her mother beamed. 'I'd be proud to see my daughter out there standing up for what's right and protecting other women. I think Richard would love to be able to tell his comrades you were getting stuck in, too.' Annie knew her mum was also desperate for her to come out of herself a little instead of always being so shy and timid – although she had never said as much to her face.

'You have to remember that your future is by no means certain any more,' her mum added with a tinge of sadness in her voice. 'Richard is at *war*. I know it's supposed to be over by Christmas – but anything could happen. It wouldn't hurt for you to build up some skills and confidence, now, would it? Just in case.' She gently squeezed Annie's hand, and Annie knew what her mum was getting at. A possible outcome she had cried herself to sleep thinking about countless times since she had seen Richard off on the train.

'I'll think about it,' Annie agreed, going back to her knitting in silence.

As they walked home that evening, her mother's words were all Annie could think about. *Would something like this really make my family proud?* It was a terrifying thought. But she did feel that she ought to be doing something more to show her support for her country and all the men fighting for it.

There's no harm applying, she finally concluded later that evening as she lay in bed. *They wouldn't accept someone like me anyway, but at least I can say I tried, and mother will be happy.*

Irene

Footsteps approached and Irene heard hushed giggling. She took her hands out of the bin, straightened her back and tried to act naturally. She didn't care if people laughed at her for rifling through rubbish in the street, but she refused to act as a sideshow for those who found her desperation entertaining.

Two young girls walked past, whispering and glancing back at her.

'Evening!' Irene called, making a point of flashing a sarcastic grin and waving at them. Both girls put their heads down, folded their arms and picked up their speed. Once they were out of sight, Irene reached back into the bin and pulled out the copy of *The Vote* she'd had her eye on before she was disturbed. She was desperate to keep up to date with the progress of the war, but she couldn't afford a paper every day. Her work at the local rag factory meant she could just about pay for her rented room. It only had a single bed and a chest of drawers, the wallpaper was flaking, there was no kitchen or bathroom and she had to share an outside toilet with three families, but after years in a children's home she was just happy to be able to shut herself away from everyone else at the end of the day. She loved having a space that was hers and hers alone. If you didn't count the rat.

Making her way home, Irene glanced down at the newspaper. It was folded over and she could see the words 'Women Police Volunteers' written in bold letters. She took a closer look and when she read that enrolment had begun, she started to feel warm inside despite the evening chill. Perhaps this could be her chance to finally make something of herself.

Of course, it was only volunteering, but what a title to tell her aunt about – and it would definitely make her factory work more bearable. She had recently managed to save a little bit of money every month by doing things like 'borrowing' newspapers from rubbish bins and eating just enough to keep hunger at bay. Her tall, already skinny frame was suffering as a result, but she liked the feeling of having some money put aside. She had enough that it meant she wouldn't have to panic about not being able to pay her rent if she got sick and couldn't make it into work for a couple of weeks. Her landlord was ruthless – he didn't care if you were on death's door, if you couldn't make your rent then you were out on your ear.

Now she wondered if she could use that money to help her fund her way through WPV training. She would need to keep saving until she joined, and even then she'd need to keep as many shifts at the factory as possible alongside the police work. She could ask her boss about night shifts. She would be exhausted but it would be worth it. She had heard the plan was to make the women fully fledged members of the force once the war was over, so perhaps this might lead to a proper, paid job – one that she would actually want to get out of bed for.

If she could become a real police officer she could finally afford to support her aunt Ruth and her cousins the way she had always wanted to. Ruth was the only one who had been there for Irene when her parents died. She'd been desperate to take her in but already had too much to cope with looking after her own children. Ruth had helped Irene through her darkest days in the children's home, and Irene had always dreamed of paying back her kindness one day. Maybe this could help her do just that.

I

November 1914

Making her way into Westminster, Maggie still couldn't believe all the risks she had taken. Not only had she lied about her age to get into the WPV, but she had managed to come up with a cover story for her father, which had actually worked – so far.

She had thought long and hard about how to convince her father to let her out of the house most days with no supervision. In the end, she had forged a letter from the head of an orphanage, which said she had been accepted in as a volunteer. All those hours stuck in her bedroom had finally paid off, as it meant she had ample time to make the letter look official.

Of course, her father had said no initially. But once she presented him with the 'official' letter he had started to relent. He eventually admitted that with the war raging on, he was busier than ever at work and had started to worry about her being at home all day with no one to keep an eye on her. That was nonsense, of course, as her mother was around most of the time. Maggie knew it was really because he hated the fact that he had less opportunity to pop home and keep tabs on her himself. He had suggested it would be good for her to get out and help the less fortunate – as if the whole thing had been his idea! She could just imagine him boasting to his friends and colleagues about what a virtuous little girl his Margaret was. *If only they knew the truth.*

Maggie had been further shocked when her application to join the WPV had been accepted without question. She had ended up enlisting Eddie's help with that. At first, she had been desperate to keep him out of it for fear of their father punishing them both if she was found out, but the twenty-one-year age limit for recruits had forced her hand. Maggie had no idea how to go about faking identity documents to add three years to her age. But she knew Eddie had a friend who had lied about his age to get into the army.

Eddie had been fiercely against the whole thing – he was terrified of what their father would do to her if he found out. 'I need to do this,' she had pleaded. 'This could be my chance to escape, Eddie.' That had done it – he wanted more than anything for her to be away from their father as soon as possible. He had agreed to get her the necessary documents and promised to cover for her wherever he could while she was training or, later, out on patrol.

When the acceptance letter had arrived, Eddie had swiped the formal-looking envelope from the doormat before their father had even looked up from his morning coffee. Once Maggie had put the orphanage story into place with her parents, she had been all set for a life patrolling the streets of London behind her unsuspecting father's back. She had been shaking like a leaf when she ate her breakfast this morning – convinced her father would have done his own checks at the orphanage and uncovered her lies. But he had bid her farewell as normal when he left the house. She was grateful his work was distracting him so much.

Now, as Maggie made her way to her first day of training, she was so nervous it felt like there was a group of dancers performing an energetic foxtrot in her belly. *Calm down*, she chided herself. Still, she couldn't help but feel frequent flushes of panic. She took a deep breath, and as she exhaled, she tried to expel all her nerves. She knew it was better to look confident in these situations; anyone acting nervous always looked shifty.

The training was taking place at St Stephen's House, part of Scotland Yard's headquarters, so she was going to be able to travel there and back every day just as if she was dropping in for a few hours to help needy children. Maggie had reassured herself that the cover story wasn't *that* far from the truth; once she was a fully-fledged member of the WPV, she *would* be helping needy children. Just in a different way.

Drawing closer to the address given in her acceptance letter, Maggie couldn't help but notice how eerily quiet her journey had been. It made her think about how much her beloved London had already changed since the outbreak of war. The hustle and bustle she had grown up around had died. People were still dashing about their daily lives, but they hung their heads and kept themselves to themselves. All the chatter and excitement had gone.

When the government had called for volunteers to fight, there had been a rush of men, desperate to do their bit for the country. The women and children they had left behind were proud of them, of course, but three months later, Maggie could see the sorrow in people's eyes: the child who had woken to find their father had left for a foreign battlefield while they slept; the red-eyed, puffy-faced wife who had received the heartbreaking telegram telling her the news she had been dreading since the moment her husband had left for the front line. And then there were the men who were unable to join in the war effort on the battlefields because they were too old or had been medically discharged – ashamed not to be helping but secretly relieved to be out of the direct line of fire.

Maggie was frightened her brother was going to head off and join the ranks at any moment. Her beloved Eddie was training to be a doctor, but he kept romanticising about life on the front and coming back a hero. He was five years older than Maggie, but she had always felt overly protective of him – like he was in fact her baby brother. The two of them were good at looking out for each other. Maggie supposed it came from years of helping each other through living with their father. Eddie was like an extension of herself and she wasn't sure quite what she would do if any harm should come to him.

Maggie pushed those thoughts out of her mind as she approached St Stephen's House. She needed to focus on looking and acting like a twenty-one-year-old, and not some teenage debutante desperate to escape an abusive father and a life of wifely duties. She flashed her acceptance letter to a stern-looking woman at the door, who directed her along the corridor and into a big hall with floor-to-ceiling windows and wooden floors. It smelt stuffy and reminded her of the assembly hall at school – a thought she immediately made a note to keep to herself.

Looking around, Maggie saw that a lot of the other new recruits were already sitting on chairs facing the front of the hall. She could only see their backs, but she could tell that they were all dressed extremely smartly, and she was glad she had put on her most formal-looking dress and tied her hair back into a neat bun. Her hatred of her ears had almost seen her leave her hair to hang down and cover them, but she knew she looked older with it tied back.

She also noticed that all the other women seemed to be middle-aged or older, and her heart sank, until she saw one young-looking face and it lifted again. Maggie made a beeline for the girl, who was sitting on her own in the middle of a row near the back. As she shuffled down the row of seats, Maggie sneaked a closer look at her face and breathed a sigh of relief – she could only have been in her twenties.

'I'm glad to find someone more my age,' Maggie said with

confidence as she sat down next to the stranger and held out her hand. 'Maggie Smyth, pleased to make your acquaintance.' Her smile faltered as the girl looked around at her with terror etched across her face. Maggie was only being friendly, she didn't see why she had to look at her like she had just announced the Germans were invading the building.

'Annie Beckett,' she said quietly, shaking Maggie's hand limply before turning back to face the front of the room.

Undeterred, Maggie tried again. 'It's all a little intimidating, isn't it?' she said in a hushed tone. Annie looked at her with wide eyes but didn't say anything, so Maggie kept babbling on as she always did in awkward situations. 'Don't mind this stuffy lot,' she whispered with a cheeky grin. 'We're the youngest and fittest ladies in here and those things are important in a job like this. They'll be coming to us for help before you know it.'

She was talking the talk well, but Maggie was feeling just about as nervous as she ever had. And she didn't get nervous a lot. One of Maggie's best skills was putting on a front. In fact, everyone at school used to marvel at how happy-go-lucky she was. She often wondered what a shock it would be to them all to discover what went on at home. The terrified girl cowering in her room as her father stormed around the house dishing out punishments to anyone who dared get in his way was a far cry from the bubbly teenager they saw in the playground.

Maggie spotted another youngish looking girl walking past the end of their row, but before she got a chance to beckon her over an angry-looking woman in a navy-blue uniform stood up at the front of the room and bellowed at everyone to sit down and be quiet. She was tall and slim, but her broad shoulders gave her an imposing presence. That, coupled with her loud, firm voice, meant that the room suddenly fell deathly silent and all bottoms were on seats within seconds. As the recruits waited for her to speak, Maggie stared at her hair. It was cut short – shorter than Eddie's. She had never seen a woman with hair that short before. She hoped all the recruits weren't going to be expected to sport similar styles – her father would surely keel over if she returned home with such an extreme cut, not to mention the effect it would have on the appearance of her ears. The short style certainly made this woman look extremely stern.

'Somebody got out of bed on the wrong side this morning,' Maggie whispered under her breath, nudging Annie with her elbow and giving her a wink. Annie gave her a nervous smile back and blushed furiously, before darting a terrified look at the woman standing in front of them. *What a stick-in-the-mud*, thought Maggie, as the woman started talking.

'My name is Sub-Commandant Frost and you will address me and any other officer of a higher rank than yourself as "Sir".' As she spoke, she surveyed the women in front of her, fixing her eyes on each one for a few seconds before moving on to the next.

'You have been chosen to be part of a very important opportunity, one that may change the way the future looks for millions of women. If we get this wrong then we won't only be letting ourselves down, we will be letting them down too.' As Sub-Commandant Frost fixed her gaze on Maggie, she could feel herself squirming in her seat. She had never felt so out of her depth in her life. She was tempted to jump up and bolt, but even though she had boasted about having youth on her side she was quite sure this giant would have a hold of her before she was even clear of her seat.

'Our main priority,' Sub-Commandant Frost continued, moving her glare to Annie, who visibly flinched and screwed up her button nose when it landed on her, 'is to protect women and children and to keep them safe from men – and from themselves. The suffrage movement has long fought for better protection for vulnerable women and children, and now we have a chance to make a difference. We can ensure perpetrators are brought to justice instead of getting away with their crimes, as they have done for too long.' Maggie could feel a rising sense of pride in the room as her new boss continued. 'The police commissioner has given us permission to patrol the streets, with a particular focus on enforcing those aspects of the Defence of the Realm Act pertaining to prostitution. You must remember, our role is one of diversion rather than prosecution. We will also be looking out for respectable young women who are having their heads turned by the men in uniform in their towns.

'We will be working on a voluntary and unofficial basis in the areas where chief constables are willing to accommodate us. We need to prove to the commissioner that our services are very much needed long-term. We already have women trained up and patrolling and I can assure you that only the best will make it through our schooling. If you don't cut it, you will be let go.' Maggie gulped, feeling more nervous by the minute.

'We need to get to any vulnerable women, respectable or otherwise, and move them on before the police arrest them for selling themselves. We also need to look out for children, who are more likely to push the boundaries with their fathers away at war. We'll maintain a presence in the courts, so any woman unlucky enough to be part of proceedings will have much-needed female support.' A woman at the front let out a big sneeze. Sub-Commandant Frost stopped dead in her tracks and stared right through the poor soul for a good ten seconds before continuing, 'We will patrol streets, parks, alleyways and any open spaces.

'Any young girls we come across will be advised to return home. Courting couples will be swiftly moved on. We'll check public houses to ensure no soliciting is taking place. For this task an air of class and confidence is essential.' Maggie straightened her back as she heard that last sentence. *At least there's one thing I will be good at.* Maggie decided she was ready to give this her best shot as Sub-Commandant Frost, who she had already decided to nickname 'Frosty', explained what they would be learning over the course of the next few weeks. It was a long list: drills, police court procedure, first aid, giving and taking evidence, general police laws, and even ju-jitsu so they could protect themselves if they got into bother.

'I hope there won't be any need for the martial arts,' Annie said anxiously as she discussed the timetable with Maggie after the talk. Everyone had been advised to move around the room 'to get to know each other', but the two of them had stayed firmly in their seats. Annie seemed a bit offish, Maggie thought, but she could tell she was just as nervous as she was. She wasn't going to go out of her way to be friends with her, but she was feeling far too intimidated to go and speak to the older women – Annie was the only ally she had right now.

Maggie felt a rush of hope when she spotted the younger-looking woman who had walked past the end of their row just before Frosty had started her speech. Her red hair was pulled back tight into a bun and she was chatting eagerly with a group of older women. She was tiny compared to them, but she held herself so confidently Maggie couldn't see her having a problem with giving off an air of authority. Maggie stared at her until she caught her attention. As soon as they locked eyes, Maggie grinned and waved at the woman. But she stared straight through her before turning away. Maggie felt her blood boil at the blatant snub. She didn't want to show her hurt to Annie, so she turned back round to face her and continue their conversation.

'Everyone else seems to already know each other,' Annie

observed, looking around the room at the groups of women who had formed and were talking enthusiastically.

'I reckon they're all part of the suffrage movement,' Maggie said. 'They're all so old,' she added, rolling her eyes.

'They don't seem *that* old,' Annie said, screwing up her nose and shooting Maggie an apprehensive look. Maggie felt slighted again – she hadn't meant to be mean.

'Goodness, I was only trying to lighten the mood,' she replied, letting out a dramatic huff, and Annie blushed yet again. The pair of them sat in silence for a few minutes, Annie chewing on her fingernails, before they were interrupted by another young woman who looked wholly out of place.

'Hi, I'm Irene. Mind if I join you?' she said with an air of false confidence Maggie recognised straight away. Looking her up and down, Maggie wondered how in God's name she had managed to get a place in the WPV. Her dress was worn and a bit grimy, and although her long dark-brown hair was clean, it obviously hadn't been cut in months, if not years, and had been put up clumsily.

'Yes. By all means,' Maggie said hurriedly, trying to smooth over the awkwardness caused by her rather unsubtle appraisal. She turned the seat in front of them round so that she could sit there, hoping that she hadn't come across as rude – but from the look of hurt on Irene's face, she didn't think she had been successful.

'I'm Annie. This is Maggie,' Annie said.

'Sorry to intrude,' Irene said quietly, looking pointedly at Maggie, and still looking upset. 'It's just everyone else in here is so much older than me and you both seem young too so I—'

'See I *told* you they were old!' Maggie interrupted, before Irene had a chance to finish. She felt her face flushing red as she realised how impolite she had sounded. She was just so nervous, and so excited that somebody agreed with her, that the words had come rushing out of her mouth before she'd had a chance to filter herself. Before she had time to apologise for her outburst, Frosty clapped her hands and brought everyone to attention again.

'We have permission from magistrates to attend the police courts and observe proceedings. If your name is called, go to the main entrance and you will be escorted to the courts,' she said. Maggie crossed her fingers and had to stop herself from crying out in triumph when her name was read out. Annie and Irene's names were called too, along with a few others, and they all trooped off together. *How exciting*, Maggie thought. She had never set foot in a courtroom. She couldn't wait to tell Eddie all about it that evening.

The fact that the three girls stood out amongst the older, burly-looking women meant Maggie couldn't help but feel a bond with her new acquaintances, despite the fact that they hadn't exactly got off to the best start. However, looking around at everyone chatting and smiling together, she felt a sinking disappointment in the pit of her stomach. She had expected to make great friends straight away, not put her foot in it again and again, nor was it quite the glamorous introduction to life as a bobby she had imagined. Still, she felt a sense of pride at what she was doing, and she hoped it would get better if she stuck it out.

Waiting for their chaperone at the front of the building with the other women, Maggie spotted the girl who had snubbed her in the hall. Thinking maybe she hadn't noticed her earlier, she decided to give her another chance. She caught her eye and gave her a friendly smile, but the girl gave her a blank look and turned away.

Although she knew she was overreacting, Maggie was upset. She was trying her best to make a go of this and get along with everyone, but she seemed to be making a right mess of it. She had been a bit of a babbling, nervous mess around Annie and Irene – so she could understand why they might not be falling over themselves to become properly acquainted with her. But this girl hadn't even given her a chance. It felt like she had kicked her when she was already down, and it had put her nose out of joint. Who was she to judge her as not worthy of even a polite smile? As the chaperone called out names to check everyone was present, Maggie made sure she paid attention when the woman who had now slighted her twice raised her hand. Sarah Brown.

2

Four chaperones took a group of six recruits each. Maggie was sent off with Annie, Irene, Sarah Brown and two older women. Their chaperone was a funny-looking woman who Maggie felt was rather out of place at the WPV. All the other superior officers were tall, sturdy and strong. But this woman was short and spindly, and her uniform hung loosely off her like it was a few sizes too big. When she revealed she was a newly qualified recruit as opposed to a senior officer, it made a little more sense to Maggie. They had taken her on for training, so they clearly weren't opposed to a slighter frame lower down the ranks.

'My name's Clare,' she told the group in a soft voice. 'I'm taking you to Bow Street police court. I've just finished training myself, so if you have any questions for me, let me know. It's all fresh in my mind!'

'Why not somewhere closer to headquarters?' one of the older recruits asked Clare as they made their way there on a crowded bus. The woman who asked the question was probably in her thirties, Maggie thought, and very well spoken.

'The staff at Bow Street have been exceptionally helpful to WPV recruits so far,' Clare explained. 'Some of the courts closer to our base have been quite obstructive. One of the magistrates makes a habit of ridiculing us, while his staff do everything in their power to get us thrown out in the middle of cases. They don't seem to understand how important it is for us to get an idea of how certain cases are dealt with.' Maggie was beginning to realise how much resistance she was going to come up against in becoming a WPV member. It seemed like it was going to be a lot tougher than she had anticipated when she had signed up in a fit of pique. 'As soon as we find court staff willing to accommodate, and even help us, we make regular visits to them,' Clare added.

As they made their way off the bus, Maggie thought she caught Sarah looking back over her shoulder at her with a look of disdain. *What is her problem?* she thought furiously as the group followed Clare down the road. But she decided to bite her tongue for now. She needed to keep a low profile and confronting another recruit in front of everyone was not the way to do that.

When they reached the court, the quiet chatter amongst the trainees came to a halt. It seemed the rest of the group were as apprehensive as Maggie. Filing into the courtroom, Maggie was surprised to see a woman already there. From what she had heard of police stations and courts, she had expected the recruits to be the only females in sight.

'Good morning, Miss Cole,' Clare said formally as they walked past her to get to a row of seats at the back of the court. 'Miss Cole is a probation officer,' Clare leaned over and whispered to them all once they were seated. Maggie was about to ask exactly what that meant when a well-dressed man walked in and stood facing everyone at a desk at the front of the court. 'That's today's magistrate,' Clare explained, motioning for them all to stand up. They did so, as did everyone else in the room. The magistrate looked around, gave a curt nod, and then sat down at the desk. Everyone else followed suit, so Maggie did the same. Clare looked down the row of seats at Maggie and the other recruits and put her finger up to her lips to let them all know they needed to stay silent.

A young woman was escorted into the room by two policemen, and Maggie tried to guess what she was in trouble for. When a charge of soliciting was read out, Maggie was surprised. Even though she was clearly poor, the woman looked smart and respectable. She realised then that she had an awful lot to learn. The woman looked around the room nervously, and Maggie gave her a friendly smile. She wanted her to know she had support. She was glad that she and her fellow recruits were there and the poor girl wasn't on her own in a room full of men, as would normally be the case. She didn't have anyone to represent her, so she spoke for herself.

'Sir, I'm awful sorry for what I done,' she told the magistrate in almost a whisper. 'It's just, I've got a little baby to feed and I can't find any work. I've never done it before.' She stopped to wipe a tear from her cheek. 'I was desperate,' she added, sobbing now. Maggie spotted one of the policemen rolling his eyes and she was filled with rage. The magistrate shuffled through his papers as he spoke to the woman – not even bothering to look in her direction, let alone at her face.

'You have a responsibility to keep your temptations to yourself,' he said. 'You can't expect men to control themselves when you behave the way you do.' Maggie was fuming now. Surely – if anything – they should both be at fault? Why wasn't the man expected to show some self-control, too?

'It sounds like it will do you good to learn how to be a decent, contributing citizen,' the magistrate added patronisingly. Still reading through the papers on his desk and sounding disinterested, he sighed before continuing, 'You will do nine months' hard labour.' Maggie gasped, horrified at the severity of the punishment. 'In these difficult times, women like you are a danger to society and need to be made an example of,' he added, finally looking the woman in the eye.

Maggie had to bite her tongue to stop herself from crying out in objection. How could he justify sending this poor woman off to prison to carry out such gruelling work for so long? Who would look after her baby? She spotted Irene sitting on her hands and she smiled to herself. She was certainly very different to Irene in a lot of ways, but she could see they were on the same wavelength regarding this.

'Please, it was me first time!' the defendant cried as the policemen grabbed her by an arm each to lead her out of the room. 'I bet the men who pay us don't get no charges!' she shouted as she was forcefully guided out.

Maggie was fighting back tears. Now she had witnessed the unfairness of the justice system towards women first hand, she wanted to stay on and complete her training even more. If they couldn't change the system, they could at least try to stop the women ending up in the courtroom in the first place.

Next up was a man who Maggie thought was probably around the same age as her father. He was well dressed in an expensive suit and held his hat in front of him with both hands. Maggie noticed straight away the officers allowed him to walk into the room by himself, and stood back at a respectful distance as he gave the magistrate his name and address. It was a far cry from the treatment the woman before him had received. He stood proudly as his charge of grievous bodily harm was read out. *He should be hanging his head in shame*, Maggie thought angrily.

She sat forward, listening intently as the man's lawyer explained how his wife had hidden some household expenses from him, and as he had tried to grab the money from her after confronting her, she had tripped and fallen down the stairs. The poor woman had cut her head open and broken her arm. Maggie couldn't help but laugh bitterly to herself at the obvious cover story – it sounded like something her father would come up with when her mother joined them for breakfast with a black eye. So, she was astounded when the magistrate went along with it.

'Is your wife all right now?' he asked in a friendly tone.

'Yes, sir,' the man nodded. 'She's back on her best behaviour.'

'Yes, well, I can understand how hard it is to keep some of these women in check.' Maggie was visibly squirming in her seat now, she was finding it so hard not to protest. Clare shot her a look and put her finger up to her lips again when she caught Maggie's eye. She was ready to blow but she took a deep breath and tried to relax. 'Because of the injuries inflicted I will have to punish you, you understand?' the magistrate continued.

'Yes, sir,' the man said with a nod of his head.

'I'm sentencing you to three months in the first division. It will be over before you know it. Next time, take more care when disciplining your wife.'

Maggie was desperate to leave so that she could let out the scream of frustration that had been building inside her ever since that odious man had walked into the courtroom. But she had to sit through several more cases of soliciting, violence and pickpocketing over the next hour. They were dealt with so quickly, Maggie found it hard to keep up. The one thing that was clear was that the men were handed lighter sentences than the women. The magistrate also afforded the men more sympathy and understanding.

'Miss Cole is very helpful,' Clare told the group as they stood to allow the magistrate to leave the court for a break in proceedings. 'If you have any questions, we can grab her outside before we make our way back to headquarters. But don't worry, you'll learn all about the different types of processes and punishments in your lessons over the coming weeks.' It seemed everyone was as overwhelmed by the session as Maggie, as not one of them asked a question.

As they walked back towards the bus stop, Maggie ran ahead after Clare. 'I can't stop thinking about that first woman we saw,' she said, trying to catch her breath. 'Her poor baby, being away from her for so long. Who's going to look after it? And then that man afterwards getting such a short sentence in comparison – and in the first division no less! He won't have to lift a finger – I've heard they get comfy beds, fire-places and all sorts in there!' She was riled again now, her voice rising.

'I feel the same,' Clare said, placing an understanding hand on Maggie's shoulder. 'It's best you try not to let it get to you so much, though. You'll see a lot of that, trust me. But that's why we're here – to help however we can.'

'I suppose so,' sighed Maggie. 'Doesn't help that woman though, does it?'

'No,' Clare agreed sadly. 'But there's only so much we can do, and this is a great start. Your passion is astounding – they'll love you at headquarters.'

Maggie couldn't help but smile to herself at Clare's comment.

'That was exciting, wasn't it?' Annie said to Maggie as she sat down on the bus next to her on the journey back to St Stephen's House. She was more animated than Maggie had seen her all morning.

'It was interesting,' said Maggie carefully. Now she had calmed down, she remembered she had struggled to follow a lot of the cases. She didn't want to give away the fact she had found it all confusing, but she also didn't want to come across overly confident. Irene sat on the seat in front of them, and didn't utter a word for the whole journey.

Back at headquarters, the group were told to get some lunch ahead of a ju-jitsu lesson that afternoon. They only had twenty minutes, so Maggie grabbed a bowl of soup and some bread, which seemed at least a few days past being edible. She sat with Annie and Irene. Sarah was sitting with two of the older recruits. *Good riddance to her*, Maggie thought.

They were too busy eating as quickly as they could to chat, and Maggie got the sense they felt as uncomfortable as she did sitting together. She couldn't think of anything to say to them. She had been drawn to them at the morning's briefing as they were the youngest in the room, but if she was honest with herself, they weren't the sort of people she would normally spend time with. Annie was too shy, and Irene was – well, she just had a different background to Maggie, and she wasn't sure they had all that much in common.

As they ate in an awkward silence, Maggie listened to the women further down the table, who were all getting to know each other. Maggie thought they must be in their forties. It felt strange to be going through training with women who were around the same age as her mother. She was surprised to hear their backgrounds; there were teachers, social workers, nurses and women of leisure.

'Have to be able to support yourself, seeing as there's no pay involved,' Irene piped up out of nowhere. Maggie looked around, confused. 'Their jobs,' Irene added, pointing discreetly towards the women. 'They must come from wealthy families if they can afford to take time off to do this.'

'I gave up my part-time job as a typist to be here,' Annie said quietly. 'We're not exactly what you would call wealthy, but the family will get by without my small contribution.'

Maggie was in the fortunate position that her parents paid for everything and hadn't insisted on her going out and finding work yet, although if she admitted that here it might raise suspicions about her age. She supposed she should probably describe herself as a woman of leisure if she was asked. Any more lies and she would surely end up falling over one of them and giving herself away. She was just about to ask Irene what she did for work, or if her family were supporting her financially through this, when a loud clap rang out through the room and everyone fell silent.

'Lunch is over!' a short and stocky man in a police uniform announced. He had small eyes, a neatly trimmed moustache and a big red boil on the end of his nose. 'I'm Sergeant Bridge, and that's how you will address me,' he added. He obviously wasn't keen on the WPV convention of calling everyone in a position of superiority 'Sir'. 'Follow me into the main hall, ladies. I'm going to give you your first taste of ju-jitsu.'

In the hall, Sergeant Bridge explained that he was retired from the police force, but he had been brought back in to help with their training. 'Who here has done ju-jitsu before?' he asked the room. Maggie was shocked as most of the recruits put their hands in the air. She, Annie and Irene were three of about six with their hands still firmly by their sides. Maggie really hadn't expected so many of them to know martial arts already. She wondered where on earth they had learned it. Sergeant Bridge looked just as confused.

'Have you never heard of suffrajitsu, Sergeant Bridge?' a voice called out from the back. Frosty, who had been standing at the door observing, broke out into a grin. *She looks a lot friendlier when she smiles*, Maggie thought.

'A lot of the suffragettes have been learning the martial arts to deal with angry hecklers who get up on stage during demonstrations,' Frosty explained.

'And to fight back against the police,' a woman to Maggie's right muttered under her breath.

'These sessions will be more of a refresher for most of the recruits,' Frosty said. 'Although I'm sure there's a lot more you can teach them, Sergeant Bridge,' she added kindly. The officer looked flustered but quickly regained his composure.

Maggie was surprised Frosty hadn't warned him that a lot of the trainees were already well-versed in ju-jitsu. But then she noticed that Frosty seemed to be enjoying having got one over on him. It was likely she hadn't had the chance to put such a high-ranking man in his place before.

'Right. Well, we'll go through some basic self-defence moves today. Apparently most of you will already know them. But seeing as I planned this lesson on the understanding you were all beginners, you'll just have to lump it.' Sergeant Bridge had come across as stern but friendly at first. Now he'd had his feathers ruffled, he looked rather forbidding. Maggie spotted Frosty smirking at another senior female officer standing at the back of the hall before turning around and leaving.

They were instructed to get into pairs, and the officer Frosty had smirked at came to the front of the class to help Sergeant Bridge with his demonstration. Maggie looked around and found herself standing next to Annie, who seemed to have followed her from lunch to the hall.

'Perhaps we should pair up then?' Annie asked timidly. Reluctantly, Maggie agreed to be her partner. She had been hoping to find a better match – someone who wouldn't be too scared to get stuck in and try out all the moves.

The recruits watched as Sergeant Bridge gently placed his hand on the officer's shoulder and twisted her arm behind her back with his other hand to incapacitate her. But Maggie found herself unable to concentrate. Out of the corner of her eye she was certain she could see Sarah glaring over at her. She was too afraid of being reprimanded by Sergeant Bridge to check, but as soon as his back was turned she risked a quick glance – only to see Sarah swinging her head away from Maggie's direction at the exact same moment. She *had* been staring at her! This was really vexing her now. What was this girl's problem?

Maggie just wanted a chance to speak to her; she was certain she would like her if only she would give her the opportunity. Annoyingly, there was no way she could confront her now – she would be kicked out on her ear if she caused a commotion before the first day was even up. She decided to focus on the ugly boil on Sergeant Bridge's nose instead. At least that way she would be keeping her eyes fixed where they should be.

When it was their turn to practise the move, Maggie was grateful to discover that, unlike her, Annie had been concentrating on the routine. She guided Maggie through it with an easy patience, and Maggie began to think she might not be so bad after all.

Sergeant Bridge took them through a few more sequences, then instructed them to practise them in order over and over, so that they became second nature. Maggie was keen to do well in this lesson – after all, the martial arts could end up saving her in some tricky situations. But she was sure Sarah was still glaring over whenever she got the chance. The fact it was distracting her from learning the ju-jitsu was making her angry. She decided to pretend Sarah wasn't there for the rest of the lesson, and made a pact with herself not to worry about her any more – she wasn't worth it.

3

Over the next few weeks, Maggie managed to keep her new resolution. The training was intense, and although Sarah continued to ignore her, Maggie chose to rise above it and instead focus her attention on learning as much as she could, and keeping her cover story with her parents in place.

So far, they didn't seem to suspect a thing. Maggie was rather enjoying making up tales of fun games and japes with the orphans in response to her father's daily grilling at the dinner table. Also, an added bonus of being out of the house for so long every day was that she avoided most of her father's moods. Although this came with guilt at leaving her mother to bear the brunt of them, Maggie reasoned that men like her father were exactly why it was essential for women to make a place for themselves in the police force. All in all, she was rather proud of herself.

So far, Maggie had always seemed to be in a different training group to the girls she had met that first day. To begin with she had been pleased, but the older women she kept getting put with were very serious. For people who were supposed to be so concerned about equality, they didn't treat Maggie like much of an equal. A few of them talked to her like she was a naughty child and the rest just bossed her around or ignored her. A lot of them had been in trouble with the police during their time as suffragettes. There was talk of lashing out at police officers, starting fires and carrying out hunger strikes. Maggie found them quite petrifying, so there was no possibility she was going to stand her ground with them.

Annie and Irene might not have been her cup of tea but at least she felt as if she could be herself around them. She had bumped into them a few times around headquarters and found herself surprisingly happy to be in their company. So, when she arrived at training that morning she was pleased as punch when everyone was given a chance to choose their own group for the day.

'It's time for you to put into practice what you have been learning in the classroom,' Frosty announced, once everyone had made it into the hall and was sitting obediently in their seats. 'You will all be going on a practice patrol,' she added, seemingly enjoying the look of apprehension on a lot of the faces in the room. Maggie could see Annie from where she was sitting and was shocked to witness her turn so pale at the announcement. Frosty spent a while recapping what their responsibilities were and what they could and couldn't do before sending them out to fend for themselves. Maggie sought out Annie and Irene straight away, but when Sarah headed in their direction, she couldn't believe the girl's cheek.

'She's got another think coming if she reckons she's teaming up with us,' she said, just loud enough for Annie and Irene to hear but not Sarah on her approach.

'Why?' asked Irene, looking confused, but Sarah had made it to the group and was standing with them, so Maggie couldn't respond. Her bravado quickly faded and she waved her hand at Irene, muttering, 'Don't worry.' Maggie huffed as the four of them made their way to collect their uniforms. She had managed to push Sarah and her rudeness to the back of her mind the last few weeks, but being on patrol with her was going to rile her up again, she could feel it.

'Gosh, it's not the most feminine outfit, is it?' Annie remarked as they headed off to get changed. The uniform consisted of a dark blue tunic-style jacket with lots of pockets. 'WPV' was spelled out in silver letters on the shoulder straps. They were also issued skirts, which reached way down past their ankles, as well as sturdy felt riding-style hats and cumbersome black boots.

'I heard someone describe it as "handsome" and I can see what they meant now,' Maggie giggled as a group of women already kitted out walked past them along the corridor. Secretly, she was relieved she was going to have all her limbs completely covered. If her father had another one of his moods, the uniform would be perfect for hiding bruises. She wasn't so happy about the hat – it was itchy and also seemed to accentuate her already big ears.

'It seems like just the kind of garb that'll get us taken seriously,' said Sarah, who up until now hadn't breathed a word to any of them, let alone introduced herself. 'I'm Sarah, by the way,' she said formally. 'Let's meet back here once we're all changed,' she added, before walking ahead into the changing rooms. *Bit bossy*, thought Maggie, but she kept that to herself. She didn't want to be accused of being mean.

The group were sent to St James's Park for their practice patrol. A tall, broad woman named Inspector Hughes was assigned as their supervising officer. She didn't seem keen on smiling and her hair was cut short, just like Frosty's. Maggie was grateful there had been no mention so far of recruits getting haircuts. She wondered why some of the senior officers seemed intent on looking so manly. *I don't fancy getting on the wrong side of her*, she thought as Inspector Hughes introduced herself.

'I will walk with you to the park,' she told the trainees, staring above their heads, 'and then you will walk the perimeter as you would on a proper patrol. I'll hold back and follow you at a distance to observe your actions, and only step in to help should the need arise.' *Brilliant*, thought Maggie, her hopes of some normal chatter with Annie and

Irene dashed. It had been made very clear to them that recruits were not to engage in conversation while on duty. *I wonder if we can get away with ditching her*, she thought mischievously. All of a sudden, Eddie's last words to her before he agreed to help with her fake papers rang in her ears.

'Stay out of mischief, Mags,' he'd said, with out-of-character sternness. 'Any trouble and they'll be straight on to Father.' That final sentence had brought home to her the importance of behaving in a way that nothing else could. She shuddered to think what would happen if her father found out about this. *Getting through this without Daddy's knowledge is more important than having any fun*, she concluded glumly as she set off towards the park with the group in silence.

On the walk, Maggie felt as though she was under a microscope. Every person they passed stared at them. It was like they had never seen women in uniform before! Although, Maggie reminded herself, a lot of them probably hadn't, actually. She could understand why they were all so interested, especially as there was a group of them. But she felt extremely self-conscious. The fact that the uniform was so stiff and uncomfortable didn't help – the skirt felt as heavy as metal and really weighed her down – and she was sure people were staring at her ears.

At St James's Park, Inspector Hughes motioned for the girls to walk ahead of her. Carefully concentrating on the correct walk and pace that had been drummed into them over the previous weeks, the girls stayed quiet and looked eagerly around them for anyone loitering.

But Maggie couldn't help herself. The lack of conversation was killing her. She risked a quick glance back and when she saw Inspector Hughes sitting on a bench and definitely out of earshot, she almost cried out in joy. 'I've got a plan,' she whispered under her breath, keeping her eyes firmly trained ahead.

'What about?' Annie replied nervously, snapping her head back to check on their supervisor.

'Shh! Eyes ahead!' Maggie hissed. She braced herself for a telling off, but Inspector Hughes didn't bite. She exhaled in relief before sharing her bright idea: 'Old Hughes is keeping a good distance. As long as we keep our voices down and carry on looking around enthusiastically, we can get away with having a bit of a chat while we walk the beat.'

'I don't know, I don't want to get into any trouble,' Annie said anxiously. As they rounded a corner Maggie glanced back again. Inspector Hughes was nowhere to be seen.

'She's obviously decided to have a little time out on the bench – she's not even following us,' she laughed. 'See for yourselves!' The group stopped and turned around tentatively, only to see that Maggie was right. 'She's just going to wait for us to do a lap of the park, the lazy so-and-so. Which leaves us free to relax until we're back in her sights,' Maggie said, clapping her hands together in glee.

'Fine, but let's make sure we keep a good eye out for anyone doing anything shifty,' said Irene.

'Yes, of course. Although given that we can't actually arrest anyone, I don't see what we'll be able to do about it,' Maggie huffed.

'We can move women on before they get caught doing something they *can* be arrested for,' Sarah said matter-of-factly. 'They should be grateful to us for giving them some guidance and stepping in before they get themselves into serious trouble. If it were me, I'd be relieved to see a WPV and not a policeman. I'd count my blessings before scarpering.'

Know-it-all, Maggie thought before replying curtly, 'Of course, I should have known *you'd* have an answer.'

'What's that supposed to mean?' Sarah said, turning around to face Maggie, her eyes wide with surprise.

'You think you're better than us,' Maggie shot back. Even though her brain was shouting at her to stop, she couldn't help herself. 'You've been giving me dirty looks ever since we started training and I want to know what your problem is!'

'I don't know what you mean,' Sarah said quietly, her shoulders slouched and her head cocked to the side, confusion written all over her face.

'Come on, ladies, we're meant to be stopping trouble, not causing it,' Annie said, stepping between the pair of them and peering back fretfully to check that Inspector Hughes hadn't started following them again. Maggie had to look again to make sure it was Annie who had spoken. It was so out of character for her to do something brave like that. She looked extremely nervous now, though, as if she regretted sticking her neck out.

'Just watch how you look at people,' Maggie snapped before walking away, praying the others would follow suit and she'd have landed the final word. *That told her*, she thought as, sure enough, everyone fell into line next to her – even Sarah, who was now looking quite sheepish. She looked across at Annie and saw her face relax. She was obviously relieved her intervention had defused the situation.

They walked around the outside of the park in an awkward silence until they came across a man and a woman lying on the grass together, barely hidden by a tree trunk. The couple were kissing passionately and the man, who was wearing army uniform, had his hand on the woman's bottom. The four of them froze and stared at the blatant display of affection nervously.

'Maybe we should go back and get Inspector Hughes,' said Annie, biting her fingernails.

'She'll just get annoyed we've ruined her tea break,' scoffed Maggie, keen to make the most of this opportunity for some excitement. She remembered the look of relief on Annie's face when Sarah had backed down from her after their cross words. *She's so jittery all the time*, she thought, *even stepping in back there had her petrified. Maybe dealing with something like this will give her a bit of a confidence boost.*

'You did well at playing peacekeeper back there,' Maggie said encouragingly to Annie. 'Why don't you take this?'

Fear engulfed Annie's face.

'We'll be right here to back you up,' Irene encouraged. It seemed that Maggie wasn't the only one who wanted to help Annie gain some assertiveness. Sarah opened her mouth, clearly about to protest on Annie's behalf, but stopped when she saw that Annie had closed her eyes and was taking deep breaths. It was almost as if she was silently gearing herself up.

'You can do this,' Annie whispered to herself firmly before she straightened out her jacket and pushed a stray curl behind her ear.

'Remember what they told us in training,' Irene said quietly, keeping her eyes fixed on the canoodling soldier and his lady friend.

'Yes,' replied Annie, letting out a long breath. 'We either tell them to go home and hope they obey, attempt to make a citizen's arrest or wait for a constable to come to our assistance,' she recited, sounding more confident now. She took another deep breath and walked slowly towards the pair. 'Excuse me,' she said, so timidly Maggie thought she sounded like a child.

'Eh?' the man looked up and saw Annie looming over him.

'Excuse me, sir, but you're going to have to move in – I mean, on,' she stammered, any hint of confidence having now disappeared from her voice. The soldier simply laughed and went back to kissing the woman – who acted like she hadn't even noticed poor Annie. 'This isn't allowed, you will *have* to move on,' Annie said, louder this time and clearly trying her best to sound more assertive.

'Yeah all right, love, move along yourself!' the man jeered, glaring up at Annie before going back to his business. The couple continued kissing as Annie stood over them watching. Any previous bravado had long since gone and it was obvious she had no idea what to do next. She glanced over at Maggie, who nodded to her in encouragement.

'Ex – excuse me,' she said again, this time even more timidly, and Maggie cringed. *Gosh, Eddie, I know I'm meant to be keeping myself out of trouble, but I think I'm going to have to step in here*, she fretted as the soldier jumped to his feet and towered over Annie, standing so close to her that his puffed-out chest was practically touching her nose. Maggie's palms started to sweat. This was not going to plan.

'What do you want now?' he roared, and Annie took a step back in fear and shock. He came forward so that he was almost on top of her again, and she looked around at the other three girls with desperation on her face. Maggie had just decided she was going to step in when the man barked aggressively, 'Come on then, love! Why don't you try telling me what to do again?' He raised his hand, and as he did so, Maggie instinctively flinched. Fear shot through her body and instead of rushing over and helping Annie, she froze – just as she did whenever her father lifted a hand to her.

The soldier slapped Annie across the face with such force that she fell straight to the ground. Irene and Sarah rushed to her side. Maggie stood still for another few seconds, visions of her father rooting her to the spot. Then all of a sudden, she snapped out of it – Annie needed her. As Irene crouched down to tend to Annie, Maggie and Sarah lunged at the soldier in unison. Their combined force and the element of surprise saw him fly backwards and fall onto his bottom with a thud.

Both girls stood over him, ready to put into practice the ju-jitsu moves they had been learning over the last few weeks. Maggie couldn't see the soldier any more. Instead, it was her father laid out in front of her, and the rage and pain of years of torment welled within her. Now she found she wanted him to try to hurt her, just so that she would be able to teach him a lesson. But the man stayed down on the grass, looking up at them both in bewilderment.

'You had best move along like my colleague said, *sir*, before we get some backup along to deal with you,' Sarah spat, with such venom and authority even Maggie felt intimidated.

'We'll take it from here!' a voice boomed from behind them. Maggie spun round and saw Inspector Hughes bounding towards them with a male constable in tow. The officer hauled the man to his feet and arrested him on the spot.

'On your way, missy. And have a bit of a think before you start misbehaving in public again,' Inspector Hughes said to the soldier's companion, who didn't hang around to argue. 'Ladies,' she added, 'you head back to HQ and I'll follow on once we've dealt with this charming young man.' The group immediately scuttled away.

'Well, you're a force to be reckoned with!' Maggie exclaimed once they had exited the park, looking over at Sarah.

'I've had enough of these men thinking they can knock us around and just get away with it,' Sarah replied with calm determination. *You and me both*, Maggie thought. 'They need to realise things are changing,' Sarah added.

'Thank you,' Annie said gratefully to the group. 'That really wasn't like they made it sound in training. I thought the uniform would help me out a bit.'

'Well, the higher-ranking officers are finding their way as

much as us, really,' Sarah said as she looked at Annie's cheek, which was bright red and slightly swollen. 'The commissioner may have given the go-ahead for them to form the WPV, but he pretty much left them to it when it came to training. I heard he gave them a list of textbooks to study and threw in a couple of sergeants to help with the physical stuff, and told them to get on with it. They haven't had many recruits through before us to test the waters, either. Don't forget, it's going to take a lot of men a long time to get used to having women in authority. And don't think just because they've let us get involved that the police are going to be any friendlier than that chap who just roughed you up, Annie.'

As everyone continued in silence, mulling over Sarah's words, she added, 'Inspector Hughes may have found a constable willing to help quickly, but they won't all be as eager. It's going to be a long road and we're going to have to stick together. Now, let's get back to St Stephen's House quickly – we don't want Inspector Hughes to beat us back.'

'Yes, let's not give Frosty any reason to turf us out just yet,' Maggie joked.

'Frosty?' Irene asked as the group quickened their pace.

'Yes, it quite suits her, doesn't it?' Maggie tried to laugh it off as she expected Sarah to scold her. But to her surprise, all three girls giggled along with her.

'So how is it that you know so much about all this?' Maggie asked Sarah. She had decided to let the dirty looks go for now and give the girl a chance. She had been friendly enough to her this morning. And, after all, someone who jumped to a colleague's defence like Sarah had just then was a good person to have around – especially in a job like this. Perhaps Maggie had judged her too quickly, after all.

'I work at *The Vote*,' Sarah said proudly, 'so I've been following the fight for female pollies ever so closely. I get to hear all the ins and outs of how it's going.'

Maggie couldn't help but feel impressed. Whenever she had managed to get a look at *The Vote*, she had really enjoyed the writing, and Sarah was clearly well-versed in the quest for the WPV. Also, her father hated that newspaper, so it was satisfying to know she was befriending one of its writers.

'I'm here to show my father I'm capable of a lot more than he realises,' Maggie said sheepishly. She felt rather foolish admitting she had signed up to show him she wasn't just a silly little girl when Sarah was obviously so serious about the cause and women's rights. But she couldn't very well tell these girls she was desperate to escape his mood swings and beatings. She hardly knew them and, besides, no matter how much she hated the control her father had over her and the fear she constantly felt in his presence, what went on behind closed doors was private. She had never even told her closest friends about what she went through at home. She often wondered if they would treat her differently if they knew the truth. Still, she spotted the disapproving look on Sarah's face and quickly added, 'and I want to do my bit during the war and help the women's lib movement!' for good measure. Keen to divert attention away from herself, she hastily asked Annie why she had joined.

'Well, my mother pushed me into it, if I'm honest,' Annie admitted. 'As you've probably all guessed, I'm not the most confident of people. She thought this might bring me out of my shell a bit. I suppose she wasn't counting on me getting knocked about before training was even over.' Her shoulders drooped and her hand moved to cradle her cheek, which was still bright red.

'Just think, what a story to tell her when you get home tonight!' exclaimed Maggie, trying to lighten the mood and lift Annie's waning spirit a little. 'I'm sure your mother will be proud to hear how brave you were, going up to that couple all by yourself. None of *us* wanted to do it!'

'Thank you,' said Annie, smiling across at Maggie. They may not have got off to the best start, but Maggie was beginning to see that Annie had probably just been feeling painfully shy on their first day. She sometimes forgot her own bravado was out of the norm. She couldn't imagine how nervous Annie must have been turning up to something so daunting all by herself. Maggie decided she would do her best to help Annie build her confidence.

'You can all call me Mags,' she said amiably. 'It's what my brother and my friends call me.' Seeing the smile spread across Annie's face made Maggie feel warm inside. She was carrying out her plan already.

'What about you?' Maggie asked Irene, who had gone very quiet all of a sudden.

'Oh, women's lib, same as you and Sarah,' she said quickly before adding, 'D'you suppose Inspector Hughes will make us fill out a report?' *That was odd*, thought Maggie. *She didn't even pause for breath before changing the subject. It looks like I'm not the only one hiding something.* But she decided to let it go, for now. There had been enough drama for one day, and she didn't want it to seem like she was prying – she needed these girls on-side. She could tell she was going to need all the support she could get to make it through this training.

4

After another couple of weeks at headquarters, Maggie felt considerably more confident about her role as a police volunteer.

She had grown closer with Annie, Irene and even Sarah since their dramatic practice patrol. They had all been worried about getting into trouble when they made it back to Frosty, but once word had spread, they had been treated almost like heroes, and had been congratulated in the corridors by the other recruits. Maggie had definitely felt a shift in their attitude towards her – the older women had stopped treating her like a silly little girl.

Even Frosty had had something to say. 'Well done for standing your ground, ladies,' she had told them the next day. 'I've a feeling that soldier will be telling everyone in his regiment to behave around WPV officers from now on. It's just the sort of word-of-mouth help our reputation needs!'

Maggie wasn't so sure that Annie being knocked about was cause for celebration, but she could appreciate the sentiment. She had to admit, the positive reaction from everyone at training had really boosted her new friend. On one of their latest practice patrols, she had even managed to move along a couple who were being amorous in a doorway. She had marched up to them with such confidence and spoken with such authority that they had scarpered immediately, much to Annie's delight – and obvious relief.

Maggie hadn't had quite so much luck when she had taken

the plunge and confronted a young woman loitering in the
street. The poor girl had actually been waiting for her husband
to come and meet her after work. She had been most offended
to be mistaken for a lady of the night. The others had found
it hilarious, but Maggie had gone bright pink and felt mortified for the rest of the day.

The girls had gravitated towards each other on tasks, and
Maggie felt a lot more comfortable being around fellow
recruits who were nearer her age. She found it funny to think
back to how badly she had misjudged Sarah, Annie and Irene
at first. Why, she'd nearly started a fight with Sarah!

Sarah was still bossy as anything and a massive know-it-all,
but Maggie had started to find it endearing. In truth, she
was learning an awful lot from her, and Sarah seemed to
enjoy educating her in return. Maggie had already picked
up a great deal of knowledge about the women's movement
just by being around her. The fact it was information she
would never have accessed through her usual channels, given
her father's attitude, made her appreciate it all the more. She
had even found herself feeling more and more passionate
about the cause – but then it was hard not to get carried
away when you listened to Sarah talking about it.

'I'm still not sure about Irene. I don't feel like I really know
her,' she told Eddie, updating him on her latest adventures
and her new pals as they walked home from the pictures one
Saturday evening.

It was a rare treat to be allowed out so late, and she had
Eddie to thank for convincing their father to agree to the
outing. Unbeknownst to him, they had met some of Maggie's
old school-friends at the picture house, and Eddie had sat a
few rows back and let his sister enjoy some time being herself.
Now Maggie felt the most relaxed she had in weeks. She
was really enjoying training, but she was finding it tiring.

'Maybe Irene just takes a while to open up to people,'

Eddie said as they wandered along the quiet streets towards home. 'Not everyone is as confident as you, Mags.'

Maggie was still convinced Irene was hiding something, but she knew Eddie was trying to steer her away from doing any digging. Eddie stopped to tie his shoelace.

'You do know that if I was on patrol, I'd be pulling us aside to check there was nothing untoward happening, don't you?' Maggie giggled, changing the subject. 'It looks like we're loitering! Just fancy that – someone thinking we are up to no good with each other!' Eddie put his fingers in his mouth and made pretend vomiting noises at the suggestion. 'You have to be suspicious of everyone,' Maggie added more seriously. 'We're only looking out for the women and making sure they don't get themselves into tricky situations.'

'What you're doing is wonderful,' Eddie said, giving his sister a reassuring smile. 'Some of the chaps at university reckon it should stop so many of the soldiers getting struck down with VD. Did you know they had a real problem with it during the Crimean War? They had more soldiers in the hospital than on the battlefield at one point – and all because of a bit of sex!'

Maggie blanched. Her brother had become quite crude since starting university and she wished he wouldn't talk like that around her. WPV training was opening her eyes to such things, but she still didn't want to hear him discussing them. Eddie shook his head in disbelief and laughed. 'Is it any wonder though, with the way women throw themselves at a man in uniform?'

Maggie *did* know about the VD problems – of course, Sarah had told her all about it. And she had also made her realise the men were just as much to blame as the women – if not more so. Thinking back to the discussion, she recalled how shocked she had been when Sarah had explained the Contagious Diseases Act to her. The Government had brought it in before she was even born. Thankfully it had been repealed, but it had given police the power to arrest any woman they suspected of being a prostitute. The poor woman would then be sent for an internal examination, which sounded just awful.

'We need to keep these women on the straight and narrow to avoid any more outbreaks. We also can't risk them bringing back that act,' Sarah had told all the girls as they sat eating lunch a few days earlier. 'The men escape any consequences, even though it's just as much down to them. They're seen as less able to control themselves. It's so unfair that the prostitutes get prosecuted and not the soldiers,' Sarah had added. It had reminded Maggie of the woman who had been unfairly punished on that first court session they had sat in on.

Maggie didn't bring this all up with Eddie. They'd had a lovely evening together and she was really missing spending time with him. She didn't want to rock the boat and start a debate on something they were clearly going to disagree on.

The following Monday at training, Maggie nipped out of a general police laws lesson to use the lavatory. She would never have got away with it with a female commanding officer, but Sergeant Bridge was a soft touch when it came to delicate lady matters.

'It's *very* important I go *now*,' she had stressed, raising her eyebrows significantly. He had immediately turned bright red before waving her off. She didn't actually need to go; she was just so bored of the lecture, she needed a breather. Pushing the lavatory door open, Maggie heard a panicked shuffling noise coming from inside one of the stalls, followed by sniffing and someone blowing their nose. *Odd*, she thought. She had expected to be alone. The female instructors never allowed toilet breaks and no one else had left her lesson. As she went to freshen up in front of a mirror, she heard whoever was in the stall at the end start sobbing uncontrollably.

'Hello?' she asked uncertainly. 'Are . . . are you okay?'

'Maggie?' came back a strangled voice from the other side of the door.

Maggie recognised it straight away. 'Gosh, Annie, dear, whatever is the matter?' she cried.

'I'm fine,' Annie managed through tiny sobs. 'I-I just need a minute and I'll be right as rain.'

'Come on now,' Maggie said, walking over to the stall. 'You don't sound fine. Come on out and talk to me.' She was met with silence. 'Maybe I can help?' she added hopefully. There was a long silence before Maggie heard Annie clear her nose again with a long blow. Then the cubicle door unlocked and Annie stepped out sheepishly. She was red in the face, her eyes puffy. Maggie held out her arms and Annie fell into them.

'I'm sorry. I'm being so silly,' she sobbed into Maggie's shoulder.

'I'm sure you're not,' Maggie reassured her, rubbing her hand up and down her back. Normally Maggie would have run a mile. She was completely out of her comfort zone; she wasn't very good at dealing with other people's emotions. Just as she never shared her home woes with her friends through a desperate need to keep it all private, her friends never opened up to her about their problems either. Maggie went around acting as if everything was rosy when in truth she was miserable because of her father. She often wondered if her friends were hiding awful secrets too. She found it frustrating that everyone at training assumed she'd had an easy life because of her family's wealth and status. So, faced with a tearful Annie, she wasn't quite sure what to do or say. She had grown really fond of her new friend and it upset her to see her in such a state. She wanted to *try* and help, at least.

'I got a letter from my fiancé at the weekend,' Annie said, pulling away gently and dabbing at the tears flowing down her cheeks with a hanky. Maggie motioned for her to sit down. As both girls slid to the cold floor, Annie told Maggie all about Richard and how they had met.

'How's he getting on?' Maggie asked cautiously. When she'd talked to her friends at the pictures, they had told her some tales that made her realise life on the battlefields wasn't quite what everyone had expected. Nearly every single one of her friends had a brother, boyfriend, father or uncle out in France. The men who were still alive certainly weren't as cheery now as they had been when they left. It was making her even more concerned for Eddie, who had been talking more and more about joining up with his university friends. Of course, Maggie would be proud of him for doing his bit. But, at the same time, she was desperate for him to stay safe. So many men weren't returning, and it had only been a few months since it all started. Plus, now Christmas was just a few weeks away, it didn't seem like it was going to be over by then any more.

'Richard says it's tough but he's thinking of me to get through,' Annie said, smiling to herself and staring at the floor, suddenly bashful.

'Good for him!' cried Maggie. 'I bet you're really proud of him – and so you should be.'

'There was just something about the tone of his letter,' Annie admitted quietly. 'He didn't seem as positive as he has done before. It's like a bit of his light is fading. When the ultimatum for Germany to withdraw its troops from Belgium expired, we were out with the crowds in Whitehall. As word spread that we were at war with Germany everyone was so excited – especially Richard. He picked me up and swung me round before giving me a big kiss. He vowed to enlist at New Scotland Yard the very next day with all his friends.'

As Annie recounted the memory, Maggie noticed how she seemed completely wrapped up in it – almost like she was there again and not sitting on a grubby toilet floor with her. It made her realise how much she must miss him. She really didn't want to go through that with Eddie. She was snapped back to the present herself when Annie continued her story.

'Richard was already in the Boys' Brigade. They were desperate for lads with even a little experience, so they took him on without question and he went straight into his regiment as a corporal. When I waved him off after his training, he was full of anticipation and excitement. His first few letters were the same.' She wiped another tear from her cheek. 'But the last few have been downbeat. He's lost most of his friends out there and that can't be good for anyone to go through, can it?'

Maggie really felt for Annie and she desperately wanted to say something to make her feel better – but what? The reality was her fiancé was in real danger and there was a good chance he wouldn't be coming home to her. She bit down on her tongue to stop herself from doing her usual trick of speaking her mind. She took Annie's hand in hers and rested her friend's head gently on her shoulder. 'What you need to do is keep being there for him,' Maggie said softly. 'Your support and positivity will get him through this. He's seeing some terrible things. He needs you to keep his mind occupied and happy when he's not in the thick of it and fighting.'

'But I feel so sad and I miss him,' Annie said, her voice breaking again. 'How can I write a cheery letter to him when I feel like this?'

'Doesn't matter,' said Maggie, sternly now. 'You go home tonight, and you write him a lovely letter full of joy and hope! You tell him how well he's doing and how everyone is proud of him and the rest of the boys out there.' She stroked Annie's head. 'And you tell him all about the training and how much fun you're having. My, I bet you haven't even told him about that couple you set straight the other day, have you?'

'He wouldn't be interested in that!' Annie giggled, moving her head off Maggie's shoulder and rolling her eyes at her.

'How do you know?! I think he'd be pleased as punch his shy, timid Annie had the courage to go up to a pair of complete strangers and tell them what was what!'

'Do you really think so?' Annie asked, mulling it over.

'Of course!' Maggie said confidently. 'And if he knows you're doing well and flourishing with the WPV, it's going to lift his spirits and give him just the boost it sounds like he needs.'

'Oh Maggie, I think you're right,' Annie said, smiling properly for the first time that morning.

'Course I am,' Maggie grinned mischievously while thinking, *thank goodness for that.* 'Now, I take it you didn't have permission to miss the first lesson?' Maggie asked. Annie nodded slowly, fear suddenly engulfing her face. She must have been so upset about Richard that she hadn't thought through the consequences of skipping the lecture.

'Don't worry,' Maggie assured her while helping her to her feet. 'I'm an expert at wrangling my way out of tricky situations. Let's freshen you up and by the time we're finished, I'll have come up with a plan.'

5

Later that day the girls met for lunch – as they had done every day since their first practice patrol together.

'Thanks again for earlier,' Annie whispered to Maggie as they sat down. Maggie gave a friendly smile and tucked into her meal. She didn't want to say too much in front of Sarah and Irene in case they asked questions that Annie would find awkward.

Maggie had opted for the stew and regretted it as soon as she took her first mouthful. 'Ugh, this stuff is so tough,' she groaned halfway through chewing. She took a gulp of her water to wash the rest down. 'I do miss Florence's lunches during the week,' she said wistfully, thinking about the way meat always fell off the bone and melted in her mouth when it was served up at home.

'You got a cook?' Irene asked, her eyebrows raised in shock. She seemed to realise immediately that she might have come across as rude, and softened her expression and relaxed her shoulders before adding, 'I mean, that's just quite fancy, isn't it?'

Maggie wondered why Irene thought her household having a cook was such a big deal. It wasn't that out of the ordinary.

'Oh, Maggie's quite the lady,' teased Sarah, giving her a playful wink. Maggie had let slip to Sarah about her private-school education a few days earlier. Sarah had been so impressed with her credentials she had offered to try and get her some work at *The Vote*. Maggie had been over the moon, until she'd realised a job at a paper like *The Vote* was something she could never get past her father. *Imagine him opening it up, his blood boiling as he reads an article about women gaining more rights – and then seeing my name next to it.* Picturing the look on his face was just delicious, but she knew it would cause everything to crash down around her. She had made up an excuse about needing to be home in her spare time to help her brother with his studies and Sarah had seemed to believe her.

'Who cooks your meals at home?' Maggie asked Irene, greedily snatching up the opportunity to find out more about her.

'Oh, I look after myself,' Irene said proudly. 'I don't need no one waiting on me.'

Interesting, Maggie thought, noting that she was obviously fiercely independent. Her old clothes and scruffy hair made sense now; she didn't have anyone to sort these things for her, or anyone to impress.

Maggie was just about to delve deeper when Annie cut in. 'My mum always has dinner on the table for me, my sisters and my pa when we come home,' she said, smiling fondly. 'I've three sisters and I'm the eldest by far – although Pa still insists on calling me his little girl. I do so love to be looked after. But we don't have a cook or anything like that. Gosh, that would be good – I think my mum would be delirious with all the extra time on her hands!'

Maggie could feel herself getting frustrated that they all assumed she had an easy time of it at home purely because her family had someone to cook for them. *If only they knew*, she thought sadly. She would gladly give up all those delicious dinners if it meant she could have a warm and loving father.

As Sarah started talking about her landlady and the meals they often shared together, Maggie accepted she had lost another chance to dig for information on Irene. She didn't want to make it obvious she was desperate to find out more, so she needed to keep her inquisitive nature in check. But trying to figure out what Irene was hiding was driving her to distraction.

Just then, another recruit came over and stood next to the group. It was Ethel, who Maggie had been paired with on quite a few tasks during the first few weeks of training. Ethel was a warm, motherly figure in her late forties. She had never spoken down to Maggie like the other older trainees had. Maggie supposed she had been paired with her intentionally, so she could give her a little guidance until she found her way.

'How are you getting on, dear?' Ethel asked, putting a hand on Maggie's shoulder.

'Oh, just dandy!' Maggie beamed, smiling up at Ethel as her friends continued talking amongst themselves.

'Now, have you heard the rumours about Grantham?' Ethel asked, sounding serious all of a sudden. Maggie shook her head, her face blank. 'They want to send two women up there to control all the "camp followers", as they're calling them nowadays,' Ethel said. 'The number has exploded since the troops arrived at Belton Park Camp.'

'Camp followers?' Maggie asked.

'Yes, dear. There are lots of unstable girls hanging around the outskirts of the camp, desperate to support the lads in any way they can. The only problem is, most of them only have *themselves* to give,' Ethel said in an exaggerated whisper.

'I've heard they're professional prostitutes out for whatever they can get from troops with a load of wages and nothing else to spend it on,' cut in Annie, who had been listening in on the conversation.

'Well, whatever their backgrounds, the problem is the same,' said Sarah. 'It's the poor women who get punished for an act that involves a man *and* a woman. They'd do well to have the army officers keeping a closer eye on their soldiers, if you ask me.'

As Sarah let off steam, Maggie found herself panicking. What if she was packed off to patrol in Lincolnshire? How would she get that past her father? A trip away was a step too far.

'Oh, don't worry, they won't send anyone as young and fresh as us,' Sarah said in a reassuring tone. Maggie looked up to see she had been directing the comment at her. She realised then that she must have failed to conceal the fear spreading across her face.

'I'm-I'm not worried,' Maggie said defiantly. 'It sounds *ever* so exciting.'

'Do you think Frosty will send a couple of her pals from the suffrage days?' Sarah asked Ethel.

'Well, I imagine that would be the sensible thing, my love,' Ethel smiled. 'I'll leave you girls to your lunch, but I'll let you know if I hear anything,' she added warmly.

'Thanks, Ethel!' Maggie called out as the older woman headed back to where she had been sitting. *I hope they don't decide to send a trainee along*, she thought anxiously. But she took comfort in the fact Sarah possessed inside knowledge. If *she* said they were set on two established officers being deployed to Grantham, then that was surely what was going to happen.

After lunch the group stuck together for another training task. 'We're going to do some role-playing this afternoon,' Frosty announced. 'You've observed various court cases and you've learned all about giving and taking evidence from Sergeant Bridge. In your groups, one of you will play the victim of an imaginary crime. Someone else will be the officer who turns up to help them. You will interview the victim and take notes. Your group will then mock up a court case where the officer will give evidence.'

Maggie sat up straighter, her eyes sparkling. Finally, something she could get her teeth stuck into, rather than just telling women to go home. She started coming up with exciting imaginary crimes they could investigate when Frosty walked over and interrupted.

'I trust you ladies will be taking advantage of the fact you have a real crime to give evidence on?' she asked.

'Yes, sir,' replied Sarah obediently.

'Your dramatic practice patrol is a perfect example,' Frosty continued. 'I look forward to hearing more about it.' She marched off to the next group.

'Well, Annie's the victim then,' Maggie said, turning to the others, 'and maybe Sarah and I can give evidence – seeing as we both gave the blighter what for?'

'Sounds good to me,' Sarah agreed. 'Irene, do you want to be the magistrate?' With that, Sarah and Maggie got to work interviewing Annie, with Irene observing until she got her chance to play magistrate.

Looking round the room at the other recruits, Maggie was surprised at how seriously everyone was taking the role play. *These women really mean business*, she thought. A few weeks before, something like this would have made her feel out of her depth. She would have questioned whether she was there for the right reasons. But now she felt like she belonged.

It had started out as a way to get one over on her father, but during the last few weeks of training she had found herself being swept up in it all. She loved the authority the uniform gave her – sometimes just seeing it was enough to make people stop what they were doing and behave. Of course, there were still people – mostly men – who were resistant to the idea of women telling them what to do. But they only ever told men what to do if their actions were putting women at risk of getting into trouble – like the soldier in the park who had hit Annie. Most of them understood that WPV officers were there purely to look out for women. And children, of course. This went deeper than simply escaping her home life, now. Maggie was proud of herself for making a go of it.

'Right, are we ready for court?' Sarah's words brought Maggie back to the present.

'I'll go first!' Maggie declared excitedly. She couldn't wait to show off her evidence-giving skills. She was delighted when Inspector Hughes wandered over just as she was getting started. She was desperate to impress the superior officers. She gave her evidence calmly, clearly and using all the correct language.

'You were very informative. You managed to put across the facts without letting your emotions take over,' Inspector Hughes told her when Irene had finished asking her all her questions.

Maggie had to stop herself from jumping in the air with joy. 'Thank you, sir,' she managed composedly. Inspector Hughes gave her a friendly nod and wandered over to the next group.

'Well done. You've been doing a lot of studying, haven't you?' Sarah asked. Maggie was overjoyed to have been given praise not only by Inspector Hughes but also someone as knowledgeable and intelligent as Sarah. She had really knuckled down the last few weeks, and Eddie had been helping her study in the evenings. She didn't know what she would have done without him.

'Thanks, Sarah,' she smiled, before swapping places with her so she could give her evidence.

Once they were finished, Inspector Hughes handed out worksheets with made-up scenarios. Each group was given a few minutes to read them and then told to act out another courtroom scene. The girls had to pretend Sarah was giving evidence in an assault case where two women had come to blows outside a pub. But instead of giving the speedy and slick responses she had rolled off for the previous pretend case, Sarah was slow. She had to keep bringing her worksheet right up in front of her face.

'You'd be able to have your notes with you to glance over, but I don't think the magistrate would stand for you making it so obvious you were relying on them,' Maggie said cautiously. She was wary of criticising someone who knew so much more than herself – but she had to say something.

'I just don't know this case as well,' Sarah said defensively. 'And it's quite complicated.'

It really isn't; it's a scrap outside a watering hole, Maggie thought. She had managed to skim read over the details in minutes and was confident she could answer questions easily with just a few glances down at the worksheet.

'I didn't get enough time to read all the details,' Sarah snapped, bringing the piece of paper up to her face again before giving her answer to the next question. 'And this writing is *so* small!'

Wow, that touched a nerve, Maggie thought as she rolled her eyes playfully and nodded in agreement. But when it was her turn to give evidence she could make out the writing just fine.

'Sarah had a bad day today, hey?' Annie commented to Maggie as they left training that evening. Annie lived in Notting Hill, so the two of them had started getting the bus home together.

'I don't understand why she had such an issue with the worksheet,' Maggie said. 'And she got so snappy with me. She's normally so calm and collected. It wasn't like her at all.'

'I quite agree. I think she might have a problem with reading,' Annie mused. 'I sat next to her in a few lessons during the first couple of weeks. She was squinting at the board for ages before taking notes down.'

'Hmm, I don't think it can be that – she works for *The Vote*, remember,' Maggie said. 'She wouldn't very well be writing newspaper articles if she couldn't read properly, would she?'

'No, I suppose not,' Annie said sheepishly. 'What a silly idea,' she added, laughing nervously.

Maggie felt bad for the tone she had taken – she hadn't meant to make Annie feel foolish. 'No, it was a valid suggestion and it's definitely an issue around reading. Maybe she has bad eyesight?' she said encouragingly.

'That could explain it,' Annie agreed, perking up, but almost immediately frowning again. 'Wouldn't they throw her out if she had problems with her eyes?'

'Yes, they would,' replied Maggie solemnly. 'We need to help her get this sorted out before it's too late. If it's obvious to us, then the bosses will cotton on soon enough.'

'But how can we help her if she hasn't even told us what the problem is?' Annie asked.

'She doesn't realise she needs our help yet,' Maggie explained, excited at the prospect of coming up with a plan to help their friend. 'We need to get to the bottom of this ourselves and then help her solve the issue. Otherwise she'll be thrown out on her ear.'

'Right,' nodded Annie in agreement.

That night in bed, Maggie set to work thinking about the best way to broach the subject with Sarah. She also pondered over how to help her solve the problem if it was indeed her eyesight that was tripping her up. It was going to be a tricky task, but if anyone was up to the job, she was.

6

The following day, Maggie found herself in a lesson on general police laws and the Police Code with Sarah. *Brilliant*, she thought, wondering if this could be her chance to get to the bottom of her friend's problem and come up with a solution. She hadn't actually worked out how she was going to magically cure Sarah's eyesight if it turned out that was the issue. But she was confident she could devise a plan once she had all the information at her disposal.

'It's nice to have a friendly face to sit next to,' she smiled as she pulled out a chair at the desk next to Sarah. Maggie normally ended up in lessons without any of her friends for company.

'Just don't start your usual chatter and get me into bother,' Sarah said with a grin as they waited for the class to start.

Maggie smiled back but she knew Sarah had been deadly serious – she didn't want any distractions. It was no surprise she took the lessons seriously; she wouldn't be such a fountain of knowledge if she didn't.

As Sergeant Bridge took the class through a list of laws and regulations, Maggie couldn't help but notice the speed at which Sarah was taking notes. She was surprised there wasn't steam coming up from her notebook, she was writing so fast.

Sergeant Bridge stopped talking and stuck a big poster to the wall. It detailed a list of rules for public house duty. Sarah suddenly stopped writing. Maggie picked up her pen and began copying down some of the points. Out of the corner of her eye she could see Sarah picking up her pen and starting to write again. She was writing very slowly now. Maggie stopped. Then Sarah stopped. When Maggie started again, she could feel Sarah surreptitiously peering over her shoulder before putting her pen to paper once more.

Are you copying me? Maggie wrote in big letters across her page. Sarah's pen stopped moving and she froze in her seat. Maggie could feel the heat radiating off her face. She didn't need to look round at her to know she had turned bright red.

Maggie knew she couldn't say anything at that moment – they weren't allowed to talk in lessons unless they were speaking to an instructor. *It's fine – carry on*, she quickly scribbled while looking up at the poster, so it appeared she was still taking notes. *But we need to have a chat after this. I want to help you.* Sarah bobbed her head slightly, and Maggie went back to taking notes her friend could copy.

At the end of the lesson they had a ten-minute break before they had to start ju-jitsu training, but Sarah fled out of the classroom door so quickly that Maggie immediately lost sight of her. 'Hey!' she called after her, but it was too late. She saw her red hair disappear down the corridor in a flash, and then she was gone.

'Why'd you give me the slip?' Maggie demanded when she caught up with Sarah in the main hall. Sarah gave her a blank look. 'You knew we had ju-jitsu together next and you left me behind,' Maggie explained, even though she knew Sarah was fully aware of what she had done.

'I don't want to talk right now, so leave it,' Sarah said quietly but firmly.

'What's happened?' Annie asked, wandering over to them, clearly sensing the bad atmosphere.

'Nothing, just—' Sarah started before Maggie cut in.

'We were right, there's something going on with her eyesight – but she won't let me help her!'

'You've been talking about me behind my back?' Sarah asked, her angry expression suddenly turning into one of hurt.

'We've been worried about you,' Maggie said sympathetically. 'Annie's noticed you struggling to read off the boards in lessons, and then you couldn't read that worksheet yesterday without bringing it right up to your face.'

'Yes, I noticed that,' said Irene, who had turned up out of nowhere and caught the end of the conversation.

'Look, keep your voices down,' Sarah hissed, looking around the hall as it filled up with recruits. 'We need to keep this between the four of us so I don't get kicked out.' She motioned for them to follow her to a quiet corner of the room, away from all the other recruits. 'The truth is, my eyesight has been fading for some time now. It started just before I signed up. I'm struggling to read things from far away; up close it's fine but anything more than a couple of feet and it gets blurry.' She looked around to make sure they were still out of earshot of anyone else. 'It's not been a problem for my work at *The Vote*, and I can get my studying done just fine and take down notes when the instructors are talking. But they keep putting up those bleeding boards!' Tears of frustration formed in the corners of her eyes.

Maggie had never seen Sarah show much emotion – she was always so formal and focused on being the best recruit she could be. It suddenly dawned on her that Sarah hadn't been giving her dirty looks or staring over on purpose on their first day. She hadn't even *seen* her.

'It's not going to be a problem,' Maggie soothed, reaching out to put a reassuring hand on her arm. 'Now we know about it, we can help you out – like I did today.'

'Yeah, but what about identifying suspects and trying to

make people out from far away? I'm struggling to make out faces, not just words!' Sarah blurted just at the moment Frosty walked into the room, and it fell silent. Maggie's heart dropped down into her stomach as all eyes turned to look at their group. *Everyone* had heard Sarah's last sentence. She looked past the other recruits and shuddered when she saw Frosty glowering in their direction.

'Would you care to tell me which one of you ladies is struggling to see what she's doing?' she asked calmly. All four of them stood dumbstruck.

'Come on now!' she said, her voice clipped.

'It was m—' Maggie started, before Sarah stepped forward and said, 'Me, sir.'

What is she doing? Maggie panicked. She had already devised a plan to save Sarah, but she had thrown herself to the wolves before giving her a chance to carry it out.

'Come and see me in my office in five minutes,' Frosty barked. She turned to the rest of the room and raised her voice. 'I will send someone else along to carry out the ju-jitsu session.' She gave Sarah one last appraising look before turning on her heel and walking back out of the hall.

'You should have let me take the blame,' Maggie hissed to Sarah as the room erupted into chatter.

'How would that have helped?' she sighed, defeated.

'Well, they would probably have made me take a sight test, which I would have aced.' She saw the colour fade from Sarah's face as she realised what was about to happen. 'I could have laughed off the comment Frosty heard, saying I must have had too much gin the night before my vision got blurry. It'd be easy to convince them a little naïve lightweight like me couldn't handle the morning after a night on the town.'

'What have I done?' Sarah groaned, running her fingers through her hair.

'They might not give you a sight test,' Irene offered hopefully.

'Of course they will!' Sarah bit back, then she rounded on Maggie. 'This is all your fault!' she shouted. 'I told you I didn't want to talk about it, but you made me. Why would you drag it out of me *here* of all places?'

'I'm so sorry,' Maggie said, but Sarah had already stormed off.

'Leave her,' Irene said softly, putting a hand on Maggie's shoulder.

As Sarah disappeared from the room, Inspector Hughes arrived to take the session. Maggie partnered up with Annie, but she couldn't concentrate. She kept getting the moves wrong and forgetting the sequences. All she could think about was Sarah and what was going to happen to her. *She's the one who most deserves to be here, and I might have ruined that for her*, she thought as she looked to the door again and again in the hope she would see her walk back in.

At lunchtime the girls headed for something to eat. Maggie wasn't looking forward to sitting down without Sarah. They had become such a close-knit group it was going to feel strange without her there. *I wonder how she's getting on*, she thought as they made their way to the lunch hall. But she didn't have to wonder for much longer.

'There she is! Sarah!' Irene cried. Maggie looked round to see Sarah walking towards them along the corridor. But her smile of relief quickly faded when she saw Sarah's face.

'Well, that's it, then!' she ranted at no one in particular, before focusing her attention on Maggie. 'You were right about the stupid sight test. And of course, I failed it!' Her body shook with rage as she continued her onslaught. 'I should never have let you talk me into opening up back there! I could have made it through the rest of training without anyone finding out!'

'I just wanted to help,' Maggie said, staring at the floor.

'Well, you just made everything worse,' Sarah spat. 'And after all the help I've given you.' She shook her head. 'I can't believe you'll all be walking the streets for the WPV while I'm getting thrown out,' she said, her voice full of bitterness. 'It's so unfair. I'm the only one who was fighting for women's lib before we got here – none of you even knew much about it until I taught you.'

Maggie knew she was right. She had educated them all. If anyone should be leaving, it should be her, not Sarah. 'I wish I could trade places with you,' she said, and she meant every word of it. She felt terrible about what had happened and wished desperately she had just kept her mouth shut and her nose out of Sarah's business.

'You're all just here for an adventure, or to prove Daddy wrong,' Sarah added, staring pointedly at Maggie. 'You don't even care about women's lib.' Through the upset she felt at having put Sarah in this awful situation, Maggie couldn't help but feel frustrated yet again at the fact that her friends had no idea about the reality of her life at home, but she pushed those thoughts away.

'Please, there must be some way around this—' Maggie started, but it was too late – Sarah was already marching away.

'Enjoy getting one over on your daddy with your little escapade, won't you!' Sarah yelled as a parting shot before disappearing down the corridor.

Maggie, Annie and Irene stood in shocked silence.

'I feel just rotten. That was all my fault,' sniffed Maggie. She didn't want to get upset here but she couldn't hold back the tears.

'You didn't mean for that to happen,' Annie assured her. 'You were just trying to help her.'

'She's right,' agreed Irene. 'They would have worked it out

sooner or later. She couldn't have gone on much longer not being able to see proper. She could've even put herself or other recruits at risk if it had led to her making a mistake.'

'That may well be,' said Maggie sadly, 'but it still didn't need to come crashing down like that. I should have kept my nose out. I always get carried away coming up with these *silly* plans!'

'Your heart was in the right place,' Irene assured her.

'Thank you, both of you,' Maggie said, giving them a weak smile. 'I think we really need to stick together from now on. Sarah was the strongest of us all. I don't know about you two, but I definitely looked up to her.' Irene and Annie both nodded in agreement.

'Let's go and get some lunch,' Irene suggested, linking arms with both girls. 'Everything feels better with a good meal inside you,' she said as they continued down the corridor.

'Can we go to Maggie's, then?' giggled Annie, and they all grimaced at the thought of the tough meat and stale bread they had to look forward to.

7

January 1915

Christmas had passed by in a flash for Maggie. She had only had a few days off training and no one had seemed to be celebrating all that much anyway. The festive cheer and the excited buzz that normally hung in the air during the week between Christmas Day and New Year in London had been replaced by a gloomy atmosphere full of dread instead of hope.

It was no surprise. When war had broken out, everyone had assumed it would be over by Christmas, so this year it had been met with deep disappointment. The families who had lost loved ones had been grieving too much to think about celebrating, whilst those with their nearest and dearest still on the battlefield had been unable to bring themselves to feel joy on yet another day when they might have been receiving the news they had long been dreading. How could they be cheery when the people they would normally celebrate with were stuck in the trenches?

Maggie couldn't help but think about all these things when she had sat down for Christmas lunch with her family. It had made her eyes fill with tears. She'd thought of poor Annie, who she'd known would be missing Richard even more than usual. As she had been forced to make small talk with her father over the meal and watch her mother wince every time she spoke for fear of upsetting him, she had found herself wishing he had gone off to war instead of Richard. It hadn't seemed fair to her that someone who sounded so caring and loving was facing such danger when someone as mean and vicious as her father was free to carry on his reign of terror. As quickly as the thought had filled her head, she had been flooded with guilt for wishing her father harm. Shame had engulfed her as she had forced herself to appreciate how lucky she was to have her whole family sitting down to Christmas Day lunch with her.

Now the break was almost over, Maggie found herself feeling desperate to get back to training to have something else to focus on. As she sipped a cup of tea and read over her textbooks in her bedroom on Saturday 2nd January her thoughts turned to the future. All the recruits were due back at HQ on Monday for a final debrief before learning where they were to be based on full WPV duty. Maggie was ever so nervous about ending up in or near her home neighbourhood.

Suddenly, there was a knock on her door. As she saw the handle start to slowly move downwards, she slammed her book shut and shoved it under the desk, nearly spilling tea all over her notes.

'Oh, Eddie,' she sighed when her brother's head popped round the edge of the half-open door. Her heart was pounding.

'Sorry,' he said apologetically, noticing the panic on her face.

'You're supposed to do the knock before coming in,' Maggie moaned, reaching down to pick up her book. She had come up with a special knock so she knew it was Eddie at her door and didn't have to worry about hiding anything to do with her secret training.

'I'm sorry, I keep forgetting,' he said, slipping into the room. 'I've just got so much on my mind right now.'

'Whatever is the matter?' Maggie asked, concern for her brother now overtaking her feelings of annoyance. She got up from her desk and sat on her bed, motioning for Eddie to sit beside her.

'I've just been to try and enlist at Kensington Town Hall,' he said.

'Oh no, Eddie!' Maggie cried, her hands shooting up to cover her mouth, tears immediately flooding her eyes.

'It's fine, calm down,' he said. She could sense the irritation in his voice, and it upset her even more. She wasn't used to Eddie being sharp with her.

'They stamped my form with "rejected" – all because I'm an inch too short!' he raged indignantly.

Relief engulfed Maggie, though she tried her best to hide it. Eddie was obviously upset and she didn't want to make it worse. He had really got a bee in his bonnet about signing up over Christmas. She had a feeling it was to do with all the recruitment posters on the streets these days – you couldn't walk anywhere without seeing one. And men who weren't enlisted were being made to feel inadequate. Maggie had seen posters suggesting men who were happy to neglect their country would be willing to neglect their girlfriends, too. She had always laughed them off, but now she realised what a deep impact they could be having on young people like Eddie.

To top it all off, their father had spent a lot of time at home over the festive break. For some reason he had been a lot more tense than usual – snapping at the smallest things. Maggie had felt as if she was constantly watching what she was saying and tripping over her words, terrified of making him angry and bearing the brunt of his fury. It had made her even more determined to finish her WPV training and set up a new life away from him.

Maybe Eddie was feeling the same. She had never

witnessed her father striking Eddie, but she knew it happened. Making the beatings private was just another way their father managed to isolate and intimidate them both. But, of course, they both knew the signs and they were close, so they talked. Eddie was the only person Maggie had ever confided in about their father. He had told her he would step in if he ever saw their father hit her. That was one reason why Maggie was relieved the beatings were kept private. After what had happened to their mother when she had tried to protect her, she could never forgive herself if Eddie was hurt in the same way.

'I thought you were five feet six inches,' Maggie said cautiously, remembering how the army had changed the minimum height back in September. Now shorter recruits could join up – and the new limit just happened to match Eddie's height. She knew the figures as she had double-checked Eddie's measurements with him at the time and been disappointed to find he was still within the acceptable window – just.

'I *am*,' he fumed, shaking his head. 'So I should be able to join now. I told them that, but the dopey old fool doing the medicals insisted I was an inch off. Now everyone will think I'm a coward, Maggie! I can't have people thinking I'm a coward!'

'But you have the form to prove you're not,' she said.

'Oh yes, and I'll just stick that to my head, shall I? No one will know unless I explain it to them. Everyone who walks past me in the street will just keep on judging me and calling me a shirker. I'm no shirker!'

'I know you're not,' Maggie soothed. 'But, you're nearly a doctor now. You'll be saving lives that way soon. That's as good a reason as any to stay here and continue your studies. *That* is the way you'll help the country, Eddie, I'm sure of it,' she added, trying to put her arm around his shoulders.

But he shrugged her off and stood up. She was searching for something to say that would calm him down, but before she could think of anything he marched out of her room, slamming the door shut behind him.

Maggie was hurt that her brother had treated her in such a way, but she was also secretly delighted he had been turned down for service. She didn't care if people thought he was a coward as long as he stayed away from those bloody battle-fields.

Later that afternoon Maggie pulled herself away from her studies to go and check on Eddie. They agreed to go for a walk to get some fresh air. Maggie hoped she could calm him down and make him see that staying put and finishing his studies was the best thing to do – for him as well as for herself. As they left their house in Bedford Gardens, they decided to head towards Kensington Gardens. It had always been one of their favourite places to walk. She had filled Eddie in on many of her wonderful plans walking around that park.

As they got near to the entrance Maggie heard loud shouting and silently scolded herself. She had completely forgotten that the 22nd Kensington Battalion used the park for exercises. *Great. This is just what Eddie needs*, she thought, imagining how frustrated he was going to feel seeing a group of men doing what he so desperately wanted to. She was about to suggest they walk somewhere else when a group of soldiers came into sight, marching towards them.

'Sorry, I didn't think,' she said as Eddie stopped and stepped to the side to let them past. Eddie stared straight ahead at the oncoming troops and respectfully bowed his head as they pounded on. When he started walking again, Maggie joined him in silence. As she battled over what to say, she became aware of a woman approaching them. She was middle-aged and smartly dressed. She was staring intently at Eddie, a look of disgust on her face, and she kept her eyes locked on him as her hand reached into her bag.

'Oh no,' groaned Maggie. She knew exactly what was coming and it was the most terrible timing.

'Not in khaki yet?' the woman shouted, pulling out a white feather and thrusting it at Eddie as she passed them. He stopped in his tracks while the woman continued walking.

'He's been rejected! He wants so desperately to fight!' Maggie called out after her – more for the benefit of the people who had stopped to watch than the woman herself. Maggie had heard of the Order of the White Feather, but she had never seen anything like this. She couldn't believe someone could be so judgemental. How was this woman – this stranger – to know the reasons behind Eddie not fighting? As she searched for something to say to comfort him, he paced ahead.

'I want to walk alone!' he shouted back to her as she tried to catch him up. Upset, she turned around and made her way home. *He'll have calmed down in time for tea*, she assured herself.

But Eddie didn't return home for tea.

'Where is your brother?' their father asked as Maggie sat down at the table with her parents.

'He, er, he said he had some studying to do with John and that he was eating at his house. I'm sorry, I forgot to tell you this afternoon,' Maggie lied, risking her father's displeasure to cover for her brother. She was really worried now. It wasn't like Eddie to stay out so long. And it really wasn't like Eddie to miss tea without having excused himself first. She braced herself for her father's reaction.

'Very well,' her father accepted, serving himself up some vegetables. His words indicated that he didn't mind, but

Maggie could tell from the look on his face that he was raging inside. She didn't dare utter another word. As they ate in silence, Maggie's mind whirred, trying to work out where Eddie might be, what he was up to and what fate lay in store for him on his return. She was just taking her last mouthful when the dining-room door burst open and in Eddie walked. He seemed to be looking very pleased with himself, but the smile was wiped from his face when a scowl took over their father's.

'Father, could I speak to you alone?' Eddie muttered, all sense of the bravado he had seemed to be carrying when he walked in now vanished. Mr Smyth rose from his chair, never once taking his steely glare off Eddie's face. Maggie's heart was racing now. She knew that look.

'I have a very busy evening ahead, Edward,' he replied sternly. 'I don't have time to listen to your sorry excuses. You will explain yourself to me when I am ready.' This was one of their father's crueller tricks – making it clear a punishment was due but making them wait for it to be dished out.

'It has to be now,' Eddie said, his voice suddenly firmer – quietly defiant.

Maggie flinched, waiting for their father to lash out. But instead he calmly walked across the room to Eddie. Once they were face to face, noses almost touching, he motioned for his son to speak.

Eddie pulled a coin out of his pocket, his hand visibly shaking as he laid it down on the table. Maggie's heart broke. It was a king's shilling. All her fears had come true. 'I'm off to do my bit for the country,' Eddie declared, now triumphant and standing tall. It was like the coin had given him a sense of confidence.

Maggie felt like she was going to bring back up the meal she had just eaten. Her eyes filled with tears as she thought about what this could mean for her poor, lovely brother. She was also fearful for the immediate danger he had just put himself in.

'They tried to tell me no, but I made them see sense,' Eddie boasted, spurred on and buoyed by their father's shock and silence.

'No,' Mr Smyth said firmly. They stood, staring into each other's eyes, neither wanting to be the first to back down. 'This will not do. You have studies to finish. Where did you sign up? I will go down there first thing tomorrow and clear this up.'

'Oh dear,' their mother wailed, putting her head in her hands and sobbing uncontrollably. Maggie was desperate to know how Eddie had managed to get in after being rejected, but she didn't dare ask in front of their parents and let slip she had known about his previous attempt to join. She rushed to her mother's side and placed a comforting hand on her shoulder. She found herself suddenly grateful for her father's political connections and hopeful he could make this all go away.

'Father, I *have* to do this,' Eddie replied, his voice louder but starting to shake again. 'I have to do my bit.'

'But what about your studies?' their mother whispered through quiet sobs. Maggie rubbed her shoulder and tried to calm her down. She didn't want their father getting any more riled up by seeing how upset this was making her.

'There might not be a university left by the time this war is over, Mother,' Eddie said passionately. 'Can't you see? We're in danger from the Kaiser – all of us. If we don't do everything we can, we shall be left with nothing. All my years of studying will have been wasted! And what if they come here and harm you? I can't sit back and do nothing. I *have* to protect my family.'

'Don't be so silly,' their father scoffed, laughing as he finally backed away from Eddie and walked over to look out of the window. He stood staring outside as the room fell silent. They were all nervously awaiting his next move, too terrified to say anything until he spoke again. The room was filled with an incredible tension.

Finally, Mr Smyth turned around and walked back over to loom over Eddie. Maggie felt the atmosphere switch in that instant. She had been scared for Eddie when she thought of the danger he would face on foreign land. Now she was worried about his safety on home soil. He was face-to-face with a different kind of enemy. Their father may not have been holding a gun, but the damage he could cause without a weapon was just as terrifying.

'Do you really think you can make a difference out there?' he sneered. They were chest to chest now, with Eddie staring up defiantly at their father. 'Have you any idea what it's like on the battlefield? A pathetic little blighter like you won't last five minutes. You'll be running home to Mummy before the first shot has been fired!'

'Please, stop!' Maggie's mother cried out. Her father looked round in shock. It was almost as if he had forgotten the women were in the room.

'I think it's time you both retired to bed,' he said, calm all of a sudden. 'Edward and I need to discuss this further.' Maggie looked desperately to her brother, who gave her a reassuring nod. She knew better than to argue with their father, especially in these kinds of circumstances. It felt like torture leaving the room, but she didn't see what choice she had. If she tried to stick up for Eddie they would both end up regretting it. She just had to hope her brother would find some sense and back down before he was beaten into conceding.

As Maggie made to leave, she felt her mother stiffen next to her. She knew she would be battling her own need to retreat to safety with the instinct to protect her son. But

Maggie couldn't let her put herself in the firing line again. She grabbed her arm, pulled her up from her chair and led her, sobbing, out of the room. She guided her to the kitchen, knowing it would be empty so long after dinner had been served up, and made sure to close the door behind them.

'He'd be safer on the battlefield,' her mother wept as Maggie set her down in a chair and wrapped her arms around her. 'I wish I could protect you both,' she added, pulling away to look Maggie in the face. Maggie was lost for words. Her mother had never spoken about her father's ways before – even after Maggie had seen her injured stepping in to help her. It was just an unspoken terror between them.

'Eddie will be fine,' Maggie tried to reassure her. But even she didn't believe that. She was worried that Eddie was finally going to stand up to their father, and she couldn't bear to think about how badly that could end for him.

'I should have done more to protect you both,' her mother said quietly.

'Don't blame yourself,' Maggie said firmly. 'We've learned how to stay out of his way over the years. We both know what happened when you tried to help me once – I don't want you to help me if it means putting yourself in danger again. Neither of us do.'

'It's too late for me,' her mother sniffed. 'I can't get away from him. Besides, despite all of this I still love him. I hate myself for it, but I can't deny it. I'm well and truly stuck.' Maggie felt sorry for her mother. She had fallen for a monster and she was destined to live out her days in his grasp. 'I want you to promise me you will leave this house as soon as you can,' her mother added fervently. 'But don't marry a suitor like your father wants you to. Girls are making something of their lives these days – go off and do something exciting!' Her mother's eyes were sparkling – Maggie had never seen her so alive. 'Whatever you do, don't stay here to try and look after me. I want you as far away from here as possible. Of course I'll miss you, but you'll be safer off on your own. Knowing you're away from here and happy will help me through the bad days.'

'Don't worry, Mummy,' Maggie smiled, despite the fact that her eyes were welling with tears. 'I'm working on a plan already.' She squeezed her mother's skeletal hand. She hadn't realised before how frail her mother was becoming. It must have happened slowly – the stresses over the years eroding her away. She was desperate to tell her mother all about the WPV and how well she was doing, had ached to share it all with her ever since signing up. She knew it would make her so proud. But she couldn't trust her. Maggie knew her mother's loyalty to her father would force her to share everything with him. She couldn't take that risk. Not yet.

'I'm devastated at the thought of Eddie going off to war,' her mother said, staring down at the table. 'But I think it's for the best. If he can survive the battlefields, then maybe when he comes back he'll have the confidence to leave this house. Your father has been telling him he's worthless for years. He needs to believe he's not so he can break free.'

'It seems like he's almost there,' Maggie said, remembering again how her brother had just stood up to their father. As raised voices echoed down the corridor towards them, she helped her mother out of the chair and guided her upstairs to bed. She didn't want her to hear what was happening, and she wanted to be waiting to help Eddie when their father was finished with him.

Maggie didn't have to wait long. She had only just settled her mother into bed when she heard the dining-room door slam shut below her. She rushed into her room and sat on the bed ready to greet her brother. She gasped when he burst in. His left eye was bright red and already swollen, and tears were streaming down his face.

'Oh Eddie,' she whispered as he sat down on the bed next to her. She tried to pull him in for a hug, but he shrugged her off.

'I've told him I'm not going, but I have to, Mags.' He took a deep breath and turned to face her so she could see the full extent of his injury up close. 'I can't stay here,' he added, his tone begging her to understand. She took a moment to process the news. She knew that, as dangerous as this was, it was for the best for Eddie. He needed to find some independence and get away from their father. Especially now he was beginning to stand up to him. A black eye was just the start – they both knew that. And as hard as it was to accept he was leaving her, she knew she would have done the same if she was in his situation. She was working on her own plan to escape, after all.

'I hope you understand, Mags,' Eddie added, now placing an arm around her shoulder. She nodded and tried to stop the tears that were forming in her eyes from spilling out. She knew there was no point in arguing with him. This was his WPV, and she had to support him – just like he had supported her even though he'd been worried about her.

'You just make sure you stay out of Father's way for a while,' Eddie added. 'Promise me that? I don't want him taking this out on you and Mother.'

'I'll be busy with the WPV,' Maggie sniffed, 'and Mother knows to have one of her headaches.' Maggie snuggled into Eddie's side and they sat together on the bed for a long time, taking comfort in each other's presence. Maggie didn't know when they would be able to do this again, so she was in no rush to end their embrace.

Eventually, she decided it was time to try and lighten the mood. 'Anyway,' she sighed, pulling away to sit up straight, 'you need to tell me how you managed to wrangle a spot on the front line after being rejected for being a shorty?'

Eddie chuckled, then put his hand up to cover his left eye. 'Still a bit sore – don't make me laugh,' he winced. He fingered it gently before continuing. 'I went down to a recruiting meeting at Chelsea Palace on the King's Road, and guess what? If I stuff a bit of tissue in my shoes, I'm just the right height to be a soldier,' he said smugly. 'I'll be back before you know it,' he grinned, putting an arm around her again.

'But who will look out for me now?' she asked, suddenly panicking.

'You don't need me looking out for you,' Eddie laughed. 'You're almost a police officer now – imagine that! You've made it through all the training on your own and soon you'll be out patrolling the streets for real.'

'I won't be a *real* police officer. And what if they put me at a station round here, Eddie? What shall I do then? How will I manage to hide what I'm doing from Father, or convince him to allow me to continue? More importantly, whatever shall I do if the worst happens to you? You're my best friend – you *have* to come back.'

'I *will* come back,' he said firmly. 'As for the rest, you'll figure it out, Mags. You always do. You think you need me, but you don't – I promise.'

The thought of life without Eddie to turn to for help and advice was scary. But she had to accept it. She had to let him go. And now their father had tried to stand in his way, she understood more than anyone his need to go – and prove him wrong.

'You must write to me whenever you can,' she said, resting her head on his shoulder.

'Of course. And the same goes for you. I want to know all about life on patrol,' he said.

'Deal,' she agreed, pulling him in closer and drinking in the feel and smell of him. They sat like that for a few minutes, neither of them wanting the moment to end. Maggie reminded herself then of her words to Annie about Richard, and she pulled away to look Eddie in the face. She was serious now.

'I'm so very proud of you, my boy,' she said, breaking into a smile and wiping tears from her eyes. After blowing her nose on a hanky, she added, 'You go and do this family proud. You'll be the best soldier out there, I just know it. And when the war is over, we'll have a big celebration to mark what a great hero you are.'

'Thanks, Mags,' Eddie sighed, slowly getting to his feet. 'I'm off to pack. I need to sneak out before anyone wakes. I'll have an early start if I'm to beat Father to it.' He seemed to be looking forward to his new challenge now they had had their chat.

As her brother walked out of her room bursting with hope, Maggie couldn't help but liken him to a cow on its final journey – too excited to be getting out of its field on an adventure to realise its real fate at the slaughterhouse. She stood up and straightened out her dress. She pushed that thought out of her head and vowed there and then to block out any negative thoughts about life on the battlefields. She would think only about what a hero Eddie was, and how he was protecting her and their country. She refused to think another thought about how frightfully dangerous this undertaking he had chosen was going to be.

So that's how they get through it, she thought. She had never been able to work out how all the people with loved ones fighting in France managed to carry on with their lives while aware every day of the devastation the enemy could bring upon them in the blink of an eye. Now she knew.

8

That night, Maggie struggled to sleep. Not only was she grappling with the fear that she would be stationed in Kensington from Monday, but now she had Eddie's departure to keep her awake, too. She had popped into his room while he was packing and told him not to wake her before leaving in the morning. She couldn't stand the thought of saying goodbye to him. So, she had bid him goodnight as usual and gone off to bed as if nothing would be changing the next day. But as she'd tossed and turned in bed, she had come up with a plan that would ensure she would get to see him off without having to say goodbye to his face – which she felt confident should save her from getting too upset.

Eddie had told her he had been instructed to head to St Martin-in-the-Fields for roll call early in the morning. From there he was to be marched off with his new platoon to Paddington Station and put on a special train. He didn't know exactly where that train was taking him yet. All he knew was that he was off to a training camp and it would be at least six months before he would see any action overseas. Maggie was already clinging to the hope that the war would be over before those six months were up.

Her big plan for the morning was to head to Paddington so she could watch from a distance as her brother embarked on his journey. But now, terrified of missing his departure, she couldn't sleep. She lay for hours cuddling her childhood teddy, Charlie. His soft, brown fur had always soothed her when she had been upset as a young girl, and she had found he continued to calm her down as she reached her teenage years. But though he was bringing her some comfort now, sleep still wouldn't come, so she got up and did some more studying to try and take her mind off everything.

She was only a few pages into her first-aid textbook when she heard Eddie creeping past her bedroom. *Gosh, he's serious about getting away before Father has a chance to stop him*, she thought. She hadn't even heard Florence or any of the other staff getting up yet. She waited a few minutes before moving, to make sure he didn't hear her. When she heard the front door being closed ever so gently, she got up and dressed as quietly as she could.

After creeping down the stairs, she tiptoed into the kitchen and left a note for Florence on the table. She was always the first to rise and Maggie knew she could trust her. *If he asks, please tell my father I've gone to church to pray for Eddie*, it read. She was confident her father would be too busy raging about Eddie's departure and defiance to question her where-abouts – but it never hurt to have a backup plan in place, just in case. Then she went to the front door and managed to open it and then close it behind her without making so much as a peep.

Maggie's walk to Paddington took her round the edge of Kensington Gardens. As she took in the pretty view, lit up by the dawn rays, she couldn't help but think about the horrible woman who had pushed Eddie into signing up. It made her angry that one small act from a stranger who had no idea of her brother's situation could shape his future so dramatically. There was no point in dwelling on it, although she knew that if she ever saw that woman again, she would surely have a problem holding her tongue.

When Maggie arrived at Paddington Station it was alive with activity, despite the early hour. Hundreds of men of all ages were heading off to various training camps. There were many tearful goodbyes being said. Maggie breathed a sigh of relief that she would be watching Eddie leave from a distance, so as not to put him through the upset of seeing her devastation. A few hours later, the concentration she had focused on every group of men being marched through the station was taking its toll – and it didn't help that she had barely had any sleep, either. She hadn't seen Eddie yet, but she was certain he must be due soon. She knew it would be just her luck that he would come through as soon as she stepped away from her look-out point in the main concourse.

Just as she was contemplating a rushed toilet break, Maggie heard the telltale sound of boots marching through the station once again. She hid behind a pillar as the group approached. When she saw Eddie's blond hair bouncing as he marched and his cherub-like face shining with excitement despite his black eye, she had to stop herself from calling out and waving at him. She so desperately wanted one last moment with him, to look into his blue eyes once more. But she knew she needed to remain strong. Pride seared through her as he marched past, head held high.

'I love you, Eddie. Please be safe,' she whispered, watching the top of his head disappear as the group of men made their way to platform three.

9

Maggie ran for what felt like hours. She raced through Hyde Park and past Buckingham Palace with no idea where her final destination might be. Darting through the London streets, she fought angrily to empty all thoughts of Eddie on the battlefield from her head. When her breathing became so laboured she could think of little else, she was grateful for the distraction despite the discomfort.

She wondered what people thought of this young woman dashing through the city in her long dress, tears streaming down her face. But strangers' opinions didn't matter to her – all that mattered was getting away from the station and to somewhere she felt safe to process her feelings.

When she found herself sitting on the steps of the WPV headquarters, she wasn't entirely sure what had pulled her there. Perhaps, on some level, she had grown rather attached to the place. It was certainly somewhere she felt at ease. Now she thought about it, it was a little like a second home to her. Sitting with only her angst and upset for company, she wondered what she was going to do to get by without Eddie.

'What are you doing here on a Sunday?' The stern and serious tone of Frosty's voice shook her back to reality. Maggie jumped up and saluted her sub-commandant. It felt strange to do so when they were both in their everyday clothes – although Frosty still looked rather smart and official.

'Don't be silly,' Frosty said, waving away Maggie's salute.

Her voice was still firm, but she had the trace of a smile on her face. 'You don't have to salute higher officers when you're out of uniform. And there's no need to call me sir out of hours, either. You can relax.' She gestured for Maggie to sit back down, and then perched on the step next to her.

Maggie wasn't sure what to do or say. She had spent the last few weeks being terrified of this woman and desperate to impress her, and now she was sat down next to her wanting a chat. *Was* that what she wanted? She didn't know how to answer Frosty's simple question about why she was there on a Sunday. She didn't want to get into trouble or sound stupid in front of someone she respected, but the truth was that she had no idea what she was doing there. She really didn't want to get drawn into a personal conversation with Frosty, for fear of letting slip anything that could reveal her true age. She would be the worst person to trip up in front of.

'I, er, I don't really know why I'm here,' she said timidly, plumping for honesty after realising she didn't have the energy to come up with a cover story. 'My brother's just left for a training camp and I started running when I left the station. I had an urge to get away as quickly as I could. My feet kept taking me, and I ended up here,' she explained. She could feel her face turning crimson under Frosty's hard gaze. She wished it was possible for the ground to open up and swallow her. Frosty let out a long sigh, and then they sat there in silence.

'I don't know what to do without him here,' Maggie admitted, trying to keep her composure.

Eventually Frosty turned to her and smiled. 'Come now, dear,' she said. 'Not one of us *needs* a man to get by. Especially not someone who is good enough to be a member of the WPV. I know this is a scary time, but you don't need your brother or anybody else to help you through it.'

Maggie didn't know what to say, so she just nodded silently, staring at her hands in her lap as Frosty continued. 'You've obviously found some sense of security in your training, and that's a good thing. If you ever feel the need to get away and just be alone with your thoughts, you should come here, if it helps you. And if anyone takes issue with it then you send them to me.' Maggie was lost for words. She thought she was going to be hauled up and disciplined for loitering around headquarters out-of-hours. She certainly wasn't expecting Frosty to speak kindly to her, with so much understanding.

'What's your brother's name?' Frosty asked.

'Eddie,' Maggie replied, smiling to herself.

'Well, if Eddie is anything like his brave and daring sister he'll be just fine out there.' Maggie felt a rush of pride. Frosty must have noticed her during training – and thought she was good. Good enough to become a fully-fledged WPV officer. She couldn't believe what she was hearing.

'Thank you. That means a lot,' Maggie said. Frosty was already getting to her feet, so Maggie went to stand up too.

'No, you stay there,' said Frosty, putting out her hand. 'You have a lot on your mind and you need some time with your thoughts. I've intruded enough. I need to get on anyway and put the list of placements together for the morning. Take as long as you need out here and I'll see you tomorrow.'

'See you tomorrow, sir – I mean, ma'am,' Maggie giggled nervously at her mistake as Frosty walked up the steps and into the building without a backwards glance.

Maggie felt honoured Frosty knew enough about her to compliment her as she had. But her good mood was shattered when she remembered the one person she wanted to boast to – Eddie – wasn't around to hear about it. *I can always tell the girls later*, she thought as she remembered she was seeing Annie and Irene at Annie's house that afternoon. They had planned to meet there to do some knitting over a cup of tea as a final get-together before they found out their placements.

Certain they would be split up and stationed with groups of older women, they wanted to celebrate the end of their training together before they all became too busy.

Making her way home, Maggie reminded herself of her plan to push all thoughts of Eddie at war out of her head. It had been a silly idea to go and watch him leaving – she should have stayed at home and pretended it wasn't happening. She could have saved herself a lot of upset. And her legs wouldn't now be aching so much. Checking the time, she found she could just about make it home for lunch. The thought of one of Florence's Sunday dinners cheered her up.

She wondered what state her parents would be in after discovering Eddie had up and left for training camp before they had risen. Her mum was probably still in bed crying, and her father calling all his political contacts trying to find a way to have Eddie sent home.

On her return, Maggie found she was correct about her mother – she could hear her sobbing in the master bedroom from the bottom of the stairs. She was pleased she had tucked herself away, even if it was to cry. It was the best place for her with her father as angry as he was likely to be.

'She's been like it all morning,' Florence whispered as Maggie stopped into the kitchen on the way to the dining room. 'She refused breakfast. You'd best get yourself sat down at the table before your father gets back. He's been raging about Eddie sneaking out all morning and I suspect he's not in the mood to be kept waiting for lunch.' Maggie gave her a grateful nod and made her way to the dinner table. Once sat down, she took a moment to close her eyes and breathe in the delicious smell of chicken that was wafting into the room. She was shaken from her daydream by her father pulling out a chair at the head of the table and plonking himself down heavily in it.

'Afternoon, Daddy,' she said with all the cheerfulness she

could muster. He gave her a stiff nod before looking back to the door, as if to check where his meal was. Maggie decided against trying to make conversation. She wasn't stupid – she could tell he was furious. There was no point in trying to talk to him when he was like that. She most certainly wasn't going to talk about Eddie.

After a few minutes, it became clear that her mother wasn't going to be joining them, and Maggie and her father ate in an awkward silence. Maggie wondered how long her mother could stay in her room crying and refusing to eat. She hoped she snapped out of it soon. It was wise to stay out of her father's way when he was angry – but too long and she could risk enraging him even more.

Maggie also pondered whether they would ever talk about Eddie again, or just ignore the fact he had defied their father to join the army. That sounded like the most likely scenario, seeing as it would leave their father's pride and ego intact.

'I'm going to a knitting meet-up this afternoon if you find that agreeable, Daddy,' Maggie said quietly as her father set down his knife and fork and made to get up from the table. 'Some of the other orphanage volunteers are getting together to knit socks for the troops,' she added and then immediately squirmed at the fact she had mentioned soldiers when her father was obviously still livid.

But he must have been so distracted by his own thoughts that the reference went completely over his head. He simply grunted and left the room.

Well, at least Eddie's insubordination has taken the heat off me, she thought, grinning despite it all. She felt bad for viewing Eddie's departure as working in her favour – but if she couldn't look on the bright side, then what was the point?

Later that afternoon, as Maggie made her way to Annie's, she felt overwhelmingly grateful for her friends. She knew

they would take her mind off Eddie leaving. And she would
be forced to put on a brave front about it – she couldn't
very well tell Annie how worried she was after all the reas-
surances she had given her about Richard.

'How is everyone? Did you all have a good Christmas?'
Irene asked cheerfully as they sat down together. Annie's
mother had joined them and supplied them with some new
patterns to work from.

'Good, thank you,' smiled Maggie. 'Although Eddie signed
up to fight this weekend and he set off for a training camp
this morning.'

'Oh my. Are you all right?' Annie asked, her eyes suddenly
wide with concern.

'I didn't even know Eddie was keen to fight,' said Irene.

'No, no neither did I,' admitted Maggie, staring down at
her knitting needles. 'Well, he'd been talking about it for a
little while, but I thought he'd realised staying here to finish
his studies was the best thing for him to do. He suddenly
got an urge to do his bit, and then he was given a white
feather and that made him rather more determined. He went
to a recruitment meeting yesterday afternoon and that was
that – he was on the train first thing this morning.' She was
trying to keep her voice chipper, but she could hear it shaking.
'Our Eddie's a tough chap though – he'll show those Germans
a thing or two, I'm sure,' she said, trying to bolster herself.
'So, how are you both feeling about tomorrow?' she asked,
changing the subject. 'I can't wait to get started properly,
and to find out where we're all stationed!'

'Yeah, me too,' smiled Irene.

'I can't believe we finally made it through the training,'
Annie said, shaking her head. 'I wasn't sure it was for me at
the start – especially after that disastrous practice patrol. But
you girls have helped me get through it and I don't know
that I've ever felt this confident about anything before.' Mrs

Beckett laid down her knitting and gave Annie a warm hug. Maggie could see how very proud she was of her daughter. She was happy for Annie, but it made her feel sad that she couldn't share her accomplishment with her parents. If only her own mother knew how much she had achieved so far. What she wouldn't give to have her father feel proud of her for making it into the WPV, instead of having to sneak around and hide it from him, scared he would lash out at her if he discovered the truth. And to have made it this far really was an accomplishment – some of the trainees had been kicked out a few weeks in as they weren't up to Frosty's standards.

'I bet your parents are as proud as me and Mr Beckett,' said Mrs Beckett, grinning from ear to ear. 'You girls are really doing your bit for the boys, you know. Annie's father won't stop harping on about his daughter the policewoman – he tells everyone he meets. He would shout it from the rooftops if he could!' Annie was blushing now, and Maggie smiled despite the sadness she was feeling. Her family could never be this close – not with all the lies and the ever-present fear of violence.

Maggie couldn't remember the last time she had sat down and done something simple like knitting with her mother. She longed to share something so special with her. She was happy for Annie, of course. But it was becoming clearer than ever to her that money and status didn't equal happiness. Annie's home was modest compared to her own, and her parents were far lower down the social ladder than her mother and father. But none of that seemed to matter to them. All of them were so happy – so loved and full of love. Maggie would sacrifice all her fancy possessions for a happy home like theirs.

'My parents are delighted for me,' Maggie lied. 'My father's always asking about the training and trying to help with my studying.'

'And now your brother's off to help the country, and all,' smiled Irene.

'What a team you make!' she added, and Maggie smiled. It was nice of Irene to say something like that, but she couldn't help but notice that in doing so, she had managed to avoid being asked for any details about her own parents and their thoughts on her joining the WPV. She knew that Irene lived alone, and she wondered if her parents even knew what she was up to. Could she be keeping it all a secret too? Maybe she and Irene were more similar than she realised. But this wasn't the time or the place to push for further information.

'I'm so sad we won't be seeing each other every day any more,' Maggie sighed.

'We don't know for certain that we won't be stationed together,' Annie said hopefully.

'I don't reckon they'd put the three youngest recruits together,' Irene said glumly. 'They're certain to split us up so we're all in with older officers to look out for us.'

'Right, well let's spend our last bit of time together doing something really fun,' Maggie declared happily, trying to lift the mood. She wanted one last hurrah with her friends. There had to be something more exciting than knitting that they could do to mark the end of training.

'Joan is helping organise a dance at Chelsea Palace tonight,' Annie's mum offered, smiling. Maggie's heart fluttered at the mention of the hall where Eddie had just made the biggest decision of his life.

Then she marvelled at the thought of going to a dance without a chaperone. She had only ever been to social functions like dances with her family – and they were normally stuffy, political affairs linked to her father's work.

'Let's go!' Maggie exclaimed, before she could stop herself. As Annie grinned and thanked her mother for the idea, Maggie suddenly panicked. How was she going to get this past her father? He would never believe that she was required at the orphanage after-hours. She quickly pushed aside her fears to join in with Annie's excitement, resolving to come up with a plan later. She didn't want to miss this.

Watching Annie and her mother, Maggie found herself comparing her life with her friend's once more. Tonight would be a full-scale military mission for her – making sure her parents didn't find out what she was up to and having the fear of discovery and punishment looming over her, tainting the experience. Yet Annie's mother was actually suggesting that she go out and have fun with her friends.

'You'll join us, won't you?' Annie asked Irene hopefully.

'Erm, I suppose so,' Irene muttered into her knitting, which she was all of a sudden very keen on getting finished.

She could sound a little more enthusiastic, Maggie thought resentfully. She wanted to ask her what was so bad about going to a dance together, but she decided not to spoil their final hours together with a confrontation.

Walking home to get ready for the dance, Maggie hoped she would be lucky and find her father out for the evening when she got back. She realised she was desperate to spend time at Chelsea Palace. Maybe she wanted to go there to feel close to Eddie, to try to understand his decision? Would she feel better if she stood in the same spot he had stood when he signed his life away? Whatever the reason, she decided it was the most fitting place to go to dance away her blues about saying goodbye to both him and her friends.

10

At the dance hall, Maggie was delighted to see her friends in a more informal setting. It was refreshing to spend time with them in such an upbeat and relaxed atmosphere. She hoped she could get to know them a little better away from the strict rules and regulations they had to adhere to at training. She had been relieved to find her mother had shut herself away in her room since Eddie's departure. In frustration, her father had gone off to his gentleman's club immediately after dinner. That was what he often did when her mother was having one of her 'emotional episodes', as she had heard him calling them. He normally returned by eleven o'clock – so she knew she had until then before there was a risk of anyone noticing her absence.

Maggie had picked out her best formal dress for the occasion – a light blue number with a delicate belt around the middle, which showed off her slim waist. Annie and Irene were waiting in the hall when she arrived, and she couldn't help but notice the stark contrast between their outfits as she walked towards them. Annie was dressed in a simple and understated black dress with white polka dots. It was plain looking, but her full bosom spilled out of the low neckline. Maggie struggled to keep her eyes off the area but tried her best when she noticed her friend was obviously feeling self-conscious.

'I told my mother this was too small for me, but she insisted

I wear it,' Annie blushed, trying to discreetly pull some of the material up to cover her.

'I'd die for curves like yours – you should be proud to show them off,' Maggie said, trying to make Annie feel better. She looked over at Irene, who was clutching her drink and scanning the room uncomfortably. 'You look nice,' she offered kindly, and Irene immediately excused herself to use the lavatory.

'I hope I didn't upset her,' Maggie whispered. 'I'd mentioned your dress, so I felt like I had to say something about what she was wearing. But I'm sure it's the same tatty old dress she had on when we met her that first day at training.'

'I thought the same,' Annie said, checking behind Maggie to make sure Irene wasn't making her way back. 'Poor love, she looks so awkward. It's like she's never been to a dance before! I had to order her drink for her – she had no idea.' Maggie laughed along, desperately hoping that nothing she did this evening would give away her own inexperience. She was beginning to understand why Irene hadn't seemed very enthusiastic about joining them – she was obviously even less accustomed to these social gatherings than Maggie was herself. She hoped she could make her feel more comfortable as the night went on. When Irene joined them again, Annie suggested they take a wander around the hall, to drink in the atmosphere.

'That sounds like just the tonic we need,' Maggie said joyfully. She had been keen to have a dance, but now she was here she realised she just wanted to spend time with her friends. She didn't much fancy abandoning them to see through an awkward waltz with a stranger. Also, she was enjoying the freedom that came with being at a dance without a chaperone to tell her what to do – or rather, what not to do.

'I-I'll just finish my drink,' Irene said nervously, still clutching her glass to her chest.

'Bring it with you,' Maggie encouraged, linking arms with her and guiding her around the side of the room as Annie walked by their side. After a lap around the hall they found a table to sit at and watch all the couples dancing. As Irene relaxed, Maggie felt her desperation to find out more about her waning. She was happy just to get lost in the music with her and Annie.

As she watched the dancing, Maggie envisioned Eddie standing in the exact same spot that she was sitting in, signing away his freedom. But she found it hard to be sad or angry now. She was proud of her brother and the sacrifice he was making. The girls started chatting and soon Maggie was laughing so hard she had forgotten about all of her worries. When the dancers dispersed for a break, the girls agreed to order more drinks.

'How are your parents after Eddie left for training so quickly?' Irene asked Maggie as they stood at the bar.

'Well, I expect my father is fuming and my mother is still weeping,' Maggie sighed. 'My father is very strict, and he didn't want Eddie to go, you see.' Talking about her father, she checked the time and panicked – it was half past ten. She hadn't realised how late it was. She needed to get home before he did – he would be furious if he caught her sneaking in at this hour. As fear took over, she made her excuses and bid goodnight to her friends before rushing back to Kensington. She felt like Cinderella!

Making her way along Bedford Gardens, Maggie could feel her panic rising. Away from the loud music, laughter and fun with her friends, she felt nervous. As she approached home, she realised that the urge to dance her depression away had taken over all rational thought. It had been a lovely evening – she decided there was no way she could ever regret it no matter the consequences. She had laughed so hard with Annie and Irene she had forgotten all about her anguish over Eddie as well as what lay ahead of her in the morning. For just a few short hours, she had felt happy and free of worry. She couldn't remember the last time she had felt like that. But with every step she took, the butterflies in her stomach became more violent, until it felt like they had enough energy to burst out of her body altogether.

As she neared her house, she resolved that the dance would be the first thing she would write to Eddie about. She might even start a letter before going to bed. Maggie wondered what he was doing right now, and if he had settled into his camp. There was no doubt in her mind that he would fit right in – everyone who met Eddie loved him.

The sight of the front door snapped Maggie back to the present. She would need to make sure she was as quiet as a mouse when she opened it, just in case her father had made it home before her. As she gripped the handle, she took a moment to pause before pushing down. She took a deep breath and started to push. Hearing a slight creak, she stopped, frozen. She took another deep breath and tried again, and felt a swoop of relief as she managed to open it without making any more sound.

She grinned at her achievement and silently closed the door behind her. She stood listening for a few moments, bracing herself for an onslaught from her father, but it seemed that either she had beaten him home, or he had returned and gone straight to bed assuming she was already fast asleep.

Maggie peered down the long corridor and saw that the kitchen light was still on, and her heart sank. *I knew it was too good to be true*, she thought as she made her way resolutely down the hall. She didn't even have an excuse lined up. Taking yet another deep breath, she pushed the kitchen door open. When she saw Florence sitting at the table, she struggled to hide the overwhelming relief she felt.

'For goodness sake, child, wherever have you been?' she asked as Maggie wrapped her arms around her. 'I've been that worried.' Maggie had known Florence most of her life, and they had always had a good relationship. But as she embraced her now, she felt a rush of love that took her by complete surprise. She was overtaken by a sense of closeness to her family's cook that she didn't understand. Maybe it was the adrenaline from the relief of not finding her father waiting for her at the table, or the euphoria from her fun evening. Either way, she had never felt so happy to see Florence's friendly face.

'Eddie asked me to look out for you, but I didn't think I'd have to be covering for you as soon as he left,' Florence whispered into Maggie's shoulder. She was broad and matronly, which Maggie found made her just perfect for a reassuring hug.

'Eddie spoke to you about me?' she asked warily as she pulled away.

'Course he did. He wasn't going to leave his foolhardy little sister to her own devices when he went off training, now, was he? Someone needs to keep you on the straight and narrow, my girl. And you'll need someone to cover for you with your father when you're out patrolling the streets at all hours.' Maggie froze. 'Don't worry, dear. Eddie told me all about your little quest and your secret's safe with me. Course it is.' Maggie relaxed her shoulders and let out another sigh of relief as she sat down next to Florence. 'Can't say I was surprised when he filled me in, mind. I know I've told you bits and pieces about the women's movement here and there, but I didn't realise you were so keen to get involved. And I was shocked you got in to the WPV – being so young and all.' Maggie felt ashamed that she'd only signed up originally to escape her father. She decided not to share that with Florence. After all, her attitude had changed completely now, so there was no point in letting Florence think any less of her.

Maggie couldn't feel angry with Eddie for sharing her secret. It felt like a weight had been lifted now that she had someone else in the house to talk to about the WPV. She was also grateful to have someone to help her get around the issue of night patrols. She hadn't mentioned her worry about them to Eddie as she hadn't wanted him to feel worse than he already did for leaving. But it was a real concern.

'So, come on, now,' smiled Florence as she got up to make a cup of tea for them both. 'Your mother hasn't moved from her bed all evening. Says it's her head but I reckon she's upset about your brother. Your father escaped to the gent's club soon after dinner – to save having to listen to her sobbing, I imagine. But you already know that, mind. I heard you sneaking out just after him, you know – you need to be more careful, love.'

Maggie suddenly felt very foolish. She had been lucky only Florence had heard her.

'Anyway,' said Florence, 'no need to worry about that. Your father won't be back for a while yet and if he is, we'll say I'm helping you through a bad head of your own.' She handed Maggie a blanket, which she wrapped around her shoulders, expertly hiding her coat and dress and making her look like a poorly patient. Maggie smiled. The small gesture made her glad that Florence was on her side. 'So why don't you sit down and tell me all about what you've been up to? I need to be in the know if I'm to help you keep this up,' Florence suggested.

As Maggie told Florence about her training, she noticed how intently she was listening. Her long brown hair was tied back, and Maggie was sitting so near to her that she could see the deep lines running around her eyes and across her forehead. She had always known Florence had a friendly face, but she realised now that she'd never taken the time to look at her closely. They chatted all the time, but Maggie was always in a rush or caught up in some excitement or other. She had never really appreciated the fact that Florence was more than just her family's cook. She really cared about Maggie, and she was like a second mother to her, really.

And now she was willing to put her job on the line to help her. If Maggie's father ever found out Florence had lied to him to cover for her it would mean the end of working in service for her – her father knew too many people and he wasn't one to let a betrayal like that go.

'Why are you risking everything to help me?' she asked suddenly.

Florence put her hands into her lap and rubbed her thighs, like she was gearing up to something. 'You remind me of my niece,' she said finally, and her eyes suddenly brimmed with tears. Maggie felt terrible. Florence knew so much about Maggie, yet Maggie didn't know anything at all about her. Especially not anything about her family. Florence rubbed her eyes and continued. 'She's called Katy and she's just a few years older than you. She started working in service for another household when she was very young. My sister couldn't wait to get her out the house and into work to make money for her. It made my blood boil but there was nothing I could do. I wanted to get her some work here with me, but yer father wouldn't have it. I think he thought having her here would distract me from my duties.'

Maggie felt guilty that her father had split up Florence's family. 'Florence, I—' she began, but Florence interrupted her with a wave of her hand.

'Not to worry, dear. It's not your fault. Anyway, the family Katy worked for had a son quite a few years older than she was. She wrote to tell me he was making improper advances and she didn't know what to do. She just wanted to get on with her work and be left alone, but he kept telling her she was *his* servant and she was to do whatever he wanted.' Maggie could sense where this was probably going, and hoped she was wrong.

'In the end she fell pregnant, the poor love. Course, she was kicked out on her ear. The family wanted nothing to do with her or the baby – even though it was their grandchild! They blamed Katy, saying she'd seduced their innocent son. In their eyes it was all her fault and he was the poor victim who couldn't resist her advances.' She shook her head sadly. 'So, now you see why I'm so proud of you for helping fight for women's rights by joining the WPV. I'll do everything I can to make sure yer father doesn't find out and stop you.'

Maggie couldn't begin to imagine the worry Florence must have felt for her niece. Her story sounded similar to so many Sarah had told her about. It always seemed to go the same way: the young women were taken advantage of or treated badly by men, and then they were blamed for it all while the men got off without facing any consequences. It was just another reason why the fight for women's rights was so important.

She felt more guilt rush over her when she thought about her original reasons for joining the WPV, and resolved to do everything for the right reason from now on. Maggie suddenly felt like this journey was really helping her grow up. She had thought she was mature before, but now she realised that hadn't been true at all. She hadn't really known anything about the real world out there. She was getting there, though.

'I want things to change,' Florence sighed. 'I want men to stop getting away with things like this and start getting their comeuppance for what they do.'

'So do I,' said Maggie with feeling. 'How is your niece now? What did she do?'

'Her and the baby are lodging with a close friend of mine in Hampstead,' said Florence, smiling now. 'I was so angry with my sister when she refused to take her in. Can you believe it? She's a selfish woman, my sister – she didn't care about what had happened to Katy, didn't care how scared she was. She was just angry the money had stopped coming in and she didn't want to worry about having an extra mouth to feed. Thank God my friend was happy to take Katy in and help her with the baby when he arrived. She'd never been able to have children herself, you see – so she was delighted at the idea of having one in the house.'

What a good friend, mused Maggie. She was certain her parents would never do anything like that for anybody they knew. She wondered if Annie or Irene would help her out if she ever found herself in a tricky situation like Katy had. Although that was unlikely, given her status, she realised. Whilst she was grateful, it felt unfair that it was something she would probably never have to find herself worrying about, while so many women were fighting those situations every day.

Florence continued. 'Katy called the little boy Fred. I go and visit every Saturday on my day off, and I send them what money I can. He's the most adorable little thing, Maggie. Although I don't know how, coming from such a terrible father.' She smiled warmly and took Maggie's hand in both of hers. 'Now you know why I'm so keen to help you, dear. As well as all that, I've watched you grow up from a little girl into a strong and determined young woman, and I'm so proud of what you're doing.'

Tears welled in Maggie's eyes. She'd had no idea Florence felt so tenderly towards her.

Florence continued. 'Don't get me wrong, yer father has

treated me very well over the years. So, I *am* going to struggle with lying to him and going behind his back to help you. Not to mention what would happen to me if he found out.' Maggie felt sick to her stomach at the thought. 'But I've heard the way he talks about women's rights and I've seen the way you and Eddie and yer mother tiptoe around him. I'm not stupid – he might not do anything in front of me, but I know a man with an uncontrollable temper when I see one. It's not right, love. I'm happy to put everything on the line to help you do this.'

Maggie felt another rush of love and gratitude. Florence really was risking everything for her. Now she had yet another reason to try her hardest with the WPV. 'Thank you,' she said, squeezing Florence's hand. 'I'll do you proud, I promise.'

'Just make sure you do yer best, love. That's all I ask,' Florence smiled.

As Maggie settled in to bed, she cuddled up to Charlie and took a long, comforting sniff of the back of his head. It felt like the weight of the worry over her impending place-ment had lifted. She had Florence to help her now and she felt invincible – like she always had with Eddie on her side. She smiled to herself and for the first time in days she drifted off to sleep without tossing and turning and fretting first. She had a feeling everything was going to be just fine.

I I

The next day, Maggie walked to St Stephen's House with Annie for the final time. They had arranged to meet Irene on the steps outside. As they sat down to wait for her, Maggie was reminded of her chat with Frosty the previous day. She hadn't told her friends about it in the end – they'd had so much else to discuss at the dance. She was just about to comment about how much she had enjoyed the get-together when Annie stood up and started waving frantically.

'There she is!' she cried, jumping up and down and beckoning Irene over.

'What's all the excitement for?' asked Maggie. She was suddenly feeling that impending sense of doom regarding their placements again.

'I'm just so desperate to know where we've all been stationed,' Annie said. Maggie could feel the anticipation seeping out of her as she bounced on the spot – so different to the timid, mousey girl she had met only a few weeks before.

'Come on, then, let's go and discover our fate!' Irene said cheerfully as she approached. She rubbed her hands together in expectation.

Maggie wished she was feeling as enthusiastic as they both obviously were. She certainly felt better following her chat with Florence the night before, but she was still nervous about the possibility of being stationed in Kensington.

Walking into the main hall, she smiled as she thought back

to day one of training when she had met Irene and Annie for the first time.

'It seems like a lifetime ago that we arrived here as strangers,' she reminisced as they found three empty seats together and sat down.

'I thought you were a nightmare,' giggled Annie.

'I was nervous!' Maggie replied, pretending to be offended. 'Anyway, I thought you were being snooty with me. But I realised after getting to know you that you'd just been really shy. Can't say that about you now,' she laughed, giving Annie a playful nudge.

'I thought you were a right odd pair,' chuckled Irene. 'And I still do!' They fell about laughing.

Suddenly, Maggie stopped and looked down at her feet. 'I wish Sarah was with us today,' she said sadly.

'We all do,' said Irene, her laughter dying on her lips. 'I'm sure she's doing just fine though. She didn't seem like the kind of girl to let a little setback stop her.' Maggie and Annie murmured in agreement.

Just then, Frosty walked into the hall and everyone stood up and saluted. 'You have all come a long way since you walked in here to start training all those weeks ago,' she said, giving her signature glare as she spoke to the room. 'I'm confident that all of you will do the WPV proud on your patrols around this great city. As you are aware, you will be expected to give *all* your time to this role.' Maggie gave a silent thankyou to Florence. This was going to be a lot easier to navigate with her support.

'The protection of women and children is our main purpose, although you will be expected to take over the lighter duties of the hard-pressed police force when needed,' Frosty continued. 'You will have seen throughout your training the swarms of women and girls of all ages who have been drawn to our city in the hopes of finding highly paid employment in canteens, clubs, restaurants and munitions works. They have poured in from the provinces with little money and no idea of the dangers threatening them. These women and girls will benefit from your guidance. There are also the wives of soldiers to consider, driven by loneliness and their anxiety for their husbands to public houses. The increase in drunkenness is a cause for concern, and is something we must deal with sensitively. Finally, of course, you will need to keep an eye out for the street women London has always been home to. It will be down to you to help guide them away from trouble. It is your job to protect all these women using your initiative and discretion, and I trust that you will.'

As she started reading out women's names and the stations they were allocated to, Maggie chewed on her thumbnail and closed her eyes. First came Paddington, and then Richmond. Each time, Maggie held her breath as the names of the recruits were read out. Wimbledon came next, followed by Marylebone. Maggie's heart skipped a beat when she heard her name. She nervously tapped her heel on the floor over and over as she waited for the names that followed. Then she looked round at her two friends in shock and relief. Both their names had been called straight after hers.

'The three of you will be stationed at Bethnal Green Police Station,' Frosty said. At first, Maggie wasn't sure if she had heard correctly – but Frosty was definitely looking at them.

Maggie wanted to jump up and down with joy, but she managed to contain herself. Not only was she going to be working with her two best friends, but she was going to be at least five miles away from Kensington and anyone who knew her family. Her parents never ventured to East London – it was far too grimy for them. She could even remember her father referring to Bethnal Green as a 'huge slum' over dinner one evening a few years before. Her mother had ventured timidly that the area had been improved in recent years, but he was adamant, and that was that – it always was when her parents had differing opinions about anything.

As soon as the final briefing was over, the room filled with the noise of recruits talking to each other about their appointments. Maggie took the opportunity to let out a big squeal.

'Who's a little bit excited now?' laughed Annie. 'After all our worrying about it, I can't quite believe they put us together!'

'You work well as a team,' Frosty's voice boomed out from above them. The girls jumped apart to face Frosty and salute. 'I must admit I had decided to split you up,' she continued. 'I'd planned on sending you all to separate stations with older recruits. I thought you needed guidance, being so young. But then I bumped into Maggie, and after our talk I had a change of heart.' She was speaking directly to Maggie now. 'I saw how seriously you're taking this and I was impressed. I went into my office and looked back over all the tasks I've seen you ladies on together. You have consistently achieved good results. It's important to have good support and influences in a role like this, and I think you will help each other more than any of the older recruits would aid each of you individually. You're the kind of friends who stick together through thick and thin.'

'Thank you, sir,' Maggie muttered, overwhelmed by what she was hearing. Now she would definitely have to fill the others in on her meeting with Frosty the previous day.

'Don't make me regret my decision,' Frosty said sternly. She gave them all a quick-as-a-flash smile before walking on to the group of women next to them.

'My goodness, what did you say to her?' Annie asked, wide-eyed.

'Not a lot really,' admitted Maggie. 'To be honest, I felt like I'd come across as a bit of a fool.'

'Well, whatever happened, you did a sterling job. I'm over

the moon we'll be staying together for the next part of this journey,' Annie beamed.

Maggie was glad her friends hadn't quizzed her on where she had bumped into Frosty and what exactly they had spoken about. She noticed that Irene was being awfully quiet. 'It's good news, isn't it?' she pressed.

Irene was biting her fingernails and staring into the distance. 'Eh?' she said, looking at Maggie in confusion.

'Gosh, how late did you stay last night?' Maggie joked. 'You're looking very pale, and you were in a world of your own there – you had better wake up before we get to Bethnal Green! I was just saying it's great that we'll be together.' Irene smiled weakly, but she still seemed distracted. 'Right, well, shall we get going?' Maggie asked, hoping Irene would snap out of whatever was the matter soon.

The group was to make its way to Bethnal Green and report for duty straight away. It was quite a way across the city, and it took them longer than Maggie had anticipated. But then she remembered that hundreds of London buses had been used to transport men and ammunition to the front since the war had begun. She pictured them being used now to get wounded soldiers to hospital for treatment, and she decided to keep her moaning about the long journey and overcrowded bus to herself.

'I suppose they'll be getting women to drive the buses and trains soon,' she mused as they navigated their way through the unfamiliar streets of East London. She couldn't imagine such a sight! But then, if someone had told her a year ago that there would be female police officers, let alone that she would have been one of them, she would have scoffed at them.

'It's a bit grotty around here, isn't it?' she added, noting how dirty everything looked compared to where she lived. Annie wrinkled her nose in agreement, but Irene looked uncomfortable and stayed quiet, staring out of the window and avoiding their eyes. Maggie immediately regretted her comment. *Does she live around here?* she wondered.

Irene had taken charge of their journey without question and hadn't even had to check on the bus route. It would certainly explain her threadbare clothes, which no amount of cleaning could disguise. And then there was her over-the-top reaction to Maggie's family having a cook. If she lived somewhere like this, then a house in Kensington with domestic servants was a whole world away. Maggie just always assumed that everyone she met was from a similar back-ground to herself. She had never mixed with anyone from a different class before.

Feeling sheepish, Maggie changed the subject. As they walked, she couldn't stop thinking about the possibility that Irene lived in the East End. She was desperate to know if her hunch was correct. But if she had learned anything over the last weeks, it was to let things like this go, so she stopped herself from prying further. Irene had never mentioned where she lived and maybe that was because she was embarrassed. Maggie didn't want her friend to feel worse. She thought about how she would feel if they had been stationed near to her home and resolved to keep her nose out.

'We're nearly there,' Irene announced as they turned onto Bethnal Green Road. 'It's that one sticking out on the corner of Ainsley Street,' she added, pointing to a big brick building just before the next turning. Maggie was relieved – the cold winter air was getting right to her bones. She wasn't looking forward to walking the streets in these temperatures every day. As they got closer, she could see a huge archway at the entrance, with a light hanging over the top, held in place by an impressive iron structure.

This was it. She suddenly became very aware of the fact she was too young to be here doing what she was doing. Her breathing quickened as she started to panic. She had become so comfortable in her lie over the previous weeks of training that she had almost started to believe it. What if the policemen here took one look at her and worked out that she was just eighteen?

Maggie thought back to her first day at St Stephen's House and how nervous she had felt then. She had made it through that and the last couple of months undetected. Surely, if she could pull the wool over someone like Frosty's eyes, then she could fool anyone. She just needed to keep up her mature act. *You can do this*, she told herself firmly as they walked up the steps and into the building.

12

Maggie let Irene take the lead as they walked up to the front desk at Bethnal Green Police Station. She was more than happy to keep her head down and let her friends do all the talking. The worst thing she could do, she reminded herself, was to draw any attention her way – good or bad.

The first thing Maggie noticed about the officer behind the desk was his incredible height. To see his face she had to tilt her head up even further than when she was talking to her father – and her father was over six feet tall. Her new colleague also had a very crooked nose, which reminded her of a witch. She stifled a giggle and immediately turned bright red when he looked straight past Irene and locked eyes with her. *Well done*, she chided herself, giving him a nervous, apologetic smile. He didn't look impressed.

'PC Bird is going to show you around,' he said, still staring at Maggie. 'But if you're not going to take this seriously then you may as well clear off home and get back to knitting or whatever else it is you've been doing that you think will help win us this war.' He was sneering now. Maggie remembered Sarah warning them that the police would probably have a mixed reaction to women joining their ranks as WPV officers. Although she had been forewarned, she hadn't expected anyone to be this openly aggressive.

'We're here to do a job, sir, and we quite intend to carry it out well,' she said, standing tall. She wasn't going to let anyone apart from her father treat her like a silly little girl. And he only got away with it because she had no choice. She could picture Eddie rolling his eyes as he read all about this encounter in her next letter. She knew she shouldn't have said anything, but she hadn't been able to help herself. She waited nervously for a reaction.

'Well, that's good to hear,' he said. His voice had definitely gone down in volume and he even seemed a little taken aback. Maggie suspected he wasn't used to women answering back. Especially not young women. She scolded herself again, just as Irene gave her a discreet nudge. Maggie knew it was a warning to keep quiet and she was more than happy to heed it.

Irene took charge of the conversation. 'Where should we wait for PC Bird, sir?' she asked firmly but politely.

'Over there,' he said, pointing to a row of chairs across from the reception desk. 'He's out at the moment – we weren't sure when to expect you. I'll get him back to the station sharpish.'

As the girls huddled by the chairs, Irene raised her eyebrows at Maggie. 'What was that?' she whispered.

'Sorry,' Maggie muttered. 'I was really nervous, and his nose reminded me of a witch and well, I just tend to laugh when I'm nervous. Then he was rude, and my tongue ran away with me.' Now Irene and Annie were giggling.

'Trust you,' said Irene under her breath. 'Now that's all I shall be able to think of when I see him.'

'Well, he didn't even think us important enough to have the privilege of knowing his name, so I hereby christen him *Witchy*,' said Maggie as the other two tried to stop themselves from laughing too loudly.

'Everything okay over there?' asked Witchy. They all stood to attention at once, nodding seriously. Maggie was glad her friends had a sense of humour. It seemed they might need

it if all the officers here were as hostile as Witchy. She hoped
he was just the exception, and everyone else would be
welcoming. But that hope soon faded. While they waited for
PC Bird, two more officers walked past on their way out of
the station.

'Oh, look,' one of them said, pointing at the girls. 'What
do you think these ladies can do, then? Maybe they're here
to fill the time as they haven't been able to find husbands!'

'Well, they can't very well arrest anyone, can they?' the
other jeered. 'They're too weak to do any proper police work
– they're just going to end up making extra work for us.
They'll be calling on us for help every time they come across
anything out of the ordinary,' he added, and they both laughed
in the group's direction. Maggie remembered to hold her
tongue this time, although it was a struggle to do so.

'Don't they realise we're here to help *women*?' she hissed,
trying to keep her voice down. 'We're not looking to take
over any of their work. And besides, constables are meant to
summon other officers to help if they come across a difficult
situation. So we can't make arrests – but if an incident was
so bad it warranted one then they would need help just like
we would!'

She had raised her voice without realising and Witchy was
now glaring at her again. Huffing, she turned away and rolled
her eyes. She was already finding this extremely frustrating.
How was she going to last even a day without blowing up
at somebody?

'Don't worry, they probably won't all be like that,' Annie
said softly. 'And besides, once we've learned the beat, I'm
sure they'll just leave us to it and we'll be able to get on
without their stupid remarks. They don't want anything to do
with us by the looks of it, and that might work well for us.'

'I do hope so,' sighed Maggie. She was worried she was
going to get herself into bother by talking back to one of

these men. She pulled at the collar on her jacket. She had thought that after wearing the uniform for a little while it would feel a little more comfortable, but she still felt awkward in it.

When PC Bird finally turned up to greet them, Maggie was surprised. Not only was he a lot younger than she had expected – he must have been in his late twenties – but he was rather fetching to look at. He also seemed quite pleased to see them, unlike any of the other officers they had encountered so far.

'You can call me Frank,' he said cheerily as he shook hands with them one by one. 'And you must salute all the other officers, but don't worry about that with me if there's no one else around.' Maggie liked him already. He was tall and slim with a thick head of hair. He had clearly tried slicking it back, but there was a big stray bit that kept flopping down in front of his eyes, which made him look endearing. 'I'm going to take you straight out on the beat,' Frank explained as another officer walked past and threw them a dirty look. Frank lowered his voice. 'As you can probably tell, your arrival hasn't met with the best of reactions – so we'll leave the station tour for another day. That's not important, though, as you'll be spending most of your time on duty patrolling.'

'Is there somewhere we can leave our clothes?' Annie asked nervously. Having come straight from WPV headquarters, they were already in uniform – but all clutched the dresses, shoes and jackets they had arrived at St Stephen's House in.

'Of course, we'll pop them behind the desk for now, and I'll have to sort you out somewhere permanent to store them as soon as I get a chance.' They watched as Frank carefully placed all their clothes on the floor at the back of the reception desk, out of sight of anyone coming into the station. He quickly explained that a shift pattern hadn't been properly worked out yet, so he was hoping they would be happy to patrol Monday to Friday until the chief constable had decided when exactly he wanted them on duty. The lack of preparation for their arrival didn't make Maggie feel very welcome, but she tried to shrug the feeling off.

Walking back along Bethnal Green Road, Maggie was relieved they seemed to have finally found an ally, but she was also concerned about what he had said regarding their arrival at the station. She hadn't been expecting to be met with open arms, but she certainly hadn't anticipated being made to feel this unwanted quite so quickly. The men could at least give them a chance to try and prove themselves.

'We'll start with the Boundary Street Estate,' Frank said. 'That will be your main priority, really. We haven't had any luck dealing with the problems there. It's mostly street women and wayward children, so hopefully they'll respond better to you ladies,' he added.

At last – someone who understands our purpose, Maggie thought.

'There are a few properties where we think untoward things might be going on, but of course no one will talk to us. With a lot of the fathers off fighting, quite a few of the little 'uns round there keep acting up, too. It's not the kind of stuff we have time for when we're run off our feet and our numbers are down.'

Maggie was nodding along eagerly – this was *exactly* the kind of work they had been trained for. She'd heard that the two recruits they had sent to Grantham had been building strong relationships with women in the area – they had sent two of Frosty's close pals in the end, just as Sarah predicted. She was hopeful she and her friends could have the same success here.

'Do you ladies know about Boundary Estate?' Frank asked.

They all shook their heads. Maggie watched Irene closely and had a suspicion she was lying. 'Well, it's about a twenty-minute walk so I'll fill you in on the way,' Frank said cheerfully.

He explained that the area the estate was built on had been one big slum up until just before 1900. It was called the Old Nichol. Nearly six thousand people had been crammed into the streets and the death rate was double what it had been across the rest of Bethnal Green. There had been families of eight living and working in one room. Crime was rife, and conditions were so bad that a book had been written about it.

'*A Child of the Jago*!' Irene exclaimed before Frank could reveal the title himself.

'That's the one,' he said, surprised but clearly impressed. 'But I thought you didn't know about the estate?'

Irene blushed and pushed a stray strand of hair behind her ear. 'Oh, well, I-I've read the book, is all. I just didn't realise it was set around here until you started talking about it,' she said, blushing furiously.

'Well, I don't meet many people who've read it,' Frank said. He was trying to catch Irene's eye, but she was avoiding his gaze.

'What was the book about?' Annie asked. Maggie was glad she had stepped in – it had started to feel a little awkward. It was as if Frank had only just noticed Irene properly and now he couldn't take his eyes off her.

'Well,' Frank laughed, finally tearing his gaze away from Irene, 'it was meant to be fiction about a little boy living in a slum. But the author had visited the Nichol an awful lot. Apparently, he got a lot of information from the local reverend. He changed the name of the slum to the Jago for the book, but everyone knew it was about the Nichol. Lots of people thought he exaggerated the criminal activities and violence of the area, but if you ask me, he was spot on.' Now Maggie understood what her father had been talking about – and why he was so against visiting the area. She made a note to herself to look up the book when she had a chance.

'London County Council cleared it all about twenty-odd years ago,' Frank continued. 'And they built a load of houses for the working classes. It's all very fancy now compared to how it was before – it was even officially opened by the Prince and Princess of Wales in a posh ceremony. They kept the existing schools and churches, but they ripped down twelve public houses. There are nearly two hundred shops on the estate and not one of them is allowed to sell liquor!' Maggie imagined residents quite easily found other ways to get hold of alcohol, but she kept her thoughts to herself. 'There's also a load of workshops for woodworkers and shoemakers who used to live in the slums.'

'Did the people who lived there before get to move back into the new houses?' Maggie asked as she rubbed her hands together to try and warm them up.

'No way,' scoffed Frank. 'Well, a few did, but most ended up spreading out among all the old properties nearby. They couldn't afford the three-shilling rent. So now we have new overcrowding problems and new slums nearby. You'll need to patrol those areas, too.'

It all seemed a little unfair to Maggie. She couldn't imagine living in such squalor in the first place, but to be forced out to make way for lovely new buildings for *other* people just seemed so terribly cruel.

As they continued walking, Irene started pulling at the collar on her jacket and when Maggie asked her what was wrong, Irene said it was chafing against her neck.

'I must say I'm impressed with the uniform,' Frank said as Irene continued to fuss with her collar. 'It does look very similar to our kit. And you look great in it.' As soon as he said it, Irene looked up into his eyes, stunned. 'I mean, you all look good,' Frank corrected himself nervously as he flicked his stray hair back and looked away. He did like her too! Maggie was enjoying this.

When they turned into the estate, Maggie was struck by the impressive, red-brick tenement blocks. The tree-lined streets housing these tall buildings radiated out from a central, circular garden that was segmented by several sets of steps leading up to a bandstand at the top. 'That's Arnold Circus,' Frank said, pointing to the garden. It was beautiful.

'I can't believe this used to be a slum,' Annie said in wonder.

'They did a good job,' Frank agreed. 'It was a police no-go area before. I wasn't an officer back then, but the older blokes have told me it was full of alleyways and nooks and crannies. Some of the gardens and alleys had been built over so it was like a maze. If you didn't live there, it was impossible to find your way around. They'd start chasing a thief, but he'd give them the slip by walking through a doorway and coming out of a house streets away. They'd be stood there scratching their heads while the other residents gathered around and laughed at them. The way they tell it, it sounded like a game of cat and mouse!'

'I can't say I blame them for staying away, then,' said Maggie, 'but no wonder the area ended up full of crime. It sounds like a terrifying place to live.' Looking around at the wide, clean streets and beautiful circular garden surrounding the bandstand, she smiled. 'They certainly did a grand job with it. There's so much open space.'

'They put in the open areas between each of the twenty blocks to make sure every living room had sunlight at some point in the day. Clever, eh?' Frank said, clearly enjoying his role of tour guide. 'There are more than five thousand people living here now. Well, minus all the men at the front. It'll keep you busy. I spoke to the chief constable and he wants you to focus on the estate, but still patrol the other streets of Bethnal Green too. There's not a lot of crime here now but you'll probably find a few bits and bobs to help you pass the time.'

Maggie frowned. 'We're not here to *pass the time*—' she started, but Irene nudged her in the side.

'Thank you, I'm sure we'll find enough to keep us busy,' Irene said loudly, drowning Maggie out. Maggie realised she had been about to let her mouth run away with her again. Thankfully, Frank didn't seem to have noticed. He was still staring at Irene and smiling. Maggie was certain she spotted Irene blushing before she looked away. But she was too riled to think any more of it. She was annoyed at the fact that just when she thought they had found someone who was on their side, he'd had to go and talk down to them like they were just bored housewives looking for a bit of excitement while their husbands were off winning the war.

'You're supposed to report directly to the chief constable, but I'll be honest with you, he's not best pleased about your arrival – just like the rest of the station,' Frank continued, oblivious to Maggie's annoyance. 'He's left it to me to act as go-between, so we'll be seeing a lot of each other.'

'That sounds wonderful,' Irene gushed. Maggie glanced over at her, surprised, and realised Irene was just as startled as she was at her little outpouring. 'I, er, I mean, that sounds like a good way of dealing with things,' Irene stuttered, trying to sound formal now. And she was definitely blushing. Maggie stifled a smile, realising that not everyone was ticked off with Frank like she was. She made a note to quiz her friend on her thoughts about their new boss once they were alone.

The group took a walk around the blocks of tenements, and then Frank took them into a few shops to introduce them to some of the locals. After about an hour of wandering around and getting to know the estate, a middle-aged woman started heading in their direction. She was wearing a long black skirt and a long-sleeved white blouse. Maggie had spotted her staring over a few times as they had been exploring. The look of purpose on her face now reminded her of the woman who had given Eddie the white feather, and Maggie worried she was going to try and harm them.

'You lot police, are ya?' she asked Irene aggressively, eyeing the girls up and down.

'We're with the Women Police Volunteers,' Irene answered proudly. The woman seemed to relax a little, but then her eyes came to rest on Frank and she tensed up again.

'I need to get back to the station,' he said quickly. 'I trust you know the way back?' Maggie nodded gratefully and waved him off. He had obviously sensed the woman wanted to talk, but not around a male officer.

'I 'eard they was sending some women in, what with all the men going off to war,' the woman said once Frank was out of sight. 'We don't often see police round this way. They don't give a stuff about our problems. I don't see that you lot'll be any different.'

'We're trained to look out for women and children – sorry, what was your name?' Maggie asked, smiling engagingly. The woman was still looking at them suspiciously.

'The name's Sally,' she said eventually. 'I'm the matron's assistant over at the central laundry, so I knows a lot of what goes on around this estate. I 'ear all the gossip.' She sounded like the perfect person to get onside. Maggie was determined to win over her trust, but she could sense it was going to take some work.

'Don't get me wrong,' Sally continued, 'things ain't half as bad round 'ere as they was before they knocked everything down and started again. There's a better class of people living 'ere now, ya see. But we still get problems now and then –

just like anywhere in London. The police don't bother coming down 'ere, and people've started thinking they can get away with whatever they want.'

She looked around nervously. It was clear she was still sizing them up. She wasn't going to trust them straight away, but that was to be expected. 'Anyway, I best be off,' Sally said hurriedly, spotting a group of women walking towards them.

'I'm Maggie, and this is Irene and Annie,' Maggie said quickly, and Sally nodded, turned and walked briskly off towards the group of women.

'We'll need to work on her,' said Irene as they watched Sally greet the group, before turning back towards them and pointing. Maggie wanted to know what she was saying. She didn't exactly look like she was singing their praises, but she hoped she wasn't being too negative.

'Should we go over?' Annie asked nervously.

'No, let's take our time to build their trust,' Maggie said. 'They're not going to take to us straight away. Remember what they said in training – if we keep up a regular presence, they'll start to see we're only here to help them. Let's take another walk around and then maybe we can pay Sally a visit at the laundry in a few days' time?' Annie and Irene nodded in agreement.

As they made their way back towards the bandstand, Maggie felt a rush of excitement at the prospect of helping the people of Bethnal Green, and she couldn't wait to get started.

13

That afternoon, the girls spent a few more hours walking around the Boundary Estate, getting to know the layout – plus, constantly moving helped keep them from getting too cold. The twenty blocks were all either four or five storeys high, and each one was named after a town or village close to the Thames.

'We'll never learn all these,' sighed Annie as they sat on some steps leading up to the bandstand trying to recite them, their breath fogging up in front of their faces every time they spoke. 'Hang on, I've got an idea,' she said, suddenly jumping up and motioning for Irene and Maggie to do the same. 'Let's go up to the top,' she said, running up the remainder of the steps. Maggie and Irene followed, keen to know what her bright idea was. The bandstand was a good few yards above street level, and once they stood at its centre they had a perfect view out across all the streets and tenement blocks. 'We can stay here and go through them as we turn around in a circle,' Annie suggested.

'Great thinking,' agreed Maggie. 'Right,' she said, pointing her finger out in front of her. 'I'm pretty sure that one straight ahead is Sunbury.'

'I thought that one was Cookham,' Irene said, scrunching her face up.

'Darn it. I was quite sure it was Henley,' Annie groaned, putting her head in her hands.

'I think you'll find that one is Shiplake!' a voice called out from midway up one of the sets of steps. The three of them turned around together and waited in silence as the owner of the voice made his way slowly up the rest of the steps. They heard huffing and puffing before they saw a man's head appear. He paused and let out a long breath. 'These days, these steps take me a bit longer than they used to,' he said, wheezing a little.

Maggie had no idea who he was, but as he advanced towards them she could see he was wearing smart trousers and a plain shirt. Although the man looked formal, his clothes weren't those of any kind of official. Perhaps he was a resident. His face was friendly, but it bore deep lines – he was clearly very old. His thinning grey hair made Maggie think he was in his seventies, at least. His oversized nose looked like her grandad's and the memory of him made her smile.

'I've lived in Shiplake for fourteen years,' the man said proudly after reaching them and taking a few moments to catch his breath. 'The name's Arthur, nice to meet you all.' He held out his hand to shake each of theirs one by one. 'I grew up in the Old Nichol,' he continued. 'I'm one of the only ones to have gotten meself a place here since they made it nice and that. Good job an' all – do you know what they used to say about the Old Nichol?' All three girls shook their heads. '"There can be no hell hereafter, we live in it already."' He chuckled darkly. 'No wonder they only let eleven of us back in! Nice girls like you lot wouldn't have lasted five minutes there, I'll tell yer that much.'

'We've heard all about it,' Annie said. 'It sounds like it was a scary place to live.'

'Oh, it weren't all that bad,' Arthur said. 'You were all right as long as you kept yer head down and didn't wander down the wrong alleyways late at night.' His gaze wandered off into the distance and he fell silent. Maggie wondered if he was thinking back to how the area used to be. If he was, then he had fond memories, if the smile slowly spreading out across his face was anything to go by. He tutted and shook his head. 'Still, at least I've a kitchen now,' he laughed.

'These places have *kitchens*?' Irene asked in awe.

'Only in Shiplake,' he said smugly. 'Rest of 'em got shared sculleries. We all got WCs too – you get to 'em through the hall or landing but they's our own.'

'Well I never,' said Irene longingly, shaking her head. They were beautiful buildings, but Maggie couldn't understand why Irene was so impressed.

'It's funny when you think the room I grew up in only had a table, two chairs, a straw mattress and a little stove,' sighed Arthur. 'Took me a long time to get used to, I can tell yer. Anyway, it sounds like you ladies need some help learning the names of all the blocks if yer going to be patrolling round here. It's not a maze like the Old Nichol, but you'd do well to get yer bearings quick.'

'How do you know what we're doing here?' asked Maggie, confused as not one of them had mentioned the WPV or said anything about what they were up to on the estate.

'It's written all over you – literally,' he laughed, pointing at her arm. Baffled, Maggie looked down and spotted the silver *WPV* letters stitched on to her jacket shoulder-straps. Now she felt silly, and she could feel her face turning red. It was going to take her a while to get used to the fact that everyone knew exactly why she was there simply by looking at her. She was so used to just blending in. 'But I knew about you before spotting you up 'ere,' Arthur added. 'I actually came looking for yer, so I could introduce meself and see if you needed any help. Old Sally told me you was here. She's a gem of a woman, Sally, she really is – but she's got a voice like a foghorn when she gets going and she loves a good gossip. You can't do nuffin' round this place without Sally finding out and telling all and sundry about it. I think the

whole estate knows what you're up to by now.' Maggie hoped
Sally had been kind when she had been talking about them.

'I've heard all about you women police,' Arthur continued.
Here we go, thought Maggie, bracing herself for the patron-
ising insults. 'I think it's a great idea,' he beamed, clearly
enjoying the shock that quickly spread across all of their
faces. 'There's some girls round 'ere need guiding on the
straight and narrow. They tend to lose all common sense
once they're around soldiers,' he added with a knowing look.
'They're not interested in listening to stuffy old men in
uniforms, and they sure as 'eck won't take any notice of their
mothers. With the fathers off at war the children are pushing
their mothers as far as they can – sometimes further, knowing
there's no one going to come home at the end of the day
and discipline 'em. I reckon they'll listen to you lot though.'

Maggie hoped he was right.

'So how do you suggest we learn our way around then,
Arthur?' Irene asked eagerly.

'Easy,' he replied, looking superior again. Maggie got the
feeling Arthur enjoyed being right about things and showing
off his knowledge. 'You got notepads, I see?' Maggie pulled
hers out of her pocket and showed him. 'Right-o. Well, best
thing you can do is draw out a plan of all the blocks while
you're standing up 'ere. Then take a walk around and label
'em up as you go. Then you've got yourselves a little map
to study and help you round. You'll know this place like the
back of yer 'and in no time.'

It was a sensible plan, and Maggie was annoyed she hadn't
come up with it herself. 'Thank you, Arthur,' she smiled
graciously. 'What else can you tell us about this place?' she
asked, hopeful they had found someone with inside knowledge willing to help them out on their very first day.

'Now, the rest you'll need to figure out for yerselves,' he
said, giving them a cheeky grin and wagging his finger

mock-sternly. 'I'm no snitch, y'see. I didn't survive life on the Old Nichol by giving up me neighbours and I'm just as loyal 'ere.' Maggie felt deflated. But then, that would have been far too easy. They were here to do a job and they needed to take the time to work Bethnal Green out for themselves and build the residents' trust.

Arthur turned and started making his way back towards the steps. 'Good luck with the map,' he called out to them. 'Come and find me if you need any help with it!' He gave a wave over the back of his head as he slowly disappeared down the steps.

They stood in silence, processing the conversation. After a few moments they heard Arthur's voice again, ringing out from the bottom of the first set of steps. 'If you want someone to sing like a canary for you, Sally's yer gal!' he shouted. Maggie dashed to the edge of the steps to look down at him.

'She won't tell us anything either, Arthur,' she said.

'That one don't take long to warm up, trust me,' he winked. He turned away again and started walking towards the next set of steps. 'Just so you know, our Sal's partial to a portion of jellied eels!' he called back, giving another wave over his head as he disappeared for good this time.

'What a strange thing to tell us,' Maggie said as she walked back to Irene and Annie, her brow puckered in confusion. They both nodded, frowning. 'Anyway, let's get our map sorted and see who else we can find to chat to,' she suggested. 'Then we'll see if we can pay Sally a visit tomorrow?'

'Sounds good to me,' said Annie, and Irene agreed. 'Funny chap, wasn't he?' Annie mused as they made their way through the gardens.

'I thought Arthur was quite sweet,' Maggie said. 'It was lovely of him to help us out. And he reminded me of my granddad – so I'm afraid I have rather a soft spot for the old chap now.' She smiled as she thought about her granddad.

She had been so close to him before his death a few years before. She often wondered how her father had ended up so mean and nasty when his own dad was so loving.

The girls were just making their way out of the gardens when three young boys ran in. Their racket dragged Maggie back to the present. 'You're not police, you're women!' one of them shouted, pointing at them. Irene, Maggie and Annie all stopped walking.

'We're Women Police Volunteers,' Maggie announced as the boys came over and stood in front of them. They must have only been about ten years old. They weren't as well presented as the children she was used to seeing around in Kensington, but they weren't too scruffy. 'Do you live around here?' she asked, trying to sound as friendly as possible.

'None of yer business,' the tallest one said, looking her up and down. The other two giggled while Maggie folded her arms across her chest. 'What sort of uniform you got there?' the same boy asked. 'You can't be police. Me pa says women shouldn't be allowed to do jobs like the police. Those jobs are for *men*.'

'Well, you can ruddy well go home and tell your father all about the female police officers you met today,' Irene said, her tone playful. 'You let him know what good officers we are.' She smiled and tipped her hat to him. 'Now, be a good boy and run along.'

All three boys stood glued to the spot, dumbstruck.

'Are you *really* police?' the shortest one asked suspiciously. He had light blond hair and a button nose that he rubbed on the back of his hand as he waited for an answer.

'Yes, dear,' Maggie said. 'We're helping the male police keep an eye on things while some of them are off fighting in the war.'

'But . . . you're women . . .' he said cautiously.

'Just because we're women it doesn't mean we can't do

the job the same as men,' Maggie laughed. 'They wouldn't give us this uniform if they didn't think we could, now, would they?'

The boys looked around at each other and shrugged.

'I guess not, miss,' the third boy said, who up until now hadn't said a word. 'Are you goin' t'arrest us?' he asked fearfully.

'We ain't done nuffin' wrong, John!' the taller boy said loudly, rolling his eyes. 'They ain't very well going to arrest us for chatting to 'em in the garden!' He was laughing now, and everyone joined in.

'Your friend's right,' Irene said. 'We'll only arrest naughty people, and so far you lot have been a bit cheeky but done nothing wrong.' The boys laughed again.

'We're off to play soldiers in the bandstand,' John said proudly. 'We pretend to shoot the Germans, and we've got bombs to blow 'em up with and everything. D'you want to play?'

'We're a bit busy,' said Maggie, 'but have fun and we'll see you around another day.'

'Bye!' the boys called out together as they raced through the gardens and towards the steps leading up to the bandstand.

As the girls carried on walking in the opposite direction, they could hear the boys' pretend gunfire and shouts.

'Why did you tell them we can arrest people?' Annie asked Irene.

'Well, we can carry out a citizen's arrest,' Irene shrugged. 'But more importantly, we don't want people to know we haven't got that power, do we? They won't listen to us if they know we can't make arrests. We're best to keep that to ourselves for as long as we can, I'd say.'

'She's right,' Maggie agreed. 'We need to do our best to hide that, otherwise no one will take us seriously – just like at the station. Speaking of which, we'll need to head back there soon if we're to see Frank before he clocks off. Shall we sort out our map and then start walking that way?'

'Yes, let's do that – we don't want to miss him on our first day,' Annie said while Irene nodded her agreement. 'Maybe we can look around the rest of Bethnal Green tomorrow?'

'Frank said to focus on the Boundary Estate. We should come back here,' Irene said quickly.

'But we need to get to know the whole area,' Annie argued, 'not just this estate. Why don't we—'

She didn't get a chance to finish before Irene cut in. 'Frank said the police don't have time to come here,' she said, sounding slightly hysterical now. 'Let's leave the rest of Bethnal Green to the men and we can focus on this patch. We can really work on getting to know everyone and helping them where we can.'

Maggie could feel the tension radiating from Irene. She couldn't understand why she was being so tetchy all of a sudden, but it definitely wasn't the right time to push her on it. 'Let's decide in the morning,' she suggested, trying to pick up the mood that had dropped so quickly. 'I'm sure Frank will be in charge of our movements, anyway.' Mentioning their new boss reminded Maggie that she wanted to quiz Irene on the blush she had caught earlier in the day. But now wasn't the time – she'd have to wait.

When they got back to the station, Frank wasn't around to retrieve their day clothes and direct them to somewhere to get changed out of their uniforms. Of course, no one else was willing to help them, so they ducked behind the unmanned reception desk to get their clothes and crammed themselves into the toilets to get changed. There weren't any facilities for women, so they squeezed into a cubicle each, in case anyone walked in midway through.

'Surely they must have somewhere we can leave our

uniforms overnight,' sighed Maggie as they all emerged from the stalls. There was no chance she could get away with sneaking such a bulky load in and out of her house every day, and anyway, she could do without lugging it across London and back again on a regular basis.

'We can check with Frank in the morning,' Irene said.

Maggie thought it seemed like a good time to try and get to the bottom of that blush. 'He's rather fetching, isn't he?' she said innocently. She watched Irene out of the corner of her eye and could see her turning crimson as she tied her shoes.

'He *is* handsome,' she agreed quietly, avoiding eye contact with both her friends.

'You like him, don't you?' Maggie jumped in. She had planned on a soft approach, but she couldn't help herself.

'Hold your horses!' Irene blustered. 'I said he was handsome, not that I want to marry him! Anyway,' she said more quietly, almost to herself, 'he'd never go for a girl like me.'

'Don't be silly,' Maggie said. 'Why ever not?'

'Look, just leave it will you? I've got to dash – I'll see you both in the morning.' And she ducked out of the room without so much as a backward glance, forgetting to take her uniform with her in her rush.

'That was odd,' sighed Maggie. 'I can't figure her out sometimes.' Annie nodded in fervent agreement. 'Do you know, we still don't know where she lives,' Maggie pondered, now tying up her own shoes. 'She always wants to meet us at the place we're going, and she dashes off so quickly – so we can never even work out which direction she's going in.'

'I think she's very private,' said Annie. 'She hasn't really told us a lot about herself at all, has she? For instance, I know about you and your parents and how strict they are. I know all about Eddie. And you know about me and my family. But what do we know about Irene?' Maggie was pleased Annie was as curious about Irene as she was. 'Ah well, I suppose we ought to fold her uniform for her and hide it away until morning,' sighed Annie.

'Yes, come on. We'll put them all behind the desk if it's still empty,' Maggie suggested. She needed to get off herself if she was to be home in time for dinner.

14

Maggie burst through the front door of her home and did a mad dash down the hallway. As she passed the kitchen, she caught a glimpse of Florence, who was beckoning her in to see her.

'Your father's not sat down yet,' she said, spotting the panic on Maggie's face and continuing to wave her in. For once, Maggie was disappointed her family weren't sitting at the table waiting for her. She was exhausted and just wanted to eat her dinner and go straight to bed. But she was also excited to fill Florence in on her first day, and she found that the unexpected opportunity to do so perked her up. She looked around to make sure they were alone in the kitchen.

Florence's face lit up as Maggie told her all about what she had been up to. Maggie wondered how her mother would have reacted if she had been able to share it with her, but pushed the thought away.

'I knew you'd be great,' said Florence smugly as she went about laying out bowls and plates for the dinner. 'What did they think about seeing women in police uniform?' she asked, 'I'm betting it's quite fancy?' She wandered over to the stove and started stirring soup in a large pan. The smell wafting up from it was driving Maggie to distraction.

'Well, it certainly makes us look the part, I must say,' Maggie mused. 'It's very stuffy looking, and rather manly I suppose. But we want people to take us seriously, so we need to look like proper police officers.'

'You got yerself one of them smart jackets?' Florence asked, giving the soup a taste and pinching her lips together in satisfaction. Maggie was desperate to eat it now.

'Oh yes, and a hat,' Maggie said, her eyes still on the soup. 'We don't wear trousers, though. We have to wear these long skirts that come right down to our ankles.' Maggie rolled her eyes. 'It's all very proper.'

'It sounds very impressive, I do wish I could see you wearing it,' sighed Florence.

'One day, you will,' said Maggie confidently. Just then, they heard footsteps on the landing above them.

'That'll be yer father,' Florence said. Yer mother's not come out of the main bedroom yet, poor lass. I think he's had enough – he's been up there since he came in from work. He keeps pacing about in the hallway and then going back in. You best get yourself sat at the table – he won't be in any mood to be kept waiting.' She took the saucepan off the heat and smoothed out her apron with her hands. 'Well done on yer first day, my lovely.' She smiled indulgently. 'Now run along.'

Maggie scuttled out of the kitchen and sat herself down at the dining-room table. She was famished after being on her feet all day in the cold, and the smell of Florence's delicious supper had got her tummy rumbling.

Maggie could hear her father's raised voice echoing through the ceiling above her, and she shivered. She knew it made him angry when her mother locked herself away like this, refusing to face whatever it was that had upset her so much. She knew he would be trying to force her to join them for dinner. She didn't blame her mother for staying put – if Maggie was being shouted at by someone, she wouldn't be keen to join them for a meal, either. She just hoped he wouldn't lose his temper completely and lash out at her.

She heard a door being fiercely slammed shut, and she knew he had given up in frustration. She breathed a sigh of relief for her mother, but hoped she herself wouldn't bear the brunt of her father's anger. Next came the thudding of his footsteps on the stairs, and then he walked into the dining room to join her. Maggie balled her fists to stop them from trembling.

'Good evening, Margaret,' he said in a clipped tone, giving her a forced smile. 'Your mother won't be joining us this evening. I'm afraid she's still not feeling very well.' Maggie wondered if her father thought her very stupid. This was one of the things that aggravated her about her parents. They still treated her like a little girl, refusing to discuss adult issues with her. She wanted to shout at him that she could cope with difficult situations, like Eddie running off to fight in the war – she was coping with that better than her parents were! She wanted to scream Eddie's name and tell her father how proud she was of him for joining the army – even if it did scare the life out of her. But what was the point in making trouble for herself? As harsh as it sounded, the angrier her father was with her mother and Eddie, the less attention he focused on her, and the easier it was to pull the wool over his eyes with her orphanage cover-story.

'The children were just wonderful today,' Maggie smiled innocently as they tucked into their soup and bread.

'That's good,' her father replied in between mouthfuls. 'I hope they appreciate all the hours you're putting in, Margaret. You do seem to be spending an awful lot of time there.'

'Oh, they do,' she enthused. 'Just this morning the matron was telling me how grateful she is for all the time I'm giving them. I think I'm really making a difference, Daddy.' She didn't want to lay it on too thick, but she needed him to keep his nose out. She was amazed he hadn't already looked into the place or popped in to keep tabs on her, as it was. The last thing she wanted was for him to storm down to the orphanage and start ordering all the people there who had never even heard of her to start appreciating his daughter more. It was one thing for *him* to treat her badly, but he was too proud to let other people get away with doing the same.

'Well, don't get too used to it,' her father sneered. 'You need to remember this is not a long-term set-up. Everything is a little up in the air with all this war business going on. Once that's settled, things will go back to normal.' He paused to wipe his mouth, and fixed her with a stern glare. 'Do you understand me, Margaret?'

'Oh yes, Daddy. Of course,' she said soberly. What she didn't add was that she was counting on the police to accept WPV members as permanent employees once life had gone back to normal. She was going to show him that she didn't need a husband – or him.

They finished their dinner in silence, and Maggie breathed a sigh of relief when her father excused her from the table. 'You'll need a good night's rest if you have another full day ahead of you,' he said. Maggie felt a twinge of guilt. But then she reminded herself that she *was* doing good work – just not quite in the way her father thought. She waved Florence goodnight as she passed by the kitchen. She was too tired for any more chatting. Her eyes suddenly felt very heavy as she made her way up the stairs. All she could think about was crawling into her bed and drifting off into a wondrous sleep.

But there was one thing she needed to do first. All day she had been planning what she would write to Eddie. Each time something new had happened she had thought about how she would tell him and imagined his reaction. She could see him smiling now when she told him about the little boys playing soldiers, and then shaking his head incredulously when he learned about her talking back to the officer at the station. Climbing into bed with a pen and some writing paper, she set to work on her first letter to the brother she was missing so much.

15

The next morning, Annie and Maggie travelled most of the way to Bethnal Green together. They had arranged to meet Irene around the corner from the station, agreeing it would be better to walk in as a group again, as there was safety in numbers. Annie had been unusually quiet on the bus, and Maggie hoped she would tell her what was on her mind. As they neared the meeting point, Annie stopped and turned to face Maggie.

'Whatever is the matter?' Maggie asked her friend. She looked like she had seen a ghost.

'Richard is coming home for a few days,' Annie spluttered, her eyes wide with fear.

'But, well – that's great news! Isn't it?' Maggie asked cautiously. She didn't understand why Annie wasn't jumping for joy. Since the war had carried on into the new year, it seemed to have now been generally accepted that it would rage on longer than everyone had first anticipated. They had started allowing soldiers home for respite, but Maggie hadn't thought Richard would be lucky enough to be one of the first.

'Well, of course I can't wait to see him,' Annie said, wringing her hands. 'I just don't know whatever I'll say to him! How am I supposed to act around him, Mags? Letters are easy – I can think about what I'm going to write and make sure I put down the right thing. What if I say something wrong or upset him?'

Maggie felt like she understood what Annie was going

through. She was going to be watching every little thing she said, terrified of distressing her fiancé. Maggie felt like that every day with her father – only if she upset him, she could end up with more than just a cross word. She couldn't very well tell her friend to count herself lucky she wasn't having to negotiate a tyrant father and advise her on coping strategies. So, she tried to comfort her as best she could – once again frustrated that she could not be completely honest.

'I think you should try to be as normal as you can with Richard,' Maggie said. 'I don't imagine he'll be keen to talk about what he's been through, so don't ask about it – but listen if he tries to tell you.' Annie nodded intently, drinking in everything Maggie was saying. Maggie desperately hoped she was saying the right things. 'He will most probably want everything to be as normal as possible for a few days,' she added.

'Right,' Annie said, suddenly full of purpose. 'That's what I shall do. Thank you, Mags, you really are the best.'

Maggie hoped she had given sound advice. She didn't feel like she was the most appropriate person to ask, but she was flattered Annie had turned to her for help. 'Let's go and meet Irene,' she said brightly.

They found her waiting on the corner they had agreed on the day before.

'You girls took your time – you got any idea how cold it is out here?' Irene demanded as she jumped up and down and blew on her hands for dramatic effect.

'Sorry, my fault,' Annie said sheepishly as they continued on their way together.

When they reached the station the girls took a deep breath in unison and walked into the building. There was a different officer manning the reception desk today. He was younger than Witchy, but looked just as grumpy. Maggie thought he looked similar in age to Eddie, but that was where the similarity stopped. This officer didn't have a friendly face like her brother, and he was most certainly not as pleasant in nature as Eddie.

'Whadda*you* lot want?' he spat as they walked over to him. They hadn't even reached the desk or managed to utter a greeting. *Not so much safety in numbers, then*, Maggie thought.

'We're WPV,' Irene announced confidently.

'I know who you are. I just thought you would've realised there's nuffin' for you girls to do round here and shoved off by now. Haven't you had yer fun?' All three stood staring at the officer, shocked. The disbelief on their faces obviously amused him, as he let out a satisfied huff and continued his onslaught: 'You can run along home now and tell all your suffragette mates that you did yer bit.'

Another officer, older by a good twenty years, was standing on their side of the reception desk openly sniggering as his colleague harassed them. Maggie thought he could have at least tried to hide his amusement at the nasty attack. But she stopped herself from saying so, and she made a mental note to tell Eddie how much better she was getting at thinking before speaking.

'Please let PC Bird know we've arrived for our shift. We'll wait right here until he comes down to meet us,' Irene said stiffly. Maggie was impressed her friend had managed to keep her cool. The officer looked them up and down, tutted and then wandered off.

'Do you think he'll collect Frank for us?' Annie whispered nervously.

'Don't worry. Frank said to meet him here at ten, so he should be down soon anyway,' Maggie said. She checked the big clock hanging at the back of the reception desk and found they were right on time, despite her unscheduled stop with Annie.

'Ah, ladies!' they heard a friendly voice booming out from

down one of the long corridors. They looked around and saw Frank bounding towards them, a big grin on his face. 'How'd you get on at Boundary?' he asked. 'I was out chasing a thief when you clocked off. Went and caught the bugger, too! I saw you stashed your uniforms behind the desk. That was a good idea. That's probably the best thing to do until we can get some kind of private area sorted for you.'

'Are we to get changed in the lav again?' Irene asked. Maggie was sure there was a twinkle in her friend's eye that she had never seen before as she looked at Frank. And she held eye contact with him for just a little longer than was necessary.

'Erm, yeah, I reckon so,' Frank said, looking apologetically at them all.

'If you think you feel unwelcome out here, then you best listen to Frank and stay away from our changing rooms!' the man behind reception added nastily as he wandered back behind the desk.

'Morning, Mitch,' Frank said stiffly. Mitch nodded in his direction but held his gaze on the girls.

'I was just trying to find out what this lot of spinsters was doing back again,' sneered Mitch, looking them all up and down a second time. The comment riled Maggie and she had to close her eyes and take a deep breath to stop herself from hitting back. She knew the suffragettes were subject to endless speculation about their sexuality and relationships, but she didn't think it would extend to the WPV.

'Come on, now,' said Frank. His tone was calm, but Maggie could see he felt anything but. His fists were clenched at his side, and a vein in the side of his head was throbbing. 'You don't need to speak about them like that, Mitch. You might not think they can get up to anything useful, but they've already agreed to take on Boundary, which'll save us all an extra job.'

'Yeah, but what good can they actually *do*?' asked Mitch. There seemed to be genuine interest beneath his scorn now. 'They're here on an unofficial basis and they don't have no authority. They'll just have to call us in for backup when they find trouble going on. So that *makes* extra work for us. God alone knows why the chief agreed to this.'

'I reckon the uniform'll act as deterrent enough a lot of the time,' Frank offered. 'Think about how people tend to scarper as soon as they see us getting near. And I bet women will go to them for help rather than coming up against them like they do with us. The Toms are pretty distrusting of us in our clobber, but they might respond better to this lot, you never know. There's no harm in giving them a chance, is there?'

'I suppose not, Frank,' Mitch said sullenly. 'Don't mean I got to like 'em being here though, does it? This place is meant for men, always has been.'

Frank ignored these final remarks and turned back to face the group. 'I thought we'd explore some other parts of Bethnal Green this morning, then maybe you can head back to Boundary this afternoon?' he suggested, as though nothing had happened.

'That sounds like a great idea,' Irene said enthusiastically. *She's changed her tune,* thought Maggie. She decided Irene had definitely taken a shine to Frank.

They quickly changed into their uniforms in the toilets and met Frank outside. He took them to an area called the Waterlow Estate. The tall buildings lined Wilmot, Ainsley and Corfield Streets, and there was a pub, The Lamb, standing on the corner of Wilmot Street. Maggie was looking forward to public-house duty. She had never once stepped foot in a pub and she couldn't wait to see what all the fuss was about.

'The Lamb's only one road away from the police station, so I don't suppose they get much bother in there?' she asked Frank as they wandered past.

'Oh, I wouldn't count on it,' he laughed. 'Blokes round here don't care where they are if they've a score to settle. We've been called to many a brawl here. And they're always far from pretty!'

'I see,' Maggie replied. She was beginning to go off the idea of public-house duty already.

'It's calmed down a lot since the war started, though,' Frank added thoughtfully. 'Most of the men are off fighting, of course, and there's more of a sense of camaraderie among the ones who are still here. Plus, there are more women going to the pubs, which always calms the men's tempers down.' He grinned.

'Well, it's a good job we shall only be on the lookout for street women and soldiers' wives spending their separation grants on drink and getting a little worse for wear,' said Annie. 'It doesn't sound like they cause much trouble, and we've our martial arts training in case anything gets out of hand.'

But Maggie was still worried. Just because they were going into pubs to make sure women weren't being bought drinks in exchange for questionable acts or getting too drunk, it didn't mean to say they wouldn't find themselves in any trouble with rowdy beer-filled louts. What if the man buying the drinks was intent on getting what he had 'paid' for? And she had heard women could get quite vicious when on the drink.

'I still can't get used to the pubs being frequented by so many women,' Frank laughed. 'We'll pop in later so I can introduce you to old Bob, the landlord,' he added, as they carried on walking along the road past the pub. 'It's a little different to Boundary down these streets, eh?' he remarked, looking up at the tenement blocks. Maggie could see what he meant. The buildings were obviously a lot older than the ones on the Boundary Estate, and she could tell they weren't very well looked after. Some of the windows on the bottom floors were boarded up, and as they passed one door a woman came out and emptied a bucket of filth onto the pavement.

As soon as the door had opened, Maggie had noticed Irene scurry round to Frank's other side, so that he was between her and the house. She had also ducked her head down. Maggie wondered why she was looking so shifty and uncomfortable – perhaps she did in fact live here, and was trying to avoid being recognised in her own neighbourhood? But Maggie didn't have time to give it much thought as Frank continued his tour.

'In some of these places you've got one family living in two rooms,' explained Frank, shaking his head. 'It's where some of the old tenants from the Nichol ended up when they were turfed out. They use one room to live and wash in, and the other to sleep in. Then there's an outside toilet that they share with a load of other families. It doesn't compare to Boundary one bit, does it?'

'Not at all,' Maggie agreed.

'The landlords are only bothered about collecting the rent,' Irene said suddenly. She had been deadly quiet since they had left the station, so Maggie was surprised to hear her chip in out of nowhere. 'They don't care about the conditions everyone's living in – only their money. They kick you – I mean, *them* – out if they can't pay up. Even if the tenants promise to get them their rent early the next week!' She was red in the face now, but she refused to look any of them in the eye and kept walking, staring firmly at the ground. 'They wonder why young women turn to prostitution. Got to pay the rent some way,' she muttered before seeming to come to suddenly and blushing.

Irene had said more than she had planned, given her crimson cheeks. The group carried on in an awkward silence, unsure how to respond to Irene's sudden outburst. Maggie was just about to try her usual course of action – a change in subject – when Frank saved her the trouble.

'I'll take you ladies to Barmy Park now,' he said.

'Barmy Park?' Annie asked. 'What on earth is that?'

'Oh, sorry – I forgot you're not locals,' Frank laughed. 'It's nothing to worry about, just a public park off Cambridge Heath Road. There's a lunatic asylum there, for the chronic sick in mind,' he said, tapping his head meaningfully. 'The Military Authorities are talking about taking it over soon – as a facility to care for wounded soldiers.'

'Where will the patients go?' Maggie asked, frowning.

'Oh, I imagine they'll transfer them to the workhouse in Waterloo Road,' Frank said. Maggie felt that that sounded a little unfair, but she decided it was better than the patients being turfed out to live on the streets – especially in this cold weather.

She looked over at Irene, who had been quiet ever since her outburst. It was clear she liked Frank, and it made Maggie sad to think she was holding back from getting to know him just because she was convinced that he wouldn't be interested in her. She decided to try and help things along. If Irene wasn't going to ask Frank for more information about himself then she would just have to do it for her.

'So, Frank,' Maggie started, keeping an eye on Irene – whose ears, sure enough, pricked up at the mention of his name. 'You know why none of us enlisted – care to tell us why you haven't joined up to fight yet?'

'Maggie!' Irene cried out in shock. 'You can't ask a man that!' She had expected a reaction from her light-hearted enquiry, but Maggie hadn't counted on Irene jumping to Frank's defence quite so fiercely. She hadn't wanted to offend him – she would never accuse him of shirking his responsibility to his country when he was already spending every day in uniform protecting the streets of London and its residents.

'It's all right, it was a harmless enough question,' Frank said, waving it off. 'I know Maggie didn't mean any harm. I actually wanted to enlist as soon as the war broke out, but my brothers made me promise not to.'

'How many brothers do you have?' Irene asked eagerly. *There you go*, thought Maggie smugly. She had opened up the communication between them in an instant and now she could sit back and enjoy the blossoming relationship.

'I'm the youngest of three,' Frank sighed. 'Always doomed to be the baby!' As he laughed, Irene chuckled along with him and Annie looked over at Maggie with raised eyebrows. They both hung back subtly to let Irene and Frank walk on ahead on their own. They listened in as he explained how his older brothers had both enlisted and his parents had been so upset that he had reluctantly agreed to stay put. 'My brothers told me our mother would need me if the worst happened to them. It's a horrible way of looking at things, but you have to be realistic in times like this,' he said sadly.

Irene reached out and touched his arm sympathetically. 'You're doing your bit already by keeping the streets of London safe,' she said.

Maggie felt butterflies in her stomach as she watched the pair of them hold each other's gaze for longer than was strictly necessary. It felt good to have that sensation for a positive reason rather than her usual one of fear.

All too soon, they had reached the gardens and had to switch back into WPV mode. As they entered the gates, Maggie noticed a drinking fountain and a sign that informed her they were in Bethnal Green Gardens. She was struck by the beauty of the place – she hadn't expected to come across such a pretty scene, having walked along the dusty streets with their unkempt houses to get there. The frost covering the grass was twinkling in the winter sunshine that had emerged during their walk. Maggie thought it looked pretty, despite the lack of flowers and colour. It was quite busy despite the cold, with adults walking around enjoying the scenery, and children running around on the grass. Maggie wished she could join in their games to warm herself up.

'It's very peaceful,' Annie said, smiling.

'Yes, but don't let this calm fool you,' warned Frank. 'The little ones are playing nice and quietly now, but they can become quite high spirited, especially when there's a big crowd of 'em. And just like anywhere else, Toms like to try and get business round these parts.' Maggie wasn't shocked – it seemed like that was an issue wherever you were in London these days. She had heard it was even worse in other parts of the country where training camps had been set up for soldiers.

As they wandered round, she saw that the gardens were split into three parts: the Museum Gardens to the north, another garden to the west and a third garden to the south. The gardens were all enclosed by wrought-iron railings. She noticed lots of people staring at them as they made their way around. A few looked as though they were about to say something, and then stopped when they spotted Frank.

'Who yer got 'ere then?' a voice called out from one of the benches as they approached.

'We've got ourselves some policewomen helping out at the station,' Frank replied proudly. Maggie knew they weren't technically policewomen, but she supposed they were there doing duties for the chief constable, and anyone in that situation would be classed as an officer. The man who had asked the question – a rotund fellow with a big bushy beard and a smart cap but tatty trousers – simply nodded in comprehension as the group continued walking past. Maggie couldn't believe he hadn't made a snide comment or questioned them on their credentials. She was unsure if it was the way Frank had described them, or if it was simply because he was with them. Anyhow, she made a note to refer to herself, Annie and Irene as policewomen from now on. The description definitely carried more authority.

They wandered around all the gardens a couple of times to get a feel for the layout, before heading back to The Lamb. Maggie felt nervous about setting foot in her very first public house. That was one thing they hadn't practised during training – they had only sat in lessons and taken notes about all the laws and what they were to look out for and challenge.

As they walked in, she was struck by the stench of the place. Cigarette smoke hung in the air, and there was an overwhelming stink she didn't recognise. It made her eyes water. She imagined it was beer, looking around at the glasses full of dark liquid in front of the customers. It wasn't yet afternoon, so she had expected the place to be quiet, but it was heaving with men in work clothes.

Every one of them stopped talking as the door closed behind Frank. He had let the girls walk in ahead of him, so now they stood in the middle of the silent room, all eyes on them. Frank walked around them and headed to the bar, so they all followed. Maggie tried her best to look confident and authoritative, but her hands were shaking.

'Morning, Bob,' Frank said cheerfully as the man behind the bar set a large glass of dark brown liquid down in front of a chap standing on the other side. Maggie had expected the landlord to look smart and imposing, but this man was the opposite. His thinning hair was dishevelled, his jumper was covered in stains and his belly was so big it had pressed into the side of the bar as he leaned over to place the drink down. He looked like he had just rolled out of bed. Perhaps he had, Maggie mused.

As Bob looked up and noticed the girls, his expression changed. Maggie wasn't sure, but it looked like he was *nervous* at the sight of them in their uniforms. 'These are the policewomen I was telling you about the other day,' Frank added as Bob gave them all a slight nod and pulled down his jumper to cover up the small flash of belly that had been on show.

'Morning,' Bob muttered. He *was* nervous! Maggie couldn't for the life of her imagine why. 'I hope you'll find everything to your liking here. I'm doing my best to keep the place in order,' Bob said quickly.

Did he think they would be stricter than Frank?

'I'm sure we won't have any problems,' smiled Irene. Annie and Maggie nodded their heads in agreement.

'I've told them what a good landlord you are, Bob,' Frank said cheerfully. 'They'll be popping in every now and then, but I'm sure they won't find any work for themselves here. Anyway, I just wanted to show them the place – we'll be off now and leave you to it for the day.' Bob smiled and gave a small wave before turning to the next customer waiting to be served.

'Women police, eh?' a voice slurred as the group reached the door. They turned to the left and saw a short, skinny man clutching an empty glass and squinting at them intently. Maggie may not have been in a pub before, but she was quite sure that he was very drunk. His scrawny physique and the way he was straining his eyes to look at them reminded her of a rat.

'Leave it, Roy,' Bob's voice boomed out from behind the bar. Roy swayed in his seat and lifted his glass in the air.

'Now, come on and tell me,' he said slowly, before using the sleeve of the jacket on his free arm to wipe his mouth, 'what do you suppose you ladies can do?'

'We're trained just as well as policemen. That's why we've been given a similar uniform,' Irene said firmly.

'I don't believe you,' Roy scoffed, slamming his glass down on the table. 'Come on, then, show me what you can do!'

he shouted. The whole pub fell silent again. Maggie could sense Annie's angst pouring out of her and she knew Frank was sure to step in at any moment. She didn't know what she could do to placate this drunken mess, but she knew she had to do something quickly before Frank took over. They would lose all hope of gaining any respect from the people of Bethnal Green if they had to be bailed out by a policeman on their second day – and because of a snivelling drunk, no less.

'I can tell you that you're in breach of the Defence of the Realm Act 1914,' Maggie said confidently, stepping forward so she was standing in front of Annie, Irene and Frank. She wasn't sure why she'd said that – she knew he wasn't in breach of anything at all – but she had blurted the words out before thinking as she felt that saying something – anything – had to be better than staying quiet.

Confusion swept over Roy's face. 'I'm not breaking no laws,' he slurred suspiciously. He didn't sound as certain of himself as he had moments before, though.

'The act states that no one is to talk down to an officer of the law – male or female,' Maggie blustered. *Just say it with confidence and he'll believe you*, she reassured herself.

To her surprise, Roy's body language changed instantly. He placed his hands in his lap, swayed again and nodded at her. 'I can only apologise, ma'am,' he muttered. It was clear he was having to concentrate extremely hard on getting the sentence out clearly.

'Just remember that the next time you're tempted to speak out of turn to any of us,' Maggie said sternly before turning back around and leading the group out of the pub.

'I didn't even know that!' Frank exclaimed, catching Maggie up as she stomped down the road. She had marched ahead as quickly as her legs would take her without breaking into a run.

'That's because it's not true,' she hissed, feeling foolish. She had just wanted to calm the situation without Frank's help undermining them, and now she was going to get into big trouble for telling a massive lie on her second day. 'There are so many rules and regulations to DORA,' she explained, 'I was fairly sure I wouldn't be questioned on it – especially not by that lout.' She waited for the dressing down, but instead of shouting, Frank roared with laughter.

'Ha!' he chuckled. 'You even had me fooled, and I've had to study it! That was great work – you really know how to think on your feet!' Maggie couldn't do anything to hide the shock and confusion on her face. 'You're not in any trouble,' he added.

'But . . . I lied,' she said nervously.

'You do what you've got to do in this job,' Frank said, wiping the tears of laughter from his eyes. 'A little white lie to calm down a silly old drunk isn't going to be a problem. And you stood up to him in a pub full of some of the toughest men in Bethnal Green. That's one hell of a first impression to make, Maggie.'

Maggie relaxed and grinned at the other two girls. Annie beamed at her, but it took Irene a few seconds to smile, and Maggie's grin dropped a notch. Was Irene jealous at the praise Frank had given her? Although she was delighted to have made a good impression, she hoped she hadn't stepped on Irene's toes. She certainly wasn't interested in him like that. She resolved to make that clear in the future.

Frank went back to the station ahead of them. As the girls made their own way there, Maggie thought back to the other faces in the pub, trying to figure out if she had recognised any from their walk around Boundary. It would be great if at least one of them had been from the estate and could feed back to the other residents how impressive she and her fellow officers had been.

16

When the girls got back to the station, they planned on picking up their lunches and heading back to the gardens to eat. They found Frank standing at reception talking to Witchy and two other officers.

'You lot heard about this?' Frank asked as they approached.

'All they do is gossip all day – they've probably got the culprit's name and shoe size already,' one of the officers said, laughing.

Frank looked uncomfortable and Witchy sniggered.

'I've already seen them put one ruffian in his place, I wouldn't underestimate them,' Frank said proudly, fixing his gaze on Maggie. She was grateful to him for sticking up for them, but uncomfortable at him complimenting her in front of Irene again.

'What's this you're chatting about, anyway?' Irene asked Frank.

'Oh, there's been a big burglary,' he said as his eyes lit up. 'Dowager Lady Parsons from Knightsbridge had all her jewels pinched from her mansion while she was hosting a ball at one of the big hotels. Proper ransacked the place they did – took everything she had, even the stuff in her safe.'

'But that's not on your patch,' Annie said, confused.

'Course it isn't,' smiled Frank, 'but they reckon the guilty fella's from round here somewhere! Word's going round that the jewels are stowed away somewhere in Bethnal Green. Isn't that the best news? We never get big cases like this – it's always shoplifters and petty thieves and prostitutes. This could really make us if we break it!' His eyes were bright with excitement, and Maggie suddenly felt alive.

'We can ask around on Boundary,' she said enthusiastically. 'We've got some good sources there who might have some information.' She knew she was exaggerating to try and impress Witchy and the other officers, but she was convinced that it would be true soon enough. Irene and Annie nodded vigorously, backing her up, but the two officers burst out laughing. Frank and Witchy stayed silent.

'What's so funny?' Maggie demanded.

'You think you can help break a case like this?' Witchy said, sneering. 'Give over, love. You're only here to deal with boring women's issues – this is way beyond your scope!'

Maggie waited for Frank to jump in and defend them, but he just stood there staring at the floor and looking more uncomfortable than ever. It seemed he felt the same, then. Maggie was disappointed – she had thought they had an ally in Frank, but now she could see he only supported them if they were doing 'women's jobs'. Without another word, the girls grabbed the lunches they had brought with them that morning from behind reception and walked back out of the station.

'We'll show them,' Maggie said defiantly, as they strode down the street. She felt furious and humiliated. She could see her friends were just as worked up as she was.

'We should try to solve the case ourselves,' Irene said firmly. Maggie almost yelped in excitement at the thought of it.

'Oh . . . I'm not sure,' Annie said nervously. 'I know they were rude, but we haven't been here long – perhaps we'd do well to keep our noses out of it.'

'Come on, Annie! If we do this then we can really show them we're serious about all of this. It's our chance to prove to them that we're not just here to pass the time – that we mean business and we can ruddy well do this job just as well as them!' Maggie was almost shouting now, and she took a deep breath to calm herself down.

Her passion seemed to rub off on Annie, though: 'I suppose it won't hurt to do some asking around.'

'Great!' boomed Maggie, now grinning from ear to ear. 'A little bit of digging won't do any harm.'

'We'll need to be careful,' Irene said. 'It's going to take people a while to get used to us and trust us. We'll need to be subtle in our enquiries, so we don't scare any of the locals away.' Annie and Maggie nodded in agreement.

They had reached the gardens. Settling on a bench, Maggie was grateful for the cumbersome WPV jacket as she rubbed her cold hands together. It may have been nippy, but she was happier sat outside than dealing with the idiots at the station. She pulled out the sandwich Florence had made her with some left-over chicken.

'I've got cheese in mine,' smiled Annie as she took a similar looking package out of her pocket. That was another good thing about the big, heavy jackets they had to wear on patrol – lots of room for carrying things. The two of them waited politely for Irene to take out her lunch.

'Oh, I had a big breakfast,' Irene muttered, waving her hand dismissively in their direction while staring off in the other direction. 'I'll be dandy until dinner time. You two go ahead.'

Maggie had been so angry at the station she hadn't even noticed that Irene had been the only one who didn't pick up any lunch. She wasn't convinced by the 'big breakfast' excuse. They sat in silence, until the quiet was broken by the unmistakable growl of Irene's stomach. Irene tried to cover it with a cough, but Maggie wasn't fooled.

Why didn't Irene just admit she had forgotten her lunch?

Or could she not afford to eat? Maggie's mind wandered back to Irene's outfit at the dance. She looked between Irene and Annie, taking note of the big difference in their statures. Annie wasn't fat by any means, but her full figure and healthy complexion made it clear she came from a family where getting hold of food wasn't an issue. She looked content, Maggie thought. Irene, on the other hand, was really quite bony under the heavy weight of the WPV uniform, and her face had a pinched, unhealthy look to it.

'My sandwich is huge,' laughed Maggie. 'I could really do with some help getting through it. I would hate for part of one of Florence's creations to go to waste.'

'I told you,' Irene said, sounding annoyed, 'I won't need anything else to eat until I get home this evening.'

'But—'

'If I'd wanted lunch, I would have brought it with me, wouldn't I?' Irene snarled, getting up from the bench and walking off on her own.

Maggie and Annie sat and ate their sandwiches in an uncomfortable silence. Maggie really couldn't face eating the whole thing now; she was too upset that she had offended her friend, and concerned that Irene was clearly hungry yet wouldn't accept help from her.

She was just wrapping up the second half of the sandwich when Irene came marching back towards them with purpose. 'Well, if you're not eating it, we can't let it go to waste, can we?' she barked, before swiping the package from Maggie's lap without even stopping. Maggie and Annie jumped up after her.

By the time they had reached Irene, the remainder of the sandwich was gone, and she was wiping her mouth with the back of her hand. 'That Florence knows how to make a sandwich,' she said, relaxed again now. Maggie smiled. She knew better than to say anything more on the topic.

Setting off towards the Boundary Estate, the girls discussed their plans for the afternoon.

'I think we should use our maps to keep learning the different buildings and street names,' suggested Annie.

'Good idea – we need to get to know the layout quickly or else we'll just be on the back foot if anything happens,' said Maggie. 'Imagine if one of those boys yesterday had played up and then run away from us. We'd have had no idea where we were going and would have ended up blindly chasing after him.'

'While we're doing that, we should stop and talk to everyone we see,' Irene chipped in. 'They won't let us help them if they don't know us. If we start building good relationships as soon as possible then they might even start coming to us when they need support or advice. And we might even manage to get hold of some good leads about the burglary. Fancy jewels like that won't go unnoticed around here.'

'Agreed,' Maggie smiled. She could feel a fire burning in her belly as she thought about presenting the burglar to Witchy at the police station. 'Maybe we should pop in and see Sally, too,' she added. 'I think persistence will win with that one.' Just as they were approaching the bandstand, they saw a young woman heading in their direction. 'Let's start with this girl,' Maggie whispered, raising a hand to catch her attention.

'Lady policemen?' the woman asked, looking their uniforms up and down, clearly confused.

'Yes, miss,' smiled Maggie. 'We're with the WPV, stationed at Bethnal Green. We're here to look out for women and children mostly, so we can help with any problems you might have. We're just getting to know everyone at the moment, so we'd love to have a quick chat. Do you live around here?'

The woman looked around uncomfortably. She had long

brown hair that looked as though it hadn't been brushed for weeks, and her clothes were rather tatty. Her pretty face was in need of a good wash, and the dark circles under her eyes looked like they could swallow a person whole if they ventured too near.

'I . . . I don't live on this estate 'ere, no,' she muttered. 'I live on Waterlow. That all right, or am I in trouble?' Her eyes widened and she looked genuinely frightened.

'Don't worry, dear, it's not a crime to walk through an estate on your own,' Annie said kindly. 'We don't want to reprimand you – we were just asking so we can get to know you, is all.'

Relief washed over the woman's face, but Maggie could tell she was still nervous as she started chewing on one of her nails. From the look of her and the way she was acting, Maggie wondered if the woman was a prostitute on her way home from making herself some money. Her training had taught her to be sensitive in these situations, and she was feeling especially cautious after her mix-up with the married woman waiting in the park for her husband during training. She still regularly cringed at the thought of that.

'Were you here visiting someone?' Maggie asked softly. She didn't want to sound accusatory or judgemental.

'If yer mean was I wiv a soldier, then that's the truth. Ain't nuffin' wrong wiv that,' the woman said defensively. She had quickly switched from timid to self-righteous. 'He bought me a drink in The Lamb last night. So lonely and sad, he was. I wanted to keep 'im company on his first night home on leave. Poor soul just wanted to cuddle.' Maggie wasn't sure she believed the last bit, but the rest sounded feasible. Maybe this woman didn't realise she had been bought a drink in return for 'cuddles'.

'Just be careful,' Maggie warned. 'The policemen around here will jump at the chance to arrest women for soliciting

– even if that's not what you're doing. And they won't touch the men, especially if they're soldiers.'

'I wasn't—' the woman started, but Maggie continued over her.

'It doesn't matter – if it looks like it then they'll come down hard on you. We just want to save you from getting into any trouble. Just have a good think before you accept drinks from strangers in the future, and before you go home with them. It could be mistaken for something more.'

The woman looked shocked now, and tears started forming in her eyes. 'I just wanted somewhere warm to sleep for the night,' she sniffed. 'It's so cold in me 'ouse, and me ma don't let me get no rest. As soon as I'm 'ome from work she's got me doing chores or minding the babies. And my gosh can those little terrors scream. Goes right through yer.'

'How old are you?' Irene asked with real concern in her voice.

'Just turned eighteen,' she whispered, wiping tears from her cheeks and looking around her fearfully. Maggie's mouth fell open in disbelief and she felt Annie nudge her in the side. She quickly closed her mouth again before the woman noticed. *Eighteen?* She had thought she was at least ten years older than her – not the same age. *Life in the slums must be tougher than I realised*, she thought sadly. She was beginning to understand just how good a card she had been dealt in life – in some ways, at least.

'Come on, love, we'll see you home safely,' Irene said, taking the girl's arm in hers. Maggie was disappointed not to have got a chance to start asking around about the burglary, but she decided that could wait – getting this poor girl home safely was more important. As they made their way back along Bethnal Green Road, they learned she was called Betty. She lived in one room on the Waterlow estate with her parents and four little sisters. Her siblings ranged in age from just one to fifteen years old. Her father tended to spend most of his wages at local pubs, so Betty was relied upon to bring in money to keep the family in their home and feed them.

'Pa never goes to The Lamb,' Betty explained. 'Bob threw him out a few months back and hasn't let him in again since. He couldn't pay his tab, yer see. Bob don't know we're related – or else I don't think I'd be allowed in neither.'

When they got to Betty's house, Irene knocked on the door before gently unlinking her arm from Betty's and bending down on one knee. Confused, Maggie looked down and saw she was tying her shoelace. Although come to think of it, Maggie hadn't noticed any laces flying loose as they had approached the street. She shrugged it off and stepped forward so she could greet Betty's mother.

'Oooh, what trouble you in now then, girl?' her mother cried when she flung open the front door and caught sight of her daughter standing with women in uniforms. Maggie was surprised at the sight of Betty's mother – she was a good foot shorter than her daughter, and her features were very harsh in contrast to Betty's soft features.

'I ain't done nuffin' wrong!' Betty shouted, pushing past her mother and stomping off down the hallway.

'Well, where were yer all night and morning? I had a right night with yer sisters and yer pa was nowhere to be found either!' her mother yelled after her, but the only response was the sound of a door being slammed shut.

'Mrs— ?' Maggie asked once the older woman had turned back around to face them.

'Connor. Mrs Connor, it is. You police, or what?' she asked, looking Maggie and Annie up and down just as her daughter had. Irene seemed to have vanished, but Maggie didn't have time to think about that right now.

'Yes, we're policewomen based down the road at Bethnal Green Police Station,' Maggie said, trying her best to smile pleasantly at the woman despite the vicious glare she was giving her. She hoped she wasn't going to have to use any of the martial arts training. 'Your daughter spent the night with a soldier. Is there any way you can make things a little easier at home for her so that she doesn't feel the need to do that?'

'I 'ope she got a good price for it,' Mrs Connor laughed. 'She ought to 'ave done – 'specially after missing a morning at work. The rent ain't gonna pay itself now, is it!'

Maggie was shocked. She had expected Betty's mother to be concerned about what her daughter had been up to, especially given her age and the danger she could have been in. She imagined what scenes there would be if *she* were ever to be escorted home by the police in a similar situation. Her father would kick her out on to the streets there and then – too angry to even punish her first. Although, she thought sadly, it seemed Betty may actually be better off away from her mother if this was her attitude.

'What's it to youse lot anyway?' Mrs Connor scowled. 'You posh lot don't give a damn 'bout us paupers in the slums.'

'That's not true,' Annie stepped in. Maggie was relieved – she was feeling a little intimidated by Mrs Connor. She may have been a slip of a woman, but she was fierce. 'We're here to help girls like Betty. She's putting herself in danger by cavorting with soldiers,' Annie stressed. Mrs Connor still didn't look very concerned.

'Has she done this type of thing before?' Maggie asked tentatively, feeling a little braver now.

'Oh, course she 'as – they're all at it,' Mrs Connor scoffed. 'How else d'you expect me to pay the rent every week when me 'usband's out drinking his wages every night and I've four little ones who don't seem to stop eating all day and bleedin' night? It's not like the soldiers are complaining, is it?' Maggie and Annie stood in silence. Maggie wasn't sure if they were supposed to answer the question, but Mrs Connor had a point.

'They come 'ome on leave and want to forget all the 'orrible things they seen on the battlefields. Poor lads. I've 'eard all about it, my dears, and it ain't pretty. All the places they used to go for amusement, like the public halls, are being taken up by the military. So, they're being thrown out on to the streets and straight into the temptations of the public houses and the loose women.' Maggie had to take a moment to catch her breath. How could a woman talk about her daughter in such a way? It was obscene.

'The kids round 'ere are running amok as there's nuffin' for 'em to do and all their dads are off fighting so there's no one to discipline 'em. Now, what do you s'pose you can do to help with that?' she finished, glaring into Maggie's eyes so hard she thought she would burn a hole in her retinas.

'Well, it's a tricky situation, isn't it?' Maggie said, trying to sound confident. She was shocked that someone like Mrs Connor had been so insightful. And she had no solution to give. Their training hadn't covered that. They were just supposed to move people on. 'Just please ask Betty to be careful. We don't want to see her in any danger, and we don't want her getting arrested for getting up to no good with the soldiers.'

''Ow about this: when you lot pay me rent, then I'll keep 'er indoors wiv me,' Mrs Connor said matter-of-factly, then slammed the door in their faces.

'That went well,' Annie laughed shakily as the clunk of the door rang through Maggie's ears. 'Can you believe how rude she was? They really have no manners around here! And I thought she'd be concerned about what her daughter had been doing.'

Maggie shook her head in disbelief. She was suddenly grateful for the roof over her head and the food in her belly, even if she did pay a hefty price for it having to live with her father. 'Now, wherever did Irene go?' Maggie pondered as they looked all around them. They turned around to head back to Bethnal Green Road and spotted her walking towards them.

'I thought I saw a little girl wandering around at the top of the road on her own, so I went to check she wasn't lost,' Irene said.

'Was she all right?' Maggie asked.

'Oh, she was gone by the time I got there. I had a search around, but she must have slipped into a house or something,' Irene shrugged.

Maggie wasn't sure she believed her, but she couldn't think why she would make something like that up. 'Well, let us know next time,' she said. 'We looked round and you were just gone!'

'Sorry about that,' Irene muttered. 'How was the girl's mother?' she asked hopefully.

'Awful,' sighed Annie. 'She was more concerned about whether Betty had made any money out of the soldier.'

The girls headed back to Boundary, ready to study their map at last. They had made it down three of the roads before they were stopped again. A young-looking man in a military jacket waved them towards him.

'You seen a scruffy-looking girl with long brown hair?' he asked desperately. 'She's got me wallet!' Maggie suddenly had a feeling Betty had got more than just a drink out of her dalliance with a soldier the night before.

'I'm sorry, but lots of girls look like that around here, sir. You'll have to give us a better description,' she replied. She knew she should head straight back to Betty's house and question her. She was certain she would find this soldier's wallet there, probably already emptied of whatever cash it had held when she had lifted it.

But she felt protective over Betty. The poor girl was desperate, and maybe the money would save her having to go out in search of another soldier to sell herself to for another couple of nights. Her mother might even give her a bit of a break. And the experience might teach this lad to think a little more with his brain, rather than what was in his trousers.

'I can't tell you more than that, I'm afraid,' the soldier sighed. 'I only got back last night, and I went straight to the pub. I just needed to clear me head of everything. I'd had quite a lot to drink when I met her and when I woke up this afternoon both her and me wallet had gone!'

'Well, I'd imagine she's long gone now, sir. It might be best to put this down to experience and be a bit more careful about who you take home with you from now on,' said Annie.

'You look like you need some more rest,' Irene added, before he could argue. 'Why don't you head home and have a nice bath, sir? It appears you're still carrying mud from the trenches on you, if you don't mind me saying. We'll take your details and we'll keep an eye out for your wallet.' Maggie was relieved her friends obviously wanted to protect Betty too.

As they waved the soldier off in the direction of his home in the Chertsey block, Maggie put her notebook back in her pocket. 'Let's have a chat with Betty and warn her not to make a habit of this,' she whispered.

'Yes, and she should probably stay away from The Lamb for a few days – at least until his leave is over,' Irene agreed.

17

That night, Maggie's mother finally joined her and her father for dinner. She was so quiet that Maggie struggled to notice any difference from when she had locked herself away. All the same, it was nice to have her back at the table with them. After excusing herself from the room and telling her parents she was retiring to bed, Maggie sneaked back down to the kitchen to talk to Florence. Sitting down to a cup of tea together, Maggie filled Florence in on the whole episode with the soldier's missing wallet.

'I'm worried I'll get into trouble for covering for Betty,' she confided. It had been on her mind all evening.

'You did the right thing, love,' Florence assured her. 'That poor lass shouldn't have stolen from the soldier, but he was taking advantage of her just as much. You'd do good to remember that.' Maggie knew Florence was right, and she felt a lot better. 'Fact yer friends all felt the same says a lot too, mind. But you need to visit this girl soon and make sure she knows not to make habits of helping herself to people's wallets from here on out. You can't *keep* covering for her. Now, tell me who else you got to know today,' she smiled, resting her cheek on her hand.

As Maggie brought Florence up to date on everything, including the burglary, she realised she and the girls hadn't got around to dropping in on Sally at the laundry as they had planned. She couldn't quite believe how busy they had been already – and they had only just started.

'We should go and see Sally at the laundry first thing,' she thought out loud as Florence cleared up around her. 'She might even have some information about the burglary.'

'That the one you was telling me about?' Florence asked. 'The one who knows everything about everyone?'

'Yes, that's the one,' Maggie said.

'Well, she's bound to know something. You ought to take her some jellied eels,' Florence suggested. Maggie looked up, confusion sweeping over her face. 'Soften her up,' Florence smiled. Maggie's face was still blank. 'Goodness, child,' Florence sighed. 'Arthur told you Sally loves jellied eels. Now why d'you suppose he went out of his way to share that with you?'

Of course! Maggie had forgotten all about Arthur's little tip – she certainly couldn't remember telling Florence about it. She must have been more tired than she realised last night, and she felt foolish for not catching on about the eels herself – it seemed obvious now.

'If someone needed something from *me*, or if they wanted to say "ta" for helping them out, it'd work a treat if they brought me some lovely, moist sponge cake,' Florence added, raising her eyebrows as she kept her eyes fixed on Maggie.

'Oh, Florence,' Maggie giggled. 'I can take a hint rather well, you know, despite missing Arthur's. Rest assured I will return home soon with a wonderful sponge cake for you!'

'It would surely be appreciated,' Florence smiled. 'And I reckon this Sally'll be goin' out her way to help you girls if you take her her favourite snack.'

Maggie got up and wrapped her arms around her. 'Thank you,' she whispered into her ear, holding her tight. They stayed in the embrace for a good while before Maggie pulled away and went up to bed. She was in desperate need of a good night's sleep before her next shift – especially if she was going to do some digging into the missing jewels.

The following morning, the girls checked in quickly with Frank at the station. They told him their plan for the day, but they left out the enquiries they were keen to carry out about the burglary. They tried their best to act normal with him, but all of them – even Irene – still felt put out that he hadn't stuck up for them when Witchy and the other officers had mocked them yesterday.

They agreed to get changed and on their way to Boundary as fast as they could manage. 'What's the point in sticking around the station waiting for the men to pick on us?' Annie reasoned. Maggie felt the same, although she was fighting her natural urge to charge around the building giving them all what for until they bucked up their ideas. It really wasn't in her nature to shy away from situations like this. But every time she considered biting back, Eddie's voice would ring in her ears like an alarm. It seemed to Maggie that even when he was far away, he was still looking out for her. She decided it was better to focus her energies on helping all the women in Boundary.

Once there, the group went straight to the bandstand and tested each other on the building and road names against their map.

'I see you took my advice,' a gruff voice called out as they applauded each other for getting them all correct. Maggie knew it was Arthur even before his head popped up. She walked over and helped him up the final few steps.

'Thank you, love. That last set really takes it out of me,' Arthur huffed, settling himself down on a bench. He took some time to catch his breath. 'I try and get up 'ere every day, though. Good to get some oxygen going around the old lungs, and I like to watch the hustle and bustle on the estate. It keeps me mind active.' Maggie was warming to Arthur. He may have come across as a bit of a know-it-all when they first met, but she could tell now he was just a lonely old man.

'I 'ear you girls have been laying down the law already,' he said. 'Don't worry yourselves,' he added as they all looked at him with apprehension. 'That showdown at The Lamb has gone down a treat – people round 'ere love a woman what can keep a man on his toes.' *How does Arthur know about that?* Maggie wondered. 'Old Sal's brother was in the pub when you had your set-to,' Arthur explained before Maggie had a chance to enquire.

'It wasn't really a set-to,' Maggie muttered, feeling coy all of a sudden. 'I just put an old drunk in his place.'

'Well, Jonny was there and way he tells it, you weren't taking no backchat,' Arthur said, looking impressed. 'And 'course, now Sal's got wind of it the 'ole estate knows. She's probably added a few bells an' whistles, an' all.'

Maggie had to stop herself from breaking out into a big grin. She couldn't have hoped for better news. She would have been happy with a Boundary resident seeing the stand-off, but someone related to Sally – now that was the biggest bit of luck!

'What you got there?' Arthur said, nodding to the small package Annie was carrying.

'Oh, we, er, we picked something up for Sally on the way in,' Annie said.

'Jellied eels?' Arthur asked shrewdly. Annie nodded and he clapped his hands and then rubbed them together gleefully. 'Smart girls!' he laughed. 'I knew you'd listen to me! Now, yer know I'm not one to tell tales on me neighbours, but you'll 'ave old Sal eating out the palm of your 'and once you take them to her, 'specially after the pub drama.' He looked at his watch. 'She has a tea break around now, so you should get down to the laundry with them eels quick smart. She'll be sat on the step outside.'

Maggie had wanted to quiz Arthur on his knowledge of any potential thieves hiding out on the estate, but that could wait. They were breaking regulations carrying the package around – they weren't supposed to carry any parcels or bags of any description whilst on duty and there was no way she was putting the disgusting eels in her pocket. They had agreed it was worth the risk carrying it in plain sight to try and get someone like Sally on side. Talking amongst themselves on patrol was against the rules and no one had pulled them up on that yet, so they were feeling confident, although Maggie didn't want to push their luck. So, heading straight to the laundry sounded like a great idea.

'Thank you, Arthur,' Maggie said as the three girls set off down the steps. They left him there looking out over the estate, a satisfied smile on his face.

As they approached the laundry, Maggie was struck by how big the building was. They spotted Sally straight away. She was sitting on the steps outside just as Arthur had promised, and she gave them a curt nod as they walked towards her.

'I 'eard yer put Jim in his place the other day,' she said loudly, before taking a big sip of her tea. 'And I saw yer helping that young scally too. She's not been round 'ere before – looks more like a slum girl. You get her 'ome all right?'

'Yes ma'am,' said Maggie. 'We escorted her all the way to her door and spoke to her mother.'

'No need to call me ma'am. You upper-class gals with yer airs 'n' graces do make me laugh. Call me Sal, will ya?'

She must be starting to trust us, thought Maggie. 'Of course, Sal,' she smiled.

'What's that?' Sal said, gesturing towards the package in Annie's hand.

'We picked up a snack on our way here, but I'm afraid we rather over-ordered,' Irene said, taking the eels from Annie and peeling back the wrapper. Sal's eyes widened and she licked her lips when she spotted the contents. 'You like jellied eels?' Irene asked innocently as she wafted the package under her nose.

'Do anything for 'em, I would,' Sal said, grinning now and craning her neck to stare at the slimy mess in Irene's hands. Maggie couldn't understand how anyone could find something that looked so repulsive enjoyable to eat. But each to their own. Suddenly, Sal hunched back down on to the step and looked up at them all suspiciously. 'Just 'ang on a darn minute,' she said slowly. 'That looks like a full portion. You sure you 'ad some or are youse lot trying to butter me up or something?' she asked.

'Oh gosh, no – of course not,' Annie said in a good imitation of taking offence. 'We were just doing our rounds with our leftovers when we spotted you sitting here. I'm sure we can find someone else to take them if—'

'No, no, no you give 'em here, I'll take 'em off yer hands,' Sal said firmly, jumping up and reaching out to Irene with such speed, it was as if her knickers had caught on fire. She snatched the package from Irene and closed her eyes, waving it backwards and forwards under her nose. Then she shoved a big handful into her mouth and groaned with pleasure as she noisily chewed the gooey mess with her mouth open. Maggie had never seen anything quite like it, and she tried her best not to retch. She had never eaten jellied eels in her life and had been disgusted when they had picked them up at a local fish shop. She had thought that had been the most hideous thing she'd seen to date, but Sal taking such pleasure in devouring them had just about taken the crown.

'We'll, erm, be off then,' Annie said uncomfortably.

Sal kept her eyes closed but managed to make a farewell noise. 'Uhm hmm,' she murmured, and gave a small wave in their direction.

They went on their way, but as they reached the end of

the street, they heard Sal shouting after them. Turning around, Maggie could see Sal wiping her mouth on her apron. She forced her face to stay neutral and not show the repulsion she felt. Sal was waving them back over, and they walked dutifully towards her.

'You girls ever need anythin', you come to Sal,' she whispered, looking around her as she spoke. She obviously didn't want anyone else to hear her offer. 'I knows all what goes on round this estate,' she added before ushering them away again and shoving another load of eels into her mouth. Excitement coursed through Maggie. The plan had worked – if Sal knew anything about the burglary, she was sure to share it with them now. She didn't want to make it obvious why they had given her the eels, though, so she kept quiet. She could bring it up the next time they saw her.

'Thank you, Sal!' Irene grinned, and they all waved before heading off again.

'Gosh, that was obscene,' Annie giggled, when they were far enough away that Sal wouldn't hear them. Maggie couldn't help but break into laughter. It felt good to let it out after having to disguise her disgust for the whole encounter.

'Leave her alone,' Irene said firmly. 'Women like Sal are the backbone of communities like this. She might be a bit rough around the edges, but I can promise you she has a heart of gold.'

'Yes, I didn't mean to be rude,' Annie said apologetically. Her face had turned bright red.

'Oh, come on, Irene,' Maggie laughed. 'The way she went for those eels!' Irene's stony face softened. She wasn't quite smiling, but she was almost there. Maggie imitated the slurping and sloshing noises Sal had made while she was eating.

Suddenly Irene was laughing too. 'Yes, all right!' she conceded reluctantly. 'I must admit, I've never seen anyone enjoy jellied eels *quite* like that! That was definitely one of your better plans, Mags.'

Maggie should have admitted the whole thing had been down to Florence, but she decided to enjoy the praise. Besides, she was sure Florence would allow her the small victory – but she would most certainly need to get her hands on a sponge cake now. 'We should ask her if she's heard anything about the jewels next time we see her,' Maggie suggested. The girls nodded in agreement.

That afternoon they chatted to a few more residents while wandering around the estate. Rather than barrelling in and asking about the jewels, they had decided to ask about anyone who had suddenly come into money. Despite slipping this enquiry into their conversations, they weren't having much luck.

They stopped to have a word with some young children who were using bad language. To Maggie's surprise, they all stared at the ground guiltily before apologising and shuffling off towards their respective homes. The uniform was having a deterrent effect on most people they met. Maybe it was worth being uncomfortable for. She also had a feeling Sal's influence may have been to thank for the positive attitudes and compliance they were experiencing. Whatever the cause, it was a good feeling to have people treat them with respect, especially given the way the men at the police station were behaving towards them.

They popped around to Betty's house to warn her about stealing from soldiers, and Maggie was pleased with herself for dealing with the situation sensitively and avoiding offending her. She was, however, put out when she realised Irene had wandered off almost as soon as they had arrived at the door. As Maggie and Annie said goodbye to Betty, Maggie really believed the young girl had taken on board what she had said, and she was confident she'd keep herself out of trouble – for the time being, anyway.

Now she just had to figure out where Irene had disappeared to and why on earth she kept vanishing whenever there was anything important to do.

They bumped into her at the top of the road. But they had to get back to the station and fill out diaries for the chief constable, so Maggie decided to focus on that instead of confronting Irene over her disappearing act.

'We need to make sure we go through our notepads and include every single conversation,' she said. 'Remember what Frosty said – we need to make them realise just how much we're doing. They need to feel like they can't get by without us.' She thought for a moment before adding, 'But maybe we should leave the part about the soldier's wallet out.' Annie and Irene agreed.

It took them a good hour to note everything down back at the station. It made Maggie realise just how busy they had actually been. 'I've got to admit, I'm rather impressed at what we've achieved already,' she said proudly as she finished up and waited for her friends. She found she was rather excited to show the chief constable and all their doubters at the station just how valuable they were.

18

As Maggie and Annie made their way to Bethnal Green together the following Wednesday morning, they talked about how quickly their time with the WPV was passing. Maggie couldn't believe it was 13th January already – if time kept flying by at this rate then Eddie would be home before she knew it. Keeping busy was a great way to distract her from the fact that he was gone.

They met up with Irene as usual and found Frank waiting for them at reception at the station. 'Chief wants to see you,' he said seriously. There was no hint of his usual cheekiness or chirpiness, and he seemed reluctant to look any of them in the eye. Maggie's stomach dropped almost to the floor. 'Get into uniform and I'll go and check if he's ready for you,' Frank added glumly, handing over the folded clothes they had placed behind the reception desk the previous day. As he headed off down the corridor, the three of them stood there, dumbstruck.

'It doesn't sound like good news,' Annie whispered nervously. 'Surely he'd only want to see us if we'd done something wrong. Do you think he's angry about something in our diaries?' Maggie was too busy internally panicking to respond. Her mind had jumped straight to the conclusion that the chief had somehow discovered her secret and she was about to get the boot for sneaking into the WPV underage.

'Perhaps we've been spotted chatting on duty,' Irene offered casually. Maggie felt annoyed that she clearly wasn't as worried about this meeting as she was. It made it clear to her once again just how much she had to lose compared to her friends, who were completely unaware of anything she was going through.

'Maybe it's about those jellied eels!' Annie cried, resting her elbows on the reception desk and placing her head in her hands.

'Whatever it is, it's nothing we can't get over,' Irene said firmly. 'Now, stand up straight before anyone walks past and sees you,' she added.

They went to get changed, and found Frank waiting for them on their return. 'I'll take you up,' he said. His tone and demeanour did nothing to reassure Maggie. They followed him up to the chief's office without a word.

Once they were sitting down in front of Chief Constable Sadwell, Maggie placed her sweaty hands on her lap and tried her best to keep her breathing under control. Sadwell was in his fifties, very wide and very bald. Maggie imagined his job must involve sitting behind his desk all day, as there was no way she could see him chasing criminals around Bethnal Green.

'Ladies,' he said after clearing his throat and shuffling some paperwork. It took a moment for Maggie to realise it was their diaries. At first, she was relieved – there was nothing in there that would give away her age. But then panic set in again. *Whatever can have riled him in there?* Her heart almost stopped when it occurred to her that he might have somehow found out that they had purposefully left out the incident with the soldier's wallet.

Chief Constable Sadwell cleared his throat again. 'It's time for me to eat some humble pie,' he said slowly, not quite meeting their eyes. Maggie's mouth fell open. 'I wasn't so keen on you ladies being stationed here. I must admit I was convinced you would spend most of your days gossiping with the no-gooders on Boundary and getting yourselves into bother that my men would have to help you out of.' *Tell us something we don't know*, Maggie thought bitterly. 'But after reading your diaries I can see you've done some sterling work already. It seems you're helping the local community immensely.'

Relief washed over Maggie as though she were sinking into a hot bath.

'The soldiers on leave around here are being targeted by prostitutes – as you well know,' the chief continued. 'You're doing a good job of moving the women on from the gardens and streets during the day. I also see you've picked up a few on their way home and warned them against making a habit of what they're up to. But the main problems are at night, when the men are weaker from drink, and vulnerable. These women should know better, but they seem to target them in the evenings. The Lamb is a popular hunting ground for them, so you would do well to start there.'

Maggie blanched as a fresh wave of panic washed over her. 'You . . . you want us to do night patrols?' she asked cautiously.

'Yes – will that be a problem?' Chief Constable Sadwell said sternly. He seemed surprised she had spoken, as if he had wanted to say his piece and for them to run along and get on with it without question.

Maggie hesitated before she replied. 'No, of course it won't be a problem, sir,' she said finally, as Irene and Annie looked intently at her. 'I, erm, I just wanted to make sure I understood correctly.'

'Good,' he said, before continuing. 'Many of the soldiers are drinking to forget, and they can act a little silly. The public are, of course, protective of them. That makes it hard for my men to arrest them when they act out of turn. I'm trusting you ladies to collect these men and escort them to safe places to sleep it off. I understand from your superiors this is something you are trained to do.' The three girls nodded enthusiastically.

As they made their way to the station's main entrance, Maggie didn't even notice the dirty looks they received from the other officers – she was too busy trying to process what had just happened. It was so far from what she had anticipated. She had known they would be expected to carry out night patrols at some point, but she'd thought they would get a little more time to settle into everything first. She hadn't even come up with a plan with Florence yet. She silently scolded herself and her friends for being so efficient.

'Thought you were in for a telling off, didn't you?' Frank asked playfully when they found him back at reception.

'You knew?' Irene cried. You could've reassured us!'

'It was too much fun watching you squirm,' Frank laughed.

'Oh, Frank,' Irene sighed, reaching out and giving him a soft nudge on the arm. There was no denying Irene had feelings for Frank now. Maggie wanted to tease her about it but held back, remembering the reaction she got last time. She decided she had too much else to worry about at the moment to risk getting on the wrong side of Irene again – and it seemed like it didn't take much to achieve that these days.

Their first night shift was to be that evening, so they were allowed to rest for the remainder of the day before heading back to the station for six o'clock. Maggie's father would be at work now, and her mother would be having tea with the wives of her father's colleagues – Maggie couldn't think of them as her friends – so it was the perfect opportunity for Maggie to get home and come up with a cover story with Florence.

Maggie needn't have worried – Florence had a plan as soon as she filled her in. She would tell Mr Smyth his daughter was so worn out from playing with the orphans all day that she had taken to her bed without dinner before he had even made it home from work. They both knew he would never dream of going into her bedroom to check on her. Maggie's mother had been uninterested in everything since Eddie's departure, so they weren't worried about her barging in and discovering her daughter's empty bed. Satisfied with the ploy, Maggie headed to her bedroom to write another letter to Eddie and catch up on some sleep.

Back at the station that evening, Witchy was on duty at reception again. 'Evening, ladies,' he said, giving them a polite nod as he handed over their uniforms. 'You're not far from here when you're checking out The Lamb. One of youse can always pop back for me if you need some backup.' Maggie didn't know how to react. The tone of his voice made it clear he wasn't happy about making the offer – but at least he was making it instead of berating them. It was like he had accepted their presence at the station – grudgingly, but it was better than nothing.

'Thank you,' Annie said as they shuffled off to get changed.

'That was odd,' Irene whispered, pulling on her heavy jacket.

'I suppose now the chief is happy with us, they must realise we're here to stay,' Annie shrugged.

'I suppose so,' said Maggie. 'Let's do our best to get through this shift without his help, though. We don't want to be owing someone like him anything. I couldn't stand to give him the satisfaction of knowing we needed him to rescue us, especially on our first night shift.' Irene and Annie nodded in fervent agreement.

'We've been doing pretty well on our own so far,' Irene said proudly. 'I can't see that a night shift will be too much harder than a day one.'

Two hours into the patrol, Maggie was beginning to realise just how wrong Irene's prediction had been. The streets of Bethnal Green were alive with men and women in drink, and young children in high spirits. They had already had to break up three groups of boys who were pushing each other around and shouting. A word of caution had seemed to calm most of them, but they had ended up escorting two of the boys home. Each time, the mothers had just shrugged their weary shoulders and admitted they had a complete lack of control over their sons while their husbands were away fighting.

'There must be a load of men home on leave,' Maggie commented as they passed yet another soldier hiccupping his way down the street. Just then, she heard raised voices. It sounded like they were coming from the next road along. Together, the girls stopped walking to try and make out what was going on, but all they could hear was shrieking. They ran to the next street and as they turned into it, they spotted a commotion up ahead. Slowing to a walk, they tried to work out how best to deal with the situation.

'I saw 'im first!' a woman cried out as she lunged at a soldier.

'Back orf!' a second woman yelled. 'I was wiv 'im last night and I'll be heading home with 'im again tonight so go find yerself someone else!' She grabbed the soldier's arm and he stumbled over his feet and on to the floor.

'He's too drunk to stand, let alone anything else,' Irene tutted. The two women started pulling at each other's hair and screaming. 'I say we leave them to it and get him out of here,' Irene suggested. When they reached the man, Annie and Maggie grabbed one arm each and yanked him to his feet. He started swaying dangerously but between the three of them they managed to steady him. Placing one of his arms over Maggie's shoulders and the other over Annie's, they walked him off down the road with Irene gently pushing on his back to give him the momentum to move forwards. The women carried on fighting and didn't even notice the girls had squirrelled the soldier away. They got him around the corner and pulled out his military ID card.

'He lives on this road – thank goodness,' Irene panted.

They were all out of breath. She directed them to the house and then ran ahead to bang on the door.

'My boy!' a woman's voice called out as the door opened. 'Thank you so much, I've been so worried!' As they leaned the soldier up against the side of the house, his mother continued, sounding like she was on the verge of tears. 'He's been like this almost every night since he got back; I don't know what to do. He's been through so much already and I know he's drinking to forget and to cope with the fact he has to go back again soon. I'm just so worried he'll get himself into some real trouble soon. If only they would give him some hard labour time, it would surely sort him out. But the magistrates won't do nothing as he's a soldier.'

She turned to her son then. 'Come 'ere, you big lump,' she said tenderly, pulling on his arm. She jumped out of the way as he toppled over the threshold and landed on all fours in the hallway. His mother nudged him, and he collapsed slowly onto his side. 'He'll be grand there til morning,' she said, as he sprawled onto his back and immediately started snoring.

'I suppose he'll be waking up tomorrow morning in that exact spot,' Maggie laughed as they walked away.

'I don't blame her for leaving him there,' said Irene. 'Imagine her trying to get that lad up the stairs and into bed – it took three of us to move him just a few steps!' They set off for The Lamb next. They had already popped in at the start of their shift and found that it was relatively quiet. 'I expect it will have livened up now everyone's home from work and had time for dinner and a few drinks,' Irene said.

Maggie's stomach flipped at the mention of dinner. She hoped her parents had fallen for Florence's tale. When they stepped into the pub, Maggie was taken aback by the cloud of smoke in the air. The stench was almost unbearable and was broken only by the alcohol fumes that accompanied it. Irene had been correct – the place was packed now.

'Picked up a bit!' Annie shouted over the noise of chatter and laughing once they reached Bob at the bar. He motioned for them to go around the side of the bar. When they had fought their way through, Bob was waiting and beckoned them into a little room. He closed the door behind them and Maggie was grateful for the silence and the break from the overpowering smells.

'Girl sitting on the table nearest the door, I think she's touting for soldiers to take 'er 'ome,' Bob whispered.

Maggie wasn't sure why he was whispering – the door was closed. But she followed suit. 'What makes you think that?' she asked him just as quietly.

'Keeps calling fellas over, having a little chat, then they push off after a few minutes and she looks put out. She's been nursing the drink she got when she first came in for the last two hours. Seems like she's after alcohol in exchange for a bit of fun.'

'Sounds a bit suspicious, I must say,' said Irene. 'We'll go and have a chat with her.'

'Thanks, ladies,' Bob said. 'Can you leave it a bit, though? I don't want no one thinking I tipped you off. I don't want this sort of thing happening in me pub, but I don't want the regulars thinking I'm a snitch or nuffin'.'

'Of course,' Maggie said. She realised what a tricky situation Bob must be in. They decided to do a round of the pub and stop to talk to a few customers on the way, before stopping off for a chat with the woman in question. As they made their way around the tables, Maggie suddenly felt overwhelmed by the smells and the heat in the pub. 'I need some fresh air,' she said as her cheeks flushed red.

'We'll be fine, take as long as you need,' said Irene, rubbing Maggie's back in sympathy. 'Poor thing – it's rather stuffy in here.'

When Maggie opened the door and the fresh air hit her

face, relief engulfed her. She had just stepped on to the pavement when she felt a firm grip on her arm. Looking round in shock, she glimpsed a man's silhouette before she was yanked so hard she almost lost her balance. Another arm came up and a hand slapped down over her mouth before she could let out the scream that had started to build in her throat. The man dragged her around the side of The Lamb and into an alleyway.

She tried to hit out at him, but he was just too strong. Terrified, Maggie desperately ran over her ju-jitsu training in her head, but it was all happening so quickly. As she struggled against him she realised he was far too big and strong for her to overpower. She had always had some warning and time to prepare in training.

'Don't scream,' he whispered urgently, stopping and pushing her up against the side of the pub. He spoke too well to be from Bethnal Green – he sounded upper class. It threw Maggie for a moment. 'It's me, Mags, I won't hurt you.' Maggie recognised the voice now. As her eyes adjusted to the dark, she could just make out Peter's features staring back at her. Peter was a family friend of the Smyths. He used to play in the street outside their house with Eddie when they were younger. He had always seemed a little odd, but Maggie had found him harmless. She hadn't seen Peter for years – not since his family had lost their chain of bakeries and moved out of the area. She supposed this was where they had ended up. But why had he grabbed her like that, and *was* he going to hurt her? She didn't know if she could trust him. As Peter released his grip on Maggie's mouth and arm, she took a step to the side. 'Hey Mags, how are you getting on?' he asked jovially.

'What was all that about?' she spat. 'You had me terrified!'

Peter laughed and looked around. 'I wasn't all that sure you would want to associate with me now I'm a ruffian from the

East End,' he scoffed. 'What with your father in politics and you all dressed up like a man. Does Mr Smyth know you're out doing lads' work in these rough parts, by any chance?'

'Of course he does,' Maggie said firmly, not quite meeting his eye as she straightened out her skirt and jacket, which had become twisted in the struggle.

'I don't believe you for one second,' Peter said shrewdly. Maggie looked down at her feet. 'I knew it!' he cried in glee. 'You always were a bad liar. There is just no way Mr Smyth, with all his respectable friends, would be allowing "his little Margaret" to strut around the East End in a police uniform!'

There was no use denying it – it really was obvious to anyone who knew her family that her father would never have given his approval for her to join the WPV. 'Please don't tell my parents,' Maggie begged. She had known she was playing a risky game this whole time, but if there was anywhere she had felt safe it was Bethnal Green. She couldn't believe she had been so unlucky as to bump into this horrible boy.

'I'll tell you what,' Peter sneered as he leaned in closer to Maggie's face. He grabbed a chunk of her hair and pulled her head to the side. He bent his head and kissed her neck, soft as a butterfly. She stood frozen to the spot as he whispered in her ear. 'I'll keep your little secret safe and sound as long as you see me right.' He grabbed hold of Maggie's right breast and as she squirmed and tried to push him away, he leaned into her harder. She was trapped between him and the wall, and now he was groping at the waistband of her skirt with his other hand. She turned her head to the side as his breath hit her face. The stench almost made her retch, it was so rotten. As he forced her head back to face him, Maggie battled over what to do for the best. She didn't want her parents to find out about the WPV, but she just couldn't let Peter do this to her.

'No! Stop it!' she shouted out, pushing at his hands, which were groping her again. But every time she shoved them away, they came back again stronger, pawing at her body and pulling at her clothes. For the first time she was grateful the WPV uniform was so heavy and thick. She didn't feel like she could fight him much longer. She was just about to give in when she heard footsteps approaching behind her. Peter had his hand over her mouth now, and the force meant she couldn't move her head to the side to see who was coming. All of a sudden, Peter's grip released and he flew away from her. She heard a loud *thwack*. Looking around, she saw Peter laid out on his back on the ground and Irene standing over him looking extremely menacing.

'What the—?' Peter muttered as he looked up at Irene. As soon as he saw her uniform he looked back at Maggie quickly before scrambling to his feet and running off down the alleyway.

'Are you okay?' Irene said as she rushed to Maggie's side. Annie was already supporting her from the other side as she shook with fear and shock.

'He came out of nowhere,' Maggie whispered through the tears she now allowed to fall freely.

'Thank goodness we came to check on you,' Annie said. 'And thank heavens Irene remembered that ju-jitsu move. He didn't know what had happened!'

'No more splitting up,' Irene said firmly. 'There's too many desperate men out there who will take an opportunity as soon as they see it. That's the kind of man we're here to protect women from.' Even in her state of shock, Maggie found Irene's statement ironic – *she* was the one who kept disappearing off on her own. But she didn't say anything. As far as Maggie was concerned, Irene could get away with whatever she wanted after saving her from god only knew what horrors Peter had planned for her.

19

Later that night, as she lay in bed trying to sleep, Maggie couldn't stop thinking about her close shave with Peter. Not being able to tell her friends the full story behind the attack had left her feeling lonely and isolated. She had been desperate to tell them the truth as they had walked back to the station together. It would have made her feel so much better to share that burden with them, and she knew they would have known exactly the right things to say to make her feel better about it all. They also would have gone out of their way to protect her from Peter moving forward.

But to confess all to Irene and Annie would mean coming clean about her age as well as her family not knowing about her joining the WPV. She was confident neither of them would share her secrets – they loved her as much as she loved them. But if she told them then she would be putting them in the position of having to lie for her, and she couldn't bring herself to do that. She wasn't prepared to drag her friends down with her if this all blew up in her face.

Maggie was terrified of what Peter might do next. Would he contact her parents? Or would he work out that she was too young to be with the WPV and go and tell someone at the station? She was desperate not to be on her own in Bethnal Green in case he grabbed her again. She couldn't even bear to think about what would have happened if Irene hadn't stepped in. But at the same time, if they bumped into him on patrol together – would he reveal everything to her friends?

Maggie wished more than ever that Eddie was here. He would know what to do. He would probably have been to visit Peter already and had it out with him. Irene had wanted to run off in search of Maggie's attacker as soon as Maggie had composed herself and assured her and Annie she was all right. When Maggie managed to convince her not to, she had faced another obstacle.

'Well, we should go and tell Witchy – get him and some of the other officers out to look for him,' Irene had raged.

'There's no way we are doing that,' Maggie had replied while desperately trying to think up a reason to stop her. 'This is our first night patrol – and you want to run to them for help within a few hours? We'll just be proving them right and we'll never hear the end of it!' Then she had changed tack. 'Please, can we just keep this to ourselves? I'm embarrassed enough as it is. All that ju-jitsu training and I was too scared and weak to do anything!' Maggie had hidden her face in her hands. Irene had pulled her in for a hug and Annie had rubbed her back soothingly.

'You've nothing to be embarrassed about,' Irene had assured her. 'It's that scally who should be hanging his head in shame. He should be able to control himself and not try and force himself on anyone who takes his fancy!'

'I got a good look at him,' Annie had said confidently. 'So, if we come across him again we can clout him even harder next time!'

Maggie was so grateful to her friends, but running into Peter again was the last thing she needed. She wanted more than anything for them to just forget all about it.

Maggie tossed and turned as she went over it all again in her head. With such a dramatic ending to her first night patrol, she hadn't even had another chance to worry about her parents realising she wasn't home late at night. She had let herself in silently and sneaked straight to bed. The house had been in darkness, so she'd known nothing had gone wrong, and she had been relieved to find Florence hadn't waited up for her – she was too mortified by what had happened to share it with her.

Eventually, she dropped off to sleep with Charlie tucked under her arm. The events of the evening had really wiped her out and she slept in far longer than usual the next day. Her father was up and at work early, and her mother had another migraine, so thankfully her late morning went undetected.

When the girls turned up for their next night shift the following day, there was a distraction to take Maggie's mind off Peter.

'We pulled someone in for the burglary,' Frank said excitedly as he bounded along the corridor towards reception to greet them. Maggie's heart sank. She had so wanted to be the one to solve that case.

'Not so fast!' Witchy's voice boomed from behind Frank as he came over to join them. 'I've just come out of the interview – he's not our man. Got an alibi.'

Frank bunched up his fists and cursed loudly. 'Sorry, ladies,' he stammered as he registered the looks of shock on their faces. 'I just really wanted to have caught him.' Maggie tried not to smile.

'Well, we've been making enquiries, so we might have a lead for you soon,' Irene said proudly. Maggie nudged her hard in the ribs. She was setting them up to be ridiculed! They needed to wait until they had some information before saying anything. She was happy for Irene to try and impress Frank – but not at her expense.

He smiled awkwardly as Witchy laughed and walked away.

'That's very kind, but it really wouldn't go down well,' he said quietly. 'Anyway, how'd you get on with your first night patrol yesterday?' Frank asked, changing the subject.

'Nothing much to report,' Maggie said quickly.

Irene shot her a sideways glance before nodding. 'People tend to fall into line when they see us coming,' she added cockily, giving Frank a cheeky look. Maggie was so relieved that Irene had backed her up, she decided to forgive her previous slip-up.

As soon as they were clear of the station, Maggie linked arms with her two friends, scowling. 'We need to step up our efforts to find out about the burglary,' she said defiantly. 'I bet we could gather more information than them in one shift if we really put our minds to it!'

'I dunno,' Irene said cautiously. 'I don't think we should upset Frank.'

'In case he decides he doesn't want to kiss you?' Maggie teased. She felt a little more comfortable with Irene since she had saved her from Peter, and brave enough to rib her again.

'Oh, hush,' Irene said playfully.

But her relaxed tone only encouraged Maggie more. 'I've seen the way you look at each other,' she said. 'Come on, admit it: you've got a bit of a soft spot for him.' She was aware she might be pushing it, but it felt so good to have some fun after everything that had happened recently.

'Well, he *is* good-looking,' Irene admitted reluctantly. She was definitely blushing.

Maggie wasn't sure where Irene's attitude change had come from, but she was enjoying it. 'I *knew* it.' She giggled.

'I bumped into him on my way out the other day and he started telling me more about his brothers and his mum,' she said. 'He's really close to his family; it's so lovely to hear him talking about them.'

Maggie wanted to know more, but their conversation was brought to an abrupt halt when they heard a man shouting further up the road. They immediately switched to professional mode and sped up to find out what was going on. Maggie could hear a woman crying.

'Is everything all right here?' Annie asked loudly. The couple, who had been standing close together, jumped apart when they heard her voice and turned around to see the three of them.

'This one won't take no for an answer,' the man, who seemed to be a soldier, explained. 'I just want a few drinks with me mates down the local and she's tryin' to get me to take her home. Can I go now, and leave her with you?'

'Please do,' Annie said, giving him an understanding smile before he walked away.

'You goin' to arrest me then?' the woman sneered. She looked young, in her early twenties, maybe, although Maggie knew now that people around here often looked older than they were.

'We're all done,' Irene smiled. 'We just wanted to stop you before you did something that could get you arrested. Please, take the evening off and just go home.'

'S'not that easy,' the woman said, wiping her eyes on her skirt. 'You lot don't get it. I don't have no home. That's why I'm so desperate to go home with someone else.' Maggie felt terrible for her. No matter how worried she was about her parents finding out her secret or bumping into Peter again, at least she had a roof over her head.

As they spoke to the woman, they found out that her name was Mary. She told them she came from a decent family and had fallen into her way of life by accident. 'There was a sense of freedom when the war started,' Mary explained, her eyes downcast, as they all sat on the pavement. 'The men was all dressed up in their 'andsome uniforms marching down the streets. They was about to go off and risk their lives for us! It was 'ard to not get carried away with it all, yer know?' Maggie didn't know, but she nodded her head in agreement, as did Annie and Irene. 'When I'd done it once I found meself trapped. I was sullied – I couldn't go home after that.'

Maggie had never thought of it in this way. She had assumed the women who did this sort of thing all started out when they were desperate and had no other option. To have come from a respectable family and then feel like there was no way back after making one mistake seemed even crueller to her, somehow. 'Now I try an' earn a living the only way that's open to me,' Mary added sadly. Maggie tried to put her arm around Mary's shoulders, but she stiffened and shrugged her off. She stood suddenly and, without another word, walked away from them. They all watched her retreating back until she rounded the corner.

'I feel terrible that there's nothing we can do to help her,' Maggie sighed. 'We can't even offer her somewhere warm and safe to sleep tonight. What a terrible way to live!'

'It's happening to more women than you know,' said Irene sadly. 'And although we're trying to help them by stopping them from getting arrested or falling into really bad company, there's not a lot we can do to *really* help them. We can't change their lives.' Maggie felt like they were failing the women, but she really couldn't think of any alternative.

'Why don't we ask Sarah for help?' Annie suggested.

Maggie looked round at her, eyes wide. 'Surely you remember how things ended with her?' she asked. 'Do you really think she's going to want to help us? Me?'

'No, perhaps not,' said Irene, picking at her nails and clearly lost in thought.

'Thank you,' said Maggie, relieved. The last thing she wanted to do right now was have Sarah shouting at her again.

'No, I mean, I think you're right – of course she's not

going to want to help us,' Irene explained. 'But she'll want to help the women we're trying to help. That's Sarah's thing, isn't it? That's what she's all about – one of the reasons she wanted to join the WPV.'

'Exactly,' chipped in Annie. 'There's no way she'd turn us away if there was a chance she could help these women by giving us a bit of guidance. And it might be a nice way to try to make things better with her. I still feel terrible about what happened.'

Maggie had to admit they made a good point. 'I just . . . don't think she's going to be too pleased to see me, that's all,' she said quietly.

'Nonsense,' said Irene briskly. 'We'll pay her a visit at *The Vote* offices together. She won't want to make a scene at work, so you can make your peace and we can find out if she has any bright ideas about what more we can do to help these poor women.'

And so it was decided. As soon as their schedules would allow, they would pop in to visit Sarah.

When she arrived home in the early hours of Friday morning, Maggie spotted a light on in the house and her stomach lurched. She took a deep breath before letting herself in. Maybe she was ready for this all to be over – the sneaking around had been fun at first but now she was tired and the run-in with Peter had really brought home to her the dangers of what she was doing. She stood at the front door, braced for whatever punishment her father had in store for her. But instead, Florence popped her head around the side of the kitchen door and beckoned her in. Maggie wasn't sure if she was relieved.

'This came for you,' Florence said eagerly. 'I didn't want to leave it out in case your parents came back down and found it.' Maggie stared at the envelope in confusion. Her name was scrawled across it in ink, but there was no address or postmark. 'I thought it were from Eddie at first – I been sneaking a look at the post 'fore giving it to yer father, so I can squirrel away any letters for you. But there's no address on it. I didn't see who dropped it off.' Maggie couldn't imagine who would hand-deliver a letter to her home. 'You going to open it then?' Florence urged. 'I've been wonderin' about it all evening!'

'Yes, sorry,' Maggie said, feeling flustered. For some reason she was nervous. She had a bad feeling about this. When she unfolded the single, dirty piece of paper and read the short note, her heart started racing and the room spun around her.

'You all right, love?' Florence asked, her excitement switching to concern.

Maggie could feel the blood draining from her face. 'I'm-I'm fine,' she managed.

'You sure? You've gone an awful funny colour, love,' Florence said, reaching out her hand.

Maggie brushed it away. 'It's nothing,' she snapped before scrunching up the paper and running out of the kitchen. She needed to get to her bedroom before the tears came and she blurted everything out to Florence.

20

It wasn't 'nothing'. Sitting on her bed, Maggie smoothed out the crumpled piece of paper with shaking hands, and read it one more time. The message was short and to the point:

> Maggie,
>   Come and meet me at my house at 7 tomorrow night.
> We have unfinished business.
>   Peter

Maggie's heart raced as she realised that if he had delivered the note while she was on her night shift, then '7 tomorrow' meant tonight! His address was scrawled on the back; he lived near Bethnal Green Police Station. Maggie felt physically sick as she stared down at his loopy, fancy handwriting, which contrasted so much with the menace behind the words. There were dark stains on the paper. She knew exactly what would lay in store for her at Peter's; he was obviously looking to finish what Irene had broken up the night before last.

Her initial thoughts were to ignore the note – she would be stupid to put herself in such a risky situation. Peter had overpowered her once before, and he would be more prepared this time. But then, she reasoned, maybe he just wanted to talk to her? Perhaps he wanted to apologise for what had happened? The Peter she remembered was a little odd, but he had always been a rather sweet boy. He had obviously been drinking when he'd attacked her. And there was no doubt he had had a rough time to end up living where he was. It was possible he felt bad about what had happened between them and wanted to make amends. Although that last sentence sounded ominous . . .

As Maggie got ready for bed, she tried to decide what to do. Now the girls had done two night patrols, they were due to work a short day shift. They would start at midday and finish at six o'clock – so she would have ample time to make it to Peter's if she wanted to. She wasn't sure what frightened her most – the thought of having to fight off Peter again or that of facing her father when he discovered what she had been up to behind his back. Then she remembered snapping at Florence – and after she had waited up late to give her the note, too. She felt terribly guilty, but she had been over-whelmed by fear when she'd seen those words on the piece of paper in front of her and she was too ashamed to share the whole story with anyone. She especially didn't want Florence, who was so proud of her and thought she had grown into such an independent woman, to know that she'd gotten herself into such bother so soon into her time with the WPV.

Lying in bed, Maggie resolved to come up with a plan on her way to the station for her shift later that day. Right now, she needed to sleep so she was rested enough to have her wits about her. Whatever she decided to do, she knew she would have to keep Peter's note a secret from Florence, Irene and Annie. Telling the girls was far too risky. If they got involved, Peter could reveal her age and bring everything crashing down around her. However much she craved their help and support, this was something she would just have to deal with on her own. If Eddie were here, he would help her figure it out. She had never kept anything from her brother, no matter how foolish she felt sharing it. The realisation made her miss him all over again, and she tossed and turned as she battled that pain alongside her anguish over Peter.

All the fussing about was making her hot, so she threw the covers off herself in frustration, knocking over a glass of water on her bedside table. She jumped up quickly to clear the mess, and as she reached down to pick up the glass, she noticed her hand was trembling. Clearly this business with Peter really had her riled. Crouched down on the floor in her nightgown in a pool of water, she decided there and then that she couldn't ignore his note – she would have to confront him and try to get everything straightened out if she were to ever stop panicking and looking over her shoulder. And the sooner, the better.

Maggie raised her head groggily as she heard a light tapping coming from the other side of her bedroom door. She rubbed her eyes as the door slowly opened and Florence walked in with a cup of tea.

'I wasn't sure what time you had to be up and out, but it is just gone eleven o'clock and your father'll be back for his lunch soon. I couldn't have him learning you were still in bed, love.'

'Thank you,' Maggie smiled gratefully, reaching out for the hot cup.

Florence handed it over, bobbed her head and retreated. 'I'll leave you to it, love,' she said quietly as she closed the door.

Maggie's stomach flipped as she remembered how horrid she had been to poor Florence. No wonder she hadn't stuck around to talk. She would have to make amends another time, though – she needed to get a move on if she was going to slip out of the house before her father came home, and make it to Bethnal Green before her shift started at lunchtime.

Maggie was running so late by the time she got to her and Annie's usual meeting spot that her friend had clearly gone on ahead. After a mad dash, she fiddled with her hair self-consciously as she walked up the road towards the station, where both her friends were waiting for her. She had run out of time getting ready and it wasn't nearly as neat as it usually was. Irene rolled her eyes affectionately as Maggie apologised and then they rushed inside to grab their uniforms and get changed.

'Don't worry, I struggled to get up for this shift after our night patrol, too,' Annie said sympathetically as they made their way see Bob at The Lamb.

Maggie was grateful to have the strange shift times to blame for her lateness. She couldn't very well admit she had been up most of the night fretting about the note from Peter. There was nothing much going on with Bob so they moved on to the Boundary Estate. Maggie had planned on picking up some more jellied eels for Sal on the way in, but she had been so consumed with Peter and what he wanted to see her for that she had completely forgotten.

'It's not like you to take your eye off the ball,' Annie commented as they wandered around Boundary. Maggie was sure her eyes had lingered on her messy hair as she spoke. 'Is everything all right?' Annie asked her. 'Your father's not giving you a hard time, is he?' Maggie had confessed to her friends that her father was strict, but she had stopped short of revealing the full horror of her home life.

'I'm fine,' Maggie said dismissively. 'I'm just tired with these long hours and all the walking around.' She was desperate to open up to Annie and Irene, but she reminded herself that it was better all round if she kept them out of it.

'Well, Sal did enjoy the last lot of jellied eels,' Irene laughed. 'Hopefully that batch will see us right for another visit. I think we should still go and see her.'

And she was right – Sal stood up to greet them when they approached her during her tea break later that afternoon. 'I've not seen you girls around for a few days, where yer been?' Sal asked, giving them a warm smile.

'We've been doing night patrols, so you've probably been tucked up in bed by the time we've wandered past,' Annie said.

'You want ter check in on Edith in the Walton building,' Sal whispered, looking around her shiftily. 'Some of the girls think she's been entertaining soldiers after hours, if you catch me drift.' Sally tapped her nose and winked at Irene as she spoke. ''Er 'usband's been away a little while now, and I guess a woman's got 'er needs. Not that I'd know – I gave up on daft men a long time ago. Far too much 'assle!' The girls promised to look into it, and conversation turned to the young women in the area who had fallen into prostitution. Annie told Sal about Mary. She admitted they had all felt terrible about not having any way of helping her out of her fix.

'You've kind souls, I can tell,' Sal said. They were all sitting on the step now, and Sal had made everyone a cup of tea. 'These innocent girls get carried away with the uniform and the danger the men are facing. But they don't realise it only takes one time for them to be too tainted to go back home.'

'That's what Mary told us,' said Annie sadly. 'I just wish there was somewhere safe we could send her, so she could break the cycle.'

Sal hesitated, a thoughtful frown on her face, and Maggie could practically see the cogs whirring in her head. After a minute, she looked at the girls and said, 'I'll take 'er in fer a while.'

'Really?' Irene asked, the shock clear in her voice.

'You think this girl is worth saving, then I'll see 'er right,' Sal said firmly. 'She'll 'ave to help me out in the laundry a course. Got to earn 'er keep. I'll tell Matron she's me niece an' I'm helping 'er out of a tight spot. I done it a few times before. I'm strong when it comes to men but I'm weak when there's a poor lass in need. Matron won't quibble so long as she's got an extra pair of 'ands fer nuffin'.'

Maggie hadn't really been listening before – her mind was still caught up in all her worries – but her ears pricked up at this. *What a generous woman,* she thought. *She doesn't even know this girl and she's willing to take her in.* She had thought Sal was just a bit of a gossip before and someone who only cared about other people if their actions entertained her. It made her feel bad for being so judgemental. They agreed to send Mary Sal's way if they bumped into her again, and promised to look out for her on their next night patrol.

They stayed and chatted for a while. They mentioned the burglary to Sal, but she hadn't heard anything. Normally Maggie would have pressed her, but she was too distracted to get involved in the conversation. 'I'll be sure to let youse know if any information comes my way. It usually does,' Sal said confidently.

They went on their way. It wasn't long before they spotted a group of young boys racing around and throwing stones. After a quick word, the lads agreed to calm down and keep their noise to a minimum. Next, the girls stopped to chat to some women in Bethnal Green Gardens. Maggie was still in her own little world and took a step back, leaving Irene and Annie to lead the conversation. She couldn't even remember what had been said when they got back to the station for a break, and had to peek over Irene's shoulder as she filled out her notes to ensure her account would match up when she put it in her diary for the chief. This Peter business was really taking over.

They were leaning on the reception desk making their notes when Frank appeared from the corridor. 'Got some good news, ladies!' he said, giving them a big grin. 'Come with me.' He beckoned them back down the corridor and opened one of the side doors. They stepped into a small room with one bare desk and two chairs. 'Best I could do for furniture I'm afraid,' Frank said, scratching his head. 'But the room is all yours! The chief decided it was time you had your own space and some of the blokes agreed to let you have this room.'

'Wow, Frank, thank you so much!' said Maggie, astounded. 'Are the others not angry at having to give up their room, though?' she asked cautiously. She didn't fancy getting more hassle and snarky comments from Frank's colleagues over a tiny room. They had made do without one for long enough. It would be nice to have somewhere to get changed, though.

'To be honest, the room wasn't used for all that much,' Frank said. 'But the fact that no one protested about you ladies having it to yourselves is a big step forward.'

'Thank you, Frank, we appreciate it,' Irene said, giving him one of her special smiles. Maggie was certain she saw Frank blushing in return, but she wasn't in the mood for romance today.

'By the way, do you know Beatrice Young from Boundary?' Frank asked as Annie and Irene both sat down. Maggie stood by the door. She recognised the name but decided to leave this to Irene.

'We've spoken to her a few times,' Irene smiled. 'Bit of a one, that girl – she was a little cheeky with us at first and seems to get herself into bother and scrapes routinely. But it's never anything major, and she's always respectful to us when we see her now. Why do you ask?'

'I've a warrant for her,' Frank explained. 'But I haven't a clue who she is and every time I go to her place she's not in. Like I told you when you started, we don't have the time to wander around and get to know everybody on first-name terms. Do you think you can point her out to me if I join you on patrol one day?'

'Of course,' Irene said. Maggie could tell from her face that she was delighted to be able to help Frank out. She was happy for her, but not as excited as she would normally have been. 'What has she done?' Irene asked.

'Failed to comply with her probation order,' Frank said, shrugging like it was no big deal. 'I really appreciate your help with this. It would have taken me a while to track her down as no one over there would be willing to point me in the right direction.'

'Hang on,' Maggie said suddenly. She had only really been half-listening to the conversation, and now it had all sunk in she could see a big problem with the plan. 'If we point her out to you and then you waltz over and arrest her in front of everyone, they'll all know we can't make arrests.'

Frank looked confused. 'But you *can't* make arrests,' he said slowly.

'I know that!' Maggie sighed impatiently. 'But we don't want the whole estate knowing! Half the reason they do as we say is because they think we can arrest them just like you can if they step out of line. Thankfully, we haven't been pushed on it yet – but this could really scupper things for us.' They all remained silent for a few moments, trying to figure out a way around the problem.

'Right, I've got it,' Maggie declared, making the rest of them jump. 'We'll find Beatrice and bring her in. She's a nice girl and I'm sure we can talk her round. There'll be less of a show if we can persuade her to come with us willingly anyway, rather than you bounding in and arresting her in front of all her friends.'

'Ah, yes – and then once you get her here, I can arrest her?' Frank asked eagerly.

'Exactly!' Maggie said triumphantly. 'So, you get your girl and we get to keep up the ruse with the locals.'

'I like that,' Irene smiled. 'Well done, Maggie.' Maggie felt good for the first time that day.

'Oh, I almost forgot,' Frank said as he rummaged in his jacket pocket. 'This was left for you at the front desk earlier.'

Maggie froze and fixed her eyes on the floor, too scared to look at what Frank had in his hands. She knew that when she looked up, he would be holding out an envelope to her and not Annie or Irene. It *had* to be from Peter. The thought of that horrible man walking into the station to leave her another threatening note made her feel physically sick. Maybe if she refused to look up at Frank then he would just turn around and leave the room, taking the envelope with him. She could pretend he had never mentioned it and convince herself that Peter hadn't been stalking around her home *and* the station twice in as many days.

'Maggie, wakey wakey,' Frank laughed, and when she eventually looked up, she could see him waving the wretched envelope in front of her face.

'Oh, it's for me?' she said, as casually as she could. 'Sorry, I was in another world there for a minute.' She snatched it from him and stuffed it into her pocket. As she did so, she spotted the same offending handwriting as before.

'Hang on, you not going to share what it is?' Frank asked.

'Yes, whoever is leaving you notes here?' Irene asked, looking bewildered.

'Ooh, is it a love letter?' Annie chipped in, giggling like a little girl.

Maggie felt trapped. She couldn't tell them, and she certainly wasn't going to open it up in front of them. 'It's none of your business,' she huffed, before storming out of the room.

She went straight to the toilets and locked herself in a

cubicle. She turned around and leaned up against the back of the door before taking a big breath and reaching down slowly into her pocket. As she took out the envelope, she saw that her hand was shaking again. *Curse you, Peter!* Bile rose in her throat as she opened up the piece of paper and read his second message:

> *I mean it, Maggie. Come to mine tonight or else Daddy will know your secret. What will he do when he finds out about all the lies his perfect little girl has been telling?*

He hadn't even bothered to sign this one. Breathing heavily as though she had just run a race, Maggie ripped the paper up into tiny pieces, threw them into the toilet, and flushed them down to the sewers where they belonged. As she watched all the bits swirl around in the basin and disappear, she knew what she had to do. She would bite the bullet and meet Peter. Her life with the WPV meant too much to her now to risk losing it. She had to convince him to keep her secret — at all costs.

21

Maggie was still trying to compose herself when she heard the door to the toilets opening and footsteps approaching. There was a little tap on the cubicle door, and she closed her eyes. *Just leave me alone*, she begged silently. *Please*. But she knew her friends were just worried about her – she hadn't been herself all day, and now this outburst . . . If it was the other way around, then she would be breaking the door down to get to them and see what she could do to help.

'I just want to make sure you're all right,' Annie's voice whispered from the other side of the door. 'You don't need to tell me anything.' *Lovely, sweet Annie*, Maggie thought. *She would never get herself into a pickle like this*. She was suddenly reminded of that first proper chat the two of them had had at headquarters. The fact that that had also taken place in the toilets made her smile.

'We really must stop meeting in lavatories like this,' Maggie said with a shaky laugh. Annie had really opened up to her that day, and she had hardly known Maggie at that point. Thinking about that made Maggie feel even more terrible for keeping something so big from her friend.

But she had to do this alone. If she told Annie about Peter then she would have to admit she had lied about her age. She knew Annie would never tell on her – but she didn't want to burden her. And, besides, the more people that knew, the higher the chances of someone slipping up and getting her into trouble. Maggie heard Annie chuckling on the other side of the door, and she opened it up and fell into her open arms.

'The other two won't ask you anything, I've made sure of that,' Annie said once they had pulled apart. 'I've left them in the middle of an in-depth discussion about the author of that silly book on Boundary that they both love so much,' she added, rolling her eyes comically. It made Maggie smile. 'Just know that I'm here if you decide sharing something might help make you feel better. It helped me when we talked about Richard,' Annie added.

After another hug they made their way to the entrance, where Irene and Frank were deep in conversation. Annie's promise held true – the pair of them acted as if nothing had just happened and Frank bid the three of them farewell before they set off for Boundary.

They spent the rest of the afternoon wandering up and down the streets on the estate, looking out for Beatrice and asking around about her. No one had seen her.

'I bet Sal knows where to find her,' Irene suggested as they sat in the bandstand. 'Come on, it's nearly time for her tea break so we can catch her if we hurry.' They found Sal where they'd left her earlier, in her usual spot. 'We haven't bumped into Mary again yet,' Irene explained. 'But we do have another favour to ask you.'

'Two in one day!' Sal exclaimed, putting down her cup of tea. 'And I already have some information to share with yer. I'll surely need some more eels!'

'Of course,' smiled Irene. 'If you can help us find Beatrice Young then you can expect another serving very soon.'

Sal's brow furrowed. 'Whad'you want 'er for?' she asked, suddenly suspicious. 'I'm all fer helping you girls out, but I ain't about to get no one round 'ere in bother. Not even for some eels.'

'We want to help her before the chaps at the station march down here and drag her in with them,' Maggie stepped in. She had decided she was going to take a back seat on this and mull over what to do about Peter, but she couldn't help but get involved now. 'She's broken her probation order and if they find her before we do, then – well, you know how they can get,' she added, raising her eyebrows meaningfully. 'We want to make sure she goes down to the station willingly and gets the mess sorted out quickly and quietly instead of being dragged down there kicking and screaming.'

Sal took a moment to think it through. 'I suppose she's best off going in with you,' she said grudgingly. 'She won't make a fuss if you explain it to 'er like that, too. She's been helping out at the greengrocer's since 'is assistant signed up to fight. But leave it a few days if yer can. She's just 'ad bad news about her brother.'

'We'll hold off for now,' Maggie said. 'And we'll be sure to bring you some jellied eels soon.'

'Make sure yer do!' Sal laughed as she picked up her empty mug and went to stand.

'Oh, hang on a minute,' Maggie said. 'You said you already had some information for us – what did you mean?'

Sal grinned and sat back down on the step. 'I'll 'ave to be quick cos they'll want me back in the laundry soon, but I just this minute 'eard some whispers about your burglary,' she said, her voice low. She was positively beaming as she spoke. Maggie thought she looked as proud as a toddler taking their first steps.

'Well, go on then – spill!' Irene cried out. The suspense was obviously getting to her as much as it was getting to Maggie.

Sal chuckled to herself. 'I bet they're certain they'll find those fancy jewels round 'ere, aren't they?' she asked, and

208 Johanna Bell

the girls nodded. 'Well, they'd do better to look a bit closer to 'ome is all I'm saying!'

'A policeman took them?' Annie asked, aghast.

'No, course not!' Sal laughed, standing up again with her mug. Maggie cringed for Annie. She had certainly come a long way since they had first met, but she still tended to act a little naïve now and then. 'Just tell 'em to get any ideas of finding the thief on Boundary out their 'eads,' she said confidently as she walked off back to the laundry. The girls stood in silence for a few minutes, mulling over what Sal had said.

'We could always ask Bob at the pub next time we visit,' Annie suggested cautiously. She was obviously wary of getting laughed at again.

'That's a great idea,' Irene said enthusiastically. The relief on Annie's face was obvious, and Maggie felt bad for the mean thoughts she had just had. As they continued their patrol around the estate, Maggie felt excited about their new lead on the burglary. She was also proud of herself for coming up with a plan that would stop anyone realising they weren't able to carry out proper arrests. But then she remembered Peter's latest note and her heart sank. She wasn't sure she was going to be so good at talking him round. Especially not alone. But she had to try.

They were due to finish their patrol at six that evening, so Maggie would have enough time to get changed and make it to Peter's place well before his deadline. She hadn't stopped in to see Florence on her way out to tell her what cover she needed, but she knew she would come up with something for her. *Even after the way I spoke to her last night*, Maggie thought with a pang of shame. The rest of the patrol was a blur for Maggie. She just wanted to get it finished and get to Peter's – the wait was making her more and more anxious.

'I've got errands to run this evening, so I'll make my own

way home,' Maggie threw at Annie as soon as she had changed back into her clothes in their new little room. She had left it until the last possible moment to mention anything as she didn't want any questions. She had also made sure she was changed before both Annie and Irene, so she could dash out of the station without anyone on her tail to see which direction she was headed in. As she ran out of the room she heard Annie call after her, but she kept going without looking back, her heart racing. Peter only lived a few roads along from the police station, so she got there early.

Standing outside, she looked up at the terraced house where Peter rented a room and took a deep breath. There were lights on in the other rooms, so Maggie reassured herself that if things got nasty again then she could scream for help and there would be lots of people around to run to her aid. *No point putting it off*, she thought with a sigh.

She walked up to Peter's door and banged on it forcefully. She wanted him to know she was feeling strong. She could hear rustling and footsteps on the other side of the door, and it made her glad she was early – she had obviously caught him on the hop. She felt like she had the upper hand now and that boosted her confidence.

The door opened slowly. Maggie tried to smile through the hatred she felt when she saw Peter's weaselly face. It had been dark in the alley so she hadn't gotten a proper look at him, and she had forgotten how rat-like he looked. His mean, starved face was a far cry from the teenager Eddie had played with in the streets.

'Hello, Maggie,' Peter said, holding out his arm to show her inside. She smiled through gritted teeth. As she walked in, he put his hand gently against the small of her back to guide her and a chill ran down her spine at the feel of his touch. 'I'm so glad you came,' he said. 'You won't regret it.'

22

Maggie looked around Peter's room. She wasn't sure if it was the cold in the air giving her goose pimples, or Peter's presence. There wasn't a lot to take in. A table in the corner was covered in stains and blotches – there wasn't even a tablecloth to hide the messy marks. Two wooden chairs sat either end of the table, although Maggie couldn't imagine Peter ever sitting there with anybody else.

It didn't really look like the kind of place where you would entertain guests. There was a tiny sofa pushed up against the wall, and on the other side of the small room there was a bed. The sheets looked as though they hadn't been washed for goodness knows how long. They were rumpled, and Maggie suspected they were exactly as Peter had left them when he had hauled himself up that morning. She started shivering.

Maggie knew life in this area was tough, but she had never actually been inside any of the rooms people lived in. She couldn't imagine having to spend time in such filth, with so little comfort. It was so far from anything she had ever experienced growing up that she just couldn't seem to wrap her head around it.

The thought of whole families surviving together in a room like Peter's brought a tear to her eye. She found herself feeling sorry for him, now. To have come to this, when he had once lived in Kensington . . . She imagined it was a lot harder to deal with these conditions when you knew how well other people were living and had experienced it your-self. How did someone go from living somewhere like she did, to *this*?

'What happened to your parents?' Maggie asked softly, forgetting all about Peter's tactics to get her here. She wanted to know how a family just like hers could end up in such a bad place.

Peter suddenly lunged towards her and she jumped back in shock. But as he flew past her, she realised he hadn't been going for her as she had feared – instead he had thrown himself down onto the sofa and was now stuffing something down the back of it.

She really was feeling jumpy. She took a deep breath and tried to relax. Peter sat back on the sofa. But before Maggie could ask what on earth he had just been doing, he distracted her by answering her question.

'Father started drinking all the profits from the bakeries,' he said matter-of-factly. 'Whenever Mother asked him to stop, he would beat her to keep her quiet.' He paused for a moment and looked at the floor. They had more in common than Maggie had ever realised. She felt a sudden connection with Peter. She knew how hard it was to live with a man who would lash out at his family – to spend your days terri-fied of saying the wrong thing or dressing in the wrong way in case it made him angry. The only person she had ever known to be going through the same thing was Eddie.

As he spoke, Maggie noticed that Peter's teeth had yellowed over the years. They, along with his hollow face, were in stark contrast to his upper-class voice – a relic from his youth. As she studied him, she thought she caught Peter's features soften, but when he looked back up at her he was stony-faced again.

'When Father eventually lost the business, he had nothing left to do but take it out on Mother. She had enough in the end. She just upped and left one day after a particularly bad beating.'

'But . . . what about you? She just left you behind?' Maggie asked, the shock evident in her voice. She couldn't believe a woman would leave her child in any circumstances. But to abandon him knowing his father was drunk and abusive was so cruel.

'I suppose she thought I was old enough to fend for myself,' Peter shrugged. 'I've no idea where she went or if she tried to come back for me. Father took his anger out on me when she left, so I didn't stick around for long.' Maggie had always thought the whole family had left Kensington together. She'd had no idea Peter's world had fallen apart so suddenly and drastically. 'I don't know where either of them are now, but I'm best off without them,' Peter added stoutly. Now Maggie really felt for him. She felt terrible that this had happened to one of Eddie's friends and they'd had no idea about any of it.

Maggie was still standing next to the door. She hadn't planned on staying long enough to sit down and talk properly – she had wanted to get in and out as quickly as possible. But when Peter got up and walked over to the table to pull out one of the wooden chairs, she found herself willing to sit and chat further.

She didn't feel like she could turn around and leave after such a revelation. Besides, she had softened to him now she knew what he had been through. That connection was there between them – even if he didn't realise it. She felt like she understood him a little more.

Florence always made Maggie a cup of tea when she was upset, so Maggie decided to try and cheer Peter up in the same way. She was doubtful he had anything in his dingy room to make tea, but she wandered over to a cupboard to take a look. Just as she was pulling the door open, Peter leaped over and grabbed her wrist, slamming the cupboard shut with his other hand. Maggie yelped and jumped back in shock.

'Sorry, private stuff,' Peter muttered, releasing his grip and putting both his hands up in the air in surrender. Maggie felt silly for overreacting, and let him guide her gently to the chair he had pulled out.

'I wish you'd stayed in touch,' Maggie said as Peter sat down on the chair opposite her. 'Eddie and I could have helped you, you know. We would have understood more than you realise. You didn't have to go through all of this on your own.' She looked around the room as she was talking. 'I can't believe you've been living like this,' she added, realising too late that she had failed to hide the disgust in her voice.

'Matter of fact, I like it here. Not bad when you consider I left home with nothing,' Peter said defensively. 'We don't all have daddies in high places, able to fork out on all the best things for us!'

'Oh, I didn't mean—' Maggie started, but it was too late. She had offended him now and in seconds he had switched from calm and composed to just as nasty as he'd been in the alley.

'There isn't anything wrong with this, you know, Maggie!' he raged. He stood up quickly, sending his chair flying back behind him. 'I've done pretty well for myself and I don't need girls like you looking down on me and making me feel bad!' He pounded his fist down on the middle of the table so hard it shook. Maggie flinched in shock.

'I'm sorry, I just—' Maggie stuttered, but Peter had moved around the table and was now looming over her, his hand raised. Maggie cowered and closed her eyes as she waited for the blows to rain down on her. Flashbacks of her father punishing her flew through her mind, and she trembled with fear.

When the blows didn't come, she opened her eyes tentatively. Peter wasn't standing over her any longer. She peered around the room and saw that he was slumped down in the corner with his head in his hands. Maggie's instincts told her to get up and run out of the room as fast as her feet would carry her – which was fast considering she didn't have her WPV boots on. But she still needed to make sure he didn't tell her father her secret.

'Are you all right?' she asked quietly, still rooted to the chair. She heard sniffling and realised Peter was crying. She was so confused. She had been certain he had been about to hit her, and now he was sitting on the floor sobbing into his hands.

'You looked just like my mother then,' Peter whispered eventually. He looked up at Maggie and wiped away the tears that were streaming down his face. 'I'm so sorry,' he went on, wiping his running nose on his sleeve. 'I can't believe I've turned into my father. I swore I'd never be anything like him. I don't know what happened – something took over me.'

Maggie found herself feeling sorry for Peter again. She believed Peter might be good, deep down. But witnessing his father's behaviour over the years had clearly affected him. She thought about Eddie then, and wondered if their father's ways would end up presenting in him. The thought made her feel sick. She got up and went to join Peter on the floor.

'You stopped yourself,' she said gently, placing her hand on his shoulder to try and comfort him. She felt like she was talking to the Peter she had known when she was little again. 'You are nothing like your father. Nothing. You know what he did was wrong – that's why you ran away. And now you can control whether or not you turn out like him.'

Peter put his hand on top of Maggie's. At first, she thought he was taking comfort in her touch. But as he grabbed her other hand and shoved her onto her back on the floor, she realised in a panic that he had tricked her. He hadn't needed her to soothe him – he had just needed her to be in a more vulnerable position so he could overpower her. And she had fallen for his crocodile tears.

Maggie tried to wriggle her way out of Peter's grip, but he forced her arms down onto the floor, above her head. Before she knew it, he had climbed on top of her and was straddling her. Looking up at his face, now inches away from her own, she saw him grinning sinisterly, and she realised with horror that he was enjoying her struggle. She writhed from side to side, but he was too strong. Suddenly, Maggie deeply regretted keeping the notes and this meeting from Annie and Irene. There was no chance of them popping up to save her this time. She was on her own and she only had herself to blame.

'Let me do this and your parents won't find out anything,' Peter said, pinning her arms down with one hand and reaching down under her skirt with the other. His eyes had come alive now. 'Just have sex with me and I'll forget I ever saw you dressed as a policeman.' Watching the excitement on his face made Maggie feel sick. He moved his hand up to grab her breast.

He was leaning on her so forcefully that she wasn't able to free her arms to try and push him off. She was struggling to breathe under his weight. 'I've told my bosses I'm here!' she rasped in desperation. Peter kept his hand on her breast but stopped the groping. He lay still on top of her and shook his head, amusement on his face.

'Is that so?' he asked.

'Yes,' Maggie said confidently. He had eased his weight off her slightly to raise his head and she could breathe properly again. 'You need to get off me or else they'll have you arrested!' She really thought he would believe her.

'You're lying,' he laughed as he started groping at her breast again. As his hand slid further down her body, Maggie wished she was in her thick, heavy WPV uniform, rather than this flimsy dress. 'They wouldn't send you alone,' Peter breathed in her ear, pressing his full weight on top of her again. She almost retched when his rancid breath reached her nose. 'Where are they now? I'd love to tell them how old you really are!'

Maggie felt tears filling her eyes as she accepted there was no way out of this for her. Even if she told Peter he could go and tell her father everything, it wasn't going to stop him forcing himself on her. He was enjoying it too much. Maggie was sobbing now. He put one of his hands over her mouth as he used the other to undo his trousers. There was no point in trying to fight back. She felt too weak to do that, anyway.

As Peter pulled her dress up and pushed her underwear to the side, Maggie found herself wishing she had never seen that copy of *The Vote*. Why hadn't she just done what her father wanted her to do and found a nice boy to settle down with? This was exactly the type of thing her father had been trying all his life to protect her from. But she had been so stubborn she had thought she'd known better.

Pain coursed through Maggie as Peter thrust himself inside her. She closed her eyes and tried to pretend she was somewhere else. She felt so foolish – for thinking she was grown up enough to join the WPV behind her parents' back and get away with it, for defying her father. But most of all, she felt foolish for trusting Peter. She had felt sorry for him, when all along this had been his plan.

As Peter pounded himself in and out of her, Maggie tried to block out his groans of pleasure. This wasn't how she had imagined her first time with a man would be. She wondered if it would be the only sexual experience she would ever get to have. He was ruining her, tainting her – who would want to touch her after this? On and on he went – it felt like it was never going to end.

Silent tears tracked down the sides of her face, pooling in her ears. She closed her eyes and tried to make her body and mind go numb, but she couldn't block out the dank smell of the room, the feel of the cold, hard floorboards against her back, the sickening noise of his excited panting as he approached what she instinctively knew would be the end of her ordeal.

When it was finally over, he rolled off her and let out a loud sigh. Maggie lay frozen, her legs still splayed. She could not move.

'Your secret's safe with me,' he said. Maggie turned her head to look at him. He was lying grinning up at the ceiling with his hands behind his head. His trousers were still open. Repulsed, Maggie felt bile rise in her throat. She quickly pulled her dress back down and shakily got to her feet, hatred throbbing in her heart.

How could he be making light of what he just did to her? He could at least show some shame. She had a desperate urge to make him understand the extent of his evil, but she felt so sore and her instincts were telling her to get out of the room as fast as she could. She didn't want to give him a chance to force himself on her again.

She scrambled to the door. As it slammed shut behind her, Maggie heard Peter laughing. His cackling rang in her head as she shoved past a woman in the corridor outside and flung open the main door. As soon as she stepped outside into the fresh air, she retched. Leaning over, she vomited all over the pavement.

As Maggie started to make her slow, painful way home, she knew what she had to do. She was done with the WPV. She would write to Frosty and tell her she wasn't returning and that would be that. A clean break would be best, she decided. Fresh tears spilled over at the thought of never seeing Annie and Irene again; they had grown so close over the last few months. But how could she face them now? She couldn't admit that she had been stupid enough to fall into Peter's trap. And what kind of policewoman was she if she couldn't fight off someone like him?

All that training had gone to waste on her, and she didn't want everyone knowing how naïve she had been. She had joined to escape her father's tyrant ways, but she had ended up falling victim to someone even worse than him. Her friends – and the WPV – were better off without her.

23

Returning home after the attack, Maggie found the house in quiet darkness. There was a note on the kitchen table from Florence to say her parents were out at one of her father's work functions. She felt a spasm of relief. She wasn't sure she would have been able to sit through dinner with them. She had planned on feigning illness and going straight to bed, anyway. Florence had gone off a day early to visit her niece and the baby, so Maggie didn't have to pretend everything was all right to her – at least that was something.

She took herself off to her room and once the door was closed, she allowed the tears she had been holding back on her journey home to flow. Climbing into bed fully dressed, she winced in pain. The evening's events flashed back to her as she felt a stabbing sensation down below. She took a deep breath and lifted the covers over her head so she could weep without the risk of being heard by any of the other staff.

Eventually, Maggie dropped off to sleep, only waking the following morning when her mother asked a maid to check on her. Maggie sent her away, telling her she was too ill to see anybody.

Later that day, there was a knock on her bedroom door. Thinking Florence must have returned home early, she called her in. But she was surprised to see her mother walking into the room. 'Whatever is the matter, dear?' she asked, her voice full of concern.

Maggie's eyes filled once again as she fought back the

urge to break down and tell her mother everything. She was desperate to confide in her and have her soothe her until everything felt better. The fact that she couldn't made her feel even more wretched, if that was possible.

Seeing the tears, her mother sat down next to her and pulled her in for a loving embrace. She wasn't normally one for showing affection, and Maggie closed her eyes and found herself getting lost in the moment. Eventually, her mother pulled away and wiped the tears from Maggie's cheeks. 'My poor child,' she whispered. 'Tell me what's wrong.'

'I just feel so poorly,' Maggie managed through her sobs. 'My head is painful, and I think I have a fever.'

Her mother placed her hand on her forehead. 'You don't feel very hot. Maybe you just need some rest. You've been so busy with the orphans,' she sighed. Maggie felt another pang of guilt at the reminder of yet another lie. 'We'll keep an eye on your temperature and let you get some sleep. If you develop a fever then we'll call out the doctor. I'll get some soup sent up for you later.' She kissed Maggie's temple and left the room.

As soon as the door closed, Maggie broke down again. The lies were piling up and all she wanted to do was tell her mother everything.

The next two days passed by in a blur. Maggie couldn't bring herself to get out of bed, let alone leave her room. It was a good job it was the weekend and she wasn't due at the station, as she most certainly would have missed her shifts and risked getting into all sorts of trouble when Annie, Irene and Frosty came looking for her. She just felt numb. All she could think about was how helpless she had been as Peter had taken what he wanted from her. Then she would get angry at herself for going to his room and putting herself in that situation in the first place.

She had so wanted her first time with a man to be special and loving. She had longed for it to be with the right man at the right time, and when she was ready. Now all of that had been cruelly ripped from her and she had been left with aches and pains and an empty heart.

She realised now that her wealthy home and background didn't mean anything out in the real world. She had been so foolish to assume her status would protect her from anything like this.

When Florence returned home on Sunday evening, Maggie convinced her to turn up at her meeting spot with Annie instead of her before their shift the next day. 'Tell her I have a fever and I'm resting,' she instructed her. She couldn't risk her friends coming to her home to check on her, but she couldn't face writing the letter that would end her WPV journey just yet. She couldn't face anything.

'Are you sure everything's all right?' Florence asked her when she had returned from meeting Annie.

'I'm afraid all this work has rather gotten on top of me,' Maggie lied. 'I just need a bit of a break, that's all.'

Florence didn't look convinced. 'Well, your friend was very concerned,' she said. 'But she said she'd tell Frank and she was sure it wouldn't be a problem.'

'You did tell her to stay away, didn't you?' Maggie asked desperately, the thought of Annie and Irene turning up at the house threatening to break her once again. Her hands started shaking and she could feel her pulse racing at the thought of the fall-out.

'Oh dear, you've gone very pale,' Florence said, wringing her hands. 'Should I call for the doctor?'

'No!' Maggie cried, panicking again. 'Please, just leave me to rest, Florence. I can't think straight with everyone coming in to check on me all the time.' As Florence retreated, Maggie felt a pang of guilt for being nasty to her yet again.

Maggie spent the next few days in her room, unable to stop running through the ordeal with Peter in her head. Every time she tried to distract herself, his pale, sweaty face would jump into her thoughts, making her feel nauseous. He crept into her dreams, too, so that in the end she tried her best not to fall asleep at all. Even Charlie couldn't make her feel any better. Finally, exhausted, on Wednesday evening she decided it was high time she wrote her letter to Frosty. She had to end this before it all came crashing down. Maybe once she was free of the WPV then she would be free of the pain Peter had caused her and she could move on. She went to her desk and pulled out a piece of paper and a pen:

> *Wednesday, 20th January 1915*
> *Dear Sub-Commandant Frost,*
>   *It is with deep regret that I write you this letter. I have to inform you that, due to personal reasons, I will no longer be able to fulfil my duties with the WPV.*
>   *I have very much enjoyed my time with the organisation, and I have faith the men in charge will see what a good job you are all doing and allow women to continue working for the police after the war is over.*
>   *With kindest regards,*
>   *Maggie Smyth*

She had to write it out twice, as the ink on the first version became smudged by the tears flowing down her face. When she had finished the second letter, Maggie realised she would have to ask Florence to hand deliver it to the WPV headquarters. She couldn't wait for it to be posted – her nerves were strung out enough already as it was. She needed to be sure that it was received and understood by Frosty. She had been so horrid to Florence over the last few days, though, she only hoped she would be willing to help her.

Just then, there was a knock at her door. Maggie placed a book on top of the letter in case it was her mother, but it was only Florence, with a bowl of soup. 'I think Mrs Smyth believes soup cures all evils,' Florence chuckled as she placed the bowl down on the desk next to Maggie. 'You'll be sick to death of my soup by the time you're better. It's good to see you out of bed, love,' she smiled warmly. Her loving demeanour made Maggie feel even worse for the way she had been treating her. Despite all that, she was still being so kind to her.

Just as she was about to leave, Florence turned back to Maggie. 'Look underneath the bowl,' she whispered, giving her a wink. Confused, Maggie picked up the soup, and her heart skipped a beat when she saw a letter underneath it – addressed to her and in Eddie's handwriting.

As excitement ripped through her body, for one glorious moment Maggie forgot all about the feelings of despair that had consumed her for the last few days, and she allowed herself to be happy. Florence had been intercepting the post ever since Eddie's departure, checking for anything for Maggie before passing it on to her father. Now, finally, she had what she had been longing for.

As Florence left the room, Maggie greedily snatched up the letter and slid to a sitting position on the floor as she ripped it open with trembling hands. She wondered fleetingly if they would ever be still again, but pushed the thought away, focusing again on Eddie. She had been waiting to hear from him for so long and now it had happened at just the right time – when she was at rock bottom. More tears fell as she read his words and felt close to him again.

January 1915

Dearest Maggie,

I was delighted to receive your letters and I do apologise for only just now getting around to writing to you. I have been so busy with all the training – they really are keeping us on our toes! Please don't worry about me, I'm having a ball and the other lads here are just grand!

We do a lot of training at local parks. We use broomsticks as makeshift rifles. It feels rather silly to be honest with you, Mags, but I'm sure they will give us the real thing soon enough.

But that's enough of that. The main reason I'm writing is to tell you just how proud I am of everything you're doing with the WPV. I was beaming with pride when I read your last letter. I knew you would do a great job, Mags, but I didn't realise how quickly you would start making a difference to people's lives! You've really found your calling, haven't you?

Please, please, please keep writing to me and telling me about your adventures on the beat. I look forward to hearing from you so much and I fall asleep with a smile on my face when I get one of your letters.

I hope Mother and Father are coping without me now. I do hope you're not suffering because of my decision. That would have been the only thing to stop me from leaving, but I do know full well you can handle yourself.

Anyway, Mags, I must go now. I have a busy day tomorrow and my eyelids are heavy with tiredness.

Sending you all my love,
Eddie

Maggie read the letter through twice. The first time she devoured it and didn't take it all in, so the second time she forced herself to slow down and read every word. When she was finished, she took a deep breath and wiped the remaining tears away from her cheeks. Her brother was so proud of her – how could she write her next letter to him with news of her departure from the WPV? She *had* to stay on – she couldn't let Peter ruin it all for her.

With just a few words, Eddie had managed to shake her out of the dark place she had fallen into. He had made her realise she couldn't let Peter win. Maggie decided the best way forward would be to deal with what Peter had done in the same way she had dealt with Eddie's departure – by pretending it hadn't happened. If she blocked it from her mind, then surely it couldn't upset her.

The following morning, Maggie ate her breakfast in the kitchen while Florence worked around her. She desperately wanted to make it up to her after her behaviour over the last week.

'Everything going all right for you, love?' Florence asked cautiously as she poured Maggie more tea. 'I must say, it's putting a smile on me face to see you down here – and eating, too. That letter from Eddie must have really lifted your spirits.'

'I'm feeling so much better today, thank you, Florence,' Maggie smiled before taking a sip of her tea. Her hands were still shaking, but not as much as they had been. Thoughts of Peter briefly pushed their way into her head, but she forced them away sharply. It was going to take a lot of effort to keep her mind off him, but she was determined to do it. And the WPV had always been good at keeping her distracted.

'I had a busy few weeks and I'm afraid to say I let it get to me,' Maggie explained, hoping Florence could forgive her. 'I'm sorry for snapping at you so much.' Maggie changed the subject quickly so Florence wouldn't pry any further. 'Thank you so much for getting hold of that letter from

Eddie for me,' she said, trying to inject excitement into her voice. 'I was so happy to read it last night.'

As she filled Florence in on Eddie's news, she felt better already. She just had to keep herself occupied so her mind wouldn't wander back to Peter and what he had done to her. She couldn't believe how close she had been to giving up the WPV – especially as that was the best distraction of all. She had hardly had time to worry about Eddie since it had kept her so busy and tired. It was the perfect thing to take her mind off anything she didn't want to think about.

Later that morning, Maggie set off for Bethnal Green. She wasn't back to her old self yet by any means, but she was feeling a little less hopeless than she had over the previous few days. She had written a reply to Eddie full of all the interesting things she had been up to. Thinking about her brother reading her letter and finding joy in her news made her smile. She could almost convince herself that the night with Peter hadn't happened. And her friends were delighted to see her back on duty.

'Oh, how we missed you!' Annie cried when Maggie walked into their little room. She hadn't had time to get word to her that she would be back in, so had made her way to the station alone.

'It's been an interestin' few days,' Irene said drily. Maggie got the impression the two of them hadn't bonded with each other as she had with each of them. It boosted her to feel like the glue holding the group together. 'I'm glad you're feeling better,' Irene added. 'This one hasn't stopped frettin' about you since your cook turned up instead of you the other morning,' she added, rolling her eyes.

Maggie gave Annie another hug. She was relieved she hadn't given all this up. But as they walked out of the police station, she started feeling anxious. With every corner they approached, she found herself fearing she would find Peter on the other side. She couldn't concentrate on what the other two were talking about.

'Don't you think, Maggie?' Irene asked as they approached the fish shop near Boundary. She had no idea what Irene was talking about, so she just nodded her head in agreement. 'Hey!' Irene shouted after Maggie as she continued walking. She hadn't even realised Irene and Annie had stopped outside the shop. 'You just agreed we should pick up some more eels for Sal,' Annie explained as Maggie stared at them both, confusion written all over her face.

She tried to snap out of it, but things like that kept happening all day. They told her everything she had missed while she had been off, but she couldn't remember any of it when they had finished. She kept trying to focus but she couldn't help but feel preoccupied. Even when they bumped into Mary and delivered her to Sal along with the jellied eels, Maggie wasn't paying attention.

'Is everything all right with you?' Irene asked Maggie as they got changed back into their clothes in their room later that afternoon. 'You still feeling a little peaky?'

'Sorry, I know I've been distracted today,' Maggie replied quietly, grimacing as she pulled off her cumbersome boots – it always felt so good to get them off her feet. She wasn't quite sure how to explain her behaviour. 'I've, erm, I've had a bit of a run-in with an old friend,' she said slowly. She hated lying to her friends, but she had to tell them *something*. The fever story really wasn't going to last much longer, and she knew it.

'Oh no, what happened?' Irene asked. She was genuinely concerned and now Maggie wished she had just shrugged off the initial question and run out of the station.

'It's just something silly and nothing to worry about,' Maggie said, trying to sound relaxed, but she could tell her voice didn't sound natural. 'It's just been playing on my mind, that's all. I'll deal with it and be back to my best soon, I promise.' Irene walked over and pulled her in for a hug.

Initially Maggie stood awkwardly, but after a second she relaxed into the embrace. She could feel the love behind it. It was so different to the farce of an encounter she had experienced with Peter, and she wasn't prepared for the way it would make her feel. She had to bite her lip to stop herself from breaking down and collapsing into Irene's arms, a sobbing mess. Composing herself, she patted Irene's back and pulled away stiffly. 'It's nothing. Really,' she said more sternly than she had planned.

'Well, we're here for you. If you decide talking will help then you just need to let us know,' Irene said. She didn't seem to have been affected by Maggie's firmness, which made Maggie feel even more rotten for lying to her and Annie. She had to get out of the room before she crumbled and told them everything.

'Thank you,' Maggie said as she pulled on her jacket, her voice wobbling. 'But I'll be fine. I'll see you both tomorrow.' She gave them as cheery a wave as she could manage and hurried out of the door, desperate to be on her own. She ran all the way home and she was exhausted by the time she got there.

'Good evening, Margaret,' her father called out from the living room as she took off her jacket in the hallway. 'Are you well enough to join us for dinner this evening?' Maggie was terrified of winding her father up the wrong way by hiding in her bedroom like her mother so often did. But she just couldn't face sitting down for a meal with her parents. She was desperate to be alone. Pretending to everybody that everything was fine and dandy was just too tiring.

'Oh Father, I do fear I went back to the orphanage a little too early. I'm exhausted and good for nothing but my bed,' she said weakly, poking her head into the room. Seeing her mother's expectant face peering back at her with concern made her heart drop. 'I need to rest. Please excuse me for dinner?'

'Very well,' he said sternly. 'Go and lie down and I'll send Florence up with some soup. You must eat.' She smiled to herself at the thought of Florence rolling her eyes when she was told to rustle up yet more soup for the sick patient.

'Thank you, Father,' Maggie whispered as she retreated to the stairs. She would have to lie to Florence now, too. *Again.* Maggie resolved to try harder to block Peter from her thoughts, as her efforts so far clearly hadn't worked.

24

Over the next few weeks, Maggie found herself managing quite well to forget about Peter. She threw herself into her work with the WPV and helped Florence out in the kitchen on her days off. She found washing dishes and hearing about Florence's niece and baby a great way to take her mind off the traumatic experience she so desperately wished had never happened.

There had been no further notes from Peter, and he hadn't breathed a word to Maggie's parents or said anything to anyone at the station about her real age. He had obviously got hold of everything he was after now and she was hopeful she could move on and forget the whole thing had ever happened.

Maggie even went to visit Sarah with Irene and Annie. Seeing Sarah doing so well at *The Vote* had lifted her spirits slightly. And the two of them even managed to clear the air.

'I'm so sorry for taking it all out on you,' Sarah gushed as soon as Maggie met her eye. Maggie had been expecting her to shout again, so she struggled to hide the relief she felt. 'I wasn't angry at you,' Sarah said, reaching out and placing her hand on Maggie's arm. 'I was just furious with the situation.' Maggie was fighting back tears. She hadn't realised how heavily the guilt of it all had been weighing down on her. 'I know you meant well,' Sarah continued. 'And I actually need to thank you as it ended up working out for the best for me – they promoted me at the paper!'

It turned out Sarah's bosses weren't bothered about her sight problems as long as she could still write. And she could write exceptionally well. She told them all about these youth clubs she had been researching for her next article, where they could send the younger women they came across. She also reminded them that WPVs were there for 'diversion not prosecution'. She had been impressed at Sal taking Mary in and suggested they find more women like her who could help those really in need.

All in all, Maggie was doing brilliantly at distracting herself. But there was one thing stopping her from blocking out that night completely. Her period was late. It had never happened before. With every day that passed she found herself feeling more anxious about what that meant.

Soon, it was all she could think about. Giving birth to a baby who looked like the monster who had raped her consumed her thoughts.

She found herself drifting off and she would often daydream about cradling a cute little newborn who would all of a sudden turn into a tiny version of Peter and sneer up at her with evil in its eyes. And the shame! She wasn't married, so if she was pregnant, she would be an outcast and her father would never forgive her for bringing such disgrace upon the family.

Maggie lost her focus once again and couldn't concentrate on anything at work. She could feel herself withdrawing from Annie and Irene, but she was helpless to do anything about it. She had no one to turn to for advice and she felt isolated and completely alone.

Once her period was more than a month late – around six weeks after the assault – Maggie finally accepted that she must be pregnant. She had no idea what to do. She couldn't bury her head in the sand and forget about this like she had with Eddie's departure and that awful night. She would start showing at some point – she wasn't sure when – and what would she do then? How was she going to explain to her father that she was pregnant, aged eighteen and out of wedlock?

She didn't even have a *boyfriend*. Would he punish her in his usual way if she was with child? Would he force her to get rid of the baby? She was certain someone like her father had the connections to arrange something like that. She couldn't imagine he would be able to stand the shame of his only daughter having a child out of wedlock. If she wanted to keep the baby – *Peter's* baby – where would she go?

Maggie thought of Florence's niece and realised that, unlike Katy, she didn't have anyone she could turn to for help. Who would take her and an illegitimate child in and look after them both? Annie and Irene were her closest friends now, but she had kept so much from them. Once it all unravelled and they learned the truth, Maggie was certain they would want nothing more to do with her. And as for her schoolmates, they were all daughters of her father's political cronies. There was no way she would be able to go to them.

As she made her way to Bethnal Green for another night patrol, exhaustion threatened to overwhelm her. Her mind was worn out from all the worry and stress, and her body was drained from all the changes going on inside it.

Sitting on the bus and watching London roll past her, Maggie contemplated staying in her seat when she reached her stop. Maybe she could just ride the bus round and round the city streets until she came up with a solution to her problem? She knew that that was wishful thinking, though.

She had spent the last few weeks thinking of nothing but what she would do if it turned out she was carrying Peter's child – and she was still no closer to figuring out what step to take next.

When the bus reached Bethnal Green, Maggie stepped off with heavy feet and an even heavier heart. She hadn't made the journey in with Annie for weeks now, instead making constant excuses about errands she had to run before and after their patrols. She knew she was pushing Annie away – and Irene too – but she was too consumed with her worries to do anything about it. When she made it to the top of the road, she spotted a familiar face. Annie gave her a friendly smile and a small wave as Maggie made her way towards her.

'I'm sorry,' Annie said quietly. 'I know you're really busy at the moment, but I've been looking for a chance to talk with you for weeks now and the opportunity just never comes up. Can we have a quick chat before we go into the station?'

'Of course,' Maggie said, feeling suddenly flustered. She was panicking that her friend was going to confront her about what was going on with her, and she wasn't sure she was going to be able to lie any more. Annie folded her arms and bit her bottom lip.

'I just need to talk to someone about Richard,' she said as tears formed in the corners of her eyes. 'You've always been so good at cheering me up and letting me know the right thing to do.'

A chill ran down Maggie's spine. *Richard's visit.* She had been so caught up in her own problems and preoccupied with her pregnancy panic that she had forgotten all about it. She must have missed it completely! She had never felt like she had let somebody down so much in all her life. And sweet little Annie, too!

'I'm so sorry,' Maggie said, placing her hand on Annie's arm. 'Richard's visit completely slipped my mind. I feel terrible.'

'You've had a lot going on,' Annie shrugged as she stared at the floor. 'He came while you were off with that fever.'

'Well, I'm here now,' Maggie said. 'Tell me all about it.' The thought of poor Annie trying to start up a conversation with her all these weeks and getting the brushoff made her blood run cold. She was an awful friend.

'Mags, it was terrible,' Annie said. Before Maggie knew it, Annie was sitting on the pavement with her head in her hands. She hadn't been expecting such a dramatic reaction. She sat down next to her and put an arm around Annie's shoulders.

'What happened?' she asked.

Annie raised her head up and stared in front of her. 'He was like a different man. He was there, but it was like he wasn't. There, I mean.' She was almost whispering, and Maggie had to strain to hear her. 'He wouldn't tell me anything about what he's been up to. In fact, he hardly spoke to me at all the whole time he was home. He hardly spoke to anybody. But no one seems to think that's a problem! I feel like I'm losing him, Mags, and I don't know what to do.' She had raised her voice for the final sentence before covering her head with her hands again.

Maggie hugged her tight. She didn't know what to say to make her feel better. She wasn't sure there was anything that would do that. Annie raised her head again and this time she looked at Maggie, her eyes desperate. 'I didn't want to say too much to you as I know you'll worry about Eddie. But it was so hard – you're one of my closest friends now.'

'You can tell me anything,' Maggie said firmly. 'You mustn't keep anything from me to spare my feelings. We're all in this together.' Annie smiled gratefully. 'All I can think is that

Richard has seen some terrible things out there,' Maggie continued. 'He may well be switching himself off from everything in the hope that it will stop it all affecting him. That could be why he's acting distantly.'

'You're probably right,' Annie agreed. 'I just wish I could help him. I've been so anxious about it – I can hardly eat!' Maggie took a moment to study her friend's face, and she realised her cheeks were hollow. Her shapely body was slowly disappearing under all the strain. Maggie had been so distracted she hadn't even noticed, but looking at her now it was obvious.

'All you can do is keep being supportive,' Maggie said. 'He might be shutting you out, but you have to just keep trying. Keep writing to him. Keep everything positive. I know it's hard when everything seems so hopeless. But he needs you to do that.' They hugged again. Maggie knew Annie would keep persevering with Richard – she wasn't the kind of girl to give up on someone she cared about so easily. Look at how hard she had tried with *her*, despite being another one to shut her out. The poor girl.

'Thank you,' Annie whispered in her ear.

'Don't be silly,' Maggie laughed, squeezing her friend tight. 'You'll probably need to remember this and say it all back to me when I'm upset over Eddie. Agreed?'

'Agreed,' Annie nodded as they pulled away and stood up. They walked the last few minutes to the station in companionable silence. It had picked Maggie up a little to be able to be there for a friend and help her feel better.

Once they reached their room, Maggie was just about to open the door when they heard a male voice coming from inside. They stopped and glanced at each other, intrigued. Maggie put a finger to her lips to signal Annie to be quiet, then she silently opened the door and they both sneaked a look. Frank and Irene were sitting in there, talking animatedly.

Maggie and Annie ducked back out of view, grinning at each other.

They stood outside the door for a few minutes to allow the conversation to come to a natural end, and as they heard Frank bidding Irene farewell, they walked in casually and greeted them both. Irene had a glow about her, and she stared after Frank as he left. It made Maggie happy to see.

But walking around Boundary later that evening, Maggie found herself feeling disconnected from her friends once again. The assault had ended up driving a wedge between the three of them. She was sure they must have noticed how withdrawn and reserved she had become. She certainly wasn't herself. But she'd shut them out and it was too late to open up now.

They stopped to talk to a group of girls who said they were on their way to a dance at a local hall. Maggie found herself standing on the periphery, lost in herself yet again. When Annie and Irene bid the girls goodnight and continued their patrol, Maggie followed slightly behind them in silence as they discussed the plan for the rest of the evening. She felt like a lost sheep, following the herd just to make it look like she fitted in.

As they made their way towards the pub, Maggie's heart started thumping hard in her chest and her hands became clammy. It had happened every time they had gone anywhere near the pub over the last six weeks. When they ventured down Peter's road, her body's reaction was even worse. She had felt physically sick the first time and even Annie had noticed.

'You look like you've seen a ghost,' Annie had remarked, stopping and taking Maggie's arm to help steady her as her legs wobbled and threatened to give way.

'I've been feeling peaky all day,' Maggie had said by way

of explanation. 'I think I must be coming down with something.' She had used that line a lot lately and she was surprised no one had sent for a doctor – especially after her days off sick. Thankfully, she hadn't bumped into Peter once since he had raped her. She hoped he felt so ashamed of what he'd done that he had gone into hiding. But she knew deep down that wasn't the case, which made her feel even more anxious.

'Come on, slow coach,' Irene teased as she and Annie waited for Maggie at the top of the road. 'You daydreaming again?' she asked as Maggie finally caught up with them.

'Sorry, these boots are giving my feet hell,' she lied. 'I'm finding it hard to keep up with you both – did I miss anything?'

'Not at all,' Annie smiled. 'We were just saying we hope Bob's in a better mood this evening,' she laughed. They had escorted a prostitute out of the pub on their last night patrol, and Bob had been unusually upset with them about it. 'I do hope it wasn't his wife we turfed out last time,' Annie giggled. 'Can you imagine?' Maggie had to smile at the thought. That would top even her training faux pas with the soldier's wife. That seemed a lifetime ago now.

'I'm fairly sure Bob must be a single man,' Maggie pondered out loud. 'I mean, can you imagine anyone marrying someone with those teeth and that pot belly?' The other two laughed and Maggie found herself chortling with them. It felt good to be in high spirits with them again. It seemed to clear her head a little and she suddenly had a bright idea.

'Why don't we ask him about the burglary again?' she suggested. The culprit was still on the loose – much to the frustrations of all the officers at the station. The girls had mentioned it to Bob a few weeks before, following Sal's revelation that the suspect was close to home. He hadn't heard anything then but had seemed pleased they trusted him enough to ask him about it. Maggie had had so much on her mind since then that she hadn't pushed to make any more enquiries on their rounds.

'Good idea,' beamed Irene. 'We could do with picking up on our enquiries again. We let the trail run cold when we should be keeping it toasty warm.' Maggie smiled with her. She hadn't even thought about the case for weeks, but now it was giving her excited goose pimples. Her joy was short-lived, though, as her stomach flipped at the sight of The Lamb. Maggie hadn't spotted Peter in there since that night he had accosted her outside and Irene had come to her rescue, but it didn't stop her panicking every time they went back. She wasn't really sure how she would react if she saw him again – and on top of that, she was worried about what he would say in front of her friends.

She walked in behind Annie and Irene. Quickly surveying the bar, she breathed a sigh of relief when she failed to spot Peter's face amongst the groups of people chatting and laughing. It was busy as usual, and Bob pointed at the side room and gave them a thumbs up as he put down a drink on the bar for one of his customers. The girls knew that meant he would meet them in the room for a chat as soon as he could, so they headed over.

Bob sidled into the room a few minutes later. He looked at them sheepishly, running his hands through his hair. 'I'm sorry 'bout the other night,' he mumbled, not meeting their eyes. 'That woman you threw out. I used to know her, if you know what I mean.' He coughed uncomfortably and turned bright red. 'Before she was, you know – what she is now. I just, I had no idea that was why she was here so I was shocked when I realised what you were doing. When the lads told me what she'd been up to I felt terrible for shouting at you like I did. I've been waiting for you to come back in so I can apologise.'

'It's all right, Bob, we're used to worse than that,' Irene joked as he finally looked up at them. 'We're good at knowing what to look out for so we can spot these things quicker than the landlords sometimes. Don't feel bad for missing it, or for your reaction.' Bob nodded gratefully and started to back out of the room.

'Everything seems to be above board tonight,' he said. 'It's just my regulars in at the moment but I'll leave you to do your normal rounds.' He left the room and shut the door behind him just as the girls burst into fits of giggles.

'Oh, that was definitely his fancy woman!' Maggie roared through the laughter. 'He was so embarrassed – he couldn't even look us in the eyes!' They continued chuckling for a good few minutes before composing themselves enough to realise they had forgotten to check in with him about the jewels. Irene went back out to the bar and returned with him in tow a few minutes later.

'We just wondered if you'd heard any whispers about those jewels yet?' Maggie asked hopefully.

'Ah, I'm afraid not, love,' Bob said. He scratched his head thoughtfully. 'A few of the lads have been a bit more flush than usual these past few weeks though – I've noticed that,' he added. 'Only thing is, I don't know their full names. Give me a few days and I can find out?'

It wasn't the greatest lead, but it was probably worth looking into. And it was sure to impress the chief when he read in their diaries about all the enquiries they had been making. They thanked Bob and left the room with him this time.

Back in the bar, Maggie's mood dropped again as she scanned the crowds for Peter's face, her heart threatening to jump out of her chest every time someone new came through the door. But he was still nowhere to be seen. As they wandered around the pub, stopping to chat to various customers, Maggie felt on edge the whole time and didn't relax until they had stepped outside on to the pavement. She took a deep breath, glad to be out of the fug of fumes and smoke and back in the fresh air. She was determined to stay focused for the rest of the patrol.

They popped back to the station for a quick break and bumped into Frank on his way home. 'How's it going, ladies?' he asked. He was the only officer who showed a genuine interest in what they were doing, even after all this time. Maggie could tell the other men had accepted their presence at the station, but none of them apart from Frank made any effort with them.

'It's a little boring tonight,' Irene said. 'There's not a lot going on, really.'

'That's good when you're on patrol,' Frank laughed. 'You shouldn't be wishing for a busy night!' He rolled his eyes playfully. 'Some women are never happy,' he joked. Irene gave him a playful nudge on the arm, and Annie and Maggie exchanged a knowing look. No matter how distracted Maggie was, it was impossible to miss the flirting between those two.

'Actually, we had reports last night when you weren't here of men trying to lure some of the girls from Boundary into prostitution. I meant to tell you earlier but I've been run off my feet. The women were hanging around Bethnal Green Gardens when they were approached. We didn't have enough officers on duty to send anyone down there. I suppose the men would have been long gone by the time we'd made it there, anyway. The girls managed to get away, but they said the group were quite forceful – they were really scared.'

Maggie was shocked. She knew this type of thing was going on at the main train stations – men were trying to entice the Belgian refugees away before they made it to the dispersal centres. But she didn't know they had started trying it with English women, too.

'The WPV patrols at the train stations must be doing a good job if these men are spreading their nets further,' Annie said, clearly thinking along similar lines.

'I think so,' Frank nodded. 'They're probably not getting much luck now your colleagues are looking after the refugees when they arrive in London. It sounds like they're getting desperate, so be careful if you bump into any of them.'

Maggie felt like it was the men who should be careful if they bumped into her. Just thinking about them made her blood boil. How dare they try to ruin the lives of women to make money for themselves. Thinking about what these women could go through in their grasp made her run-in with Peter flash into her head and she had to act quickly to shake it free before her anger took over and she started screaming.

'I doubt word has made it around yet so there'll probably be more girls in the gardens this evening,' Frank said.

'We should go straight there now,' said Irene. 'I can't stand the thought of them getting their hands on any of our girls. Just who do they think they are?' She had turned red and her fists were clenched. The three of them bid goodnight to Frank and set off with a renewed purpose. Maggie hung back and took a few deep breaths. Her reaction before had taken her by surprise. She had done so well at blocking the attack out that she must have suppressed all her feelings of anger towards Peter. Her worry over being pregnant had upstaged her angst, anyhow. Catching up with Annie and Irene, she hoped she could keep her cool if they ran into any of the men Frank had mentioned.

25

The gardens seemed quiet, so the girls wandered around for twenty minutes, talking. Well, Annie and Irene talked while Maggie drifted off into her own little world yet again. She found herself feeling a bit deflated. She realised she had been looking forward to some excitement, perhaps a chance to revenge herself on a deserving man.

She reminded herself of Frank's words about how they shouldn't wish for a quiet patrol to be any other way. The fact was, when she was busy on patrol, she didn't have time to think about the baby. There, she had said it: she was having a baby. She couldn't be in denial about it – it was going to happen. Finally accepting it felt strangely freeing.

'Shall we head over to Boundary?' Annie suggested. 'If we bump into anyone there, we can warn them about these men. At least then we'll be starting to get the word around in case they come back another evening.' Irene and Maggie nodded.

As they made their way towards the nearest exit, they spotted three young women heading into the gardens. Maggie recognised them from Boundary.

'It's the police ladies,' one of the girls said amiably. She was tall and thin with scraggy hair in desperate need of a brush.

'Evening, girls,' Irene said cheerfully. 'You know what we're going to say, don't you?' she asked. They knew full well they shouldn't be loitering somewhere like this after dark.

'Come on,' another of the girls groaned. She had red hair,

hanging in ringlets down to her shoulders. 'Boundary's so borin'', and we can't spend time together at any of our 'omes!' she added wearily.

'Why not?' Maggie asked.

'You try gettin' the three of us into a room already filled wiv kids and chaos,' the tall girl answered darkly. 'You can't 'ear yourself think, let alone 'ave a conversation! Even if you could, you'd soon be dragged off to 'elp wiv some chore or another.' Maggie felt foolish. She still often forgot how different these people's lives were to her own. 'Besides, it's not like we're goin' to come to any harm 'ere, is it? There's never any trouble 'ere – that's why we like it,' the girl added.

'Well actually, being around here at the moment will *only* get you into trouble,' Irene warned. 'There have been some nasty men doing the rounds, trying to get young ladies like yourselves into mischief.'

'What do you mean?' the redhead asked, startled.

'They're trying to get women into prostitution,' Maggie explained. She had decided it was better to be matter-of-fact about it, so there was no doubt they had fully understood the situation.

'Oh, don't worry 'bout us! We can look after ourselves,' the girl responded proudly as her friends nodded their heads in agreement. Maggie wondered if any of them had ever come close to having to sell themselves to help their families keep a roof over their heads, or to eat – like poor Betty. They almost certainly knew people who had, she was certain of it. She didn't understand how they could be so blasé about it.

'I'm sure you can,' said Maggie, 'but these men mean business, and they might not give you much of a choice. They won't just leave you be if you turn down their offer to go with them. If they want you, they will make sure they have you. You need to be really careful.' The girls weren't looking quite so confident now, and Annie and Irene were staring at Maggie. She must have sounded rather too fierce.

'I don't mind admittin' that's made me a little worried,' the tall girl said, placing her hands nervously into her pockets and looking around her. Her bravado had vanished. Maggie felt bad for making her feel nervous, but it was for her own good.

'Well, come on then,' Annie cajoled. 'We're on our way to Boundary so we'll walk back with you. You can have your natter in one of your homes. It might be a little crowded but at least you'll be safe, eh?' All three girls looked reassured and smiled gratefully. They turned around and started walking back out of the park with Maggie, Irene and Annie. It wasn't quite the excitement Maggie had been after, but at least it had kept her mind busy for a few minutes. And she could talk to the girls on the way back to the estate, which would distract her further.

They were only just out of the gates when shouting in the distance made them all stop in their tracks. The six of them stood perfectly still, trying to make out where the noise was coming from and what was going on. It sounded like a commotion on the other side of the gardens. Maggie could hear a woman yelling, but she couldn't make out what she was saying.

'Girls, you're going to have to make your way home together. Keep your heads down and get inside as quickly as you can – do you understand me?' Irene said firmly. All three of them nodded in agreement, looking terrified. The shouting had clearly spooked them. They set off at speed without another word, clinging to each other for reassurance. Maggie was confident they would be running all the way home.

Once they were out of sight, Irene led the way back through

the park, with Annie and Maggie close behind her. When they heard a man's raised voice, followed by a woman's piercing scream, they all instinctively broke into a run.

Approaching the gates on the other side of the gardens, Maggie could make out a tall, beefy-looking man grappling with a woman. She was about a foot shorter than him. It appeared she was giving a good fight, but it clearly wasn't enough. Even as she fought back fiercely against him, he was managing to edge her out through the gates and onto the pavement.

'Get off me!' the woman yelled as the man tried to pick her up around the waist. She was kicking out at him and punching and slapping him in the chest, but he was still too strong for her. As the girls drew closer, Maggie could see a car waiting on the side of the road, lights on and engine running. She felt sick to her stomach as she realised what was happening. The man was trying to force the woman into the car. Once that happened, she stood no chance. And there would be no way for them to help her. Maggie *had* to stop this.

Seeing this clearly strong woman fighting back against a man with more strength than her lit a fire in Maggie's belly. First, the memory of her father striking her mother as she stepped in to protect her flashed into her mind. As she sprinted towards the couple, her run-in with Peter in the alley next to the pub burst into her head, followed closely by the night he had managed to violate her. With these thoughts came all the emotions she had been battling ever since. The anger. The rage. The shame. The sadness. The aching loneliness. The sense of hopelessness. She felt it all rise up inside her and just as she reached the couple, it exploded out of her and she hurled herself at the man.

For a split second, Maggie thought there was a wild animal in the gardens – until she realised the guttural cry she could hear was coming from her own mouth. As she made contact with the man, he let go of the woman and lost his balance. Maggie stayed with him and ended up flat on top of him when he landed on the ground on his back with a thud.

His body went limp – it was like he had been stunned into submission. Still, she took her right arm and placed it around the back of his neck before grabbing hold of the scruff of his top. Her ju-jitsu moves were finally coming in handy. She wanted to make sure the bastard didn't get away. Gaining confidence from the man's lack of protest, Maggie took a moment to catch her breath while she reminded herself how to finish the move and get him into a more secure position.

Everything fell silent and still, and Maggie looked the man straight in the eyes. She grabbed hold of his arm and was just about to pull it under her armpit and pin it there to disable him, when he suddenly roared and bucked, and threw her off him. She rolled to the side and saw him stand up. Out of the corner of her eye she spotted Annie and Irene reaching the woman and comforting her. Maggie realised she must have been going at some speed to get to the scene so much quicker than the other two.

Still lying on her side, she turned her head and noted that the car had vanished. Maggie got to her feet, angry that the driver had managed to get away. The man was staring straight through her. She would normally have felt terrified in a situation like this, but her hatred and anger were still bubbling over.

As she glared back at her most recent abuser, she suddenly realised in a moment of clarity that Peter's attack on her wasn't her fault. She shouldn't have been wasting all this time blaming herself when the only guilty party in the situation was *him*. She may have been naïve turning up at his room alone, but it was Peter who had chosen to violate her.

To her, this man was Peter, and this was her chance to show him he couldn't win. Her sense was blinded by rage.

'What do you think you're doing?' she demanded fiercely. She was ready for a fight – ready to make him understand women were not his property, and that he should treat them with respect. But instead of arguing with her, the man looked shocked. He was obviously used to women being scared of him.

'Maggie,' Irene said as she approached them both slowly. Maggie didn't want her to step in and help. She wanted to deal with this brute on her own. Irene's voice startled the man, and he finally looked away from Maggie. He looked panicked when he realised a second woman in uniform was coming towards him.

Like a cornered animal, he lashed out, shoving Irene to the ground. Maggie jumped forward to try and protect her friend, but as she did, the man grabbed her by the collar of her jacket and pushed her into the road.

It all happened so quickly. Maggie tried to steady herself, but the man had thrust her with such force that her feet gave out from under her. She flew through the air, her arms flailing as she tried to stop herself from falling. As her body started dropping to the ground, she looked to her right. Bright headlights flashed in her face. She accepted in that moment that there was nothing she could do. A loud screech tore into the night as the driver of the car slammed on his brakes, but it was too late.

The next thing Maggie could remember was coming to in the middle of the road. Everything looked blurry. She could just about make out a figure leaning over her. She heard a soft, comforting voice, and it took her a few moments to recognise it as Irene's.

'Take your time,' she soothed. 'You're going to be just fine, I've got you.' Maggie felt reassured by her words. She blinked and blinked until she could finally see Irene's face above her. She was cradling her head gently. Someone else was holding her hand.

Maggie tried to look around to see who it was. 'Argh!' she cried out as pain shot through her body.

'Try to stay still, help is coming,' Annie said gently. That was who was holding her hand, then. *Of course*, Maggie thought. *Silly me*. As she drifted in and out of consciousness, she caught little snippets of their conversation.

'He'll be long gone,' Annie was saying in a hushed voice. 'Just stay here, please. We can't have you getting hurt too.'

'But we can't let him get away with this,' Irene was arguing.

'Leave it – we can track him down another time,' Annie said, her voice unusually firm. Maggie wasn't surprised Irene wanted to give chase. She would have been the same if anyone had hurt her or Annie. But she was glad Irene listened to Annie and stayed put – she was running her fingers through Maggie's hair now and the feeling was overwhelmingly comforting. Maggie drifted off again, and as she came to this time, her friends' voices seemed more concerned than they had sounded previously.

'We really need to move her soon,' Annie was saying. 'Why is he taking so long?' She sounded panicked now. Suddenly Maggie felt a wrenching pain in her abdomen. *The baby*, she thought, as she finally passed out altogether.

26

Maggie woke with a start. Confused, she stretched out her arm, feeling for Charlie's soft, comforting fur. Somehow, she had expected to be in her own bed, waking up from a terrible dream. But as she peered around, she didn't recognise anything in the room. The pale curtains were drawn shut, so she knew it was still night-time, although she had no idea as to the hour. She didn't know whose bed she was lying in, but she breathed a sigh of relief when she spotted Irene and Annie standing by the door. When they looked over and saw she was awake they rushed to her side.

'We're here and you're safe,' Annie soothed, grabbing hold of Maggie's hand. 'Can you feel any pain? How do you feel?'

'Give her a minute,' Irene said. 'She's only just come round.'

'Sorry,' sighed Annie. 'You've been out for so long. I've just been so worried.' Maggie wondered how long she had been unconscious for. More importantly, how she had got from the middle of the road to this bed – and whose bed it was. Before she could ask, a stern-looking man with glasses and a moustache approached the bed.

'Wha-what's happening?' Maggie asked nervously, squeezing Annie's hand.

'Don't worry, he's a doctor,' Annie explained. 'Mrs Wenman over there,' she said, pointing to an elderly lady in the corner of the room, 'saw everything and she wanted to help. This is her house. Do you remember what happened?' Maggie winced and closed her eyes again as she nodded her head slightly. Everything ached. The doctor had left her side now and was talking to a man by the door.

'The driver of the car that hit you went to get help and brought the doctor back,' Annie continued. 'He doesn't think there's any lasting damage. We should be able to get you home soon.' Maggie closed her eyes again and said a silent thank you. She felt a rush of protectiveness for the baby, which she hadn't expected at all.

The fear of losing it had made her realise that she did love her baby, after all. It may have been conceived in a rage of hate and bitterness, but she would cherish and love it as fully as her heart would allow. She pictured herself playing in a park with a little version of herself, and she felt a rush of maternal love. She decided her baby was a little girl, and she smiled weakly to herself.

'Thank you for coming so quickly,' Irene was now saying to the doctor as he packed up his medical bag to leave. Suddenly, Maggie screamed out as an excruciating, twisting pain shot through her stomach. Everyone stopped talking and froze, staring at her. The doctor rushed to her side again.

Just as the pain was easing off, Maggie felt a warm sensation between her legs. She opened her eyes, which she had been squeezing tightly shut, and looked up at the doctor. He was looking at the bedsheets. Tentatively, she peered down and panicked when she saw they were now soaked with blood. She looked back at the doctor and as he looked sadly into her eyes, she knew what he was asking her. As her lips quivered and tears streamed down her face, Maggie nodded. The doctor slowly shook his head. She knew in that moment that the baby was gone. Her little girl. Another shot of pain ran through her and she drew her legs up to her middle before passing out.

When Maggie came to for the second time, the doctor, Mrs Wenman and the driver had left the room. She looked slowly around, blinking. Annie and Irene were sitting on chairs either side of her.

'Welcome back,' Annie said quietly, reaching up and running her hand gently over her forehead. Maggie felt so comforted by her touch. But then the evening's events raced back into her mind, and she looked up at Annie, fearful for what she was certain she was going to have to tell her. Maggie could still feel the warm sensation between her legs, and it felt like there was padding down there.

'Oh Mags,' Annie sighed sadly. She broke off eye contact to stare at her lap.

'Maggie, did you know you were pregnant?' Irene stepped in for Annie who was now wiping tears from her cheeks and still couldn't look her in the eye.

How on earth was she going to explain all of this? She contemplated playing dumb, but she was so tired of lying. She stared at Irene, tears welling in her eyes and her bottom lip trembling, and slowly nodded.

'She's . . . gone, isn't she?' Maggie asked quietly.

Irene nodded sadly and squeezed Maggie's hand. 'I'm so sorry,' she whispered.

Maggie closed her eyes and took a deep, shuddering breath. The baby was gone. She had spent the last few weeks terri-fied of what having a child would do to her life – how it would ruin everything for her. So it seemed so much crueller that the baby had been violently snatched away from her just as she had learned to love her.

As she tried to process the flood of emotions hitting her, the doctor walked back in. 'Oh good, she's awake,' he said, and Maggie wished she wasn't. 'I'll just examine you again, and then you should be able to go home. That will be the best place for you to get some rest and recover,' he added.

The girls left the room and Maggie kept her eyes closed as the doctor poked and prodded her and carried out all the relevant checks. She knew he was just doing his job and helping her, but she couldn't help but feel violated all over again. She desperately wanted to be on her own to deal with everything she was feeling.

'Right, let's get you home, then,' Irene said with purpose, once the doctor had signalled for them all to return to the room. She helped Maggie sit up slowly. Every movement sent a pain shooting through her abdomen. As Irene and Annie helped her off the bed, Maggie came over all wobbly.

'That will be the blood loss,' the doctor explained. 'I've put some padding down there to try and soak up as much as possible, but you will probably keep bleeding for a while.'

Maggie groaned. Why couldn't it all just be over with now? Did she really deserve such a persistent reminder of everything she had been through and everything she had just lost? 'The rest of your injuries are superficial cuts and bruises,' the doctor continued. 'You'll be sore for a few days, but you should be fine.'

They slowly helped her to the door. As Irene opened it, she paused and looked back. 'I don't think we can take her on the bus,' she said.

'Oh, heavens no. She's far too weak for that,' the doctor said. 'I was assuming this young man was going to drive her home?' he added, pointing at the driver of the car, who was stood outside.

'Of course. It's the least I can do,' the man said eagerly. Maggie looked at him for the first time. He must have been in his twenties. He looked pale and terrified. She felt bad for him. He was probably happily going about his evening when *wham*, she had flown straight into the path of his car, giving him no choice but to hit her. She wasn't angry at *him* – there was nothing he could have done to avoid what happened – she was angry at the man who had pushed her.

'We've already told you it wasn't your fault,' Irene told the driver sympathetically. 'There was nothing you could have done. This is all down to that brute.' He nodded sadly, staring at Maggie with such sorrow in his eyes she felt like she might break down there and then. All she could think about was playing with her little girl in the park.

'A lift would be much appreciated,' she smiled weakly, trying hard to pull herself together. She couldn't see herself making it home any other way.

'We'll come with you,' Irene said firmly, linking her arm with Maggie's and pushing the door wider.

'No, no, it's fine,' Maggie said, desperately trying to think of a way to persuade her friends to let her go alone. She couldn't even begin to imagine how she would explain all of this to her parents. She needed to slip into the house unnoticed, not with a noisy entourage. 'The doctor said I'll be all right, so there's really no point you both going so far out of your way to escort me home.' She tried to dig her heels into the floor to stop herself being carried forward and through the door, but she was too weak.

'Maggie, we don't know this man – he could be anybody,' Irene whispered urgently into her ear. 'We agreed to stick together after that alleyway scare and this is no different. You are *not* going on your own.'

'I can drop you both either home or back to the station after we've taken your friend home,' the driver offered. 'It's really not a problem. I'm not carrying on with my plans for the evening now, anyway, so I have nowhere to be.'

'Right, that's that settled then,' Irene said, and Maggie knew there was no point in arguing with her. They were making their way slowly down the stairs now, and she was out of ideas – and energy. Once outside, she found herself allowing her two friends to help her into the car.

As they drove away, a sense of dread filled Maggie. It seemed to stretch out into the road ahead of her as she stared out through the windscreen. She prayed her parents were both soundly asleep when they arrived in Kensington, and that she could sneak out of the car and into the house without any fuss.

Maybe she could give the driver a different address? Her friends wouldn't insist on seeing her into the house, would they? That would definitely get her caught. And they were all still in uniform, so there was no way on earth she was going to be able to explain her way out of it – even if by some miracle, Irene and Annie didn't actually speak to her parents.

Maggie started feeling clammy as panic set in. Her heart raced as she thought of all the possible outcomes. She felt like she was going to be sick. She wasn't sure if it was the impending sense of doom she was experiencing that was causing the nausea, or the blood she could feel she was still losing. She hoped she didn't bleed over the leather seats. She had probably ruined that poor woman's spare bed sheets, she realised in horror.

In the end, she was too exhausted to come up with any grand plan. She gave the driver her real address and just hoped for the best. That would have to do.

When the car pulled up outside Maggie's house, Annie gave her a gentle nudge. Rubbing her eyes and looking around in confusion, Maggie realised she must have drifted off to sleep for the rest of the journey.

'I'll be fine, you stay here,' Maggie said, suddenly snapping out of her sleepy state. The grogginess she had felt consumed by when Annie had roused her had quickly disappeared. The need to protect her two worlds from colliding had taken over and adrenaline was coursing through her veins.

'We're going to help you to the door,' Irene said resolutely as she stepped out of the car. Maggie flinched as Irene slammed the door shut behind her. It was like she *wanted* to wake her parents. She suddenly realised she hadn't addressed the baby issue with either of them. She had drifted off in the car before she'd had a chance to sort that out. They had both been very sensitive about it, and had obviously picked up on the fact she didn't want to talk about it. Would they bring it up in front of her parents, though? She decided she had even more reason to keep them in the car and away from her family. 'Come on then, out you come – nice and slowly,' Irene encouraged, as she opened Maggie's door and held out her hand to her.

'Please, be quiet,' Maggie groaned. 'I don't want to wake my parents.' She could almost taste the desperation in her voice, but Irene seemed to be completely oblivious.

'Don't be silly,' Irene scoffed loudly. 'You need looking after and that's what parents are for.'

Maggie knew Irene was only trying to help, but she really was making everything worse. She was just about to bite the bullet and tell Irene and Annie everything when she saw a bright light flicker on out of the corner of her eye. Her heart sank down into the pit of her stomach. She didn't need to look up to know that it was coming from her parents' bedroom.

With resigned acceptance, she allowed Irene to help her out of the car. There was no use confessing to her friends now. They would find out soon enough. They stood by the motor as the hallway light came on, and then watched on in silence as Maggie's father opened the front door to stare out across the road at them.

'There you go,' said Irene tenderly as she rubbed Maggie's back reassuringly. 'Parents always know when their children are in trouble. You're so lucky you have them both to look after you,' she added with a sadness in her voice.

'You can go now,' Maggie said faintly. 'Please don't walk me to the door.'

'If you're sure?' Irene asked, and Maggie nodded.

'You've done enough,' she whispered. Irene smiled and Maggie was grateful she hadn't understood the real meaning behind her words.

'We'll let the chief know what happened and that you won't be in for a little while,' Irene added. 'I can't imagine you'll be ready to get back on patrol tomorrow. He was very relaxed when you had that fever, so take your time and don't rush. We want you back to full health! We'll see you when you're ready.' The mention of the chief made Maggie's pulse race again. She looked at Irene, fear in her eyes. 'Don't worry, we won't tell him the *full* story,' Irene said quietly.

Maggie knew she meant the baby and she smiled gratefully. As annoyed as she was at Irene for waking her father, she knew she was only looking out for her. She was lucky to have such understanding friends, and she had a lot of explaining to do when she saw them next. That was if she ever made it back to Bethnal Green. She had no idea how her father was going to punish her, but she was sure he wouldn't be allowing her to carry on her work with the WPV.

As Maggie made her way to the front door, she was glad Irene and Annie had listened to her on one thing and not walked her to her father. She had enough explaining to do as it was. She flinched as she heard the car door slamming shut. *Thanks for that*, she thought, looking up and spotting the curtains next door twitching. Then the sound of the engine disappeared into the distance. At least her friends weren't going to witness whatever was coming next.

Maggie couldn't even bring herself to look at her father. When she reached the threshold, he grabbed her by the arm and yanked her into the house. He clearly didn't want the neighbours to get any more entertainment out of them that evening. Once the door had closed, Maggie risked a glance up at him. Now they were in the light, he was staring at her uniform in disbelief.

'Are you going to tell me what this is all about?' he said with an icy calm, and Maggie flinched, knowing she was in for it. Ashamed, she broke off eye contact and looked down at her feet. She saw a puddle of blood on the floor and realised why her father wasn't as angry as she had expected.

His rage had been overshadowed by shock that his daughter was standing in front of him bruised and bleeding, rather than sleeping soundly in bed. He was speechless. She found she couldn't look at him again – her gaze was fixed on the pool of dark red liquid on the floor. As another drop hit, her head suddenly felt light. Swaying to and fro, she tried to steady herself. She felt her body giving way beneath her and then her father's arms were around her waist, catching her just before she hit the floor.

When Maggie woke up, she was in her own bed and it was dark. As she recalled everything that had happened that evening, she burst into tears. She was mourning the baby she had never wanted and dealing with the shock of being thrown into the path of a moving car. But most of all she was fearful of what her parents already knew, and what they might find out.

She could just about make out her WPV uniform hanging over the back of her desk chair. There was no way she could talk herself out of that now, she decided. She would have to come clean. But they would never understand about the baby – they might just forgive her for the WPV lies, but she *had* to keep that to herself.

Maggie drifted in and out of sleep. She wasn't sure how long she had been in bed when there was a knock on her bedroom door. 'Come in,' she said weakly. She smiled when she saw it was Dr Heath, their family doctor. She had known him her whole life and he had helped her through many an illness and scrape. Then she realised what he might discover if he examined her and her pulse rose again. Her father walked into the room behind Dr Heath. He wouldn't even look at Maggie.

'Thank you for coming out to us so late at night. Like I was saying,' her father said to the doctor, 'I'm concerned about the bleeding . . . between her legs. Our maid has put some towels down on the bed, but she said it doesn't seem to be stopping.' He was talking about her as if she wasn't even there, but Maggie was too ashamed to speak up. Her father left the room and she tried to hold back her tears as Dr Heath examined her silently. He had always been so warm and friendly towards her, but she knew that wouldn't be the case any longer. She imagined her father must have told him about the WPV uniform, and the bleeding probably spoke for itself. Within minutes he would be confirming her shameful secret.

'Did you know you were with child?' he asked when he had finished. Maggie was surprised at the gentleness of his voice. She had expected him to be outraged as she knew her father would be. What must he think of her to end up in a situation like this? She couldn't answer him. She turned her head into the pillow and wept until he left the room, knowing that at that very moment, he would be informing her parents.

27

When Maggie eventually stopped sobbing, she could hear voices outside her bedroom door. Everything was muffled, but she could make out enough to know that it was her father and Dr Heath talking. Dr Heath was speaking very quietly and calmly, when out of nowhere her father exploded. At that point he raised his voice so much that Maggie could hear everything.

'You're wrong!' he roared. Then Dr Heath was mumbling again. He sounded apologetic. 'There must be some kind of mistake!' Maggie's father yelled. Dr Heath was talking again, and then it fell silent. Maggie heard footsteps moving down the corridor. Trembling, she waited for her father to return. She heard the front door being slammed, and then stomping coming up the stairs. She braced herself as her bedroom door flew open and her father walked in.

He was standing at the head of her bed in two strides and he stayed there staring coldly down at her for what felt like hours, but was probably only about thirty seconds. Maggie tried to stop herself from shaking as she looked up at the anger in his eyes. His face was bright red with rage and he was shaking with it. All of a sudden, Maggie felt her head spin to the side with such force her neck jolted. She cried out in pain and brought her hand up to her cheek. Her father had slapped her. Taking deep breaths, she tried to recover from the shock. It had come out of nowhere, and was definitely meant to humiliate her more than hurt her – although he had managed to achieve both.

'Look at me,' he spat. Slowly, she peered up at him again and tried to contain her sobs. 'You have a lot of explaining to do,' he said, his voice thick with venom. Tears streamed down Maggie's face as she tried to work out where to start, but her mind was blank. Blind panic consumed her as she realised she didn't know how to talk herself out of this one. 'I'm waiting,' he said, his voice louder now. Maggie wondered if he was going to add to her pain by beating her properly, or if he would take pity on her and spare her.

'I'm sorry,' she finally whispered, her voice breaking as she spoke. It seemed like a good place to start. 'I was hit by a car,' she added meekly, hoping that might evoke some sympathy.

'*Pregnant?*' he said in quiet disbelief. His voice was softer now, but he still sounded angry. 'You were brought up better than this. Tell me who the father was. *Now.*'

'Daddy, please,' she begged. 'Please don't punish me even more. It wasn't my fault, you have to believe me.'

'Why would I believe anything you say?' he roared, and she flinched, certain he was going to hit her again.

'Where's Mother?' Maggie asked weakly when no more blows came. Maggie had always been so strong and independent. She often found she was the one to comfort her mother when she was having a tough time. But now, for the first time that Maggie could remember, all she wanted was a hug from her mother.

'She's taken to her bed,' her father said, letting out a long sigh. 'You didn't think she would take this news well, did you? You know how she gets.' Now Maggie could add guilt for upsetting her mother to the list of emotions she was currently battling.

'Right then,' Mr Smyth continued, sounding more frustrated than angry. 'If you're not ready to tell me how you came to be with child, why don't you start by telling me what *this* is about?' As he spoke, he grabbed Maggie's WPV jacket off the back of the chair and thrust it onto the bed next to her. She had no choice. She had to tell him everything. No matter the consequences. At least she didn't have to worry about him harming the baby now. The thought of her little girl made her well up once more.

As she started explaining how she had gone behind his back to sign up for the WPV, Maggie could see her father becoming angrier than ever. She left out the fact that Eddie had helped her, of course. He had enough to deal with.

'And where exactly have you been parading around in this uniform, trying to do men's work?' her father demanded. She had known he wouldn't understand. But at least he was giving her a chance to explain instead of doling out more punishment straight away.

'Bethnal Green,' Maggie whispered. 'That's where I ran into Peter. Do you remember Peter, who Eddie used to play with outside?'

'Oh, so that's who got you into this other mess is it!' Mr Smyth exploded. 'I always said that family was trouble!' He was so incensed now that Maggie could see spittle flying out of his mouth as he shouted.

'Daddy, it wasn't my fault!' Maggie replied, sitting up despite the pain. She was shouting too, now. Her fight had suddenly come rushing back. She needed him to know she hadn't fallen pregnant willingly. She was so ashamed and embarrassed about what had happened to her that she hadn't confided in anybody. But she couldn't let her father think she was going around offering herself to all and sundry. He didn't let her explain, though.

'I've heard enough, Margaret,' he said stiffly. 'First your brother, and now you. I don't know what your mother and I have done to deserve such disobedient children. All we've ever done is try to provide the best for you both and this is how you repay us.' He closed his eyes and shook his head before pinching the bridge of his nose and sighing again.

'Daddy, please,' Maggie started, desperate to talk herself out of whatever he had planned for her. But he wouldn't let her speak.

'You have let this family down,' Mr Smyth continued. He was looking Maggie in the eye now, and she felt his gaze burning straight through her. She was getting ready to brace herself. He had never looked at her like that before. 'You have been lying to us all this time. And you've brought shame upon this family in every way. You are not welcome under this roof.'

Maggie was stunned. She had been expecting him to lash out at her, not throw her onto the streets. 'But, wh-where will I go?' she asked desperately. She had played out all kinds of different scenarios in her head, imagining how her father would react when he found out about the WPV – and later about the baby. But this outcome had never crossed her mind. She had heard of girls being thrown out of their homes after getting themselves into situations. A lot of the prostitutes she and the girls had spoken to on patrol had fallen into their way of life after being disowned by their families. But they were from different backgrounds. That didn't happen to girls like Maggie. At least, that was what she had thought.

'You should have thought about that when you got yourself into this situation,' Mr Smyth said coldly. 'Dr Heath says you'll be back to full health after a few days' rest,' he continued. 'As soon as you are back on your feet, I want you out of my house. Do you understand?' Maggie nodded silently, and her father walked slowly out of the room.

Her fight disappeared just as quickly as it had returned moments before. She sat in shock, trying to work out what she could do and where she could go.

Before she knew it, the sun had come up and light was streaming through her windows, heralding the start of a new day. She hadn't even managed to get up and close the curtains. There was a gentle tapping at her door. Hopeful it was her father, ready to take it all back and forgive her, Maggie straightened herself up. But it was Florence who walked in. Maggie was so happy to see a friendly face that she burst into tears.

'Poor love,' Florence whispered, running over to the side of the bed and pulling her in for a cuddle. 'I haven't got long – your father hasn't gone into work today and if he catches me in here with you, I'll be done for. He has forbidden all the staff from talking to you.' Maggie realised Florence was risking everything for her, yet again. Whatever would she do without her? 'I wish I could help you, dear,' Florence said sadly. 'But I have to send all me spare money to me niece.'

'I know, Florence,' Maggie sniffed. 'And you've done more than enough for me already. I couldn't ask for any more.'

'If me friend had a bigger house, I'd send you there, I truly would,' Florence said.

Maggie nodded and smiled gratefully. 'Your niece is so lucky to have you,' she said, taking hold of Florence's hand and squeezing it tight. 'What am I going to do?' she added desperately, as a fresh wave of tears poured down her face. Now they had started, she couldn't keep them in. She wasn't used to showing people emotion like this. She saw it as a weakness. It was much easier to put on a strong front, anyway. But Maggie found that she was able to let herself be vulnerable with Florence.

'Yer friends will see you right, I'm sure of it,' Florence said with confidence.

'But I've not been honest with them,' Maggie spluttered. 'I kept all of this from them,' she said, motioning to the area below her waist.

'You didn't tell me neither,' Florence said. Maggie looked up quickly, afraid Florence was going to turn on her now, just like her father. But she saw warmth in her eyes, not anger. 'I know you would have had yer reasons,' Florence said. 'God only knows what you've been through. I know you're a sensible girl, so I'm imagining you had an experience similar to my niece.' She stopped and closed her eyes briefly before continuing. 'What makes it worse is that I was rooting for you to help change things by joining the WPV, not get caught up in it all.'

'Oh, Florence,' Maggie whispered through tears. 'I should have spoken to you. I'm certain I wouldn't be in this awful mess if I had.' Maggie suddenly felt foolish. Why hadn't she just asked for help?

'I wish you could've shared it with me – it might've made you feel better,' Florence said. 'But you weren't ready to talk about it, and that's just fine, love. But you *must* tell yer friends now. You need their help and, from what you've told me about them and my brief meeting with Annie, I know they'll be only too willing to do whatever they can to help you out of this muddle.'

Maggie hoped Florence was right. She realised with a heavy heart that the WPV and her two friends were all she really had at this moment in time. She was going to have to tell Annie and Irene everything. 'I'm sorry I've been so snappy with you,' she said sadly. She felt incredibly guilty for the way she had treated Florence the last few weeks.

'I won't hear it,' Florence said firmly. 'You were going through something. I know that's not yer normal way.'

'Florence, you're too kind to me,' Maggie replied. She heard heavy footsteps going past her door, and then the stairs creaked. Her father was on his way downstairs.

'I'm out of time,' Florence whispered. 'Please, love, go to yer friends for help. They'll understand. And keep in touch with me. I'll keep an eye on the post like I've been doing, so you can write to me here. And once yer settled I'll pass on anything from Eddie.' She got up from the bed. 'If there is ever anything you think I can do to help you then you must ask me. Do you understand?' Maggie nodded obediently. Florence pulled her in for a quick embrace before hurrying out of her room, silently closing the door behind her.

Maggie was all alone again – only now she had an idea of what to do next. But would Annie and Irene really help her? Would they even be able to? Annie lived with her family and they were very respectable – would they take her in after what had happened? Her own father had thrown her out like she was one of the prostitutes – is that how everyone would see her now?

Maggie still didn't know enough about Irene to be sure she was even in a place to help her out. But she knew that if either of her friends were in a sticky situation like this, then she would do whatever she could to help them. She had to trust that they felt the same about her. Even after she had spent the last few weeks pushing them away.

Maggie decided she didn't have much choice but to ask for their help, anyway. She resolved to confess everything to them as soon as she was well enough to make it back to the station. She breathed a sigh of relief that she didn't have to worry about missing her shift today. She just needed some rest, she thought to herself as she lay her aching head back down on her bed and drifted off into a deep sleep.

28

When Maggie woke up, every bone in her body was aching. As she tried to turn over on to her side, she felt a dull pain in her abdomen and realised with a start that she was still bleeding. Fresh tears stained her pillow as grief and devastation took hold again. She spent the whole day in bed, refusing to even raise her head when Florence came in with a bowl of soup. She couldn't face eating, so left it to go cold. She must have been asleep when Florence returned to fetch the tray, as it was gone when she woke up again.

The following morning, Maggie crept out of bed before sunrise to use the bathroom and try to clean herself up a little. She was so exhausted when she got back to her bedroom that she crawled back into bed and stayed there for another day. This time, when Florence brought her up soup, she managed a small smile of acknowledgement. She was grateful to her friend for not trying to talk to her or comfort her – she just wanted to be left alone. Her father must still have been enforcing his ban on any household staff talking to his daughter, but Maggie felt only relief. She finished the soup within minutes then fell back to sleep, finding that the empty bowl had been collected when she woke.

The following morning, four days after the accident, Maggie was surprised to wake up feeling stronger and almost refreshed – a feeling she hadn't experienced for what felt like a long time. The challenging WPV shifts, and the stress of living in constant fear of being caught out by her father or somebody else she knew had resulted in restless nights and utter exhaustion. Not to mention the added trauma she had been dealing with since the attack. And then there was the baby she had been growing inside of her, which had seemed to sap any remnants of energy she'd had left.

She was still grieving for her little girl – she was all she had thought about during the short time she had spent awake throughout her imprisonment in her room, and her ghostly figure had haunted her dreams. But she had come to accept that what had happened was for the best. Now, it was almost as if everything being out in the open had lifted all the extra weight and worry from her shoulders. Maybe that was why she had been able to sleep for so long – for the first time in months despite the fact her life was unravelling and her parents had all but disowned her. This conclusion brought her screaming back to reality and the awful situation she was in. Instantly, her heart dropped along with her mood.

Maggie had enjoyed a glimmer of hope that her father would calm down given a few days to think things over, and have a change of heart. She was his only daughter, after all. And his only child at home, right now. But as she sat up in bed and spotted the suitcase sitting just beside her bedroom door, her hopes were dashed. He must have seen to it that it was delivered to her room while she was recovering – ready for her to pack up and leave with as soon as she was fit to. Just as he had ordered. It was callous, and the action stung her to her core. He really wasn't going to give her a chance to explain.

As for her mother – well, she hadn't even come in to see her since she had returned home bloody and bruised. Was she too frightened of what her husband would do to her – to them both – if she visited Maggie's room? Or was she so ashamed of her daughter that she couldn't even look at her? Did she not want to hear what had happened from Maggie herself? Or had she just taken what her husband had told her as gospel? Maggie suspected she had been holed up in the master bedroom crying since the doctor had left. She was torn. While she was heartbroken to be leaving her mother to be the sole outlet for her father's abuse, she was also devastated that her mother had not found the strength to defy her father to get Maggie's side of the story. Or even just to say goodbye. Maybe she was better off without either of them.

Now she knew there was absolutely no way her father would relent, she decided there was no point in staying any longer. She finally felt fit enough to be up and about, so she needed to leave this house before her father physically removed her. And the sooner she went on her way, the sooner she could work out what to do next.

Once she was gone, Maggie wondered if her parents would just stop talking about her, as if she didn't exist. They had erased Eddie from the family history the day he had departed for training – without a second thought, it seemed. So, it was certainly feasible they would do the same to her. The thought was like a knife to her chest. Would they ever speak about her – or to her – again? What would they tell Eddie? Their friends? How would they explain their missing daughter to everyone they knew? They certainly wouldn't be running around shouting the truth from the rooftops, that was for sure.

As Maggie contemplated her new life, fresh tears filled her eyes. But she brushed them away defiantly. She had to stay strong today. She was going to have to keep her composure while revealing everything that had happened to her to her friends. A breakdown at the police station just wasn't an option.

She could see the male officers rolling their eyes and tutting about it now. What joy they would find in seeing their suspicions that women couldn't cope with police work proved correct! She might have been feeling sore and vulnerable and like she just needed a good sob and a loving cuddle, but she wasn't about to let them think that they had been right all along. No, she would hold it together – at least until she was away from judgemental eyes.

It was going to be tough – but she needed to consider the alternative. If by some miracle her father relented and allowed her to stay at home, she would most certainly have to give up the WPV. Everything she had worked so hard for would end up being for nothing. She would lose Annie and Irene. And, after walking on eggshells for goodness knows how long, afraid of her father losing his temper with her, she would most definitely end up having to marry a suitor chosen by him.

She thought about her mother playing the dutiful wife, and never doing anything with her life that *she* wanted to do. Despite everything, that wasn't a life that Maggie wanted. So maybe, as tough as it was right now, this was for the best?

Looking around her, Maggie wondered how she could possibly pack up her whole life into one small suitcase? Where would she even start? As she contemplated what to take, she realised she was probably going to be better off making a completely fresh start. This was going to be hard enough without constant reminders of her old life around to upset her. It was strange to think of this as her old life. But it was now. And it was best left behind. She would just have to block it out, like she had done with all her other worries.

Maggie carefully folded up a few dresses and packed them along with some underwear, and her writing pad and pencils. She closed the suitcase with a heavy heart. Then she looked over at Charlie. That bear had been her best friend at one point, before she and Eddie had grown close. He had always been her biggest comfort, and she had turned to him a lot over the last few weeks. She was desperate to take him with her – one cuddle could lift any sadness she was feeling, if only for that moment. But he would be a continual reminder, and she had already decided she needed to move straight on. With a pang, she put him to one side.

Next, she pulled her savings box out from under her bed. Over the years, she and Eddie had been sent money from rich relatives for every birthday and Christmas. They had never wanted for anything – their father may have been cruel, but he was always generous with his wallet – so they had both been able to save up quite a stash in their bedrooms.

Eddie had started saying recently that he was going to use his to buy a car. Maggie knew they had nowhere near enough for that, but she indulged her brother's dreams. She had never really thought about what she would use her money for, but she certainly hadn't counted on it coming in handy for this. She grabbed the notes and coins now and stuffed them in her jacket pocket without even counting them.

Making her way along the corridor, Maggie noticed the door to the main bedroom was closed. Her suspicions about her mother had been true, then. She hoped she never ended up as weak as her. At the top of the stairs she took a deep breath and got ready to walk down them for the final time. She was still a little sore and she winced as her feet touched each step. She paused halfway down. From that spot she could see into the lounge.

Peering in now, Maggie spotted her father on the sofa, avidly reading a copy of *The Vote*. His face looked strained as he stared at the words in front of him. How ironic, she thought to herself, that the newspaper that started all of this was what he would read as it ended.

She was so distracted that she forgot to avoid the creaky step, and it groaned loudly. Her father stopped reading and looked straight at her, and Maggie's breath caught in her throat. She wasn't sure if she could cope with more shouting, or another lecture. But what happened next made her feel worse than any of that possibly could have done. Her father's face turned instantly stern and angry. He fixed her with a stone-cold stare for a matter of seconds before turning his attention back to the newspaper.

Maggie stood, rooted to the spot, willing him to look up at her again, smile and wave her down to join him. She so wanted him to tell her he had made a mistake ordering her to leave. But as she stood and watched her father studiously ignoring her presence, Maggie realised he had cut her out of his life already. It was that simple for him.

Just then, Maggie noticed him looking up at the chair opposite him and shaking his head with a warning glare, before going back to the paper. Her mother was sitting there, knitting. So she wasn't in the bedroom. *Mummy,* she pleaded in her head, *don't make me go! I'm scared and I'm sorry!* She wasn't brave enough to say any of it out loud.

She stared longingly at her mother, willing her to look up. When she did, tears welled in both their eyes as they gazed sadly at each other. Her mother placed her knitting down on the floor and made to stand up. Hope raced through Maggie. But then she heard her father's cruel snarl. Immediately her mother sat back down, picked up her knitting and continued with it with shaking hands. Maggie stayed still as a statue, desperate for her mother to defy her husband this one time. But she refused to look up again and Maggie watched as a single tear ran down her cheek.

Trying to stay strong, Maggie reminded herself of what it would be like for her if she remained in the family home. *It's better for you to go – you'll be able to live your own life the way you want to live it,* she told herself. She thought back to her mother's words to her when Eddie had signed up – she wanted her to get as far away from her father as possible. Maggie looked down at the WPV uniform that was hanging over her arm, and proudly ran her hand over the back of the jacket to straighten it out. She lifted her chin and squared her shoulders. Then she picked up her suitcase again and made her way down the remaining stairs.

When she got to the front door, she chanced a look back down the hall. Florence was standing at the kitchen doorway. Even with the distance between the two of them, Maggie could see that her face was blotchy, and her eyes were puffy. She knew Florence couldn't come to her – her father would go mad if she did – but they were both out of his sight now, so Maggie blew Florence a silent kiss and smiled sadly. Florence pretended to catch the kiss, and then she brought both her hands to her heart.

Maggie turned away quickly and opened the front door. She couldn't stand to look at Florence any longer. The tears were already streaming down her face and she would surely break down if she stood there another second. As she stepped outside, the heavy wooden door slammed shut behind her. It was the first time she had ever made any noise leaving the house for WPV duty. She felt liberated already.

Maggie took another deep breath and then exhaled slowly. *This is a good thing*, she reminded herself again. She knew it would be hard at first. But once she got herself settled and started her new life properly, she would look back on this moment and be grateful it had happened.

She thought about all the men on the front line, putting their lives at risk and fighting to keep her and everyone else in the country safe. She thought of Eddie, going through gruelling training so he, too, could risk everything to save so many others. And she thought of all the street women she had encountered over the last few months, who had no choice but to sell their bodies to keep a roof over their heads or put food on the table for their families.

Maggie knew her friends wouldn't let it come to that for her. They would look after her and they would help her set up her new life. Maggie had freedom, and that was a lot more than many people could claim right now.

29

Maggie found herself at Bethnal Green Police Station long before Annie and Irene. In her haste to bid farewell to her old life, she had arrived an hour early for their patrol.

'Good morning, dear. It's good to see you back,' the officer behind the main desk said as he tipped his hat when she walked in. She didn't even know his name, but none of the officers ever spoke that kindly to any of the girls. She was so thrown by it that she didn't respond, and just continued on her way.

She bumped into Witchy outside the WPV room. 'Here, let me get the door for you,' he said, rushing to hold it open and guiding her through with his arm. 'You come and let me know if you need anything,' he added as he closed the door again on his way out. Maggie was flummoxed. Where had the dismissive attitudes gone? Why was everyone being so respectful, all of a sudden?

She got into her uniform and while she waited for the others, she thought about how best to confess to her friends that she had been lying to them about her age and her family's support all along. Then, of course, there was the story behind the lost baby to deal with. Her musings were interrupted by heavy footsteps moving along the corridor in her direction. She looked up at the door and was relieved when Frank's friendly face poked around it, smiling at her.

'Someone's keen,' he grinned, looking at the clock on the wall behind her. 'And I wasn't expecting to see you back so soon – it's only been a few days, hasn't it? How are you doing?' Maggie sat up straight, her heart thumping in her chest. A tingle ran down the back of her spine and she felt boiling hot all of a sudden as panic engulfed her body. What did he know? Irene had *promised* her she wouldn't say anything to anyone about the baby. Had she stayed true to her word? Irene was close to Frank – Maggie hoped desperately that she hadn't revealed her secret to him. Because if she couldn't trust her friends, what was she going to do?

'From what Irene says, you took a nasty hit protecting that girl,' he said, looking impressed. 'You're a bit of a hero round here now – all the lads are eating their words!'

Thank goodness, Maggie thought, sinking back down into her chair. 'Is that why everyone is being so nice?' she asked.

Frank beamed. 'You've been the talk of the station. Everyone is so impressed with your determination to get hold of that man no matter what. There's been a real shift in attitude towards all of you.' Maggie was pleased, although at the same time she was slightly put out that it had taken her being struck by a car for her and her friends to be taken seriously. 'Are you sure you're fit to be back?' Frank asked, sounding concerned. 'Irene said you might be off a while and it's only been a few days.'

'I'm, er, I'm fine now. Thanks, Frank,' she smiled. 'Has there been any news on the man who did it?' she asked hopefully.

'I'm afraid not, but don't you worry – we're putting everything into tracking the brute down. We won't let him get away with what he did to you.' Maggie smiled gratefully. Now she felt terrible for doubting Irene. Of course she had stuck to her word! 'Still looking a little pale there, though,' Frank observed, walking further into the room for a more thorough inspection. Maggie had never felt more under the spotlight.

'I am still feeling a bit peaky, I must admit,' Maggie said.

'But I was desperate for some fresh air and company. An afternoon on patrol will do me the world of good, I'm sure,' she said with confidence.

'Well, you take it easy,' Frank said. He looked very serious now, and more concerned than ever. 'And don't be afraid to come back for a sit-down if it gets a bit much.' Maggie nodded. As he disappeared off down the corridor again, she breathed a sigh of relief. She needed to stop doubting her friends.

Hearing the telltale clip-clop of ladies' shoes on the hard floor, she sat up straight to look presentable for either Irene or Annie's arrival. Plastering on her best brave grin, she felt ready to greet them and stay strong. But as soon as Irene came through the door and met her eyes, Maggie realised it was no good. She wasn't sure if it was the joy at seeing her friend again, or if she was having a delayed reaction to leaving home. Either way, she couldn't stop the tears flowing.

'Oh Mags,' Irene sighed, dropping her things and rushing to her. She knelt down on the floor in front of where Maggie was sitting and pulled her in for an embrace. Maggie couldn't help it – she was full-on sobbing now. 'Don't worry, just let it out,' Irene said reassuringly.

Maggie had never let her guard down like this in front of anyone – not even Eddie. It just wasn't her way. She was so used to having to keep people at arm's length so that they didn't find out the truth about life with her father. But she felt so comfortable in Irene's arms, and such a sense of relief letting go like that. It was as if all the secrets and worries she had been carrying for so long were slowly lifting. It wasn't over yet, though – she still had to tell her friends the full story. As she geared up to talk, Annie entered the room.

'You shouldn't be back yet,' she said, sounding panicked. She ran over to Maggie and Irene, placing her hand gently on Maggie's shoulder. 'Is everything all right?'

'My parents threw me out,' Maggie said quietly, staring at the floor. She wiped the tears from her face and sat up straight again. She cleared her throat. She was ready. Crying like that had revitalised her and she now felt strong enough to tell them everything without breaking down again. Which was a good job, as she could hear officers' voices in the corridor and the door was still open. She hoped no one had wandered past while she was sobbing. Irene went to close the door, then brought the other chair over to sit next to Maggie. Annie leaned up against the desk. They listened intently as Maggie told them in a hushed voice how she had lied about her age to get into the WPV, and the truth about her father.

'I had no idea,' Annie whispered, shocked when Maggie was finished. 'I always just assumed you were around the same age as me.'

'You do act very grown up,' Irene agreed, nodding.

'Well, I only added a couple of years, so it was no big deal really,' Maggie said. 'But I knew I could get into a lot of trouble if anyone found out, and that if I told you, you might also get in trouble for knowing about it and not reporting me. I'm sorry I kept it from you, but I was trying to protect you. Can you ever forgive me?'

'Don't be daft,' laughed Annie. 'It's a harmless thing – and we never actually asked you your age, so you didn't outright lie to us!' Maggie loved Annie's innocence and her ability to make her feel better about just about anything. 'As for your father, I had no idea. We knew he was strict, but he sounds just rotten, Mags. How awful to have to live with the threat of that over you day in and day out!' Irene shot her a warning look. 'Sorry, I mean, I know he's your father . . .'

'Really, don't worry,' Maggie said. 'You're right. He *is* rotten. Rotten to the core. But I've never actually admitted that to anyone until now. It's not really something you talk about, is it? I suppose I felt ashamed that my lovely privileged life wasn't all it looked to be on the outside.' Now those two confessions were out of the way, Maggie felt a little better. She had never dreamed that telling anyone the truth about her father would make her feel good, but she certainly felt lighter now.

She couldn't relax yet, though. She still had the Peter situation to address – and the baby. Neither of her friends had brought that up yet, but she knew they must be desperate to know the story behind it. She took a deep breath and started from the beginning.

'I *knew* there was something up with that chap,' cried Irene, jumping in when Maggie had only got as far as the encounter with Peter in the alleyway. 'I should have kicked him where it hurts once I'd slammed him to the floor,' she muttered, shaking her head.

'So that's why you didn't want us to report it?' Annie asked.

Maggie nodded. 'I couldn't risk Peter telling them my real age, and telling my father about the WPV. I felt terrible keeping it from you both, honestly I did. But I thought I could deal with him on my own. I stupidly believed he would just go away and leave me alone – especially after you gave him what for, Irene.' Irene's face softened, and she gave Maggie a half-smile. Maggie could tell she was going over the ambush in her head and relishing it even more now she knew the truth about Peter.

'Wait a minute. That letter you got at the station, the one that upset you. That came soon after that night. That wasn't him, was it?' Irene asked.

Maggie nodded and explained about the threats. She took a moment to gather herself before telling them about the attack. This was the first time she had spoken about it out loud. If the events of the past few days hadn't made it all seem more real, then this certainly would. But she couldn't pretend it hadn't happened any longer. Her friends deserved to know the truth. And she couldn't expect them to help her if she was still keeping things from them.

As Maggie went over the details, she could feel her friends' eyes boring into her. She stopped herself from looking up at them. This was hard enough already – she would definitely start crying again if she saw their sympathetic faces. She needed to get this done so she didn't have to talk about it ever again.

Once Maggie had finished, the three of them sat in silence. Annie was kneeling on the floor now and holding Maggie's hand, and Irene had her arm around Maggie's shoulders. They were taking it all in. Maggie was floating in the relief of finally having unburdened herself of the awful truth. But did they think she was foolish for visiting Peter alone? What if they thought it was all her own fault for being so silly? She looked nervously over at Irene and saw her fists were clenched tight.

'Maggie, I swear to you,' Irene started in a slow and barely controlled voice, 'if I ever see that man again, he will live to regret what he did to you.' She was pale and shaking with rage – Maggie had never seen her so angry. How she wished she had taken Irene along with her that evening!

'We knew there was something going on,' Irene added as she got up again and paced the room. 'You'd closed yourself off to us and we didn't want to push it. We hoped you'd open up to us in your own time. I'm sorry we didn't help you. I wish we could have done something!'

Maggie was stunned – she had expected her friends to be angry with her for keeping everything to herself, not apologising.

'I should have told you. It's not your fault, please don't feel bad,' Maggie begged. The last thing she wanted was for them to feel guilty. 'Mostly, I felt silly,' Maggie admitted quietly. 'I still can't believe I was stupid enough to go to his place on my own, let alone stay after he raised his hand to me. No wonder I ended up his victim.'

'Don't you dare even think that again!' Irene said fiercely, suddenly full of rage again. In a shot, she was kneeling by Maggie's side. 'None of this was your fault,' she said firmly. You have to believe that. I'm not just saying that as your friend – it's the truth, and anybody who heard your story would agree.'

'She's right,' Annie said, squeezing her hand. 'This is all down to Peter. You did absolutely nothing wrong, Mags. He's the one who couldn't control himself. He lured you there after planning it all out. You mustn't blame yourself, you just mustn't.'

Maggie gave a grateful nod. It felt good to hear them say it after spending so long blaming herself for what had happened. 'Anyway,' she said, desperate to move on from the topic of Peter, 'the most pressing problem at the moment is the fact that I've been thrown out of my home and have nowhere to go after we finish today's patrol.'

'Gosh, yes,' said Annie, her brow crumpling. 'I can't believe your parents threw you out after everything you've been through.'

'Well, I lied about the WPV and my father was so angry about that he wouldn't even let me explain about the baby. He probably thinks I've been using the uniform to get my wicked way with soldiers down alleyways,' Maggie whispered. 'Honestly, I'm devastated he could think that of me. But I'm also relieved I didn't get his usual type of punishment.' She swiped at a lone tear that had escaped from her eye and was making its way down her cheek.

'It doesn't matter how you got pregnant, Mags,' Irene said sympathetically. 'He's an awful man for kicking you out onto the streets after what happened. I'm sorry – I know he's your father. But I have to be honest with you.'

'It's all right,' Maggie said sadly. She couldn't really argue with what Irene was saying. And she hated to admit it, but she wasn't even sure if the outcome would have been any different if he had allowed her to explain how she had really become pregnant. Most likely he would have somehow made that out to be her fault, too.

'So,' Maggie started, this time with hope in her voice. 'I've got nowhere to go, and you two are my closest friends.' She let the sentence hang in the air between them, praying that one of them would step in and offer her a place to stay.

'Maggie, I'd help you in a heartbeat if it were up to me – but we have a full house,' Annie said apologetically. 'My aunt couldn't stand to be in her own house after my uncle went off to fight, so she's staying with us, along with all my cousins. Me and my sisters are sharing our bedrooms and my aunt is on the sofa,' she added.

Maggie was sure Annie must have mentioned that, but of course she had been in her own little world for so long she hadn't taken it in. They both looked to Irene, who was deep in thought. She jumped a little when she looked up and saw their expectant faces. 'You live alone, don't you?' Annie asked her. Irene nodded slowly. 'Wonderful!' Annie cried. 'So, Maggie can stay with you?'

Irene's face froze.

Maggie didn't understand – she had her own place so why wasn't she jumping at the chance to help her? 'I-I really don't have anywhere else to go,' Maggie whispered. She hadn't expected to have to plead for help. It was humiliating. Why didn't Irene want to take her in?

Irene sat motionless for a few moments longer. When she finally looked up at Maggie, she seemed worried.

'Look, I haven't been completely honest with you, either,' she admitted.

Maggie had always known Irene was hiding something. After all, she and Annie still knew hardly anything about her. But she didn't get her usual sense of triumph out of knowing she had been right all along.

'Of course you can stay with me, Mags,' Irene continued. 'You can stay as long as you need. But you need to know that I don't exactly have the grandest digs.' She looked down at her hands in her lap and scoffed, 'Especially compared to you and Annie.' Looking up again, she smiled nervously. 'Just . . . just don't expect too much, that's all I'm saying.'

'It doesn't matter, I don't care about any of that!' Maggie exclaimed. 'I'm just so grateful to have somewhere to go! I've been so scared.'

'Come on, now, we wouldn't see you on the streets, would we?' Irene said jokingly.

'Well, you had me worried for a moment there,' Maggie said.

'Just understand that it's not going to be what you're used to. You'll have to share a bed with me, for a start,' Irene added seriously.

'But at least I'll *have* a bed,' Maggie declared gratefully, clasping her hands together.

'And there will be no cook making you dinner every evening. No one to make the bed for us.'

Maggie got the idea now, so she wasn't sure why Irene was trying so hard to hammer it home. 'I'm so grateful, Irene, really I am,' she cried, tears pooling in her eyes. Irene still looked apprehensive, but she embraced Maggie warmly when she held out her arms to her.

'Right, well that's settled, then,' Annie smiled. 'Now we just have to work out what we're going to do about Peter.'

Maggie pulled away from Irene abruptly. 'We're not going

to do anything about Peter,' she said firmly. She was feeling stronger already now that she wasn't in such a vulnerable situation, but she just wanted to put the whole thing behind her.

'You're not going to let him get away with this, surely?' Annie asked in shock.

Maggie caught Irene flashing Annie a look of warning before she cut in. 'We don't have to worry about that now,' Irene said calmly. 'Annie, let's get changed and then we'd better get out on patrol before we're pulled up for being late.' Annie nodded grudgingly.

As the three of them headed towards Boundary, where they always liked to start their patrol, they chatted and laughed together. Maggie realised they hadn't done that for a long time. Things had definitely been different since her run-in with Peter. She felt sad that she had isolated herself from her friends like she had. She was glad it was all over and that she could finally move on. She was ready to start her new life – one where she was an independent young woman making her way in the world without having to answer to anybody else.

30

Boundary was busy, which was perfect for Maggie as it kept her distracted. That was something she was always grateful for, but particularly on the day she had been thrown out of her home, disowned by her parents and compelled to talk through her attack for the first time. She may have felt like some weight had been lifted from her shoulders, but she was still carrying around an incredibly heavy load of sadness.

On their travels, the girls bumped into Sal. She was taking her tea break with Mary in tow. Maggie was struck by how different Mary looked compared to the day they had dropped her off at the laundry. She had colour in her cheeks now, but there was something else, too. A sense of life radiated out of Mary. It was like she had given up when they had spoken to her previously, but now she had something to live for. Sal had saved her.

'I'm so proud to have helped turn that girl's life around,' Maggie said as they wandered up and down the tenement blocks following their catch-up with her and Sal. 'To think I could have lost all of this if my father had allowed me to stay at home. There's no way he would have let me carry on with this. And I don't see how I could've got away with sneaking around any more.'

'Maybe being thrown out was a blessing in disguise,' Irene said. 'Just remember that my place isn't what you're used to.'

'You don't have to keep warning me,' Maggie laughed. 'You're hard up, I understand. It honestly doesn't matter a jot to me.' Irene looked worried again. Maggie wondered once more what her friend was hiding. As they rounded a corner, they spotted Arthur walking towards them.

'Hello ladies,' he smiled. He was always genuinely pleased to see them, but today his grin was only half there. It was clear he was trying to be cheerful, but his face was tinged with sadness. They helped him up the steps to the top of the bandstand. As they sat next to him on one of the benches, he revealed what was getting him down.

'One of the lads is gone,' he sighed. 'Phillip, from Marlow block. I'd known him from a boy. Lovely lad, he was. Just turned twenty. It's no age at all.'

'I'm sorry, Arthur,' Annie said, as she put an arm around his shoulders to comfort him. A single tear ran down his left cheek as he looked out over the estate.

'His mother got the telegram this morning,' Arthur continued. 'Her only son, killed in action. Came straight round to see me. I don't think she knew what else to do.' He wiped the tear away and looked at the three girls sitting next to him. 'It's such a waste,' he whispered. 'And what for? When is this all going to end? We keep sending our boys and men out there and more and more of them are failing to return. How much longer can we do this for?'

Maggie didn't know what she could say to make Arthur feel better. She was feeling just as hopeless as him. No one had the answers to his questions, least of all her and her friends. All she could think about was Eddie and how, in just a few short months, he would be heading out to the front line. She looked over at Annie and knew she was thinking about Richard.

Arthur patted his knees and made a visible effort to buck himself up. 'Anyhow, I best get back to Sheila – that's Phillip's mother. She's been howling like a wounded animal all morning, and I thought it best to give her a bit of space. I needed a break from it, too, to be honest. But I don't want to leave her alone too long.' The girls nodded, and Annie jumped to her feet to help Arthur up. Once they were at the bottom of the steps, Arthur bid them farewell.

'You must let us know if we can do anything for Sheila,' Irene said before he left them. 'Even if you want us to sit with her for a while, so she's not alone. That way, you can have some space to grieve yourself.'

'Thank you, dear,' Arthur smiled gratefully. 'I might just take you up on that next time you're around.'

'Any time, Arthur,' Irene said, as they waved him off on his way.

The three of them were a little more subdued for the rest of the patrol. It seemed the reality of the war had hit Annie and Irene as hard as it had Maggie, after hearing about Phillip. His death was a chilling reminder of the horrors that so many were facing at the moment.

At the end of the shift, Maggie realised she had forgotten all about her personal troubles for a little while – but the suitcase sitting waiting for her in their room at the station brought the reality crashing back to her in an instant. Then she remembered she was about to move in with Irene, and she felt a flush of excitement. She was finally going to learn more about her guarded friend.

As Irene led her through Bethnal Green, Maggie started feeling anxious. They were walking down Peter's road. 'You don't live on this road, do you?' Maggie asked, her voice quavering.

'No, but it's nearby,' Irene sighed. 'Look, I told you I don't have much, Mags. Please don't make this more humiliating for me than it already is.' Irene walked on ahead of Maggie, clearly offended. *Oh no*, Maggie panicked. *She thinks I'm getting upset about the area she lives in!*

'Hang on, wait!' Maggie called out as she picked up her pace to catch up with Irene, the suitcase feeling heavier by the minute. 'I wasn't being funny because I thought this was where you lived.' She grabbed Irene's arm to make her stop so she could speak in a quieter voice. '*Peter* lives here. In that building there, in fact,' she said in a tremulous whisper. '*That's* why I was panicking.'

Irene's face softened. 'Oh lord, I'm so sorry,' Irene said as she linked Maggie's arm in hers and quickly led her on down the road. 'There's another way we can go from now on. It's a little further to walk, but I'd rather that than risk you bumping into him. No wonder you were so on edge.'

Maggie breathed a sigh of relief, although the feeling of angst didn't fully lift until they had made it to the next road. It turned out Irene only lived three roads along from Peter. It was a little close for comfort, but Maggie had nowhere else to go. As they made their way up the stairs to Irene's room, Maggie wondered if it might be a good idea to confront Peter, after all. With her friends there for backup, of course. If she got a sense of resolution and made sure he knew not to come after her again, she would certainly feel more comfortable living so near him. At the moment, his presence and the threat of him attacking her again was looming over her like a heavy raincloud ahead of a thunderstorm.

Maggie decided to think about it. Her friends would make sure she was never left alone, and for now, she needed to concentrate on making sure she didn't offend Irene when they walked into her room. She needed to push down any negative reaction that might jump to the surface and replace it with a positive, happy expression.

'Don't worry, you don't have to pretend,' Irene smiled as she looked over at Maggie's already grinning face. Irene hadn't even opened the door yet. Maggie laughed nervously. She had been caught out and she felt foolish.

Once the door was opened, though, and she had time to take in the room and its contents, she felt uneasy. Not only was it just a few roads along from Peter's place, but it was very similar. Same floor, same layout, same sparse décor. And cold. Very, very cold. She was pleased she had brought a thick shawl with her. Maggie heard a light scratching noise coming from one side of the room and froze.

'Oh, don't worry, that's just the rat. He's harmless,' Irene said. 'I keep meaning to give him a name, but I can't find one to suit him.' She was so blasé about it. Maggie tried to act unbothered, but she wasn't sure she felt all that thrilled about sharing a room with a rodent. She would just have to keep her worries to herself, though.

Studying the room further, she got the nasty feeling that when she needed to relieve herself, she was going to have to traipse outside and use the same toilet as at least five other people. She shuddered. *Stop it*, she scolded herself. *Stop being ungrateful. This is better than being on the streets.* But now she understood why Irene had kept her living conditions to herself.

'I swallowed my pride to let you come here,' Irene said, as she sat down on the bed and took off her shoes. Maggie knew she was terrible at hiding her emotions. She had failed again, and Irene must have seen the disgust and disappointment on her face. 'I thought your need was greater than my dignity,' Irene added quietly. 'It's not a lot but I call it home. Hopefully you can too.'

Maggie felt guilty for coming across so unappreciative. It had clearly taken a lot for Irene to open up and reveal this part of her life. And if growing up with her father had taught her anything, it was that a big house and lots of money didn't make you a nicer person than someone living in a slum – or close to a slum in Irene's case.

'I really do appreciate this,' Maggie said as she sat down on the bed next to her friend. 'It's not the surroundings that matter – it's the company.' She was shocked to see tears welling in Irene's eyes. It was a lot from someone who hardly ever showed her softer side.

'That's so kind,' Irene sniffed as she held out both arms wide. 'Come here, you silly so-and-so!' As they hugged on the bed, Maggie realised she truly didn't need the plush surroundings she had grown up with in order to be happy. She would ask her about the lavatory situation when the need arose – she wasn't ready to know all the details about that yet. And she could do with some time to work on hiding her emotions, clearly.

They lay down on the bed together and Irene sighed contentedly. 'It's a big relief that you know about my circumstances,' she admitted. 'It was exhausting keeping this from you and Annie. I was never able to fully open up and get to know you both properly. And I was always so worried about getting found out.' Maggie realised that she and Irene had more in common than she thought.

'I know exactly what you mean,' Maggie said earnestly. 'Now we can both just be ourselves. No more secrets.' She paused for a moment while she thought about how hard Irene must have worked to keep this from everyone. 'You must know people around here, then?' she asked her. 'You must have been so annoyed when they placed us here.'

'Yeah, it was just my luck,' Irene laughed glumly. 'I haven't lived here a long time, but there's a few people I've got to know. There's some girls on Betty's street who'd probably recognise me. And that road we escorted that drunk soldier to – I was terrified someone would spot me there.' It was all falling into place now for Maggie.

'So that *is* why you kept ducking off,' she said triumphantly, realising her previous suspicions had been correct. 'But what does it matter? Surely you didn't think Annie and I would think any less of you?'

'I suppose I've just always felt a little ashamed of the way I live,' she said sadly. She was no longer looking Maggie in the eye as she spoke. 'It's different for you and Annie – you've grown up around money. I grew up in a children's home – it was a very different way of life, let me tell you. You two have never been judged for being poor, like I have. I think I just didn't want it to change your opinion of me.'

Maggie was sad to hear about Irene's childhood. She was keen to know how she had ended up like this, and what had happened to her family. But she knew her friend had opened up far more than she was comfortable with already. She didn't want to push it. She started telling Irene about how Peter had ended up in the area, in the hope it might encourage Irene to share her story. But that just gave Irene the excuse she needed to weave the suggestion of confronting Peter into the conversation again.

'I might have to admit defeat on this one,' Maggie sighed. She turned over on to her side so she was facing Irene. 'I wanted to just forget it had ever happened. But I've spent the last six weeks or so terrified of bumping into him and I suppose this could be one way of stopping that.'

'You need it over and done with for good,' Irene urged. 'And that good-for-nothing toad needs to understand that he can't do that to women and get away with it.'

'I can't run away from it any more,' Maggie agreed firmly. 'Especially not if I'm going to be living in such close proximity to him as well as patrolling near his place.'

'That's decided then,' Irene said firmly. 'Annie's on board, I know that much. We'll go and pay the rat a visit tomorrow. We'll do it in uniform – really put the frighteners up him!' Maggie wasn't sure Peter would be fazed by their WPV kit – he had tried to attack her in the alleyway when she was wearing it, after all. But she nodded and smiled along with Irene. It was better that she was riled up like this and feeling confident when they went to see Peter. She just hoped with all her heart that this wouldn't end up being another of her big regrets. She seemed to be having a lot of those lately.

A short while later, Irene got up and got dressed in even shabbier clothes than Maggie had seen her in before.

'Where are we off to?' Maggie asked optimistically. She had been dreading the thought of spending all afternoon and evening cramped up in Irene's tiny room. And she was desperate for the toilet. Hopefully there would be an indoor lavatory wherever they were going so she could put off braving the outside one just a little longer.

'Ah, erm, I'm off to work,' Irene said sheepishly. Maggie couldn't hide her confusion. 'The WPV may be work to you, Mags, but remember it's a voluntary role. How do you think I'm managing to pay for this room? It might not seem like it's worth much, but I still have to pay a fair whack to keep it.' She paused for a moment while Maggie's brain went into overdrive. 'I don't have Daddy's money to fall back on like you and Annie and all the other well-off recruits,' Irene added, her cheeks reddening.

Maggie was panicking again now. She hadn't even *thought* about how she was going to fund this new life. She could probably make the small amount she had brought with her stretch to a few weeks – not that she'd counted it, money wasn't something she had ever had to worry about – but after that, well, she didn't imagine her father was going to be sending her any cash to help her along.

Irene started putting on her jacket as she explained further. 'I was working at a factory before and they let me keep some of my shifts – the ones that work around our patrols,' she said. 'I'd already been saving up for a rainy day when I applied for the WPV, so I had some money set aside to make up for the shifts I'm missing out on. It's given me a bit of relief but things are still very tight.' The incident with Irene's 'forgotten' lunch now made sense – she couldn't even afford to feed herself. Maggie felt a pang of guilt for imposing on her already struggling friend.

'You must be exhausted!' Maggie said. 'It's all I've been able to do to keep up with the WPV work. I can't even begin to imagine how hard it would be to do a factory job on top of that.' Irene really was a tough old thing, she thought to herself. 'And you've never once complained about being tired,' Maggie mused.

'Well, you might have to think about taking on some shifts there with me, Mags,' Irene said as she reached for the door. 'I'm not expecting you to pay any rent, of course. But I can just about feed myself at the moment, let alone another mouth. They're always looking for more hands – I'll ask for you if you want?'

Maggie nodded gratefully. She was going to have to toughen up. 'But not just yet,' Irene added. 'Once you're fully back to health, I'll get it sorted. You still seem a little shaken up. Rest up this afternoon. Enjoy having the bed to yourself before I get back and take up most of the space – I'm used to stretching out!' Irene laughed as she pulled open the door and walked out.

As Maggie sat in the silence, she realised her friend was right, she was still a little shell-shocked. It was all so over-whelming. She lay back down on the bed and curled up into a ball. She was asleep within minutes, despite feeling that her bladder was about to burst.

31

When Maggie woke the following morning, she was surprised to find Irene lying in bed beside her. She hadn't even heard her coming in the night before.

'Good morning, sleeping beauty,' Irene giggled as Maggie rubbed her eyes and stretched her arms up in the air. 'You were out for the count when I got back – you didn't even stir when I flopped into bed next to you.'

'I suppose my body's still recovering,' Maggie said, yawning.

'You don't have to go in today, you know,' Irene said, serious now. 'I can get around Frank for you.'

The reference to Frank perked Maggie up. 'I'm *sure* you can,' she teased, moving her eyebrows up and down quickly and making kissing noises.

Irene put her hands over her eyes and groaned. 'Oh, stop!' she cried. Her face had turned crimson. She rolled over to face Maggie and her expression became sombre. 'I really like him,' she admitted, biting her bottom lip.

'Shock, horror,' Maggie laughed. She was surprised that Irene was finally admitting her feelings and realised she must trust her more following their heart-to-heart, but thought it was best to keep things light-hearted. 'I could see that the moment you met him!' Irene had her hands over her eyes again and was shaking her head from side to side. 'I don't see what the issue is,' Maggie said. 'Just tell him.'

'Come on, Mags,' Irene said scornfully. 'You really think

someone like Frank is going to be interested in a pauper like me?'

Maggie felt terrible that Irene felt that way. 'You're worth ten of any of those other posh recruits – myself included!' she said passionately. 'Of course he's interested in you, Irene! I've seen the way he looks at you. And the two of you are always sneaking off for private chats. It really upsets me that you would put yourself down like that.'

'I'm no good at any of that romance stuff anyway,' Irene huffed as she got out of bed. 'So, don't you go getting any of your ideas. No interfering. And I mean it,' she added firmly, wagging her finger at her friend.

Maggie had no intention of trying to play matchmaker, though. A few months ago, she would have been hatching a plan immediately. She would probably already have one in her head, in fact. But she had finally learned that her big plans tended to end in nothing but trouble. She would leave Irene and Frank to it. If they were meant to be then she was sure they would work it out eventually, without her help.

'Are you going to stay here and rest?' Irene asked as she started getting dressed. They were due into the station for another day shift.

'No, I'll come in,' said Maggie. 'But I'll be a little late – so if you could work your magic on Frank, that would be helpful,' she added with a playful wink. She had decided to risk a visit back home while her father was at work. 'I'm going to say a proper goodbye to my mother and Florence,' she explained to Irene. 'It broke my heart leaving them without so much as a word yesterday.'

'Well, you can walk with me to the station,' Irene said firmly. 'You'll be all right from there, but I don't want you going anywhere near Peter's on your own. I can show you the other route.'

Maggie nodded gratefully. They agreed that Maggie would

get back to the station in time for the girls' first break. 'I could do with the distraction of being on patrol,' Maggie sighed. 'And besides, I want to get this Peter thing over and done with so I can move on properly.' She winced as her bladder burned.

'I have a chamber pot, you know,' Irene giggled, seeing the look on Maggie's face as she struggled out of bed. 'I know that hobble,' she added when Maggie looked up at her. Irene pulled a pot out from under the bed. 'I'm going to go and use the outhouse, so you can relieve yourself in privacy. But you'll have to empty it before we go. I'll let you use it, but that's where I draw the line,' she added, mock-sternly. Maggie giggled, then stopped herself – her bladder was too full for that.

They made their way to the station, avoiding Peter's road. Irene had been right – it was a longer route. But Maggie would have walked three times the distance to steer clear of that building. They said goodbye at the station and Maggie's mood dropped as she made her way to Kensington – she couldn't even call it home any more. She feared going back to see her mother and Florence one last time was going to make things harder for her, but she couldn't leave things as they were.

Standing at the front door, she took a deep breath. If she was wrong about her father being at work, then this could end up being a terrible mistake. Exhaling, she knocked quietly and breathed a sigh of relief when Florence opened it almost immediately.

'My darling!' Florence cried as Maggie threw herself into her open arms. 'I just wanted to say goodbye properly,' Maggie sniffed as she was ushered along the hallway to the kitchen. She wondered why Florence was in such a hurry to get her into the room, until she looked up and saw a khaki uniform. Eddie was beaming from ear to ear. They embraced, tears running down both their faces, as Florence watched on. When they finally parted, Maggie realised her mother was there, too.

'I'm so sorry,' Maggie whispered through her sobs.

'You've nothing to be sorry for,' her mother said, pulling her in for yet another warm hug. Once everyone had calmed down, Maggie, Eddie and their mother sat down at the table while Florence made a pot of tea.

'I need to tell you the truth about what happened to me,' Maggie said nervously. She guessed Eddie had been filled in on recent events, although she was confused about how he had managed to get back from training. She was keen to find out but that could wait – she was desperate to enjoy some time with him and she couldn't do that until this was off her chest. Florence poured them all a cup of tea then placed her hand on Maggie's shoulder and gave it a gentle squeeze.

'I'll give you some privacy now, but come and find me before you head off,' she whispered.

Once the kitchen door was closed behind her, there was a heavy silence in the room. Maggie took a deep breath and told Eddie and their mother about her run-in with Peter outside The Lamb. They looked shocked and upset, but stayed quiet and let her continue.

She was grateful for the lack of interruption – she just wanted to get it all out as quickly as possible. She told them everything, and then finished with the fact she had confessed all to Annie and Irene, who were going to look after her now she had been thrown out of home. When Maggie was finally finished, she stared into her cup. Her mother grasped her hand in both of hers and bowed her head.

'Where does he live?' Eddie asked calmly. Maggie looked up, confused. 'I'm going straight there,' Eddie explained, his voice shaking with rage now.

'Eddie, no,' she pleaded. Who knew how much things could escalate if he barged in there now, full of anger and seeking revenge? As much as she wanted Peter to get his comeuppance, she didn't want to risk Eddie being harmed in the process – or ruining his career, both in the army and later as a doctor. She also didn't much fancy the men from the station having to go to Peter's to break up the fight, and finding out what had led Eddie there. 'The girls and I have a plan,' she assured him. 'Now they know, I'm safe. And we're going to make sure he never comes near me again.' She hoped.

'Mags, this is serious. He needs to be warned off properly. The thought of him touching you again . . .' he trailed off and Maggie noticed his fists were clenched.

'Please, let me deal with this,' she begged. 'I've grown up a lot over the last few weeks. I need to do this myself, so I can move on from it.'

Eddie's demeanour softened. 'I'm sorry I wasn't here for you,' Eddie said, his anger morphing into sadness as his eyes brightened with tears. 'I always knew there was something off with that bastard.'

'You don't need to apologise,' Maggie said soothingly. 'It's Peter who needs to say sorry – and me and the girls will make sure he does. Trust me on that.'

'All right, Mags,' Eddie sighed. Their mother was still gripping Maggie's hand silently, so Maggie decided to give her some more time to process the news.

'Anyway, how did you manage to get leave so quickly?' Maggie asked, trying to lighten the mood.

'Mother wrote to me a few weeks ago,' Eddie said, smiling over at Mrs Smyth, who had now raised her head to smile sadly back at him.

'I was so worried about you,' their mother said, rubbing Maggie's back tenderly. 'When you put on that illness and fever, I didn't believe a word of it.' Maggie looked down at the table sheepishly. 'Then you claimed to be feeling better, but you were acting like a ghost of yourself – pale and withdrawn. I desperately wanted to help, but I didn't know what to do, how to make you open up.'

'But, you didn't know where Eddie was – how did you manage to write to him?' Maggie asked, looking at them both in puzzlement.

'That's where our dear Florence comes in,' Eddie piped up. 'Mother confided in her and she confessed we had been in contact, and passed on my address.' Maggie was shocked their mother had taken so many risks to share her concerns with Eddie. It meant a lot to her. She felt bad for feeling disappointed in her for not standing up to her Father when she had left.

'Anyway,' Eddie continued, 'I wrote back, knowing that Florence would catch the letter for us before Father got to it. I told Mother to write to my supervisors telling them an aunt had died and asking them if I could return home for the funeral. It was a bit of a punt, but it worked. Of course, I'd never have done that normally, but I was just so worried about you.'

'I can't believe you both did all that for me,' Maggie whispered.

'Of course we did,' Mrs Smyth said. 'I might be too terrified of your father to stand up to him to his face, but I will always fight for you behind the scenes if I can. I'm so happy you came back today – I was heartbroken not to be able to say goodbye to you, but you know what your father's like . . .'

'It's all right,' Maggie said. 'I understand – you did the right thing. I wouldn't have been able to forgive myself if he'd harmed you because of me.' Their mother was sitting in the middle of Maggie and Eddie, and she now placed both her hands on top of the table in front of her. Her son and daughter placed their own hands over them, and they sat in silence – nobody wanting to be the first to start the inevitable goodbyes. Who knew when they would all see each other again?

Finally, Maggie decided she would have to be the one to break up the embrace, as she had to get back to the station. She started mentally preparing herself to leave. Before she could say anything, though, the kitchen door flew open. There was a loud crash as it banged against the wall. They all looked up, startled, to find Mr Smyth standing in front of them – his face full of rage.

32

The four of them stared at each other in silent horror. Finally, Maggie's father broke the quiet.

'Well, isn't this cosy?' he sneered, his voice thick with sarcasm and venom. Maggie could feel their mother's hand shaking beneath her own on the table. She was terrified, and Maggie felt the same. 'I see you couldn't hack life as a soldier – run back to Mummy before you even made it onto a battlefield, did you?' he added smugly, glaring at Eddie.

Before anyone could respond, Eddie shot up out of his chair and walked calmly towards their father. Maggie's heart raced in her chest as she willed her brother to turn on his heel and just head straight out of the room. But he reached their father and stood in front of him, nose to nose.

Eddie spoke slowly and firmly. 'I came home to make sure Maggie was all right, seeing as you didn't give a damn.' Maggie was desperate to stop her brother putting himself in the firing line for her sake. This was all her fault – Eddie would never have had to come back if she hadn't got herself in such a mess. But she was at a loss as to how she could help him now he had squared up to their father. She closed her eyes, refusing to watch Eddie being harmed.

'What, that little harlot?' their father cried out before laughing cruelly. Maggie opened her eyes again to see he was pointing at her.

Suddenly, Eddie brought his right arm back behind him, his fist clenched tight. Maggie heard her mother gasp and then there was a loud *thwack* as Eddie's bunched fist made contact with their father's nose. The older man's face was swept to the side with the force, and when he raised it back up again, blood was pouring from his nose into his mouth.

Mr Smyth stared at his son in shock. Maggie knew she needed to get Eddie out before their father composed himself enough to retaliate.

'Go to Florence as soon as we've left. Stay in her company until he's calmed down – he won't hurt you in front of her. I love you,' she whispered hurriedly in her mother's ear before leaping up out of her chair and running over to Eddie. She grabbed his arm and dragged him across the kitchen. It was as if he had been in some kind of trance, but he snapped out of it when they reached the door and he ran through it behind Maggie.

'I see the army has given you a bit of courage, at least!' they heard Mr Smyth yell out as they reached the front door. 'You're never welcome in this house again – either of you!'

His words rang out behind them as they raced down the street. They stopped at the end of the road. Maggie looked back to check their father hadn't followed them. 'I'm worried about mother,' she gasped, huffing and puffing as she tried to catch her breath.

'She'll be fine,' Eddie said confidently. 'She knows to stay out of his way for a few days.' Maggie tried to believe him – there was no question of them returning so she had to trust he was right.

'That felt delicious,' Eddie said, breaking into a wide grin. His eyes were suddenly bright with life. 'Did you see his face?!'

'Oh, Eddie,' Maggie giggled. The adrenaline was still racing through her veins after the shock of what had just happened. 'I can't believe you did that! He was stunned!'

Eddie ran a hand through his hair and sighed. 'I'm afraid

I just lost it,' he said, looking back down the road towards the house. 'When he said that about you – knowing what you've been through – I saw red.'

'Thank you.' Maggie couldn't believe he had finally stood up to their father. 'You were so brave back there, and I'm so proud of you. It's what you needed to do – to make sure you're truly free of him.' Her worries about Eddie going to war lifted slightly. He could certainly look after himself. Maybe their mother had been right – joining the army had made Eddie realise he wasn't worthless after years of their father telling him he was.

'I'd better start making my way to St Pancras,' Eddie said sadly, looking at his watch.

'Oh no, you're not leaving again already?' Maggie asked, dismay engulfing her. She had only just seen her brother again – and now he was heading straight back? They had so much more to talk about. She was upset she hadn't had a chance to say a proper goodbye to Florence and her mother as she'd planned, and now precious time with Eddie was being stolen from her.

Thinking back to their talk with their mother just now, Maggie felt confident she could write to her in time and try to organise a secret meeting. Florence would catch the post for her – and she might even manage to come along. The idea boosted her spirits – but not enough to help her feel ready to say goodbye to Eddie.

'I only got one day of leave,' Eddie explained sadly. 'I stayed with a friend last night as I knew father would be home. So my time is up now.'

'Well, I suppose this is goodbye, then,' Maggie whispered as fresh tears filled her eyes.

'You have to promise me one thing before you go,' Eddie said.

'Anything,' Maggie replied, and she meant it.

'Don't keep anything from me again, do you understand? We've only got each other now. I don't care if I'm away training or fighting – if you need me then I can find a way back or I can get help to you. I've proved that now, haven't I? I'll never let you down.' Maggie had to agree. Yet again, her brother had pulled through for her, against all odds. She promised not to keep anything from him again, no matter how much she knew it would upset him. They embraced one last time before Eddie jogged off along the road.

Watching him disappear around the corner in his smart uniform, Maggie smiled. She was on her own again, but she didn't feel lost or alone. She had Eddie, Irene and Annie – and with them by her side, she knew she was going to be just fine.

33

As Maggie made her way back to the station, she was excited to tell the girls about Eddie's revenge on their father. She made sure she was dressed in her uniform and sat waiting in their room at the station when it was time for their tea break. When Irene and Annie walked in, the three of them fell into a group hug.

'It's good to be back together properly,' Annie smiled. Maggie knew just what she meant. Now that everything was out in the open, she felt like they had a fresh start. There were no secrets holding anyone back or causing them to push the others away. She felt so close to these girls and she didn't want to hide anything from them ever again.

They decided to go straight to Peter's, and Maggie was relieved to be getting the confrontation out of the way before she could spend any more time worrying about it. It was late morning now, but from what she had gathered about him, it was likely he would still be sleeping off the night before. They hoped banging on his door would wake him up and catch him unawares, giving them the upper hand from the start.

When they got to Peter's door, Maggie stood in front of it, and Irene and Annie stood just out of sight, a few steps away, so that Peter would think Maggie was alone.

'We're ready to pounce if he tries anything,' Irene assured Maggie in a whisper as she took a deep breath and prepared to knock on the door. 'You will not be going into that room alone.' Maggie's heart was pounding so hard she could hardly hear what Irene had said. She didn't want to look scared, so she tried her best to put on her bravest face.

The butterflies in her stomach went into overdrive as she tapped on Peter's door. They waited a minute, but there was no noise coming from the other side. She looked over at Annie and Irene, who were both nodding eagerly at her – they wanted her to knock again.

'Harder this time,' Annie urged her.

'She needs some help,' she heard Irene saying, before her hand reached out in front of Maggie and pounded on the door five times. She struck the wood so hard that the noise echoed. In a flash, Maggie was standing on her own in front of the door again. They heard a cry of confusion, followed by cursing. They had obviously woken Peter up. Maggie looked over at her friends, who were grinning. She felt braver now. He was going to be disorientated and confused.

There were a few loud footsteps, followed by some coughing. Then after some shuffling from the other side of the door, it swung open and Maggie was staring Peter in the face. She could feel bile rising up her throat. Her whole body started to shake as the memories of her attack came flooding back. Her body was desperate to flee, to get away from him as quickly as possible. But then she remembered her friends were here to support her, and she felt strong again.

Peter's expression changed from one of confusion to amusement as he took in the sight before him. 'Back for more?' he laughed as he rubbed sleep out of his eyes. Maggie stood frozen to the spot. All her strength had evaporated. Even half-asleep, Peter was able to render her powerless and weak.

'Right, that's it,' she heard Irene's voice boom out from behind her. Before she knew it, her friend was shoving Peter back into his room. Annie grabbed hold of Maggie's hand

and pulled her in before closing the door behind them. 'How dare you speak to her like that after what you did!' Irene was shouting at the top of her voice now.

But Peter just smirked. 'Come off it, you women are all the same,' he sneered. There was a strong smell of spirits in the room and Maggie suspected he might still be intoxicated from the night before. His room smelt like a pub. 'We all know she enjoyed it as much as I did,' Peter added, grinning menacingly at Maggie. That was it for her. She'd had enough of being scared of this man. Something in her snapped.

'That's a lie!' Maggie screamed, stepping forward so she was inches away from Peter now. 'You attacked me in this room, and you tried to do the same that night in the alley. I didn't want any of it and you need to know you can't do that to a woman!'

'Well, whatever makes you feel better about it, love. You've said your piece, now get out,' Peter said in a bored voice.

Maggie realised her words had had no effect on him at all. She didn't need to enlighten him. Just as she had thought, he knew what he had done was wrong – he just didn't care. But she had confronted him and made him see that she wasn't scared of him any more – that was the main thing. Still, she felt crushed.

'Stay away from me or you'll regret it,' Maggie hissed, with more venom in her voice than she had thought possible. She really did hate this man. 'If you so much as breathe anywhere near me then I'll make sure you're put away for a very long time,' she added, her eyes locked on his. Infuriatingly, Peter laughed in her face.

'You haven't got any evidence of anything, so how exactly are you going to "put me away"?' he asked, raising his eyebrows. Maggie was stumped. He had called her bluff and she was about to look very foolish.

Bell*Johanna Bell*

'Oh we're not afraid to stretch the truth a little to get what we want,' Irene's voice piped up from behind Maggie. She silently thanked her friend for stepping in and helping her.

'Yes!' Maggie exclaimed, feeling powerful again as Peter's brow furrowed, giving away his worry. 'Just remember, we've got a lot of friends at the police station who would be willing to help us out,' she added. She turned to leave before spinning back around to add triumphantly, 'And you can go running to my father if you want to – see if I care!' Part of her hoped he did pay a visit to her father. He was likely to be so wound up by the very mention of his daughter that he might give Peter a piece of his mind – using his fists.

Maggie once more turned around to leave and saw Irene and Annie both sitting proudly on the sofa, their arms folded. They had obviously enjoyed watching her stand up to Peter. 'Come on, ladies, let's leave this poor excuse for a man to sober up, and get on with our day,' Maggie said confidently. She was just about to start walking towards the door when she noticed both her friends' faces fill with horror.

'Don't you dare!' Annie yelled out, jumping up. At the same time, Maggie felt her collar being pulled back violently and she flew backwards with the sudden force. Then Peter's hands were clasped around her neck.

But then just as she tried to catch her breath, it was over. She was flung forward again as Peter suddenly let go of her. It had all happened in seconds.

Maggie turned around to see Annie holding his arm up against his back.

She had twisted it back to incapacitate him – just like they had learned during that very first ju-jitsu session. Peter was wincing in pain. Maggie couldn't believe what she was seeing – Annie was so small compared to Peter, yet she had full control over him now. She couldn't help but laugh.

'All right, all right!' he shouted, shifting his weight from one leg to the other and trying to break free from Annie's grip.

'Apologise to Maggie and we'll be on our way,' Annie growled. Maggie had never heard her sound so fierce. Peter scoffed and Annie twisted his arm further up his back until he cried out in pain. 'Say you're sorry – and mean it!' Annie roared.

'I'm sorry!' he yelped. Maggie looked over at Irene and they smiled at each other. Maggie walked up to Peter. She longed to bunch up her fist and smash it into his face. But she knew lowering herself to his level – and that of her father – wouldn't help.

'You stay away from me,' she snarled, forcing him to meet her eyes. 'If you ever try to hurt me again, I promise you you'll regret it.' With that, Annie loosened her grip on Peter's arm and walked round to Maggie's side to stand with Irene. Peter rubbed his arm as they marched out of the door. Maggie slammed the door behind her with all her strength, and was shocked at how much she enjoyed it.

'Well, that was something else!' Irene cried happily as they spilled out on to the street. 'You clammed up at first and I thought I was going to have to do all the talking for you, but the old Maggie burst back! And Annie! Well, I don't even know who that was back there, but I really like her!'

'I couldn't let him hurt Mags again,' Annie shrugged. Then she broke into a huge grin. 'I don't know what came over me, but it felt so good to put him in his place,' she giggled.

'It was brilliant to see him lose all the control,' Maggie said.

'What was also great to see was this,' Irene said gleefully, pulling something out of her pocket. It took Maggie a few moments to realise that it was a diamond bracelet. It glistened in the sun as Irene turned it over and over in her palm. Maggie and Annie both gasped.

'We didn't go there to *steal*,' Annie whispered, looking around her in panic.

'Think about it,' Irene said as she slipped the bracelet back into her pocket. 'You've seen Peter. You've seen his place. He's as well off as I am – there's no way this bracelet belongs to him.'

'So . . . whose is it?' Annie asked.

'Who has just been burgled of thousands of pounds' worth of jewellery?' Irene asked coaxingly.

'Gosh!' Maggie yelped, throwing her hands up to cover her mouth when the penny finally dropped. 'Do you really think it's hers?'

'The Dowager from Knightsbridge'? Annie asked, her eyes wide.

'Lady Parsons. I *know* it is,' Irene said proudly. 'Frank showed me photographs of some of the pieces that were stolen – this is definitely one of them. We've only gone and solved the biggest case Bethnal Green Police have ever had to deal with – us three girls on our own!'

They all jumped up and down, squealing with joy. 'If it wasn't actually Peter then he's certainly implicated and will be able to lead them to the culprits,' Irene said confidently. 'Someone like Peter will sing like a canary as soon as he's arrested. He's full of front, especially with women – but put some men in uniform and a prison sentence in front of him and he'll tell them everything he knows!' Maggie was certain Irene was right about that. She may not have got any remorse from Peter – but this was ten times better. This really was revenge.

'Hang on, where on earth did you find it?' Annie asked.

'I could feel something digging into my back when I sat down on the sofa,' Irene explained. 'One of the diamonds was poking out from behind the cushion. Peter must have shoved it there when we banged on the door. We shook him up more than we could ever have hoped. Goodness knows what else he has hidden back there!'

Maggie thought back to her first visit to Peter and remembered how he had lunged to the sofa. They needed to get officers there straight away – she was certain they would find a stash in his little cupboard, too.

'Right, we'd better get it to the station immediately,' Maggie said excitedly. 'Before he realises anything is missing.'

'He's probably gone straight back to bed,' Annie said scornfully.

'I can't wait to tell the officers we've found their man – and then see Peter's face when they uncover the rest!' Maggie cried. This really had turned everything around for her.

All three of them started running to the station. The snakes that had been writhing around in Maggie's stomach before her latest encounter with Peter had transformed into butterflies of anticipation and excitement. When they got to the station, they grabbed the first officer they saw, who was standing at the reception desk chatting to Witchy.

'We've found the jewellery thief!' Maggie cried triumphantly as they screeched to a halt just under his nose.

'Of course you have,' he said dismissively. 'And I'm the King of England. I'm busy,' he sighed, before turning back to Witchy and continuing their conversation. Deflated, the girls started walking towards their room.

Just then, a sergeant appeared at the other end of the corridor and started walking towards them. 'Sir,' Irene said eagerly. 'We have some important information for you.'

'I'm on my way out, ladies,' he barked, as he brushed past them without so much as looking in their direction. It seemed the respect Maggie's accident had garnered for them had started wearing off already – and didn't mean anyone believed they were capable of actual police work.

'No one will take us seriously,' Maggie huffed as they

walked despondently into their room. She sat down heavily
on a chair and looked up at her friends. 'We can't arrest him
ourselves!' she cried, throwing her hands up in frustration.

'Who do you want to arrest?'

Maggie jumped up when she heard Frank's voice. Finally
– someone who would listen to them! Irene stepped in quickly.
She grabbed Frank's arm and pulled him into the room,
closing the door behind them.

'Easy, now,' he joked. Then, seeing how agitated they all
looked, he became serious. 'What's going on?' he said with
a frown.

Irene pulled the bracelet out of her pocket and dangled it
in front of his face. His eyes opened wide and his mouth
dropped open. 'That's Lady Parson's,' he gasped, snatching
it from her. 'Where did you get it?'

'We had some personal business with a chap down the
road,' Irene explained, choosing her words carefully. 'We
popped in to see him this morning and I found this hidden
down the back of his sofa. I'm sure there must be more, but
no one will listen to us and he'll surely hide it all once he
realises we have this.'

'*I'm* listening,' Frank said firmly. As Irene gave Frank all
of Peter's details, Maggie paced the room nervously. Frank
went to leave but Irene grabbed his arm.

'We want to come with you,' she said.

'You know I can't allow that,' Frank said quietly. 'As much
as I'd like to.'

'We cracked this case,' Irene cried indignantly. 'It's only
fair that we get to see his face when you find the rest of the
jewels!'

'I'm sorry,' Frank said, his voice gentle but firm. With one
last look into her eyes, he broke away and ran off down the
corridor. Just minutes later he was running back past their
door with a handful of other officers.

'We could always follow on after them,' Annie suggested hopefully.

'No,' said Maggie firmly. 'We'll let them bring him in. Frank will make sure we get our credit. If Peter sees me and thinks I'm gloating he could very well blurt out something about my age, anyway. I don't want to give him any excuse to drag me into things. Also, I think I've done my fair share of defying orders, don't you? It might be time to do as I'm told.' Irene and Annie each put an arm around her, and they held the embrace for a good few minutes before breaking apart.

The girls waited for what felt like hours but was probably only around thirty minutes. They paced the room, unable to focus on anything else. Maggie decided to take the opportunity to thank Annie properly for jumping in and helping her at Peter's. 'I still can't believe you overpowered him like that,' she grinned.

'Remember that timid girl we met on the first day of training, Mags?' Irene joined in. 'If I'd told you she'd be bounding in to save you from a terror like Peter then, you would've laughed!'

'I certainly would have done,' Maggie agreed.

'The WPV has helped me grow so much,' Annie said, looking emotional. 'I'm much stronger as a person. I have much more energy now I'm not using it all up on being terrified of everything.' Maggie was shocked. She knew this had been a journey for her friend, but she hadn't quite realised the extent of it.

'I bet your family are so proud of you,' Maggie said. 'We both are,' she added, and Irene nodded in agreement.

'My father says I'm like a different person,' Annie smiled. 'I can't wait to tell Richard about how we cracked the burglary case. I just hope he makes it back to see how much I've changed.'

'He will,' Maggie said firmly. 'Richard and Eddie will both make it back, and we'll all go to a dance together! With Irene and Frank, of course,' she added teasingly. Irene flushed bright red, and Maggie decided not to push it. 'How has the WPV changed you?' she asked her instead.

Irene looked thoughtful. 'I've realised people from all walks of life can be friends,' she said. 'And that I can achieve anything I put my mind to.'

'I think we can all agree with that,' Maggie said. 'I've learned I don't have to put up with men pushing me around. I know it's early days away from home, and I've a lot of hard work ahead in order to support my new life. But I'm ready and I'm excited to stand on my own two feet. I don't feel trapped any more.'

'You're going to be just fine,' Irene said, walking over and giving Maggie another hug.

'Hey, I know! Why don't we ask Sarah to write about us solving such a big crime on our own in *The Vote*?' Annie suggested. 'It's exactly the kind of publicity the WPV need!' Maggie's stomach flipped at the idea. The thought of her father opening up the paper and reading about her success was just delicious! 'We could even see if they'd start a monthly column,' Annie added. 'We could meet up with Sarah every few weeks and give her the most interesting bits from our diaries to write about.'

'A lot of people would certainly be shocked if they found out how much we actually do,' Irene said thoughtfully.

'Yes,' Maggie agreed. 'And that would mean Sarah would be able to make a difference with the WPV after all – despite having had to leave.'

Just then there was a commotion in reception. Maggie darted out of the room and along the corridor. A sea of officers were entering the building. In the middle of them all, Peter's head bobbed up and down as he struggled with the men restraining him. They stopped briefly at reception and he looked in Maggie's direction. As soon as their eyes met, he started cursing and swearing.

'You!' he shouted, as the officers started dragging him off down the corridor towards the cells. 'You'll pay for this!' he hissed back over his shoulder before he disappeared around the corner.

'They got him!' Maggie cried, running back into the room. Annie and Irene let out yelps of joy, and Frank appeared in the doorway just behind Maggie. He was huffing and puffing, but after taking a few moments to catch his breath, he filled them in on what had happened.

'Not only did we find the missing jewels,' he said excitedly, 'but his room was also full of loads of other illegal stuff! He had forged money tucked away in there, evidence of blackmail – you name it, he was into it. We opened up a little cupboard and a whole hoard came tumbling out!' Maggie thought back to her first visit again, when Peter had been so desperate to stop her opening that cupboard. How close she had been to discovering his crimes in that moment! 'You girls really uncovered a nasty piece of work there. He won't be going anywhere for a long time,' Frank said with a satisfied grin. 'He's not very smart, that one. I mean, he was clever enough to carry out the burglary undetected, but imagine keeping hold of all the jewels for so long – it's like he was waiting for us to find him!'

Maggie wondered why Peter hadn't sold the haul straight on and used the money to get himself out of Bethnal Green. She could only imagine he just didn't have the relevant contacts – given his upbringing. Her thoughts were interrupted by Annie grabbing her for a hug. They both burst into tears.

Maggie looked around for Irene just in time to see Frank sweeping her up into his arms. Maggie quickly spun Annie around so she could see, too. They cheered as Frank dipped his head to place his lips on Irene's, and they shared a short but passionate kiss. When he pulled away, he kept his arms wrapped around Irene's waist and looked deep into her eyes. 'I've wanted to do that since the first day I met you,' he said.

'The feeling's been mutual,' Irene whispered, flushing crimson and tucking some stray hairs behind her ears nervously. Maggie was so happy for her friend.

Frank gave Irene another quick kiss, before heading for the door. Just before he left, he paused and turned back to them all. 'Oh, there was one more thing,' he said, laughing to himself. 'That chap has really got it in for you girls. He even started ranting and raving about Maggie being too young to be here.'

Maggie's heart started racing. Was this finally it?

Frank shook his head and laughed again. 'I've never heard anything so ridiculous,' he said. 'Anyway, I've got his interview to prepare for. You best get out on patrol and I'll see you all later.'

Maggie flopped down into a chair as he left and put a shaky hand to her pale cheek.

'No one will take him seriously,' Irene assured her. 'He just sounds desperate.' Maggie nodded, deciding to try to believe her. Besides, nothing could ruin the high she was feeling after seeing Peter dragged away to the cells kicking and screaming. All she had wanted was to confront Peter so that she could move on from what had happened, yet she had ended up helping to put him behind bars! She hoped with all her heart that he would rot in jail.

Not only that, but she had witnessed Irene's first kiss with Frank. She was over the moon for her, and had noticed that she hadn't stopped grinning since Frank had left them.

They somehow made it through their shift and were looking forward to an update on Peter when they got back to the station. Frank was waiting in their room for them. 'He's been charged and he'll see the magistrate tomorrow. It won't be good for him,' he said, a wide grin spreading across his face.

Just then, Witchy entered the room. 'The chief wants to see you ladies,' he said with a grave face.

In an instant, Maggie's high was flattened. Her pulse raced as she panicked that Peter's claims about her age had been believed. Trying to keep herself composed, she followed behind as Witchy led them all up to the chief's office. But when they walked in, they stopped short at the sight that greeted them.

There was an older-looking woman sitting behind the chief's desk, and the chief himself stood behind her. The woman had silver hair, piled up on top of her head in an elegant bun. Her clothes were gloriously over-the-top, and she had a definite air of old money about her.

'Ladies, I'd like you to meet Lady Parsons,' the chief said seriously. Maggie was dumbfounded. She imagined she must have come to the station to identify her jewels – but why had she asked to see *them*?

'I told Lady Parsons about your great detective work, and she wanted to thank you personally,' the chief explained, still sounding very formal. 'These are the women who found your jewels,' he said proudly to Lady Parsons.

'Thank you, dears,' she said quietly. 'As I've always said, if you want a job doing properly then you should ask a woman to do it,' she added, her eyes twinkling mischievously. The chief shifted uncomfortably but managed a small smile when Lady Parsons looked up at him. Maggie loved this woman already. 'You should be very proud of yourselves,' Lady Parsons continued. 'I wanted to say thank you. Not only are those jewels priceless, but they mean a lot to me personally – each one has a story behind it. That bracelet you found, for example, was given to me by my late husband on our wedding day. I also wanted to reward your hard work. I know you don't get paid to do these patrols, and I think that's rather outrageous.' She handed them each an envelope before signalling to Chief Constable Sadwell that she needed help standing up.

'I'll be making rather a large donation to the WPV because of you three,' she added once she was on her feet. They were all too stunned to respond properly, but they each muttered a wide-eyed 'thank you' as the chief escorted her out of the room. As soon as she was gone, the girls raced back to their room, opened their envelopes and counted the money.

'Mags,' said Irene excitedly. 'Have you seen how much she's given us?' She was almost squealing now. 'If we pool our money, I think we could afford to rent a proper flat in a half-decent area!'

'Won't you miss your rat?' Maggie joked, before grabbing both of Irene's hands and jumping up and down with her. When they had calmed down, Maggie turned to Annie. 'What will you do with your money?' she asked.

'Well,' Annie said thoughtfully, 'they're saying the war could go on for a long time yet, and my house is so cramped. I could do with having my own space while I'm waiting for Richard to come home.' She looked at them both hopefully. 'I'm asking if I can move in with you two,' she said when neither of them got the hint.

For a moment, both Maggie and Irene were speechless. Then they looked at each other, and back at Annie. 'Of course!' they both said at the same time.

'The Bobby Girls together under one roof,' Irene said, rubbing her hands together gleefully.

'The Bobby Girls?' Maggie asked. 'That's rather good, I must admit – I wish I'd thought of it myself!'

'Why thank you,' Irene grinned. 'Come on, then, Bobby Girls,' she laughed as she started getting changed. 'We have flats to view!'

As the girls left the station, they linked arms. Maggie felt so grateful for her friends. For so long now she had been in a dark and desperate place, and suddenly it felt like everything was going to be all right after all.

And this was only the *start* of her new life. Watching the sun set as she walked along Bethnal Green Road with Annie and Irene, she felt content and happy – and ready for whatever came next.

If you'd like to know more . . .

I enjoyed researching the WPV and what London was like during the First World War so much. If you're interested in learning more about it all, here are some of the sources I found most useful:

Books

- *The Pioneer Policewoman, Mary Sophia Allen* (originally published by Chatto & Windus, 1925)
- *Feminist Freikorps: The British Voluntary Women* Police 1914-1940, R.M Douglas (Praeger Publishers, 1999)
- *Women on Duty: A History Of The First Female Police Force,* Sophie Jackson (Fonthill Media, 2014)
- *From Suffragette To Fascist: The Many Lives Of Mary Sophia Allen,* Nina Boyd (The History Press, 2013)
- *All Quiet On The Home Front: An Oral History Of Life In Britain During The First World War,* Richard Van Emden and Steve Humphries (Pen & Sword Military, April 2017)
- *City Of London in the Great War,* Stephen John Wynn (Pen & Sword Military, May 2016)

Websites

britishnewspaperarchive.co.uk

The British Newspaper Archive is a partnership between the British Library and findmypast to digitise up to 40 million newspaper pages from the British Library's vast collection, over the next ten years. I had a great time reading through issues of *The Vote* from all the way back in 1914!

londonist.com

This website is home to some great information about the Boundary Estate, including photos of what it looked like back in the early twentieth century.

Acknowledgements

Warm thanks to everyone who has encouraged and supported me in the writing of *The Bobby Girls*.

To my editor, Thorne Ryan, at Hodder & Stoughton – thank you for being my biggest cheerleader. Your encouragement, guidance and awesome suggestions have been invaluable. You were a dream to work with.

I must also give a big thankyou to Fiona Ford, who championed me when her agent was looking for a writer. Kate Burke at Blake Friedmann is also now my agent and I will forever be grateful to her for taking a punt on me – as well as giving me the onion bedroom tip!

The Imperial War Museum Research Room played a huge part in my information-gathering, and I'm grateful to all the staff for being so helpful and friendly.

Big thanks to Hewy, for enduring soft-play hell on countless weekends so that I could write in peace – and thank you, too, to our little cavegirl Emma, for being so into Waffle the Wonder Dog and her puzzles that I was also able to write a lot when she was at home.

I must also thank my mum for her endless encouragement and for letting me run countless ideas past her. Thank you for talking me down when my plotlines were getting too wild!

And I'm grateful to my dad for never moaning when I didn't answer his calls because I was too deep into writing to look up. Thank you for waiting patiently until I finally remembered to call back.

Finally, special thanks to my wonderful granddad and cousin – who sparked my interest in the great wars. They will both forever hold a special place in my heart.

The Real Bobby Girls

This photo of Commandant Margaret Damer Dawson and Subcommandant Mary Allen was an image I came across a lot during my research. I was always struck by how strong and proud they looked.

WOMEN POLICE OFFICIALS.
BY MRS NOTT BOWER.

It is a curious thing that many people seem quite amused when the necessity for appointing women police is first suggested to them. Apparently the chief idea conveyed to their minds is one of stalwart Amazons in blue serge hauling drunken navvies to prison. It needs but a little reflection to show how far this picture is from the ideal in the minds of practical workers.

The mental image this excerpt from *The Vote* threw up into my mind really tickled me!

This picture board of a well-dressed lady taking down a policeman using 'suffrajitsu' made me smile – especially as she manages to keep her hat on in all but one of the photos.

Find out what happens to Maggie, Annie
and Irene next in

The
Bobby
Girls'
Secrets

Available for pre-order in paperback
and ebook now

HODDER

Bookends

When one book ends, another begins...

Bookends is a vibrant new reading community to help you ensure you're never without a good book.

You'll find exclusive previews of the brilliant new books from your favourite authors as well as exciting debuts and past classics. Read our blog, check out our recommendations for your reading group, enter great competitions and much more!

Visit our website to see which great books we're recommending this month.

Join the Bookends community:
www.welcometobookends.co.uk

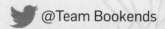 @Team Bookends 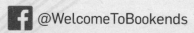 @WelcomeToBookends